MARTIN SIXSMITH

SPIN

A Novel

PAN BOOKS

First published 2004 by Macmillan

This paperback edition published 2005 by Pan Books
an imprint of Pan Macmillan Ltd
Pan Macmillan, 20 New Wharf Road, London N1 9RR
Basingstoke and Oxford
Associated companies throughout the world
www.panmacmillan.com

ISBN 0 330 42676 1

1 3 5 7 9 8 6 4 2

A CIP catalogue record for this book is available from
the British Library.

This book is a work of fiction. Names, characters, places,
organizations and incidents are either products of the author's
imagination or used fictitiously. Any resemblance to actual events, places,
organizations, or persons, living or dead, is entirely coincidental.

Typeset by SetSystems Ltd, Saffron Walden, Essex
Printed and bound in Great Britain by
Mackays of Chatham plc, Chatham, Kent

This novel is an amused and affectionate look at the worlds of politics, journalism and big business.

The incidents and characters in the book are not real . . . yet.

ACKNOWLEDGEMENTS

Thanks are due to my family,
Who suffered with me stoically;
To Ed, and DavidMariaKatieLiz at Macmillan,
Who all performed heroically.

PART ONE

PART ONE

1

SEPTEMBER 2006

'JON ADAMS?'

'Here.'

Oh, when the fog comes down . . .

'Julie Braeburn?'

'Here, sir.'

. . . the thick, the clinging fog, the fog that swirls and blackens thought . . .

'Peter Dalglish?'

'Yeah.'

. . . does it come to smother our faults, to hide our deeds from human eyes?

'Rory Fenton?'

'Present.'

Dan Curragh, sixty-four, decades a hill walker, never so seized with the cold mountains' dread.

'Jenny Haddow?'

'Here.'

Dan the teacher, Dan the leader.

'Evie Kilburnie?'

'Present, sir.'

Dan, whose voice was shaking.

'Sally Lawless?'

Sniggers.

'Yeah. Here.'

And now the fog and now the night beginning.

'Leanne Lockerbie?'

'Yeah.'

How can this be? How can this be?

'Philip McNab?'

'Here.'

To start with twelve and return with eleven?

'Paul Nisbett?'

No reply.

'Paul Nisbett?'

So is it him?

'Paul Nisbett?'

Paul the tough guy, Paul the swaggerer?

'Paul, are you here?'

Dan felt a shock of relief.

If it's him, he'll make it.

Of all of them, he's the one to beat the mountain.

'Paul Nisbett? Is it him who's missing?'

A quick infusion of hope after panic.

'Nah, sir. He's over there having a fag.'

Hope dashed.

Back to the nightmare.

'Cathy James?'

'I'm here sir, but it's Clare – Clare's not here.'

'What do you mean, Cathy?'

Don't panic, Dan.

'She's not here, sir. She's not here any more.'

Don't panic, Dan.

'Are you sure? Has anyone seen Clare?'

Silence.

'Cathy, you're her best friend—'

'Yes, sir. I don't know where she is.'

OK. OK, Dan Curragh. Think.

The fog's thick; she could be here.

'Clare! Clare O'Leary! Are you here?'

Clare the quiet. Clare the timid. Don't let it be her.

'Cathy! You two are always together. When did you last see her?'

'I don't know, sir. It's the fog. And Clare's gone. I'm scared, sir!'

Sit down, Dan.

Take stock.

One child down.

No way we can go back with one child down.

'Ian, we need to call Mountain Rescue. We need to get them out here right away. That's the first thing. Right? Then we need to decide who goes looking and who stays here. OK? . . . And where's Selwyn? What's he doing? . . . No, wait. Wait. We mustn't move from here till we talk to Mountain Rescue. They'll tell us what to do. Have you got the mobile? Come on, Ian! Ring them now!'

Ian Murray. Ten years younger than Dan. New Project, like Dan.

'Right, Dan. OK. What number do I ring?'

Why does my back hurt?

What am I doing here? What's down there?

I want to go home.

*

Home.

'What do you think, Frank? It's getting dark. Do you think they'll still be up in the mountains? I hope they're all right.'

'Of course they're all right, Eileen. It's organized by the council. It's the youth club. They know what they're doing. Stop worrying.'

'Hello, nine nine nine? What? . . . No, I don't want any of those. No . . . Yes, it is an emergency. I want Mountain Rescue . . . Yes, we're up in the mountains . . . What? It's Ian Murray. I'm a councillor. I'm one of the leaders of the trip.'

I'm scared.
    It's too dark. It shouldn't be this dark.
    I want to be at home.
    Top of the Pops is starting.
    Why can't I feel my legs?

'We'd better record *Top of the Pops* for Clare, Frank. They're not going to be back in time now, are they? Can you do it, please? Get up off your backside and do something, Frank!'

'You're asking me what my phone number is? I don't know. I'm ringing on a mobile, of course . . . Yes, it is my mobile . . . No, I don't know the number.'

I've got to look down. I can't.
    It's the only way out. I can't climb back up there.
    I must have fallen.
    Why is it dark? The last I remember it was light.

*

'No, I don't know exactly where we are. It's completely fog-bound up here and we've been going round in circles. But we've got a child missing. Can you please hurry up and come and help us? . . . I think we're near the top of Ben Donnan.'

'It's The Darkness on *Top of the Pops*, Frank. Have you put a tape in for Clare? What, have you just been sitting there? I can't believe it. Put the bloody tape in, Frank!'

'Yes, I told you: I'm Ian Murray . . . I'm a Project party councillor from Exxington District Council. It's our youth scheme . . . we've got eleven children here . . . we started with twelve.

'And we've got an adult missing too. We haven't seen either of them for about two hours now.

'The child's called Clare O'Leary. She's twelve. I'm worried about her . . . she's not very tough. Very timid . . . quite frail, you know.

'The adult's Selwyn Knox . . . he's a New Project councillor, too. He's the one who runs the youth scheme . . . It was his idea to bring this expedition up here . . .

'I wish we hadn't come on the bloody trip. It's too late now, but I wish we'd called it off when the weather warning came out. It's just, you know . . . Yes, OK . . . Sorry . . .

'Well, yes, *we're* all OK. No injuries, no . . . Yes, we're all warm and safe here. We've got food, but I want to find Clare and get this lot down as quick as possible.'

I can't look down.

I want my Mum.

Mummy, it's Clare! Can you see me, Mum?

*

'Frank, I'm really worried about Clare. Perhaps we should call the school.'

'It's got nothing to do with the school, Eileen. It's the council youth scheme or something. And, anyway, we haven't got their number. So just calm down, they'll be back in a bit.'

'Oh, Selwyn, there you are! Where the hell have you been? We've been going spare here.'

'Hi, Ian! Don't worry, Dan – I'm fine. I've been looking for Clare, but I don't think we'll find her in this fog.'

'What do you mean, you don't think we'll find her? We've got to find her. We can't go back without her! Ian's been on the phone to Mountain Rescue. They're going to send a helicopter. Then they're going to get the rest of the children down out of here.'

'Oh, right. So when's the helicopter coming, Dan?'

'I don't know, Selwyn, for Christ's sake! Ian's on the phone to them. They'll be coming as soon as they can.'

That's funny. I'm starting to feel warm again.
Why am I feeling warm?
It should be freezing here.
And I'm feeling warm.

'You know Clare O'Leary, don't you, Selwyn? You're in charge of the youth scheme. Do you think she'll be all right out on the mountain on her own?'

'I don't know, Ian. She's quite little and she's very nervy. I'm worried about her.'

'But she'll be all right won't she, Sel? She's not going to die out there or anything, is she? She's not, is she? Sel? Why did we come on this bloody trip, anyway?'

*

I'm getting warmer.

I feel OK now.

'This is BBC Radio Strathclyde. Some pretty atrocious weather conditions out there tonight. There's a weather watch in force for the whole of western Scotland, so if you're driving please do take extra care.

'Now, we're getting reports of a party of local school children stranded on a mountaineering expedition. The Mountain Rescue service has been alerted and a helicopter is reported to be on its way to pick up one child who's said to be injured. We have no further details on that breaking story, but we'll keep you informed as soon as we hear more.'

'That's the phone, Frank! Can you get it, please? I've got the dinner cooking here!'

Please, let me go home . . .

If you let me go home, I'll never argue with Lily again.

I'll never be cheeky to Mum and Dad.

I want to go home.

'Mountain Rescue here. Is that Ian Murray's phone? . . .

'Oh, OK. So who's that then? . . . Selwyn Knox did you say? All right. Hello, Mr Knox. The helicopter's on its way to you now.

'We'll be looking out for your party, so can you please make yourselves visible. That means spreading out as much brightly coloured material as possible on the ground where you are. Use tents or groundsheets – anything bright. And please light a fire so we can spot you as quickly as we can. I don't suppose you've got any flares with you, have you? . . . OK, not to worry. We'll be there soon.'

*

'Eileen, it's your sister. She says she's been listening to Radio Strathclyde and there's been something about a school party in trouble in the mountains. I told her not to worry because Clare's not on a school party, it's the council youth scheme.'

I'm getting warmer again.

And now I know how it's going to end.

I read it in my book; I'm just not sure what sort of bird it is.

It looks like an eagle, but I know it's not an eagle.

'I can hear the helicopter, Ian. Can you hear it, Selwyn? I'm sure I can hear something. Listen carefully. This damn fog muffles the noise.'

'Oh, Frank, I'm worried. It doesn't matter what they call it. School, youth club, council – it's school children up in the mountains. And I'm sure it's Clare. I just know there's something wrong.'

'Ten o'clock. BBC Radio Strathclyde news. This is Nigel Tonbridge at the news desk.

'Our headlines tonight.

'A party of Strathclyde school children is reported missing on a hiking expedition in the Ben Donnan area. The party, organized by the Exxington District Council youth scheme, set out this morning before weather conditions started to worsen. It's thought the party of twelve children, reported to be aged between thirteen and sixteen and led by three council members, were caught in the dense fog that descended over the region in mid to late afternoon. Mountain Rescue helicopters are now scouring the area, but there are unconfirmed reports that one child may be missing.'

*

It's an auk!

That's what it's called! An auk.

I remember it now from my book.

'Yes, it is the helicopter, Ian. I can see its lights now. Can you see it, Selwyn?

'I think it's going to try and land.

'Children! Everybody stand up and start waving.

'Here's the helicopter. It's coming to rescue us, so everyone stand together in a group and start waving so the pilot can see us.

'Move over to those rocks, children. The pilot wants us to move over there, so he can land on this flat bit of ground. Quickly, children! Go now!'

An auk.

A great auk! That's it.

He's coming to take me home.

When little children get lost, he always comes to carry them back to his nest, where it's warm and soft and safe.

'Hello, is that Mrs O'Leary?

'Hello, Mrs O'Leary. It's the duty officer at Exxington District Council here. I just wanted to let you know that there's been a bit of a problem with the youth scheme expedition. Now you don't need to worry. We're doing everything we can and we've got the Mountain Rescue people out, so everything's going to be all right.

'Mrs O'Leary . . . ?'

'Hello, I'm Captain Peters. Who's in charge here? Which of you is Mr Murray?'

'Hello, Captain. I'm Selwyn Knox and I'm in charge. Let's get the children on board, shall we? And let's get everyone home as quickly as possible.'

'Yes, I'm here . . . I'm here. I'm sorry . . . it's just I can't take it in. Clare's only twelve, you know. She's so little. And she shouldn't really be going out hiking like that, only it's organized by the youth scheme, you know, and Mr Knox said it would be safe. But now we've got the newspapers ringing us and saying Clare's been injured or something. I just don't know what's going on and I'm so worried . . . but you did say she's all right, didn't you?'

'Yes, Captain, I know we've got a little girl missing, but we have to be logical about this. We need to get these children back to safety or we'll have more of them dying from cold or frostbite. We can't help Clare O'Leary at the moment, but we can help the others. So let's get them all back home while the other helicopter and the search parties carry on looking for Clare, all right?'

'Hello, Mrs O'Leary. It's the council duty officer again. Just to say that the Mountain Rescue people have been on. They've located the main party now and they expect to have them back here in an hour or so. Unfortunately, they haven't found Clare yet, but they say you shouldn't worry because they've got search teams and two helicopters out looking for her and they say they hope to find her as quickly as possible. So don't worry, Mrs O'Leary; the best thing you can do now is stay by the phone and wait until I ring you again, or the Mountain Rescue people or the police get in touch. Is that all right? . . . Mrs O'Leary—?'

'Is that Selwyn?
    'Selwyn, it's Bob Travers here. Thank God you're back. And

thank God we've got most of the kids back. But what the hell's happening about Clare O'Leary?

'We're all very worried about this. It's not looking good for the council, you know . . .

'We were the ones who set this thing up; and we're the ones who're going to get blamed if anything's happened to the girl . . .

'I've already had the media ringing me, Selwyn, and it's pretty unpleasant, I can tell you. As council leader, I'm getting it right in the neck. They want to know why we let the trip go ahead in such bad weather and what safety measures we took.

'You know, they're saying we breached government safety guidelines. But I've checked: there *are* no bloody guidelines! So I don't know what they're on about, really.

'But that hasn't stopped London getting on the phone to give us a bollocking. The leadership are absolutely furious. They say we're a major New Project council and this could hurt the government's image. I've told them that's nonsense, but you know what control freaks this New Project lot can be.

'Anyway, they're sending somebody up here for a meeting first thing in the morning. What? . . . No . . . no, I don't know who it is yet. We'll find out in the morning. Anyway, they want the whole of the Project group here without fail. So make sure all three of you who were up on the mountain get in here by eight o'clock, OK? Tell Ian and Dan. All right?

'Yes, I know you've got to make a statement to the police. Go and do that now, then get some sleep. But you need to be here in the morning to tell this guy from London exactly what happened. They've really got it in for the council – and that means me and you. We're in trouble if we can't give a good account of ourselves.

'And another thing, Selwyn: the media are camped outside the

O'Learys' house. They know it's Clare who's missing. So keep away from there, OK?'

'This is BBC Radio Strathclyde with the seven o'clock news.

'Just one headline this morning and it is, of course, the continuing story of the little schoolgirl who's missing in bad weather following a hiking expedition that went disastrously wrong.

'Clare O'Leary, who's twelve and comes from the Exxington area, is still missing this morning, despite intensive rescue efforts, which have continued throughout the night.

'Search teams are combing the area near the last sighting of Clare, but the Mountain Rescue helicopters, which would normally lead an operation like this, have not been able to operate since fog and driving sleet forced them to return to base. Earlier one helicopter managed to bring back eleven other children and the three Project party members of Exxington District Council, who had taken the expedition into difficult mountainous territory despite weather warnings from the Met Office. No council spokesman was available for comment this morning, but on the line now is Captain John Peters from the Mountain Rescue service: Captain Peters, can you tell us what went wrong?'

'Gentlemen, can I call this meeting to order, please? I'd like to start by introducing Geoff Maddle. Geoff's here from party headquarters in London. The national Project party — or the government — which is it, Geoff? . . . OK, the national Project party it is — they're the same thing, of course, but Geoff's officially from the party, even though he's an adviser to the New Project government, is that right? . . . OK, Geoff. Thanks.

'So London have sent Geoff here to help us deal with the way we, er . . . deal with this very unpleasant incident.

'As council leader, I'd just like to say that it was most unfortunate that this expedition ended in the, er . . . unfortunate way it did.

'But I'd like to add that we mustn't give up hope. The missing girl is still missing. So she isn't dead and we can only hope that things turn out all right after all. I think we have to hope that—'

'Get real, Bob. The girl's dead. Even the Mountain Rescue people say she couldn't have survived a night out in weather like this. Didn't you hear them on the radio this morning?'

'Just wait a minute, Tommy. Wait! You weren't up there on the mountain. It's no good jumping the gun here. I think we have to have a policy to follow in case she's alive and a policy in case she's dead.'

'What do you mean a policy? This is a little girl we're talking about here, Bob. How can we have a policy? We've cocked things up and we have to say so. We can't play politics with a little girl's life.'

'No, of course we can't. We've all got children . . . or we've all got mothers and fathers at least.

'So we're people first and foremost, of course, but we're also the public face of the New Project party and Geoff is here to make that point to us all.

'So before we all get carried away . . . no, wait. We can't all talk at once!

'We'll all get the chance to have our say.

'Order! Gentlemen! Wait! Please—

'What we have to do first is introduce ourselves so Geoff knows who we are. And then I think we'll hear what Geoff has to say.

'And, don't forget, Geoff is speaking for the Prime Minister. Whatever Geoff says to you all this morning, it's the same as if

Andy Sheen was saying it himself. Is that clear, everyone? That's right, isn't it, Geoff?

'Right, let's tell Geoff who we are. First of all, I need the three of you who were leading the expedition to make themselves known to Geoff.

'First, Dan Curragh. This is Dan Curragh, Geoff.

'Dan's been a mountaineer for very many years. There isn't anyone more experienced at mountain walking than Dan in the whole of the region, is there? And Dan was in the SAS, weren't you, Dan, so he knows all about survival and rescue and things . . . What? The TA – OK. The TA Dan was in.

'And second, here's Ian Murray, Geoff. He's a master butcher and he's been a member of Exxington District Council for fifteen years – fifteen is it, Ian? So he's very experienced as well.

'And last of all is Selwyn Knox. He's the leader of the council's youth scheme, so he knows a lot about young people and to some extent it was his idea to take this expedition out there, wasn't it, Selwyn?

'Selwyn? . . . where's Selwyn?

'He was here earlier, wasn't he?

'I know I talked to him on the phone. I'm sure I did because I told everyone on the New Project group they had to be here. Does anyone know where Selwyn is?'

Selwyn Knox had not slept during the whole of that terrible night.

After two fraught hours at the Mountain Rescue HQ, talking to the search leaders on the radio link and trying to guide them to where Clare might be, then giving endless statements to one police officer after another, all the while churning over the events in his head, he could not sleep even when he got back to his flat at three a.m.

As mug of coffee followed mug of coffee and the night ticked away, Selwyn brooded on the images of sleet, fog and rock that were burned on his brain and gave him no peace: the thought of Clare; the blackness of the fog descending on the mountain; sight extinguished; sound deadened; no voices, no cries; then returning to the group; Dan's voice; the dread cold of fear in his heart; the mental rally as he attempted to take control; the celestial apparition of the helicopter; the surge of adrenalin; the return of lucidity in conversation with the pilot—

Now, Selwyn, now!

Stay focused – stay calm!

You're facing your biggest test yet so keep the ice in your heart – stay in control.

They're out to get you – they've always been against you – you've only yourself to rely on.

You're down now, they'll try to keep you down. But every setback is an opportunity. Don't just survive this: use it, use it to grow stronger, use it to advance. You're not one of them – you're different, stronger, better. You're marked for the future – don't forget the future – your future will change things – and today is make or break for you.

'OK, so it looks like Selwyn isn't here. Maybe he overslept or something. Can someone try his phone, please? Meanwhile, I'm going to hand over to Geoff from party headquarters. And I want you to listen carefully to what Geoff has to say because the way we handle this crisis could determine all our political futures. We've got local elections coming up soon, I don't need to tell you that. And Geoff's got his own concerns about the party's image at the national level too, haven't you, Geoff? I think we all need to remember what Andy Sheen has always said: "What we do is important, but it won't count for anything if we don't present it right." So Geoff's going to tell us now how we need to go about presenting this crisis. Geoff—'

'Thanks. Morning, everyone. Sorry I've had to come at such a difficult time. I'm here 'cos the Prime Minister and Charlie McDonald are concerned about what's happened in Exxington. They're both very sad about the little girl and her family, of course, but most of all they're concerned because this was an expedition organized by the New Project party. I'm not saying anyone did anything wrong, I'm sure you all had the best intentions. But when things happen that have the New Project party's name attached to them, we can be sure our enemies will be delighted that things have gone wrong for us. The opposition will be meeting at this moment to figure out how to use this against us. And don't forget we've got Prime Minister's Questions coming up, so Andy Sheen is going to face a grilling in parliament. And that's really why I'm here now: what I need from you is a clear explanation of everything that happened up in those mountains. Then we need to agree a very clear story that we all stick to. We mustn't end up contradicting each other because it'll make us look guilty and that's exactly what our enemies want – we don't need it. We need to stick together. We need to agree a line to take and we need to get your other guy – what's his name, Selwyn Knox? – involved in this. We don't want any loose cannons on this story. OK? So why don't you go first, Ian Murray, and tell us exactly what you remember about yesterday, starting from when the expedition set off, and then talk us through exactly who did what and who went where? All right?'

'You don't have any children, do you, Mr Knox? It's not easy bringing them up. You spend your whole life building them up, creating them, then they start to leave you. Or that's how it feels. The whole time you feel them growing away from you. But if you're lucky you can know they're still yours. They're still with you. When you wake your daughter in the morning she looks like a grown up twelve-year-old, but in that minute when she's coming round from sleep, waking from a dream, you know . . . she's suddenly back to the little one she used to be. It's hard to explain. She's all soft with sleep and when she opens her eyes she looks at you just the way she used to do when she was small. And then you can see that inside she's still the same; still the lovely child she was when she was little; you can see that she's full of goodness and simplicity and love. Oh, Mr Knox, how can this have happened?'

As he walked out to seize his destiny, Selwyn Knox glanced in the hall mirror of the O'Learys' terraced house. He looked stern. He looked determined. He smoothed his beard with the palm of his right hand.

There are moments in a person's life when the future is decided. You need to recognize them, you need to seize them. Only the strongest can seize their destiny. Only the strongest can act with mental clarity and decision – and I have been given that gift – I have been given the talents and the power. I am strong – I won't be looking back in twenty years and regretting opportunities I missed—

'Good morning, ladies and gentlemen.

'You've been here most of the night. Thank you for doing your job with such devotion.

'I know you are all concerned about Clare.

'I know you want to talk to Mr and Mrs O'Leary.

'And I know you want to hear from the council, who organized this expedition.

'Well, I'm here. My name is Councillor Selwyn Knox. Mrs O'Leary is here too, and we'll do our best to answer all your questions.

'But first let me say how terribly stricken I feel this morning. Stricken by the weight of last night's events; stricken by the anxiety and fear of a mother waiting for news of her child; stricken by the force of a mother's love.

'We all know the burden Mr and Mrs O'Leary are carrying as we wait to hear about Clare, as we hope for her safe return from the mountain but fear for her safety.

'So let our first thoughts be with Clare and with Clare's parents. As human beings, we owe that to ourselves.

'But let me say, also, that I am here to answer any questions you may have about the council's role in these events. As a two-term New Project party councillor myself, I can say that I at least have absolutely nothing to hide. This has been a tragic accident. If anyone has acted incorrectly, then I'm as determined as you are to find out the truth and take any action that is necessary. I can say quite categorically—'

'Mr Knox! We want to talk to Mrs O'Leary—'

'Mrs O'Leary, how do you feel about what has happened to Clare?'

'Mrs O'Leary, are you angry at the way the council has handled this?'

'Mrs O'Leary—'

'Wait! All of you! One at a time. Don't shout! Don't you know Mrs O'Leary has been through a terrible ordeal? Now Mrs O'Leary has a short statement to make and then I'll take any further questions. Eileen, are you all right? Are you going to be able to talk? OK, be quiet everyone and listen to what Mrs O'Leary has to say because this is all she'll be saying today.'

'Thank you, Selwyn – Mr Knox, I mean. I just want to say

that I love Clare very much. She is my youngest daughter and she is a lovely girl. I know she is in danger, but we are praying to Our Lady to keep her safe. We're praying . . . I'm sorry . . . I'm sorry . . . that's . . . I'm sorry . . .'

'It's all right, Eileen. Don't worry. Just the last bit, remember? The bit about the youth scheme. OK?'

'Yes . . . yes . . . I just want to say that Clare has been a member of the council youth scheme for the last two years and she has always been safe on it. And she has always enjoyed the activities Mr Knox has organized. And we have never had any problems at all. Is that all right?'

'Thank you, Eileen. Now I want to say—'

'Mrs O'Leary, have you been told exactly how Clare went missing?'

'Mrs O'Leary, how did the supervisors all manage to lose sight of Clare?'

'Mrs O'Leary—'

'Now stop that! Stop shouting! Can't you see Mrs O'Leary is upset? She's been very brave coming out to talk to you. You can't expect her to answer all those questions—'

'It's all right, Selwyn . . . it's all right . . . Can I just say to all of you that Mr Knox has been a good friend to Clare ever since she was ten and she joined the council youth scheme. In fact, he's been a friend to our whole family. So I want Mr Knox to answer your questions. He can speak on behalf of me . . . if you'll excuse me, I just can't say anything else just now . . . I'm sorry . . . I'm really very sorry—'

'Right, everyone! Leave Mrs O'Leary alone. You've had your statement. Leave her in peace. Thank you. Now, I just have a couple more things to say on behalf of Exxington District Council.

'The whole of the New Project group are devastated by what has happened to Clare. The decision to take the expedition into the mountains yesterday was made by the council as a whole. It was a collective decision. The trip was led by very professional, very experienced guides. And the decision to set off yesterday morning was made before the bad weather started. There was never any suggestion that the weather was going to turn, and anyone who says the bad weather was predicted by the Met Office is just kidding themselves.

'It is true that I was one of the leaders of the expedition. I can't go into details of what happened up in the mountains because the relevant authorities are still investigating what happened and I cannot be seen to pre-empt their conclusions. But I can tell you that I was not the man who organized this outing. I have no axe to grind and I certainly have nothing to hide. What I can tell you is that I didn't support the idea of the trip. In fact, I had severe reservations about it and I think bad decisions were taken by some of those in charge of the expedition, although I don't want to point the finger of blame and they will have to speak for themselves . . . when the time comes, that is.

'I will just say that when things went wrong up on the mountain there was a lot of panic among those who should have known better. When the weather turned bad – and conditions were atrocious, I can tell you – it was me who took charge, while the others were dithering around at base camp. I went looking for Clare, I did all I could, so my conscience at least is clear.

'As Mrs O'Leary told you, I have known Clare and her family for a long time. It is no exaggeration to say that in some respects Clare knew and respected me as a father to her. So what happened yesterday was absolutely heartbreaking for me . . . excuse me a moment . . . I'm sorry, I just need a moment . . . I can tell you, in all honesty, I loved Clare like a father . . . I'm sorry . . . what was I saying? Yes . . . so, as a result of what I suffered yesterday, I have decided I could not live with myself if I didn't now do everything possible to ensure a tragedy like this never happens again. It's scandalous that despite many promises there are no legal guidelines to ensure that such trips are carried out with the maximum safety for the children involved. So I hereby pledge to all of you that I will not rest until this question has been tackled properly. From today onwards I shall be devoting myself to leading a campaign for new government guidelines to increase safety regulations for trips like this one, whether they be school trips, youth club outings or any other expedition.

'And I can tell you that this campaign will be waged at national level, not just here in Exxington but at Westminster! Because there can be no higher cause than the safety of our children, our children who are the future of our whole society. And I can tell you that I, Selwyn Knox, will be at the heart of that great campaign.

'Thank you very much, everybody. I would like to end by asking us all just to take a couple of moments of silence to turn our thoughts to Clare O'Leary, who is missing in the mountains, for believers among us to pray for her salvation, and for all of us to express the hope that Clare will be found safe and well and that she'll be back here soon with her loving parents.'

But what Selwyn Knox could not hear at that moment was the voice of Clare herself, poor Clare, lying in the mountains—

'I know he's coming. I know the great auk is coming,' said Clare, her eyes now burning from the pain and fever, but burning too with hope and looking to the happiness that lay ahead.

'The great auk is coming.'

And Clare was right, because what happened next was exactly as she had foreseen it.

With the utmost gentleness, the great auk swooped down to the ledge where Clare was lying.

Even though a tear was running through the feathers round his noble eyes, he smiled his great auk smile at her and Clare felt comforted.

And then, just as she had known he would, the great auk cradled her in his powerful claws – taking infinite care not to crush or hurt her.

With a mighty beating of his powerful wings, he rose from the sluggish pull of the earth and hovered briefly over the mountain ledge.

Clare felt the relief and thrill of weightlessness.

Then the great auk soared into the sky, carrying his precious cargo to the safety and warmth of his noble nest.

In Exxington, outside a terraced house on a council estate, a mobile phone rang moments later and a member of the media listened to a message from his newsroom.

'Mr Knox . . . Mrs O'Leary. I'm sorry to interrupt. We've just heard. Clare's been found.'

2

GEOFF MADDLE was watching the television in the council leader's office with a growing sense of anger.

The story had been too late to make the papers, so that was OK.

On the radio the *Today* programme had given in to its current anal fixation with the faltering economic situation, running item after item slagging off the government for things that any reasonable person knew were beyond its control, like the state of the stock market, the crisis of British manufacturing or the collapse of Marconi and all the other crap news.

Geoff had felt his usual fury with the insidious John Humphrys and his weasely undermining of all the government's achievements, his fixation with attacking it over GM, and his refusal to give any government minister a fair hearing in interviews more like public lynchings than exchanges of views.

It was further confirmation – if confirmation were needed – that the PM was right to spurn the *Today* programme in favour of *Richard and Judy* and *Tonight with Trevor McDonald*. They were the shows real people followed and took notice of. Not like *Today*, with its audience of sad bastards in the Westminster village, the saddo journalists and political observers who were more concerned with observing the fluff in their own navels than doing anything relevant to the real concerns of real Britain.

Anyway, the consequence of all that – all those sad *Today*

programme obsessions – thought Geoff with some relief, was that the dead-girl story had actually come well down the programme's running order and that it had been played low-key, with no opposition spokesman and no real attempt to exploit the political implications of the New Project council connection.

So not bad, a score draw there, Geoff thought.

But then he had switched on the end of *Breakfast* news to keep an eye on how the story was playing on the telly and – to his amazement – had come in on the middle of Selwyn Knox's impromptu press conference at the girl's family home.

Geoff found it hard to believe his ears.

In all his years as a professional media director, in all the hundreds of stories he had managed for New Project, he had never heard anything so badly controlled and so ill-disciplined as this. What had happened to the 'culture of no surprises' the party had inculcated in all its workers and officials?

This was exactly what he had warned those bloody councillors *not* to do!

Not to go off spinning a line that hadn't been cleared by Downing Street; *not* to start shooting from the hip with freelance versions of the story, however convincing and however clever.

Geoff Maddle's fury with Selwyn Knox grew as he heard Knox expand his maverick line of special pleading and self-justification. Yeah, right! That all sounds pretty good for Selwyn Knox esquire, Geoff fumed, but what's it going to do for the rest of us? What's it going to do for the party? It won't take the media long to spot that Knox is dumping on his colleagues; it won't take them long to come round here asking who's to blame, who it was that made all those mistakes superhero Selwyn had to try to put right – what a fucking shambles!

'Bob! Bob Travers! Get down here now! Have you seen what's running on the telly? It's your man, that bloody Selwyn Knox.

He's on *Breakfast* news and he's off spinning his own line on this story. It's bad news for you guys, I can tell you. You're the council leader and he's dropping you and the New Project group in the shit. This is exactly what I was sent up here to stop happening. You get him on the phone right now, mate, and tell him I want him here in this office in less than half an hour. Tell him I'm going to have to ring Downing Street about this and it's not good news for you or for me or for anyone—'

'Good morning, Downing Street.'

'Put me through to Charlie McDonald.'

'Who's calling, please?'

'It's Geoff, Geoff Maddle.'

'Good morning, Mr Maddle. Putting you through now.'

'Charlie, is that you? . . . Yeah, OK, mate. How you doing?'

Geoff Maddle had known Charlie McDonald for twenty years. They had worked together as junior reporters at the Brixton Newspaper Group, where Charlie's colour – a deep west African brown – and his size – six feet seven inches in his undarned socks – had helped protect Geoff's pasty white, scrawny English ass on numerous occasions in a variety of professional and personal scrapes. In the bars of Brixton, they had shared more pints than they cared to remember, more stories than most hacks get through in a lifetime and more women than either recalled or would admit to. Both of them were New Project through and through and fired with a grim determination to get their party into power 'by hook or by crook – whatever it took!'

Geoff had gone on to work for the National Union of Journalists, fronting its PR effort and doing his best to defend its anaemic leadership from the overwhelming opinion among hacks that, when it came to standing up for its members, the NUJ packed all the punch of a blancmange.

And Charlie had taken the job as chief political correspondent for the *Daily Mail*, a move that had prompted much amazement and ribald hilarity among his friends and colleagues. Charlie's reply, when challenged over how a pillar of the black community and the Project party left could write for the right-wing *Mail*, was to laugh and ask whether his questioner had never heard of the fifth column or the then much-vaunted tactic of entryism.

It was the run-up to the 2005 general election that had brought the two of them back together.

As a political journalist, Charlie had long moved in elevated political circles, getting to know and admire national figures like Alastair Campbell and Hugh Gavno. He had a high intellectual regard for Campbell's political writings and a more physical appreciation of his outpourings in certain male-orientated organs – the sort of writer whom one reads, in Alfred de Musset's memorable phrase, with one hand.

Charlie's ethnic and social background – the archetypal ghetto boy made good – and his undeniable physical presence had earned him a high profile among the chattering classes.

His job gave him access to high places and he spent the late nineties and early noughties cultivating his links with the coming men of the New Project party. His friendship with Andy Sheen, the young lion who was rescuing Project from the unelectable doldrums of Militate, proto-communist trade unions and self-destruct-button squabbling, was reflected in a noticeable softening of the *Mail*'s tirades against New Project.

Charlie was even credited with suggesting the party's Procter & Gamble-esque brand name, New Improved Project (or NIP, as it was joshingly called by Old Project diehards), and the PR campaign that went with it. Privately, he used to say that New Project was located somewhere between the party he had grown up in and the newspaper he was now working for, and he didn't mean it entirely as a joke.

When the election was announced, Andy Sheen had asked Charlie how he would feel about coming to work full-time for the party. Sheen's explanation of the role seemed nebulous, but Charlie immediately spotted the potential it offered. Few people in those days realized how powerful the New Project spin doctors were to become, how much influence the imperatives of presentation would soon have over the substance of party policy-making. But from Andy's sketchy job description Charlie knew that he could be at the pinnacle of that power and influence. He was delighted.

After a little diplomatic hesitation, Charlie McDonald went back to Andy Sheen with a few additional demands about his title (director of strategy and communications), office (next to the PM in Downing Street with a window overlooking the garden) and formal powers. Sheen promised him the incoming Project party government – no one had any doubt they'd be elected – would give him all the power he needed.

When New Improved Project were duly voted in, Andy Sheen became the voice of the country's conscience, a righteous, ethical, trustworthy Prime Minister, and he took his protégé with him.

As a non-elected official, Charlie McDonald's job was supposed to make him a back-room boy, but his colour, his attitude and his size meant he didn't stay in the shadows for long. His natural street-wise, no-nonsense authority had worked on the streets of Brixton and it worked equally well in Whitehall. It wasn't long before even the toughest MPs and ministers understood that when Charlie spoke they needed to sit up and listen.

Having thus secured his own future, Charlie McDonald set about recruiting the people he wanted to work for him.

Few were surprised when his first port of call was Geoff Maddle. Charlie wanted people he could rely on in a tight corner, people who would punch their weight in a scrap and who wouldn't be too squeamish about some of the things they might be asked to do in the name of the party. Geoff had all of these qualities: in Charlie's eyes he also had the invaluable attributes of complete trustworthiness, complete discretion and complete devotion to the cause. His experience in PR at the NUJ was a bonus, as was the fact that he was so pissed off there that he leapt at the chance to work with his old mate.

In the months since New Project had come to power, sweeping Labour out of Downing Street, the two of them had built a ferocious team and an equally ferocious reputation. Now Downing Street had become the most efficient, most revered and most feared PR outfit in the whole of Europe.

Foreign governments sent their Charlie McDonald wannabes to study at the court of the master: to learn how carrots, sticks, black eyes, blackmail, saccharine and smears, seduction and schmooze can all be deployed to keep the government at the top of the news agenda; how the media could be flattered or cowed into submission; how difficult journalists could be neutralized; and how inconvenient stories could be killed by kindness, by cunning or by cutting some bastard's balls off.

It was Geoff who had become the most accomplished exponent of the last technique. He was Number Ten's fireman, despatched to quell the flames of any hot news that looked in danger of singeing Andy Sheen's immaculate coat tails. His work was behind the scenes and all the more effective for it.

Success for Geoff Maddle was when a story did not appear; when a dog did not bark. For him no news was most definitely good news. Let Charlie and the others do the clever stuff, plant the positive stories, manipulate the facts to make them fit the government's preferred agenda, mould journalists and editors until it became second nature to them to know what Andy Sheen wanted and simply to write it. Let Charlie get on with all that; Geoff was happy going out and twisting a few arms, stuffing a few mouths, keeping his nose and Andy Sheen's arse as clean as possible.

And that was why he was here now in the back of beyond, in Exxington, where a New Project party council's stupidity had got a young girl killed.

'Listen, Charlie, have you seen what's going down this morning?'

'I saw the GM story on the front of the *Guardian* – ugh; the usual crap from Humphrys on the radio; and we've got a few helpful previews for Andy's speech at the Guildhall tomorrow. Your dead-girl story turned out OK, I thought. Is there something else I should know about?'

'No, Charlie. It's the dead girl I'm ringing you about. We kept it low-key overnight. It didn't make the papers, at least not in a big way. But we've had some stupid fucker from the council mouthing off.'

'What do you mean from the council? Is he a councillor?'

'Yeah. It's a bloke called Selwyn Knox and he's just done a presser outside the girl's house here. You must have missed it – they carried it live on *Breakfast* news.'

'Right; I've just come back from the eight-thirty meeting, so I haven't had the telly on. I've heard of this guy Knox, though: he was at the party conference last year making a big fuss about himself. Not a bad operator. What's he been saying?'

'Well, he's been defending himself, of course; saying that it wasn't his fault and he'd tried to stop the expedition before it set off – which is a bit rich, considering he was the one who ran the youth scheme and considering we know it was his idea to take them up into the mountains.

'Anyway, I suppose that's fair enough; but the thing that pisses me off is that he's trying to blame his mates and the council as a whole for the cock-up. He's talking as if we're doing some kind of cover-up here, as if we've got something to hide.

'And the worst thing is that he's trying to cover himself in roses by attacking the government for not having proper safety rules for school trips. He's setting himself up to lead some sort of campaign for legislation to regulate youth expeditions and that sort of thing. So he's coming out of this looking like the good guy in the white hat.'

'OK, Geoff. We don't want that. Not today of all days. Andy's speech tomorrow is the top story on our News Grid for more than a week. We can't afford to have that overshadowed by some loner promoting his own political career.'

'Yeah, that's definitely what's behind all this. It's the Selwyn Knox show and "Notice me please ... I want to be an MP." That's what Knox is up to, Charlie.'

'Right. Let me just think about this for a minute. The first thing we need to do is put out a news sponge to soak up some of the hacks' attention. I'll think of something – maybe we could do the Alice Sheen starts nursery school story, or perhaps I'll use the stuff about that Tory MP and the backhander allegations—

'Anyway, don't worry about that; that's not your problem. What *you* need to do is neutralize Knox. You need to stop this school-trip legislation campaign before it starts, Geoff. I don't know if you've followed it, but we've been having a real ding-dong with the education select committee over school trips ever since those lads were killed canoeing in France.'

'Yeah, I saw that. Some problem with the unions, isn't it?'

'Basically, if we introduce regulations, we'll have the teaching unions down on us like a ton of bricks; they're shit scared we'll use any legislation to prosecute their members every time little Johnny gets his knee scraped on a school nature ramble. It'd mean teachers and youth-club leaders would down tools and refuse to take children out anywhere. And we can't have that happening.

'Anyway, the PM doesn't want to hear another word on the subject: we've managed to slip the select committee a few sweeteners to keep them quiet, but if this guy Knox starts up the fuss again, we'll never hear the end of it. So we need to shut him up. Will you see what you can do with him? Have we got any useful information on Knox from the records?'

'No, we haven't. That's the problem, Charlie. While I was travelling up here last night, I got the boys at headquarters to run a check in Lancelot, to see what we could dig up on all the Exxington rednecks. I ran the check on all the council members 'cos I didn't know which ones would turn out to be the trouble-makers. Anyway, we've got something on nearly all of them. The one with the biggest list against his name is a bloke called Ian Murray, by the way: he's a dab hand at fiddling his expenses and we know he's used his influence on the Exxington housing committee to get council houses for at least three of his relatives. So he would have been easy; we could have screwed him over, no trouble. The problem is that Knox came out completely clean. You know, I think that's the first time I've ever seen Lancelot not come up with something on a subject: Christ knows, we spend enough time and effort collecting and sifting all the dirt we keep in there!'

'OK, Geoff. Don't worry. If you can't threaten him, you'll just have to reason with him! And if that doesn't work, try a bit of sweet talking. Tell him Andy Sheen knows who he is and rates him as a future MP or something – all he has to do is agree to drop this barmy campaign idea he's talking about. Think that'll do the trick?'

'I'm not sure. You said yourself Knox is good at making a fuss – I take it we're not really going to offer him a seat, are we?'

'Mmm—' Charlie McDonald hesitated. 'I don't know, Geoff. Maybe, maybe not. I told you he did well at the party conference. And I know it's a pain in the arse what he's been up to today, but you have to admit it shows he's got guts. You've got to hand it to him: he's turned a pretty bleak story into something potentially very positive for himself. That's a talent we could use. It's not everyone who has the nous to do that sort of thing. And it's not everyone who comes up clean after we've dug through their records in Lancelot! Ha! I dread to think what you and I would have against us if they ran a check on us, mate! Anyway, just size up the situation. See what you can do to keep him quiet without promising him anything. But actually, you know, if you can't manage that, Andy *has* got a couple of safe seats going spare for the next election. Come back to me if you think we'll need to use one of them on Knox. OK?'

'OK, Charlie. I'll see what I can do—'

As he put the phone down, Geoff Maddle felt a surge of anger. He didn't know Selwyn Knox, he'd never even met him. But instinctively he disliked the man.

Geoff was still smarting from Knox's TV appearance, which he saw as a deliberate challenge to his own authority: he'd told the councillors to keep their mouths shut and Knox had gone shooting his mouth off; he'd told them they had to agree a party line and Knox had gone to the press with his own version of events.

So, no team player – that was for sure!

But at the same time, and it pained him to admit it, Geoff was impressed with Knox's performance. It had been clear to him from the outset that Knox was the man in the hot seat and that if anyone was going to get blamed for Clare's death it was Knox. Knox was the man who ran the bloody youth scheme and – according to everyone except Knox himself – the man who had organized the trip to the mountains. And yet here he was on the TV, as bold as brass, painting himself as the hero of the hour: not only had he counselled against the trip, he had – in his version of events – kept his head when all around him had lost their marbles.

And how clever of him, thought Geoff, to do all that emoting on camera: in the eyes of the media, Knox was pretty bullet-proof now, a friend of the family, a father to Clare and almost as upset by her death as the mother herself. How could anyone be callous enough to suggest that maybe Selwyn Knox should take some – if not all – of the blame for what went wrong?

And Geoff couldn't help admiring the final master stroke of Knox's performance: leaving the media with something to throw the story forward, something to distract them away from Selwyn Knox and someone else to chew on. By dropping in the safety campaign right at the end, Knox had shifted the spotlight away from himself and straight onto the government. Now the government was the villain for not having regulations to stop accidents on mountains! What a devious bastard!

Nine fourteen a.m. 'Ride of the Valkyries' ringing on the mobile.

Always a welcome event for Selwyn Knox.

Always a sign that someone wanted him, needed him, was taking an interest in him.

'Knox here.'

'Selwyn, it's Bob Travers and it's bad news. You'd better get down here pronto. The guy from London is hitting the roof. He's on the phone now to Charlie McDonald in Downing Street and he says he wants to see you right away. Can I tell him you're on your way? You are on your way aren't you, Selwyn?'

'Yeah. Tell him I'll be there. It's about my statement to the press, is it?'

'Damn right it is. You've put your foot in it there, good and proper. You're not going to be London's blue-eyed boy any more after this, I can tell you. You can wave goodbye to a seat in parliament.'

'All right, Bob, keep your hair on. We'll see. Tell Maddle I'll be there in a couple of hours; there's a few things I need to do first.'

'A couple of hours? He's not going to like that. He says—'

Knox cut the connection.

The Valkyries were riding again.

And this time the ring was tinged with something else.

Not fear. Not panic.

But apprehension – an unaccustomed doubt whether the summons from the outside world would be the harbinger of new glories, accolades, promotions.

'Hello, Knox here.'

'Oh . . . hi, Selwyn.'

The voice was familiar, but somehow hesitant.

'Who's that?'

'It's Nigel – Nigel Tonbridge from BBC Radio Strathclyde.'

'Oh, Nigel. Of course. How are you?'

Selwyn was back in his stride now. A local journalist. Something he knew how to deal with. 'Do you want a quote on the tragedy? What happened was awful and we need to learn the lessons for the future. Safety on school trips and youth club outings needs to be codified and policed by the government. Is that OK?'

'Yeah, that's fine, Selwyn. I got all your stuff from the news conference as well, so we're OK on that. I'm just ringing about something different.'

'Oh yeah. What's that? Fire away.'

'It's a bit tricky, Sel. I'm not sure how to put this.'

For the first time in the conversation, Knox hesitated.

'Well, I can't guess what it is, Nigel. You'll have to tell me.'

'OK. I've been speaking to Ian Murray.'

'Yeah . . . and? What's he saying?'

Murray the councillor, old school Project party . . . Knox knew from council meetings that Murray was a plodder. Thorough, but lacking imagination. No future in the New Project party. Not like Selwyn Knox.

'Well, he had a couple of things to say about you, Sel. He said you broke ranks with the council; he says you didn't turn up for the councillors' meeting on the Clare O'Leary tragedy—'

'Yeah, so what? Somebody had to get out there and talk to the press. Those old farts don't realize you can't spend hours wittering away to yourselves when the media needs to be given some proper information. They'd still be in there now if I hadn't gone and done it – that's not for quoting, by the way.'

'Yeah, Sel, I know that. But what Murray's saying is that you went out on a limb. You didn't stick to what the council wanted to say about the tragedy.'

'Oh yeah. Like what?'

'Well, you know Murray. He won't go into details. He's a bit old schoolish. But he didn't sound happy with you at all. In fact, he sounded pretty angry.'

'Yeah? So what?'

'Look, Sel. Reading between the lines, I think they're all a bit pissed off with you. Partly because you've come out of this looking like the hero of the hour, partly because they've all been made to look stupid. And partly because they're shit scared the council's going to get blamed for the whole thing. If you're the only one who actually went out looking for the kid after she went missing and all the others just ran round like headless chickens, it doesn't look good for them, does it?'

'I can't help that, Nigel. I've made my position clear – that I was against this trip in the first place. That I wasn't convinced it met even the most basic safety standards. And that I did everything in my power to find poor little Clare when she went missing – despite the panic in the group leaders' ranks. And now I'll be lobbying hard for national legislation to make school trips and youth club outings safe in the future. It's going to be my crusade, Nigel, and I'll take it to the national press, to parliament and to the government. We need proper guidelines for the supervision of children when they're taken out on trips like this. I'm going to make sure something is done about this scandal.'

'Yeah, I know, Sel. It's a good issue to take up. It'll do you no harm either. But what Murray is saying is more to do with what actually happened up there on the mountain.'

Selwyn Knox hesitated again, and this time Nigel Tonbridge noticed it . . .

'What exactly is Murray saying, Nigel? I need to know what he's been saying to you.'

'Well, what he says, Selwyn, is that he saw no evidence of your heroics up on the mountain.'

'Of course, he didn't. He was pissing around at base camp while I was out looking for the bloody girl.'

'Yeah. Murray doesn't dispute that. He's not trying to make himself a hero. But he is saying that you hadn't been with the party for quite a long time before they noticed Clare was missing. And that you only came back much later.'

'Nigel! You weren't there. I was. Conditions up there were

atrocious. You couldn't see a yard in front of your nose. No one knew where anyone was. We all got lost and started going round in circles. It's no good one member of the team trying to stir up trouble for the others.'

'I don't think Murray is trying to do that. OK, he's pretty annoyed about you missing the councillors' meeting to speak to the press. But he's not trying to do a whitewash on this. I think he's unhappy at the way you've been portrayed as the good guy in the white hat and made all the rest of them look like idiots.'

'OK, so he's not proud of messing up. What's that got to do with me?'

'Listen, Sel . . . the thing is – Murray's saying that you and Clare both went missing *before* the fog came down. And that you came back much, much later, on your own. So for one thing they had no idea what you were doing all the time they were regrouping. And for another Murray claims that when you came back you said straight away you'd been out looking for Clare. He says no one had told you anyone had gone missing, so there was no way you could've known about Clare – *unless you were with her when she got lost!* Were you with her, Selwyn? How did you know Clare was missing? Were you with Clare O'Leary when she disappeared? . . .'

There was a pause on the line. Then Knox, his voice strained, rattled.

'Look, Nigel! I'm not going to stand here and listen to you calling me a liar! I know what I did! I tried to save Clare!'

Selwyn Knox was flustered. He knew he was flustered and he knew it was showing. He was angry with himself for letting it show. He prided himself on not letting things show.

'The others can say what they like, Nigel. They messed up. It's their fault. And I did my best to put things right. I'm still doing my best to put things right. To stop this sort of thing happening again in the future. So how dare they try to blame me? How dare they try to excuse themselves and blame me? They've got absolutely no evidence of anything . . . of any of what they're saying . . . they're trying to drop me in it to save themselves, Nigel. That's what they're doing!'

'Look, it's not me who's saying this. It's Ian Murray. He's Project party. He's your colleague. All I'm doing is telling you what Murray has said to me.'

'And all I'm saying is that if you broadcast any of this you won't have a leg to stand on. There's nothing behind all this. Nothing at all. Murray and the others have got no proof of anything. I'll string the bastards up if they repeat it again – and I'll string you up too!'

'Look, Sel—'

'They've got no evidence of anything. What can they say? They were all pissing around doing nothing at base camp and I was out there trying to save the girl. What can they say against that?'

'Look, Sel, don't have a go at me—'

The phone call was abruptly terminated. Nigel Tonbridge was left with a dialling tone and the first vague suspicions that he might actually have a story.

3

SELWYN KNOX didn't arrive at Exxington District Council until eleven o'clock. Two hours, five strong coffees, a lot of thinking and numerous phone calls after Geoff Maddle had first summoned him.

Geoff Maddle was not happy.

Geoff Maddle was not used to being dissed by redneck councillors from the back of beyond. Even if they might become Charlie McDonald's or Andy Sheen's little favourite.

'Where the hell have you been? I told you to get down here straight away!'

'Good morning, Mr Maddle. My name is Selwyn Knox.'

'I know what your bloody name is, mate. Don't piss around with me. You know who I am and you damn well know who sent me here. So you'd better start explaining what the hell you think you're up to.'

'I'm not sure what you want me to explain. I've been doing my best for Exxington District Council and for the Project party. I take it you know that I've been comforting Clare's parents in my role as youth scheme leader?'

'Too damn right I do. Me and several hundred thousand other people saw you all over the television this morning. And who gave you permission to do that? No one bloody did! I didn't. Charlie McDonald didn't. Andy Sheen didn't. So what do you think you were up to?'

'All right, Geoff. I know I should have cleared it with you, but it just happened, really. I was at the house trying to help the O'Learys – I thought you'd approve of that, showing the Project group in a compassionate light and so forth. But then all the media and the TV crews turned up and they kept asking Eileen O'Leary to go out and talk to them. Now I knew we needed to control the situation – you guys are always telling us we should control news situations and not let the story get out of hand, right? And I knew that if Eileen went out on her own she could have said some very damaging things, you know, about the council – and about Ian Murray not doing anything to make sure Clare didn't wander off and get lost up there in the mountains – so I had a quick word with Eileen and told her that she should just make a short statement. I told her not to answer any questions because the media always try to distort whatever you say. I said I'd answer any questions on her behalf, and she agreed because she trusts me. I've known Clare and her family for two years now under the Project group's "Help the Community" initiative – we've been doing some pretty good work on that, Geoff, I'll have to tell you about it sometime. It's certainly got New Project a good name with the poorer voters, New Project voters, Geoff, people who are going to keep Exxington New Project—'

'Look, Knox, cut the crap! You know what I'm talking about. It's all the stuff you've been saying to the media that's got Charlie McDonald pissed off – and Andy Sheen too. They want to know why you made yourself out to be the hero in all this and left the council to carry the can.'

'Geoff, I had to do it! No one else from the council was standing up to be counted so someone had to talk to the press. Otherwise they would have just written whatever they wanted and that wouldn't have been good for the Project party. Your guys in London, all the New Project spin doctors, they're always telling us, "Never leave a story without a comment. Never let the hacks write unguided because they'll get it wrong." Now that's just plain good sense. And that's all I was trying to do! I mean, let's get real on this one: there's been a pretty big cock-up; it's some of our councillors who are to blame, and the flak's coming our way. So I reckoned the best thing was to be up-front, to say, "OK, someone made a mistake, mistakes happen, mistakes are human; Ian Murray is basically a good guy, but he should never have been leading that expedition up in the mountains. He messed up, but – hey – there was nothing evil about what happened up there. He just took his eye off the ball." And you know, Geoff, I think people will respect us for that sort of honesty. They'll see we're human too. So it's no longer Exxington Council that made the mistake, it's no longer the New Project party that's in the dock: it's just one old codger who bit off more than he could chew. And another thing: can I tell you why I was a bit late coming here to see you, Geoff? It's because I've spent the last two hours giving exactly that message to all the media—'

'You've what? You mad bastard! Who told you to do that? You must be joking! You've been doing all the press calls—?'

'Yes, Geoff, but don't get angry. Let me tell you what the response has been. It's been really good—'

'Wait a minute! Why does Exxington Council employ a press office? And why have I just spent all morning telling that press office what to say if the press ring for a comment? Why have you been doing a job that someone else is trained to do . . . and . . . and paid to do?'

'Oh, Geoff, if you knew the council press office the way I do, you'd know you can't rely on them for anything. I always do my own press work. That way you can be sure the message gets across without any intermediaries and without any cock-ups. I don't want to tell you of all people how to suck eggs, but I always find the media respect a politician much more if he talks to them direct instead of hiding behind press officers, you know. Anyway, let me tell you how this story is running with the media. I've talked to virtually all the nationals and our local contacts, and they all agree this was an unfortunate tragedy and nothing more. One or two of them are going to have a go at Ian Murray, but not as a councillor, just as a bloke who got out of his depth. And the overriding emphasis in all the papers is going to be on poor Clare and the human tragedy. It's not going to be a political story, I can promise you that. You can relax—'

Geoff Maddle thought for a moment.

'Are you completely sure of that, Selwyn? You're not spinning me a line, are you? Because if you are—'

'Absolutely not, Geoff. Absolutely not. The press are swallowing what I've been telling them. But I'll be completely honest with you – there's just one guy who's got me a bit worried. We've got a reporter at our local BBC station up here – name of Nigel Tonbridge – a bit of a wanker, really, too big for his boots, real bigot, anti-Project, poodle of the Tories. He's been out to get the New Project group for months now and I think from talking to him he may have a go at the council for lax safety practices on this trip—'

'What makes you say that? Has he got something we don't know about? What's his angle?'

'I don't think he's got an angle exactly. He's just talking in general terms, you know, about the council's record on safety and how they shouldn't have let the expedition go up the mountains. That sort of thing. But I know Tonbridge and he's likely to use this as a political football. I'm pretty sure he's going to have a go at the Project party for not introducing proper safety legislation for school trips—'

'Oh, shit! That's exactly what we don't need. That'll really stir things up. And that's something else I need to speak to you about, Selwyn, by the way, about this daft idea you've got for some sort of safety campaign. We're going to have a problem with that one. But look, first things first. First we've got to knock this Tonbridge guy on the head. How did you leave things with him?'

'Well, we've got a bit of time, Geoff. His show's on air this evening at five o'clock and I said I'd get back to him with something this afternoon. But to be honest, I think we need to do something about him before then. I think we need to put Nigel Tonbridge back in his box! Actually, there is one thing I was just wondering about. You've got that computer at headquarters, haven't you? What's it called? Lancelot, isn't it? – the one that keeps all the useful information on politicians and people you think might be anti-Project? Do you think there's any chance you could have a look on it for something on this Nigel Tonbridge guy? We'd have to be pretty quick, though, that's the only problem—'

'Hah! Don't worry about that, mate. Lancelot is quicker than quick! I could put the call in now and we'd have all the gen on Nigel Tonbridge back with us in no time at all.'

'Well, do you think you could do that for me, Geoff? It would be really useful – and then I'll get back to Tonbridge a.s.a.p. and make sure he doesn't dump on the Project party. And then perhaps we could talk about my campaign for school-trip safety legislation—?'

There are few feelings in the life of a journalist to equal the intensity of emotion involved in tracking a scoop. When that scoop combines the pathos of human tragedy, the revulsion of human depravity and the whiff of political scandal, the emotion can be overwhelming.

Nigel Tonbridge was on a high.

His thoughts roamed incessantly between the horror of Clare's lonely death, the enormity of the allegations he alone was privy to and the possibility that a man like Selwyn Knox could actually be a murderer. Selwyn Knox the youth scheme leader, Selwyn Knox the pillar of the community, the sanctimonious holier-than-thou puritan with a gleaming future as a New Project MP? Surely not.

And even as Nigel churned over all the implications of what he knew, or felt he knew, another thought lurked in the back of his mind – consciously repressed, constantly resurfacing – a premonition that this story could be the turning point in his own career, the breakthrough all journalists seek and few achieve. The anticipation of what it could lead to filled his mind with images of fame and success: Nigel Tonbridge, the investigative journalist; Nigel Tonbridge, the righter of wrongs; Nigel Tonbridge, the guest of chat shows and national TV debates. It was a somewhat ignoble thought when a young girl had just died, but he found it hard to shake off.

First, though, he had to convince the guardians of BBC Radio Strathclyde that his story was kosher and that he, Nigel Tonbridge, should get on the air and tell the world.

Nigel's news editor, George Young, was one of those hacks who probably enjoy being referred to as hardbitten, the type of journalist who's been round the houses and come back with a few bumps and scrapes to prove it. For George, scandal was not new. Forty years in the BBC, forty years of competent, unspectacular news processing had left him, if not exactly cynical, then at least hard to impress. And George knew his journalistic law. He was the man who'd been copy-tasting on the BBC's general news desk in Broadcasting House in London the night news of John Profumo's affair with Christine Keeler had broken. George had dropped the story because he wasn't going to risk the Secretary of State for Defence suing the Corporation for defamation. Ever since then he had been known as 'the man who spiked Profumo'. Nigel knew he would have a fight on his hands.

'Listen, son,' George replied, after pausing to digest the story Nigel had breathlessly spilled out, 'I'm going to give you some good advice. That's a pretty good story and it'd be hot as mustard for any journalist who can stand it up. But right now it's a passport to disaster. Just think about it for a minute. You've got a girl dead up a mountain. You've got a local councillor, Calvinist pillar of the community – no previous, no fangs, no dribbling saliva – and you're going to tell the world he's a child murderer? Not on my radio station, you're not! I'd need a lot more proof than you've given me before I'd let you loose on the airwaves with that story.'

'But, George, *you* think about it, too. This is the biggest story we've ever had up here – well, except for the spy in the shipyard last year. You know it's our chance to put Radio Strathclyde on the map. This Selwyn Knox is a big fish in the Project party. He's going to be an MP pretty soon, you know – some people are saying he's a natural to be a minister in the government. So are we going to let him get away with it? Are we going to let someone like that run the country when we know he abused and killed a little girl? You can't let that happen, George. We've got to run with this story.'

'Keep your hat on, son. I didn't say I want to let him get away with anything, *if* he did it. And that's a pretty big if. Look, what have you got? You've got a councillor who says he thinks Knox took the little girl off and didn't come back until she was dead. But did anyone see him molesting her? Did anyone see him do her in? No. And has your councillor told the police about it? I thought it was *their* job to keep monsters out of government, not mine.'

'George, he's been to the police and they told him to get lost.

The problem is Knox is best mates with the Exxington cops – I think he's best mates with everyone who has any clout round here. Anyway, Murray was basically told to keep quiet. The police and all the other journalists I've spoken to have decided this was just a tragic accident and that Selwyn Knox is the best thing since Mother Teresa. It's no good hoping PC Plod will sort this out for us because he won't.'

'OK, I can see that, Nige. But put yourself in my place, lad. If the police are saying it was an accident, then in my book that means to all intents and purposes it was an accident. We're not paid to go out on a limb to contradict the strong arm of the law. That's not our job, is it?'

'Well, maybe it isn't, George. But how will you feel tonight if you go to bed knowing you were the only person who could stop a child abuser and murderer getting away with it and you'd done nothing?'

'Hang on a minute, Nigel. I didn't say we weren't going to do anything. I've got grandchildren, you know. I'm as upset as you are. It's just that I don't want to go off half-cock with a story that's going to collapse and drop us all in the shit. So you just calm down a bit and tell me again exactly what you've got. For a start, will your councillor – what's his name? Ian Murray – will he back us up if we do go public? Will he come on air and repeat what he's said to you? Can you get the girl's parents to finger Knox? Will Knox say anything himself?'

'George, look, I'm chasing all those leads. I've got calls in to everyone. But this is a difficult story and it's not going to be handed to us on a plate. At some stage we're going to have to be brave and start the ball rolling. We may not get it cut and dried before we hit the air with it, but once we go public I'm dead sure we'll get people confirming what we say about Knox. He must have abused other little girls too, I reckon. We just have to be the ones to start the ball rolling on this story.'

'Well, you probably haven't come to the right man if that's what you want to do, son,' said George with a wry smile. 'I'm the man who spiked Profumo, remember? Anyway, I'll tell you what I think. If we're serious, we're going to have to clear the story with the BBC lawyers; there's no way we can avoid that, whatever way you look at it. And at the moment I haven't got a leg to stand on if I go to them with what you've told me. At the very least, you're going to have to go back to Ian Murray and get him to put something on tape. Then you'll need a statement from the family. And you'll have to run it past the police. OK? Do you think Murray will stick to his guns?'

'Yeah, I know he will. He was absolutely certain of what he was telling me. He said he'd discussed it with Dan Curragh, the other councillor who was up there, and they both agreed it was really fishy about Knox and the girl. But let's get this straight: if I get Murray to go firm on this, you'll let me put something out on air?'

George thought for a moment and grunted. 'Yes, I suppose so. It was a terrible thing about that little girl. If there really is something going on, someone's got to stand up and be counted.'

He didn't show it – he never did – but Selwyn Knox had an anxious few hours while he waited for Maddle and McDonald to interrogate Lancelot, waited for the dirt on Nigel Tonbridge that would put God back in his heaven and restore Selwyn Knox's universe back to its usual, pristine, calculated order.

Five o'clock was the deadline. The five o'clock show on BBC Radio Strathclyde – 'Drive Time, Tonbridge Time'. It was coming fast.

And he had a few shocks to deal with in the meantime.

The Valkyries now were bringing Selwyn calls he would rather not receive.

'Is that Mr Knox? Hello ... Selwyn? Yes, it's Eileen here, Eileen O'Leary. I'm sorry to bother you. It's just we're very upset ... we're very upset about Clare, you know ... and we need to ask you something. Is that all right? We've had the police on the phone. They took us to identify Clare's body ... oh God, oh, Holy Mother of God ... I can't ... I can't ... no, it's all right. Wait a minute, Mr Knox ... what I need to ask you ... the police have asked us ... asked me and Frank, you know ... asked us if we want an autopsy done on Clare—'

'What? When did they ask you that? That's ridiculous. I talked to the police and they said they wouldn't be doing one. Who told you—?'

'No, Selwyn. They didn't say they have to do one. They just asked us if we want one. They said it was usual to do one in the circumstances.'

'Yes, usual but not strictly required. That's what they told me.'

'That's right. They told us the same. They aren't obliged to do one because there's no foul play involved or anything, and they say they don't want to put us through more than we've already been through—'

'Yes. That's right, Eileen. There's no need for an autopsy. Did you tell them that?'

'Yes, we did. That's what we thought too. But they said we had the choice if we wanted one. And, you know, I just thought: what if there has been something wrong up in the mountains? What if it wasn't just an accident?'

'Eileen, look, I was up in the mountains. I know nothing happened to Clare. It was just a terrible accident. And you know I loved Clare like a father. So I just want what's best for her and for you. Think of her. Her poor little body has been through enough. We don't want anyone cutting her up with a knife, do we?'

'No . . . I suppose . . . no . . . you're right, Mr Knox. We'll tell them . . . OK. That's decided, then . . . I'll tell Frank to drop the idea . . . OK . . . right . . . I'm sure you're right. There's just one other thing . . . can I ask you about it? We've been refusing to talk to the press, like you told us, you know . . . but there's just one of them who's been pestering us . . . and actually we know him, and we'd like to talk to him if you don't mind . . . it's a boy called Nigel Tonbridge, who was in my little brother's class at school and now he's working for the BBC. He says he wants to talk about Clare and what she was like and things—'

The sharpness of Knox's response took Eileen by surprise.

'Listen, Eileen! There's no way you or Frank should talk to Nigel Tonbridge! He's not interested in Clare or her memory. We're the only ones who respect Clare, who loved Clare. You, Frank and me: we're the only ones. Tonbridge is like all journalists. All he wants to do is exploit Clare's memory and your tragedy to make his name as a journalist. He's only thinking about himself, take it from me. There's no way you should talk to him – all right? You trust me, don't you, Eileen?'

'Yes, but—'

'So you're not going to talk to him, are you?'

'No, I suppose not—'

'If he rings again, just tell him you can't talk to him and that I'm handling all questions so he should talk to me, all right? In fact, I'll ring him now, so you don't have to worry—'

'All right, Mr Knox. Thanks . . . thanks very much.'

'BBC Radio Strathclyde, Nigel Tonbridge speaking.'

'Yeah, hi. It's Selwyn Knox here.'

'Oh, yes. Thanks for ringing, Selwyn. I need to talk to you—'

'You've been pestering the O'Learys!'

'What? No I haven't. I just rang them for a comment. I was at school with Eileen Bates, Eileen O'Leary, that is—'

'I don't care. Just stop it. Stop ringing them. Enough has happened to them. They don't need people like you pestering them at a time like this. I've got a statement on their behalf. You'd better write it down because this is all you're going to get. Are you ready? "Mr and Mrs O'Leary have suffered a great loss. Clare was a lovely child and will be greatly missed. The best thing now is for everyone to let Clare's memory rest in peace." And that's what you'd better run tonight, Nigel. That and nothing else. I'm referring to our earlier conversation. You know what I mean.'

'Well, look, Selwyn. I can't do that. You know I can't. I've got a pretty heavy story here, you know, the Ian Murray allegations and all that, I can't just drop it. Not unless you can tell me what really happened up there in the mountains. I need the truth, Selwyn. Can you give it to me?'

There was a brief pause. Then Knox, emollient now, suddenly helpful: 'OK. OK. Look, Nigel, don't do anything rash. I'll get back to you this afternoon. You're not on the air till five, are you? Don't do anything before then, OK? If you play this properly, I may have something for you in an hour or so. Something really big. But you have to hold on and not run the rubbish you've got from Murray. OK?'

'Yeah. OK, Selwyn, I'll wait. But you're going to give it to me straight, aren't you?'

'I am, Nigel. That's a promise. Just wait until you hear from me. OK?'

*

'Hello, this is Ian Murray's voicemail at Exxington District Council. I'm not here at the moment, so please leave a message and I'll get back to you as soon as possible. Please talk after the tone—'

'Murray, it's Selwyn Knox here, you bastard. It's one o'clock. You've been speaking to the press. You know what I'm talking about. Well, it's all crap that you've been telling them. It's absolutely untrue. There's not a shred of evidence and you're making some really libellous allegations. Oh, and another thing. Don't think I don't know about your expenses' scam: it's up to about twelve thousand pounds now, isn't it? And how your sister-in-law jumped the queue for a council house. I don't think those little facts would help your career if they got out – in fact, *you* probably wouldn't get out for six months minimum! So think about it – and you may decide you want to get on to Tonbridge and tell him you made a mistake. Which you most certainly did—'

'George, can I talk to you?'

Nigel Tonbridge was bringing his editor bad news.

'Yeah, come in, Nige. Had any luck standing up your big story?'

'Well, it's a bit tricky. It's sort of "good news, bad news". The first thing is that I've just rung Ian Murray again to ask him if he'll put something on tape.'

'And?'

'Well, I think he's been nobbled. He won't talk to me any more. He says he made a mistake when he rang me this morning and he's retracted everything he said.'

'Oh, well, that's the end of that one!' To Nigel's annoyance, George Young sounded mightily relieved. 'To tell you the truth, I never thought we'd get the story past the lawyers. It all sounded so tenuous. And Selwyn Knox, well . . . he's such a respected man; such a big fish in this town—'

'Yeah, but hang on a minute, George. For me, this doesn't kill the story. I think Murray's been warned off. He was so certain this morning. And now he's saying exactly the opposite, contradicting himself. It doesn't add up unless Knox has scared him off somehow. Anyway, the other thing is . . . I told you there was good news, bad news. Well, the good news is that Knox rang me himself, unprompted. So I reckon he's pretty worried about this story. At first he tried to warn me off; but when he saw I was serious he changed his tone completely and he's promised to ring back this afternoon before the show goes on air. He says he's got something really big to tell me. So if you'll authorize it, what I'd like to do is set up a tape to record his conversation with me – you know, covert taping. It's a bit tricky under BBC guidelines, so we'll have to testify that it's in the public interest. Is that OK? Then I'll get him to talk about what happened on the mountain and if we can get him on tape in his own words, we can definitely run something on the show, can't we, George?'

'Hmm. Maybe—' George Young looked dubious.

Nigel Tonbridge took it as a yes and went to set up the tape recorder.

'Good afternoon, Nigel, Selwyn Knox here. I promised I'd ring you back and I always keep my promises.'

'Oh, great. Thanks, Selwyn. Just wait a minute while I go to another phone. Don't hang up if the line goes dead for a moment. OK? . . . Right. Here we are. Now, Selwyn Knox . . . what do you have to say to me, Mr Knox?'

'Just a couple of things, Mr Tonbridge. The first is that you have been threatening me in a most scandalous way. Your allegations are, of course, completely false and what's more they are highly libellous.

'You have no evidence, no witnesses and no testimony to support your allegations. Since I am completely innocent in this matter, I can only put your behaviour down to a highly unprofessional political bias on your part against the New Project party, a bias that does you and the BBC no credit at all.

'My second point is that if you persist in repeating the sort of thing you have been saying, and in particular if any mention of it is ever made on air in any shape or form, I will see you in court in less time than it takes to say "record libel damages".

'And don't think you'll be able to count on any support from your corrupt and prejudiced former informant on the council because you won't.

'Finally, just in case you are recording this conversation, Mr Tonbridge, I want to make something very clear to you. I want you to know that I am aware of things about you and your past that show you in an extremely unfavourable light.'

Nigel felt as if a charge of electricity had surged down the phone line and rattled his headphones.

'What's that? What did you say?'

Knox's voice was calm, exaggeratedly deliberate.

'I said I know about your guilty secret, Nigel. I know what happened with you and your father—'

Nigel felt the electric shock in his ears; felt it burning in his brain.

'I don't know what you mean—'

'Oh, but I think you do, Nigel. I think you most certainly do.'

At four p.m. a white-faced Nigel Tonbridge was in George Young's office for the regular pre-show planning meeting.

'Sit down, Nigel. You look whacked. How's the big story? Did you get anything on the tape?'

For a moment Nigel sat motionless, deep in thought. Finally, he looked up and mumbled, 'No. I guess you were right, George. There's nothing in the story. There's nothing on the tape. In fact, the machine didn't work. And anyway Knox seems pretty innocent. He didn't really have anything to tell me. Nothing we could use. I must have got a bum steer from someone. I think we'd better forget it, if that's all right with you.'

Not surprisingly, it was more than all right with George Young, the man who spiked Profumo. 'OK, that's that, then. Now, let's have a think about a new lead for the show. I think the Clare O'Leary story has pretty much run its course. No one else seems to be covering it any more, so I think we can drop it. Now, if you agree, Nigel, I think we should lead the show on the investigation into the state of the town swimming pool. Apparently, there are loose tiles and dangerous seating. It seems someone had to have tetanus jabs after sitting on a rusty nail. So let's see if we can get the public health inspector to come on the show – OK?'

That evening in the Exxington Arms, Geoff Maddle was finally starting to loosen up. The dead-girl story had gone away with no damage to the party and Geoff was toasting his success with what was either his fourth or his fifth whisky.

'Anyway, well done, Selwyn, mate! I don't mind telling you, I listened to the opening headlines on that Nigel Tonbridge show with a bit of trepidation. So when they led on the swimming pool and the fat lady with the rusty nail in her arse I was well pleased! And not a mention of dead girls or New Project party councils. Charlie's just been on the blower from Number Ten and he says the first editions of tomorrow's nationals are looking pretty good, too. So well done. We got a result there. We'll have to get rid of that dope Ian Murray, of course. You know that, don't you? Don't you lose sleep over Murray, mate! I've told him he has to step down on health grounds. No great loss, if you ask me. The only thing is, Selwyn, you'll have to drop your bloody school-trip safety campaign – it's a pain in the arse, to tell you the truth. It's really embarrassing the government, you know. Andy's in deep shit with the teachers' unions and the select committee, so he's asking you as a favour – and Charlie and me are asking you, too – to drop it, mate. OK?'

Knox was a man to recognize his chance when he saw it. He thought for a moment, smiled and said, 'Hey! If Charlie Mc-Donald and Andy Sheen want me to drop it, what can I say? But listen, Geoff, we're all politicians and we all live in the real world. I've done you one favour today and now you're asking me to do you another one. So what do I get in return?'

'Well, you've got balls, mate, that's for sure! You were pretty ruthless dealing with the media too – pretty ruthless and pretty smart. And, you know what, that's the sort of attitude we like. I reckon you could go far. I know Charlie and Andy think pretty highly of you too. So if you're looking for a pay-off for today, why don't you think about coming to join us, say, on the media-management side of things – down in London, I mean. Get out of this dump, eh?'

But Selwyn Knox had his sights set on bigger things. 'I was thinking about a seat, Geoff. I'm a natural for an MP. Can you give me that?'

Geoff Maddle broke into a grin. 'Hey, hey! Somehow I thought you might say that. Well, that's not something yours truly can deliver, but you know what? I do know a man who might be able to. What do you think? Shall I get him on the mobile and see what he says?'

Geoff Maddle dialled a familiar number, went through a familiar switchboard, heard a familiar voice and passed the mobile to Selwyn Knox.

The following day, 11 September 2006, two hijacked planes crashed into Canary Wharf, wiping out Britain's tallest building and two thousand lives.

In Whitehall, a New Project party special adviser sent an email suggesting it was a good day to put out some of the difficult news stories the party would prefer the media to overlook.

In Exxington, Clare O'Leary was buried; so was Selwyn Knox's school-trip safety campaign.

In Downing Street three weeks later, Prime Minister Andy Sheen found time to sign – although not to read – the note that Charlie McDonald had written for him to welcome their latest recruit.

Dear Selwyn,

Terror and war are looming again. We need determined, ruthless people like you. Come and join us as an MP. Help us protect the values of our society.

Yours,
Andy Sheen

PART TWO

4

FEBRUARY 2011

SELWYN KNOX gazed at his own image in the brightly lit mirror of the chrome and glass en-suite bathroom attached to his ministerial office.

Knox liked the new Department of Commerce building on Marsham Street: it was clean and bright; it was sparse, bold, modernist; it looked to the future; it was not mired in the past.

He used to say the building mirrored his own character.

It was four years since he'd shaved off his beard and he felt the clean-shaven look was in keeping with the dynamic, pared-down, stripped-for-action image he and the New Project party were striving to convey.

It was four years since Selwyn Knox had become an MP.

The Canary Wharf tragedy had enflamed Prime Minister Andy Sheen's lust for revenge and in February 2007 he'd called a snap election on an 'Endorse the Next War' ticket.

At Sheen's invitation, Knox had contested and won a difficult campaign in a Scottish constituency vacated by an Old Project dinosaur who Charlie McDonald had helped persuade to step down.

And it was now two years to the day since Knox had landed his first cabinet post, rising by way of junior ministerial jobs in education and environment to become one of the youngest – if not the youngest ever – Secretary of State for Commerce.

As he stared into his face in the mirror, Knox reflected on his rise and rise; but his gaze did not soften with emotion. It remained hard and inscrutable. If his progress were to continue – which he knew it must – those eyes would have to stay cold, stay ruthless, stay merciless.

Knox did not blink even when Sonya Mair, his political adviser, tapped gently on the bathroom door.

Another minute went by. He passed his hand over his face, switched off the bathroom light and walked in darkness through the connecting door to his office.

As he slumped into the leather armchair, Sonya shrugged her shoulders and let the slip she was wearing slither to the carpet.

In the evening gloom, her body was silhouetted in the moonlit window and her luminous skin glowed like a siren's, calling men to their doom. The languor of her movements, her sensuous grace – at once serene yet arousing – were the language of her siren tongue. Her flesh voiced pleasures that men with eyes and ears unbound were fated to struggle against and then succumb to – ineluctably to drown.

She sensed Knox's eyes lingering on her flesh. Her body moved faster; her nails brushed hurried patterns on her naked skin.

She slid across the room, moving closer, still not looking him in the face.

She enjoyed this foreplay, this moment of maximum exposure. She enjoyed unveiling her naked flesh to a man's probing stare; she enjoyed hiding her eyes to allow men's gaze unhindered access to her body, to its intimate vulnerability, its welcoming secrets.

Sonya knew that this moment of anticipation, of contact

achingly delayed, could not often be prolonged, that physical invasion rapidly followed the invasion of men's eyes.

Now, though, she waited and as the waiting was drawn out she began to sense something other, a deviation from the rite's habitual course.

Now the moment of transition – the moment of turbulent, fleshly onslaught – was slow in coming.

Knox's gaze was on her – she knew it, she felt it, but where was his expected touch? Where were his hands invading her body? Why was her anticipation not eliciting a response?

She risked a furtive glance from under lowered eyelids.

She saw her boss on the green leather armchair, slouched, as when she had last looked at him. His eyes were fixed, intent, rapt almost, but devoid of desire, devoid of expression.

Her flesh shivered under Knox's gaze.

She was puzzled, unused to this absence of complicity, alarmed to discover his lack of participation in the rite she had been performing – and had mistakenly believed he was sharing.

She drew closer to her boss; she leaned over him, tall, slender, naked.

'It's no good, Sonya,' Knox said petulantly. 'It's not right . . . we need to try something else—'

'Jack! Your car's ready! The driver says the police barricades are all operating between here and Downing Street, so you'll need to leave soon if you want to get there on time. Shall I tell Tim?'

Jack Willans did not look pleased. The prospect of a stop–start drive through the anti-terrorist searches all the way from Dock-lands to Whitehall was bad enough; the thought of the grilling that lay in store for him from Andy Sheen and Charlie McDonald was infinitely worse.

'Yeah, OK, Linda. Tell Tim to hurry up. And tell him to bring the Operation Colditz papers with him. I'll meet him downstairs in the garage.'

2011 was shaping up to be a crucial year for DRE plc.

The fallout from the early struggles over Iraq in the first half of the noughties, back when Labour was in power, and the subsequent Allied invasions of Iran, Syria and Saudi Arabia had been a disaster for most of the top FTSE 100 companies. The Stock Exchange had fallen dramatically and had still not recovered significantly.

But for defence stocks the lengthy series of Middle East Wars, now universally known as the MEWs, had been a godsend.

Years in the doldrums following the Cold War had been replaced by full order books and production lines working at a pace not seen since the heady days of the Second World War.

As chief executive of Britain's number-two defence company, Jack Willans had made his own name and a fortune for his shareholders.

DRE's weapons systems had been deployed in virtually every phase of the long-running MEWs, from the initial air war when DRE laser-guided bombs had wiped out the bulk of the region's industrial base, through escalating deployment of ground forces, when DRE's night-sights and battlefield communication systems had been widely used in the fierce hand-to-hand fighting, to the still continuing guerrilla wars, in which DRE's short-range ground-to-ground projectiles were repeatedly unleashed against the mosques and so-called 'civilian hospitals' sheltering enemy troops.

So for a long time DRE had been flavour of the month, the darling of the New Project party and exploited relentlessly by government ministers whenever they needed an example of British enterprise to hold up to the rest of the world. For Jack Willans, success had brought a seat in the House of Senators and the self-interested but nonetheless prestigious attentions of a gushing Andy Sheen.

Flattering profiles in the country's leading journals had been followed by nominations as Businessman of the Year and a middle-rank place in the *Today* programme's Man of the Campaign awards.

Through it all genial Jack had kept his feet firmly on the ground, shrugging off the adulation of the City with a ruddy-faced smile and his frequently repeated claim that 'I was just in the right place at the right time.'

In fact, Jack Willans had never been much of a publicity seeker.

When the MEWs had really hotted up and business began to boom for DRE, the board had brought in a top PR man, Stephen Hadley from Granwick Communications, to handle the deluge of media attention. With requests for press and broadcast interviews pouring into DRE's Docklands headquarters from leading media figures in virtually every country, Hadley used to say his job was money for old rope.

But even Stephen Hadley couldn't crack the Jack Willans nut: instead of seizing the free publicity as Stephen constantly urged him to, Jack would respond with a wry grin and a slightly pained expression. 'But, you know, I did a pile of media engagements last month. Let's give the public a bit of a rest from my ugly mug, hey?'

When the media became insistent and the PR people told him he really should reconsider, he would reply, 'Why don't you get Tim to do them?'

But using the irascible Tim Stilwell, the finance director who ran DRE's mergers and acquisitions division under a rule of terror, substituting barked orders and tantrums for Jack Willans's charm and charisma, was a suggestion Stephen Hadley and his communications directorate were never keen to take up.

Tim Stilwell's secretary leaned her head round the door and coughed quietly. Stilwell did not look up.

'Er, Tim—'

'What is it, Deirdre?'

'Er, Senator Willans says it's time to go. You've got your Downing Street appointment at nine. And he says will you bring the Colditz strategy paper, please?'

Tim Stilwell uttered an oath and grumbled his way from the fifth floor to the basement garage. As he slumped into the back seat of the BMW, his greeting to Jack Willans was less than effusive.

'So we're off to see the lovely shiny Sheen, are we? I hope he's not going to give us any shit over Colditz!'

'Me too, Tim. But I don't think he's going to be very happy—'

'So what's he going to do? Take your senatorship back?'

'Oh! Don't mention the senatorship, Tim!' Jack Willans smiled wryly. 'I reckon they only gave it to me so I'd be their tame businessman – backing the PM's loony schemes and helping them bash the unions, you know. And I keep getting slagged off for not going to the House of Senators enough – I think I went twice last year. Did you see that article in the *Guardian* saying I've got the worst attendance record of any of the new appointed senators since the Upper Senate was created? I have been loyal to Andy, though, so he can't fault me on that – it should be useful when we tell him about this Colditz thing.'

'It had bloody well better be, Jack. By the way, let me do the talking in Downing Street. If Sheen and McDonald give us any grief, I'm not going to roll over and surrender just because you're a pal of Andy Sheen's. OK?'

Jack Willans depended heavily on the hyperactive Tim Stilwell. A charismatic chief executive was one thing – and Jack was genuinely popular with the staff – but everyone in DRE recognized that it was Stilwell who pulled the strings in terms of the financial aggression, deal-making and marketing strategy that had brought DRE its very profitable relationship with the UK military and the Ministry of Defence. What was more, Tim Stilwell was well aware of Jack's dependence and treated him accordingly.

'Look, Jack, the first thing we need to say to Sheen and McDonald is that they owe us one for everything we've done for the war effort. They'd be in even deeper shit than they are now if we hadn't fixed those night-sights for the occupation forces. How many British soldiers are dying in Iraq and Iran and Syria? About a hundred a month, isn't it? Well, without our night-sights I reckon we'd be losing a hundred a day and that's no lie. So the first thing to get straight is that they are in our debt, not the other way round. Then we need to remind them that DRE's success is about the one bright spot in their crappy economy at the moment. And who is that success down to? It's down to us, Jack. So when we tell them it's time for a change, they'd better believe we know what we're talking about. The plain fact is that the defence market has changed, and it's not our fault—'

By now the BMW had negotiated the army checkpoints and police chicanes along the Embankment and was drawing up to the armoured gates at the Whitehall end of Downing Street. The Portakabin which had previously housed the Number Ten security screening unit had been replaced after the failed Stinger attacks of 2008 by a permanent installation of brick and armoured glass: a business-like army captain briskly relieved Jack and Tim of their mobiles, belts and writing implements and exchanged their shoes for pairs of standard issue slippers. He apologized for this latter precaution, explained that it had been introduced in response to the growing spate of shoe bombers, but he said they were welcome to keep the slippers as souvenirs when they collected their belongings on departure.

Once inside the front lobby of Number Ten, the two men felt as though they had entered another world. After the impersonal efficiency of the security checks, the homely familiarity of a largely unchanged Downing Street was a pleasant token of continuing normality. The policeman checking their laissez-passer was reassuringly genial. Young policy unit officials wandered back and forth in casual shirts and sweaters, Tracey Emin wood-and-wire sculptures stood on rosewood tables and nine-year-old Alice Sheen sat on a hard-backed chair in the corner waiting for her driver to take her to school.

Within a few minutes, a smiling secretary had appeared to usher Jack and Tim along the corridor to the back stairs and up to the first floor. Depositing them in an empty, pastel-coloured conference room overlooking the garden, she took their orders for tea and coffee and apologized for the PM's late arrival: he was, she said, on his way back from a working breakfast with the Secretary of State for Commerce at the D of C. On hearing this, Tim Stilwell grimaced and put his hands together in an image of mock prayer: both Jack Willans and the departing secretary smiled at the allusion to the notoriously pious Selwyn Knox.

Tim Stilwell used the delay to give his chief executive a final pep talk.

'OK, Jack, so we tell Sheen we're getting out of defence, we tell him why we're doing it, and we tell him why we're selling to EES. You can do that bit. You can tell him the MEWs were good for us at the time of the big invasions. That's clear and we're not arguing with that. But now things have begun to change, and not for the better as far as DRE is concerned. We've seen an end to the big offensives. Now it's just a war of attrition. A guerrilla war. Skirmishes with the terrorists and all that, but nothing major since we destroyed Damascus and Tehran. So no more need for the big laser-guided bombs, no more need for ground-to-air missile systems. And that's not good news for DRE; we expanded pretty dramatically when the war was at its height and we've over-stretched ourselves. We've left ourselves badly exposed – although that's for you to know, Jack, not for Andy Sheen and Charlie McDonald. When we see them, we don't give any hint of weakness, OK?'

At that moment the doors of the conference room burst open and Andy Sheen swept in, followed by the towering figure of Charlie McDonald and a retinue of officials and minders. Sheen was a man who radiated youth and vigour. He dominated the room, just as he dominated every room he entered. He was Britain's boldest, most radical Prime Minister in decades and he never let you forget it.

'Good morning, gentlemen. Jack, how are you? Haven't seen you in the House of Senators for a while – only joking! And you must be Tim. Hello, Tim. I know all about your exploits, of course. Now sit down everyone, please. Let me introduce Charlie McDonald – he's my director of strategy and, as you know, much more powerful than I am . . . ha, ha! And Geoff Maddle. Geoff is Charlie's very capable right-hand man. Now I think we want to keep this quite tight, so Cedric, Billy, Julie, Helen and the rest of you – could you all go and make yourselves useful elsewhere, please? Thank you. We've got an hour scheduled for this meeting and I'll kick off. Now, Jack, I hear you're scheming to get out of the defence market. I hear you want to sell your business to English Electronic Systems, so I'm going to tell you straight away: I don't think that is a good idea!'

Jack Willans's face fell through the floor.

Apart from himself, Stilwell and the three other members of the highly restricted Operation Colditz team, no one was supposed to have any idea of DRE's plans to escape from the contracting defence market – to do a Colditz, as they'd jokingly called it. And yet Andy Sheen knew all about it; he even knew who DRE were planning to sell to: English Electronic Systems, their major British rivals – their only British rivals – the only other major defence firm in the UK.

Jack was almost lost for words. 'Er, Andy, I'm not quite sure what you're telling me here. Do you know about the Operation Colditz plan? How did—?'

'Jack, I'm the Prime Minister. It's my job to know what is going on in this country and to know it in good time. I know all about your plans. I take it that *is* what you wanted to talk to me about this morning?'

Tim Stilwell told Jack later that at that moment he looked like a rabbit caught in the headlights of an onrushing Ferrari. Far from negotiating from a position of strength, Jack Willans spent the next fifteen minutes firmly on the back foot, outlining all the problems the slow-down in the MEWs was causing for DRE, and revealing how desperate the company was to restructure.

It took a firm kick under the table from Tim Stilwell to get Jack to shut up and hand the floor over to his deputy.

'Thank you, Jack. Thank you very much. Now, Prime Minister, I think I heard you say that you don't believe DRE should get out of defence. But I am here to tell you that that is exactly what we are going to do. And I'll tell you why. The defence market is shrinking. There are no more big orders like the ones we had a few years ago. So DRE has several options. We can retrench; we can cut costs, downsize and carry on with the military communications gear. The night-sights business could break even, too. But it won't maintain the momentum we've had over the last eight years; it won't maintain DRE as the shining light of your ropy national economy, Prime Minister. And it would mean closing factories. It'd mean job losses, too, lots of job losses. Now I don't think you want that, do you? You don't want to see the one company that has done well for New Project and for Britain go down the drain, do you? So I think you should listen very carefully to what I'm offering you this morning. A business like DRE needs to stay dynamic, it needs to move forward to stay alive. So we are going to move forward. We're going to be positive. We're going to get out of defence and into bio-engineering! We're going into gene therapy, life extension and – best of all – into human cloning. There's no doubt whatsoever that it's where the future lies. Bio-engineering and human-cloning technology are what defence was eight years ago: a market about to boom; a market with everything going for it—'

Charlie McDonald looked at Tim Stilwell and couldn't disguise a shudder of distaste. Who was this little runt to come here and threaten the Prime Minister of Great Britain? Who did he think he was talking to?

Andy Sheen, though, was maintaining his usual calm. He knew Willans and Stilwell held some strong cards, the talk of bio-engineering was intriguing and, most importantly, he knew the trap that he and Charlie McDonald had planned for DRE's unruly bosses was still poised to spring shut around Tim Stilwell's bony ankles. He nodded and asked Stilwell to continue.

'Well, just think about it, Prime Minister. The world's been a pretty dodgy place since the Middle East went up in flames. The terrorist attacks here have made people think about life: they've seen Canary Wharf, they've seen the gas victims on the Piccadilly line, they've seen the people killed by poison in the water supplies, and what do they think? They think: it could be me next! I might

71

not still be here by the time Jeb Bush and your good self finally manage to sort the Arabs out! So what's their next thought? They think: maybe I should have a look at this bio-engineering lark; maybe I'll be a goner myself, but at least DRE could help me live on in some shape or form by cloning my DNA. Human cloning – it's a natural human desire and DRE could help satisfy it in a big way. And think about gene scanning: they've got technology that'll read your genes like an open book. It'll tell you what diseases you're going to get, how long you're going to live – it'll almost tell you who's going to win the Grand National. It's the biggest thing around. People want to know their futures; insurance companies want to know their customers' futures. And now's the time to do it! There are three US bio-tech firms and half a dozen start-ups that we've identified as potential takeover targets. It would make DRE Britain's world leader in a market that's going to be the next big thing. Think about it, Prime Minister. It's the way forward. It's good for DRE, it's good for Britain and it's good for Andy Sheen. All you have to do is give us your blessing and not make problems for us over selling off the defence business.'

Andy Sheen looked at Charlie McDonald, then turned back to Willans and Stilwell and smiled. He felt like a man who was about to spring his master stroke.

'Well, gentlemen, I hear what you are saying. I understand why you so desperately need my approval for your plans. Now let me tell you why I shall oppose your defence sale as you are currently proposing it. As Prime Minister, I must protect the interests of the people of this country. And I would not be doing that if I let you sell off your defence business to EES. Why not? Because DRE, as you well know, is one of only two British defence firms capable of filling the vast majority of contracts from the Ministry of Defence. If DRE sells out to English Electronic Systems, it would leave one firm – EES – in such a dominant market position that they would have a monopoly. Every time a big purchasing contract came up, they would be able to hold the MoD to ransom. The taxpayer would suffer, the British military would suffer, the whole country would suffer. Do you seriously think I could honestly countenance such a situation arising at a time of conflict in the Middle East?'

Tim Stilwell's face was darkening ominously.

'So let's be clear, then, Prime Minister. Let's be quite clear. Are you saying you're going to use the Competition Commission to block our plans?'

'Oh, Tim, I'm a reasonable man. I can see how much this means to you and what a tricky position you are in. I want to help, I truly want to help—'

Tim Stilwell heard the note of conciliation, but he also detected a trap. 'So what do you propose? What do we have to do to get approval for this sale?'

Andy Sheen let the trap spring shut. 'Quite simple. If you want me to approve the sale, you sell to the French.'

For a moment there was silence. Then Willans and Stilwell both began to speak at once. Willans put his hand on Stilwell's shoulder. Stilwell knocked his boss's arm aside and elbowed him sharply in the ribs. With a face the colour of an overripe aubergine, Tim Stilwell clasped his hands in a rictus of rage.

'I can't believe you are saying this, Prime Minister! If you know so much about this deal – as you certainly seem to – then you know the French are offering us a pittance! You know English Electronic's bid is the only one we can accept, the only one that'll give us the equity we need to get into the bio-engineering market—'

'Well, I'm sorry about that, Tim. You know my very strong preference is for a common European defence policy and a common European defence industry. This country needs to do much more to prove its European credentials. In fact, I am on record as having told President Le Pen that any rationalization of the UK defence industry will certainly involve France and Germany too. So if you want to sell – and I sense that you have a pressing need to do so – then the answer is simple: forget EES and sell to the Europeans.'

Tim Stilwell's face had been turning a deeper and deeper shade of purple. Without a word, he rose to his feet, picked up his papers and walked out of the room. Jack Willans was on the point of saying something to Andy Sheen, when Stilwell reappeared at the door and yelled, 'You ungrateful bastard, Sheen! You bastard! Come on, Jack. We're leaving—'

The following morning Tim Stilwell and Jack Willans were trying to pick up the pieces of their shattered business strategy. One fraught hour in the pastel-coloured meeting room in Downing Street, one moment of rage from Stilwell, had left Operation Colditz in tatters and DRE's future looking bleak.

'It's a bugger, Jack, and we need to do something about it pretty damn quick. That bastard McDonald will be spinning their version to the Sunday papers even as we sit here. I just hope Stephen Hadley has enough guts and enough clout to get our story about the frigates into the press. We've got to show Sheen that we can play hardball with them and that we're not just going to roll over and die. At the moment, the only hope I can see of saving Colditz is to kick the government in the balls and keep kicking them until they beg for mercy—'

On the floor below DRE's director of communications Stephen Hadley was drinking tea with the company's chief engineer.

'Milk and one sugar, please, Peter. Thanks for seeing me. It's a bit urgent, actually. Jack and Tim have just had me in and they want me to put out a story to the Sunday papers. It's a bit hush-hush, so keep it under your hat, all right?

'Now Tim wants us to get this story in the *Sunday Times* and their deadline for copy in the business section is tomorrow afternoon, Friday. I don't know why it's so early – to do with sharing the presses in Wapping, or something. Anyway, that's the way it is. So what I have to do is get all the facts together a.s.a.p. and give them to Matthew Koblenz – he's the business editor and I know him from way back – so that he can get the story on the front page if possible. That's where you come in. It's the MoD frigates story I want, and you were chief engineering manager on that project, weren't you? Not a happy time, by all accounts. What I'm after is the stuff about the cost overruns and the MoD's cock-ups that kept changing all the specifications . . . you know, all the stuff we kept quiet about at the time to save the government's face. Well, now we're out to rub the government's nose in it, so don't hold anything back.'

The following Monday it was a grim-looking Charlie McDonald who strode into the eight-thirty meeting in the Downing Street press office, clutching his Arsenal mug and a copy of the *Sunday Times*. As he threw the paper on the table in front of him, McDonald made a show of holding his nose between the finger and thumb of one hand and pulling an imaginary lavatory chain with the other.

'So who's responsible for this, then?' he growled, glaring at a front-page headline: 'Government Wastes Taxpayers' Millions on Frigates that Can't Sail Straight'.

'This is dirty work from someone and I want to know who!' McDonald looked menacingly round the table. 'No one knew about the steering-gear cock-up. Or at least no one did until yesterday morning. So was it some wanker at the MoD who leaked it, Toby?'

McDonald stared accusingly at Toby Singlet, the overawed-looking press chief from the Ministry of Defence.

'Er, no, it wasn't anyone at our end, Charlie. In fact, we're all so ashamed of the frigates story that I can't imagine it would even cross anyone's mind to speak to the press. I did a quick mole hunt yesterday, just to make sure I was right. Our guys are clean. Actually, the *Sunday Times* have got so much detail that they must have seen a copy of the enquiry we carried out with DRE once the faults were discovered. And I know for certain that all our copies of the report are accounted for, and the only other people with copies are DRE themselves—'

A few hours later, up in Marsham Street, Selwyn Knox was preparing for his working lunch with representatives of the driverless vehicle industry, when Sonya Mair poked her head round the door. 'Phone for you, Sel. It's Charlie at Number Ten.'

Knox picked up the receiver and nodded to Sonya to listen in on the spare extension on the coffee table.

'Hello, Charlie. Selwyn here.'

'Hi, Selwyn. Just check your people aren't monitoring this call, will you?'

Knox replied quickly and deferentially – the tone that everyone adopted with Charlie McDonald. 'It's OK. I've sent Jeremy out to lunch and I can see there's no one in the outer office. It's just me and Sonya here. So fire away.'

'It's about this DRE proposal to sell off their defence business, you know, and go into bio-engineering and cloning technology or whatever.'

'Yeah, yeah. I've seen the advance reports. I would have thought that's going to run into trouble on monopoly grounds. It'd leave English Electronic Systems as the only defence manufacturer and that'd put the poor old MoD over a barrel every time they ordered a new tank. I can't see that being approved.'

'I'm sure you're right, Sel. And that's good news for me and for Andy. But what I'm saying to you is that when the deal comes to your people for approval, you need to make sure the Competition Commission turn it down. Don't leave it to chance – tell them there's only one decision they can make. OK?'

'Yeah, Charlie, sure; but you know . . . technically, things have changed since the old days of the Monopolies and Mergers Commission. The Competition Commissioners are independent now, they aren't directly answerable to me as Secretary of State any more. So I can't actually tell them what to decide, like we used to do with the old MMC. If the CC decide to block a deal on monopoly grounds, that's their decision; and if they decide to let it go through, it's their call and theirs alone. We made a big thing out of saying we wouldn't interfere – a bit like the Bank of England and interest rates, really. I suppose I could tell them what to do, but it would be breaking all the rules—'

'I don't think you heard me very well just then, Selwyn. I said when the deal is referred to you, you need to make sure the CC vetoes it. And that means one hundred per cent sure – OK?'

'OK, I get it. I hear you loud and clear, Charlie. I was just explaining the legal position, that's all. You know I'll make sure everything turns out the way you and Andy want it. In fact, I don't think there's even going to be a problem in this case. We don't have to worry: I've already had a look at what DRE are proposing and I can tell you there's not a cat in hell's chance of the Competition Commission letting it through. The monopoly supplier argument is so strong the commissioners will block it for sure. So take it easy, the sell-off's going to be blocked. Tell Andy it's a done deal.'

'That's the stuff, Sel! Great. And thanks very much. I'll let Andy know we're OK for knocking back Willans and Stilwell. And it couldn't happen to two nicer blokes, right? See ya, mate!'

5

Jack Willans and Tim Stilwell were men in despair. Operation Colditz was looking increasingly hopeless with every day and with every phone call to Downing Street and the Department of Commerce.

All the good will from Jack's past service to the New Project cause seemed to have gone out of the window following their disastrous meeting at Number Ten. Tim Stilwell calling the Prime Minister an ungrateful bastard to his face had certainly done little to foster warm emotions and a helping hand for the defence sell-off.

Downing Street was now using its tame poodles in the media to attack DRE with more venom than Jack – or any FTSE 100 chief executive for that matter – had ever experienced at the hands of New Project's mighty spin machine.

Charlie McDonald had responded to DRE's leaked story about the faulty frigates with a long and savage series of articles planted in the business and political press. All, without exception, were aimed at undermining DRE's previously high reputation: exposing the faults in DRE's gear which had 'put our boys at risk in the heat of battle'; and – most damaging of all – pointing out the unacceptable harm that would be inflicted on the UK's war effort at a time of international crisis if Senator Willans and Tim Stilwell were allowed to sell their defence business to EES.

As the man on the receiving end, Jack was taken aback by the firepower Charlie McDonald and his spin doctors were able to muster.

Even more was he taken aback by the complicity of the British media in reporting what Downing Street and McDonald dictated.

It seemed that the journalists who had queued to fête him and sing DRE's praises for the past eight years had suddenly forgotten all that had gone before; now they were falling over themselves to do him and his company down. The only explanation, thought Jack, was that the hacks were either hopelessly beholden to McDonald and his crew for past misdeeds, or they felt an over-whelming need to curry favour with the man who distributed coveted news from Number Ten exclusively to his favourites.

Most willing to do his master's bidding – and this was no surprise to those who knew him – was Dave Sopwith, political correspondent at the *Chronicle* and so intimate with Downing Street that ribald journalist colleagues used to swear they could spot Dave's nose and blinking eyes protruding from the crack of Charlie McDonald's arse.

It was Dave Sopwith who delivered the coup de grâce to DRE's hopes of completing the sale to EES. In a malevolent splash, he 'revealed' that DRE had 'deliberately ripped off the taxpayer on a series of defence contracts to the tune of £750 million'. The article was stuffed with damning details of inventory pricing, purporting to show that DRE had overcharged the Ministry of Defence for tanks, missiles, rifles, machine guns and virtually every item of kit the British army had ever ordered from them. At the same time, Sopwith claimed, the company had failed to deliver much-needed consignments of body armour, whose absence had left the troops badly exposed. As unanswerable proof of DRE's demonic cupidity, Sopwith printed a 'secret' government memo showing that the company had charged the MoD 'fifty pounds per roll' for every pack of desert-proofed toilet paper our boys had taken into battle in the Middle East.

The government, Sopwith informed his readers, was seeking an immediate freeze on DRE's financial operations – including the buying or selling of any business assets – until the overcharging scandal had been explained to Downing Street's complete satisfaction.

Jack Willans knew Dave Sopwith; he knew Sopwith had exaggerated and distorted the facts; he knew the source of Sopwith's information was the man sitting at Andy Sheen's right hand; but he also knew that for DRE the game was up – Operation Colditz was dead. DRE and with it Jack Willans were on the downward slide to disaster.

Sonya Mair fixed her lipstick and strolled into Selwyn Knox's office, closing the door behind her and settling her shapely rear on the arm of the easy chair in which her boss was stretched out reading Dave Sopwith's front-page exposé of Senator Willans's evil deeds.

'Hi, Sel. Everything OK?' she whispered, making a pretence of not disturbing his concentration.

'Yes it is, thank you. I've just about sorted out the Rover sale. Looks pretty certain that the Cambodians are buying it. We should do a photo opportunity with their Trade Minister and the Cambodian board members in front of the Churchill statue on Parliament Square. Apparently they're going to drop the Rover name and rechristen it CamCars. Quite clever, really – gets the Cambodian reference in without reminding people they're actually buying something that's going to be made in the paddy fields and jungles, eh? Anyway, Rover's been a millstone round our neck ever since George Simpson sold it to the Germans in the nineties – and ever since Stephen Byers got his knickers in a twist when BMW decided they wanted rid of it too. But enough of that. What good news is the lovely Sonya bringing me?'

'Well, a few things. I've got Rachel Thomson to agree to profile you in the *Telegraph*. She says she's particularly interested in where you buy your clothes and have your hair done. I told her she can come and have a look at the labels and inspect your parting! I said we don't want it to be totally girlie, though, and that we'll withdraw the interview if she doesn't write about your political ambitions. Rachel's fine, actually, but she won't write a heavyweight piece. In the end, I did a deal with her: I told her if she'd include the line, "Selwyn Knox, increasingly seen as a credible successor to Andy Sheen as Project party leader," we'd let the photographer do a shot of you changing your shirt. And she bought it. That's OK isn't it, Sel?'

'Yeah, I suppose so. Did she ask about Ruth?'

Sonya Mair gave a fleeting but undisguised grimace at the mention of Selwyn Knox's long-time live-in girlfriend, or partner as he called her.

'Yes she did, actually. She asked if she could do the interview at your flat or at the house in the constituency, with Ruth there in the background. But I said no. It's not that I've got anything against Ruth, Sel. It's just that there's such a lack of chemistry between you two that things are painfully obvious. Rachel might start speculating – or write something dodgy, you know what I mean. And then Ruth's looking so, well – so old these days. It just isn't quite right for your image. You know there was all that gossip last year about her being just a "token girlfriend"? The last thing we want is to start all that running again. So, anyway, I told Rachel we'd do the interview here in your office or not at all. So that's fixed.

'Now, the other thing is the civil servants. I've been having the same trouble again ... some of them are getting really bolshie. Most of them'll do what I tell them all right, but there are one or two who've started quoting the civil service code at me, or whatever their prissy little bible's called, saying they're not obliged to take orders from party political advisers like me and that they have to be neutral and non-political and ethical and all that crap. Well, it just won't wash, Sel! I know that's the formal position, but they should know Andy and Charlie have made it pretty clear they don't give a toss for their code of ethics. It's New Project that calls the shots now and the bloody civil service had better do what we say. Anyway, if I tell you who the trouble-makers are, will you haul them in here and tell them they have to do what I tell them? Actually, there's one in particular I think you'll need to get rid of: can you give him his marching orders, please? Then I thought we might make an evening of it tonight. What do you think?'

The civil servant whom Sonya Mair had fingered to the Secretary of State as a hopeless trouble-maker was sitting in the sanctuary of his poky office in an outlying annexe of the Department of Commerce.

While the department's Marsham Street HQ was clean, bold and forward-looking, this backwater would have been recognized with no difficulty at all by civil servants of the Northcote–Trevelyan era. It was dark and dusty, cramped and slightly malodorous, but it was here that the big issues were examined: issues like which strategic business deals, disposals, takeovers and mergers would be allowed to go ahead and which would be blocked; issues which affected the UK's biggest conglomerates and the future of the UK economy itself.

For some time now Barry Clynes had been looking hard at an application from DRE to sell its defence arm to English Electronic Systems.

From the moment the application had dropped on Barry's desk he had known there was no chance it would ever get past the Competition Commission. The country couldn't allow itself to end up with a single defence manufacturer cornering the market – the new heavyweight EES, bulked up from swallowing DRE's plants, patents and production lines, would have eaten the poor old MoD for breakfast.

Perversely, though, Barry had left the DRE application to gather dust for some weeks now. Not because he had any doubt about its outcome – it had to be blocked – but because for some reason he had found himself the target of an annoying campaign, led by Selwyn Knox and Sonya Mair, to bully his team into making the decision they were going to make anyway.

Barry was a bluff Mancunian and he didn't take kindly to being leant on. He believed that if the British civil service was meant to be independent and not subject to the whims of party political apparatchiks, and if the government had agreed that the Competition Commission should be objective and impartial in its decisions, then that was how things should be.

Barry despised the blatant crassness of Charlie McDonald's spin campaign to demonize DRE through the media; he resented Sonya Mair's attempts to tell him what to do; he hated New Project's arrogance in assuming that the civil service could be used for its own party advantage instead of serving the interests of the nation as a whole with political impartiality and integrity.

After repeated sessions of nudging, cajoling and threats from Knox's hyperactive political adviser, he had coined the nickname by which she was now universally known: 'Miss Night-Mair'. When they saw him looking careworn, sympathetic colleagues would ask, 'Been Night-Maired again, Barry?'

But even Barry Clynes's stubbornness had a limit, even Barry

Clynes's prickly principles were not immune to the brute force he was now subjected to.

The day after Sonya Mair and Selwyn Knox had their conversation about difficult civil servants, Clynes was summoned to the Secretary of State's office and told to veto DRE's application. If he didn't, Knox told him, he should prepare himself for a transfer to a new post adjudicating disability allowances at the Benefits Agency in Leeds.

The following day Knox and Mair had their way. The document Knox wanted was on his desk and all was well with the world – the application by DRE plc to sell its defence business to English Electronic Systems plc was to be 'disallowed by the Competition Commission on monopoly grounds' and the decision could 'be announced by the Secretary of State for Commerce at a time convenient to him and his department'.

Selwyn Knox smiled a smile of satisfaction and picked up the phone to Charlie McDonald.

'Good stuff, Selwyn.' McDonald sounded delighted. 'Well done. Don't make the announcement just yet, though. I need to look for a prominent date for it in the News Grid. We don't want this being overshadowed by any other big news from another department, do we? Talk to ya later—'

Sonya Mair was a New Project true believer.

She had believed in and worked for the Project ever since her earliest experiences of student activism at Redbridge University. A close personal and political friend of Andy Sheen and Charlie McDonald, she had performed the remarkable feat of maintaining good relations with the man in Number Eleven at the same time. Harold Delph, the Chancellor of the Exchequer, was a very different kettle of fish from Andy.

Where Andy was visionary and inspired, Harold was down to earth and pragmatic; where Andy believed in moral imperatives and his mission to improve society, Harold believed in a strong pound and watching the pennies; Andy wanted to be remembered as a crusading Prime Minister, Harold wanted to be remembered for balancing the books – he certainly wouldn't let Andy Sheen drag the country into the Euro if it was going to throw his accounts out of balance.

Even on the war issue the two men took different routes to the same conclusion: Andy believed in expanding the war in the Middle East because that was ethically the right thing to do; Harold had at first opposed the war on grounds of cost, only coming round to the idea once Washington had promised him that any expenditure he incurred would be more than reimbursed by spoils and oils from the conquered countries.

In the tensions that existed between Numbers Ten and Eleven, between Andy and Harold, Sonya Mair was an invaluable, irre-placeable go-between. For Knox, having Sonya as his helpmate was like a platinum-plated entry card to both camps and to all sources of influence in the government – few ministers could say they enjoyed the same access.

But Sonya was also something more. Her feminine instinct was as powerful as her political instinct. Her charm could be switched on and targeted like a laser-guided missile. Few could resist her and she knew it.

Strangely, the objects of her charm offensives were usually acutely aware of the deliberate and calculated nature of the way she was treating them – Sonya Mair rarely if ever did anything without thinking it all through in advance – but, astoundingly, they didn't seem to mind. The phenomenon was worthy of study by the anthropologists – seasoned politicians and hard-nosed journalists would melt in the sunshine of Sonya's smile, even while a small internal voice was saying, 'Watch her, mate, she's not doing this because she likes you; she's doing it because she's after something.' The problem was that a louder voice at the front of their mind was saying, 'Never mind about that; look into her eyes and let yourself drown!'

If she wasn't hammering you to death, Sonya was achieving the same result with a smile and a flutter.

She brought Knox something that no one else had ever done or ever could do. She brought him the secrets of other men's minds.

At DRE, things were going from bad to worse.

When the nerve-racking weeks waiting for the Competition Commission's decision grew unbearable, Jack Willans decided he must confront Tim Stilwell to discover the reason for his obsessive insistence that Colditz was their only possible salvation.

Jack and Tim had spent the morning in the City trying to reassure their big investors – pension funds, unit trusts and insurers – that DRE remained a good bet in the long term. Jack had spoken warmly about future prospects if the move out of defence was completed – it was, he said, a potential gold mine for investors who could buy low now and watch the share price rocket when cloning technology and gene scanning came online. But when he started to argue that the prospects remained good even if DRE were forced to stay in the defence market, he suddenly noticed Tim Stilwell's face had lost its usual composure and his lips were mouthing something that Senator Willans could only guess at.

In the company BMW on the way back to headquarters, six years of accumulated annoyance and resentment with Tim Stilwell boiled over into sudden anger.

'Look, Tim, what the hell is going on? I need to know what you're up to. Why are you so worried about our defence business? What's wrong with it?'

Tim Stilwell had obviously decided he too had had enough of the pressure. 'Well, Jack, you asked for it. You want to know what's up? I'll tell you: we're broke! We've got nothing left. Everything's gone down the pan and if we can't flog the business to EES you and I are finished. If Selwyn Knox and the bloody Competition Commission announce they're blocking it, you and all the other suckers can wave goodbye to any future at all.'

The rest of the journey passed in silence. After thirty years at the peak of British industry, Jack Willans was staring disaster – unmitigated and terrifyingly final disaster – in its leering face.

As the BMW pulled into DRE's underground garage, and at the very moment Jack stepped out of the car to walk to the lift, Albert Topping died.

Albert was fifty-nine, a smoker, a drinker and a former miner.

The doctor told his widow it was perhaps no surprise the heart attack had been so violent. Even if medical help had arrived the moment Albert collapsed in his constituency office, it was unlikely anything could have been done to save him. As it was, it had been a quiet afternoon and it was probably one or two hours before Albert's constituency agent had arrived and discovered the body.

Andy Sheen was informed thirty minutes later. 'Oh no, Charlie. Did you hear that? Albert Topping's died. He was only fifty-nine, I hadn't realized. I guess he just looked so much older. Means a by-election I suppose. Safe seat, though, isn't it?'

'Albert Topping? He's Tyneland East isn't he? Yes, he is. Oh, fuck! That's where the bloody shipyard is, Andy. What's it called

. . . Schoerner's. And you know what that all means. We're really up shit creek now!'

Selwyn Knox was feeling pretty pleased with himself.

The Rover deal had been completed and he had had a very good press. The Churchill statue pictures were flattering and had been widely used. Rachel Thomson had included the key phrase in her *Telegraph* piece as Sonya had promised, and he'd had several calls from political hacks asking him if he saw himself as a future leader of the Project party.

To all of them Knox had used the time-honoured phrases: that he was not seeking any other job than the one he was currently doing to the best of his ability; that the party had an outstanding leader in Andy Sheen; but that if in the future, for whatever reason, his party were to call on him, he would be ready to answer that call.

The one sour note had been a telephone call from a dyspeptic Harold Delph, who reminded him that leadership questions were not something any minister should be commenting on and that it was in the party's best interests to discourage press speculation on the subject. Knox had, of course, concurred, but when he put the phone down Sonya Mair, who'd been listening on the other extension, burst out laughing. 'What he's really saying, Sel, is that it's OK for Harold Delph to talk about the next party leader, but it's not OK for anyone else! Unless they're tipping Harold Delph for the job, of course!'

The two of them glanced around. They both knew there were civil servants in the outer office for whom loyalty to Knox was not number one priority, so it wouldn't do for them to know too much about his ambitions, or those of his right-hand woman.

'I'm off to Number Ten now, Sel,' Sonya said. 'Charlie

McDonald's having a drinks party for the press. He wants me to reward the helpful hacks with a glimpse of cleavage and cane the bad boys until they beg for mercy. OK? I'll see you this evening: don't forget.'

It was a subdued Andy Sheen who put in an appearance at Charlie McDonald's media drinks party. Sonya thought Charlie himself was in his gloomy, overhanging eyebrows mood.

Dave Sopwith was there, doing his best to cheer up his mentor and protector, but McDonald wasn't having any of it. Hacks who asked what the matter was were told the news about Albert Topping had dampened the mood, but Sonya knew that neither Andy nor Charlie gave a monkey's about Topping, an Old Project fart who had never got with the new party. Sonya knew there must be something else, so she deliberately stayed behind after the party to find out what was on Charlie's mind.

'It's bad news, Sonya. Old Topping's gone and died at the worst possible moment. The daft bugger, he could never do anything without fucking up! The problem is Schoerner's, the Germans – you know, the ones who're closing the naval shipyard up there? Well, fuck me if it isn't in Tyneland East, Albert's constituency! The Krauts wanted to close it nine months ago, but we got them to postpone it while we tried to look for a buyer. Well, you know all that – we couldn't find anyone daft enough to buy the place, 'cos the MoD aren't placing the big naval contracts any more. You can't sail battleships across the Iranian desert! So, anyway, Schoerner's called us two weeks ago to say that they've waited nine months while we faffed around and they're closing the place down now whether we've got a buyer or not. They're making the announcement next week in Hamburg and we've not been able to make them change their minds.'

'So it's the by-election that's the problem then, is it, Charlie? How many redundancies are we expecting?'

'Twelve fucking thousand when you take all the support industries into account. It's meltdown time up in Geordieland, Sonya girl, and it couldn't have happened at a worse time. There's going to be a lot of angry voters up there.'

'Yeah, but come on, Charlie: we're not going to lose the seat, are we? It's safe New Project, isn't it?'

'Yeah, in theory. But ever since the formation of this NewLib party, we aren't as invincible as we used to be. Bloody Ken Clarke leaving the Tories and taking all the pro-Europeans with him caught us on the hop. If he'd just set up some Tory-wet-pro-Euro party, we couldn't have cared less. But he was pretty smart. Linking up with the LibDems and the Labour rump was a fucking master stroke. Together they're a real opposition now and we haven't been used to that, have we?

'Crap name, by the way, "NewLibs" – sounds like something I'd have dreamed up fifteen years ago. Anyway, they're on a roll and they know it. They're really popular up in Tyneland even without this Schoerner close-down and if we don't do something, we reckon the NewLibs are in with a real chance. If we can't get someone to buy the yard now, and if half the constituency get thrown on the dole, the anti-Project protest vote'll hand it to the NewCraps on a plate. And if we lose Tyneland, think of all the other seats we could lose. We could see the heartlands going down like dominoes. It could set the whole New Project edifice crumbling—'

'How did the drinks go, Sonya?'

Selwyn Knox looked up from his papers as Sonya Mair walked into the office. It was ten o'clock and Knox was doing his usual late-night swotting.

'Not good for Charlie and Andy: they're down in the dumps. But I've got an idea that might do you and me some good, Sel. Can I go off and do a bit of freelancing this week?'

Jack Willans had been trying without success to talk to Sonya Mair for the past two months. He knew the influence she could wield over the Competition Commission's decision. But every approach, every phone call and letter, had been met with a wall of silence or a curt instruction to make his request 'through the proper channels'.

Now here was the woman herself, sitting on the black velvet sofa in Jack's office and looking even more gorgeous than her pictures in the papers.

When Jack emerged briefly to collect the two white coffees his secretary had prepared for them, even Linda couldn't help commenting – and only half in jest. 'She's a bit of a looker, Jack. You'd better stop panting and keep your wits about you if you don't want to end up doing something you might regret.'

Jack smiled sheepishly and went back in with the coffees. His pleasantries about how hard she was to get hold of were met with an arch smile. 'You can get hold of most things if you try hard enough, Senator Willans.'

Amid the banter and the flirting – Jack was aware he was being targeted by the Sonya Mair charm, but like most men he was more than happy to step eagerly into the role of willing victim – her opening gambit was delivered in a deceptively offhand aside. 'I see DRE's in a bit of a mess, isn't it, Senator Willans?'

Jack almost fell through the floor. 'Er, no, not that I know of, young lady. What makes you say that?'

'Well, it seems I must know something you don't know, then. Didn't you know your accounts are up the spout and you'll be lucky to survive another six months?'

'Er, that's not my understanding. May I ask what gave you that idea?'

'Information is my business, Senator Willans, but it's your problem, not mine. I'm not here to threaten you, I'm here to help.'

Sonya Mair slowly crossed and uncrossed her legs. She looked fixedly at Jack Willans's ruddy, battered face to see if his eyes would wander down towards her carefully exposed thighs. They did. Sonya smiled.

She continued: 'Just imagine something for me for a moment, Senator Willans – Jack. Just imagine that I am Father Christmas and that I'm bringing you what you most want in the world at this very minute. Think of the one thing that would make you happier than anything else. And imagine I'm here to tell you that I can get it for you. What would you think about that?'

Jack Willans's jaw dropped open and his white coffee spluttered onto the black velvet of the sofa.

After that things happened very quickly indeed, as they often do in the pragmatic worlds of politics and big business.

As soon as questions of personal fortune – financial or political – come into play, it is instructive to note how quickly and easily deals that once seemed unthinkable can be struck; how gratifyingly everyone's vital interests can be protected.

Jack Willans called a full board meeting of DRE plc in the company conference suite and explained to a flabbergasted array of non-execs, managers and accountants that he had decided to buy the Schoerner shipyard in Tyneland East.

The board's objections, expressed in a flurry of horrified speeches from around the table, ran broadly along the following lines.

– We need a shipyard like a hole in the head.

– That particular shipyard is an even bigger white elephant than most because it's geared for exactly the deep-draft naval vessels that the MoD has said it's got no intention of purchasing for at least the next decade.

– Schoerner's is losing money hand over fist.

– The yard's pension commitments are enough to bankrupt us on their own.

– The workforce are wreckers and skivers.

– And, anyway, our plan is to get out of defence and into bio-engineering and human cloning, so why the hell would we buy another military shipyard?

Jack listened to them all patiently and told them the deal would be signed the day after tomorrow.

At about the same time, Charlie McDonald rang an astonished Dave Sopwith to tell him he had to write a new splash on the DRE question. This time, the *Chronicle* needed to explain that DRE was actually an outstanding exemplar for British industry, that its management team were among the most gifted in the world, and that the company's proposed move into bio-engineering and human-cloning technology would put the UK at the forefront of a vital sector in the future development of the world economy.

Selwyn Knox called Barry Clynes into his office for another meeting.

He showed the gob-smacked Mancunian a 'redraft' he had made of Barry's earlier announcement on the DRE–EES deal. There weren't many differences between the two texts, Knox told him, but one that Barry spotted straight away was that the word 'disallowed' had been replaced with the word 'approved'.

On seeing what Knox had done, Barry Clynes muttered, 'Bugger this for a bowl of cherries – I resign,' and walked out of the Secretary of State's office never to return.

On the night New Project won the Tyneland East by-election, Selwyn Knox took Sonya Mair back to his pied-à-terre in Dolphin Square, Westminster. She was still there the next morning. In north London Sonya's husband noticed her absence again and gave a resigned sigh.

That evening Andy Sheen called a smirking Selwyn Knox to Downing Street to congratulate him on a job well done. Over a glass of pink champagne, the blue-eyed boy asked if the PM had shared Harold Delph's annoyance at seeing Knox spoken of in the press as a future leader of the Project party. Andy Sheen looked at Charlie McDonald. Both of them looked at Knox, shook their heads and smiled most encouragingly.

6

THE MOVIE mogul Sam Goldwyn used to say a verbal contract was not worth the paper it was written on.

For weeks after Selwyn Knox's celebratory meeting with Andy Sheen and Charlie McDonald, the jibe haunted him with increasing bitterness. It was unlike him to be carried away with the excitement of the moment. He had, he felt, broken his own golden rule at Downing Street that night: he hadn't pinned Sheen and McDonald down to an undertaking they could not renege on. It was all very well for them to give him a nod and a smile; it was all very well for them to hint at his prospects for advancement – but where was his guarantee? Where was the proof? Where was the route map to the destiny he knew should be his?

It was another month of anxiety and self-reproach before Knox finally discovered his worrying had been unnecessary. Andy Sheen and Charlie McDonald were as good as their – unwritten – word. On a sunny Tuesday morning in Downing Street, the Prime Minister unveiled the first instalment of Knox's advancement with grace and no little panache.

'So look, Selwyn. You and I go back a long way, don't we? I can remember back in 2006 when we had that little trouble up in Scotland – Exxington, wasn't it? I don't recall all the details, but I do know you acquitted yourself remarkably well that day. I remember getting notes from Charlie here, and from Geoff Maddle, saying you were MP material. And they were right.

'You've had a pretty rapid rise, Selwyn. Merited, of course. And what I will say is that every time we've come up against a problem of some sort you've not let us down. You and Sonya Mair. So we're indebted to you. We really are.

'Now Charlie showed me something quite interesting yesterday. I've got it here. Here it is. It's the little note I sent you back in September 2006, remember? It was just after Canary Wharf and we were all pretty jumpy at that time. Anyway, this is what I wrote to you: "Dear Selwyn, Terror and war are looming again. We need determined, ruthless people like you. Come and join us as an MP. Help us protect the values of our society. Yours, Andy Sheen." Yes. That's it. Now that was a very special time, of course. The civilized world was under attack. We didn't know what to expect next. Emotions were running high.

'I'm not quite sure, by the way, whether I really meant to use the word "ruthless" there, did I, Charlie? Didn't I mean to say "dedicated" or something more like that? Oh well, it doesn't matter. If Charlie says ruthless, then ruthless it is. But ruthless in a positive way, ruthless in the sense that we are all ready to do everything necessary to save this country from disaster; we're ready to be ruthless with ourselves, to bear any sacrifice – and ruthless with others, of course, if they stand in the way of our programme.

'Civilized values are under threat in the modern world, Selwyn, and that threat comes from many sources. It comes from the terrorists who seek to destroy our world and our civilization. And we have been ruthless with them. We have borne all the sacrifices that have been demanded of us, including the loss of young British and American lives. I have not flinched. I have remained determined in the face of adversity. I have remained, yes – ruthless, because I know my actions are serving the greater good.

'Now I am telling you all this because I am about to ask you to follow my example. I am about to ask you to take on the same heavy burden of responsibility; the burden of ruthlessness and self-sacrifice in the name of a cause we all believe in.

'I said earlier that the threat to our values comes from many sources. Sadly, international terrorism is not the only threat our society is facing. There is another less obvious, but perhaps more insidious, more dangerous threat. And that is the threat from within our own society. You know, sometimes I look at what we have done in Iraq and Iran and in Syria and Saudi Arabia, and I think: yes, we have protected ourselves, we have protected our values from the outsiders who would destroy what we stand for.

'But what an irony – what a bitter irony – if we were to allow the very values our brave troops have fought and died for in the Middle East Wars to be undermined and corrupted from within. What a terrible indictment, what an insult to their memory, if our lack of vigilance here at home were to negate what they have achieved on the battlefields so far away.'

Andy Sheen paused and looked Selwyn Knox straight in the eye. He had long felt that Knox shared his own moral beliefs, his own dedication and commitment, his own selfless desire to bring succour to the people of Britain. This was a man he trusted as pure, honest, modest and free from personal ambition. Now was the moment to put that trust to the test.

'Selwyn, I want you to do here at home what I have done in the Middle East. I want you to take on the domestic threat in the way that I have taken on the foreign threat. And I want you to triumph in the way that I have triumphed.

'Charlie here will explain all the details. He will tell you how the new Department for Society is going to work. How it is going to wipe out the inner rottenness that is spreading through today's society: the antisocial values that are threatening our way of life; the ungrateful individuals who are spreading poison in the form of dishonesty, disrespect, greed, immorality, laziness and all the negative phenomena such attitudes engender – drug addiction, crime, teenage pregnancies, irresponsible parents, desertion, single-parent households, benefit fraud, bogus asylum seekers – all the things that threaten us – all the manifestations of the enemy who lives among us – the enemy in our midst—

'It is a very big brief, Selwyn. I do not disguise that. Creating a Department for Society is a brave move. People will criticize us. Perhaps they'll say we are over-ambitious. Perhaps they'll say society cannot be saved from itself. Perhaps they'll even say there is no such thing as society. But we know better. The Department for Society. It is a radical concept and we need a big man to be our Minister for Society. Are you that man, Selwyn? Can you step into those shoes?'

Selwyn Knox returned the Prime Minister's unblinking gaze, thought for a moment and nodded his head gravely.

'Yes, Prime Minister. I am – and I can.'

Knox's meeting with Charlie McDonald was fixed for ten o'clock the following day. He told Sonya the meeting would be decisive for his future and for hers. If this Department for Society was going to work, he told her, it would have to be thought out properly and in minute detail. He also told Sonya that Andy Sheen's concept had struck him as woolly and a little naive. He was hoping Charlie McDonald would be able to tell him more clearly what it would involve, exactly how its responsibilities were to be defined and where the boundaries would lie between it and the Home Office.

For her part, Sonya was considerably more sanguine. Where Knox saw problems, she saw opportunities: 'Look, Sel, for a start, Andy is going to be on your side in any turf war. He's never been a fan of the Home Office. So you've got the whip hand there, for sure.

'And your other advantage is that our department will be able to take a real overview of the problem. Everyone knows drugs and crime, unemployment and parental abuse, teenage mums, shirkers and benefit fraud are all interconnected, but up to now they've been dealt with by different government departments, and you know the Keystone Kops effect that always creates. All that talk about "joined-up government" at the end of the nineties and the start of the noughties was just guff.

'What you've got now is the chance to rise above all that. You've got the Olympian overview – you're basically an uberminister, Sel. That's what you are, an uberminister! ... Seriously, though, I think Andy was right about how many social problems can be traced back to this underlying malaise thing. It's down to people who just don't know how to behave as a part of society – all the yobs and antisocial elements – and if we can start to tackle them, I think we can really impress him. And you know what that means for your future, don't you? Andy won't be around for ever: you've got to start thinking about that. I know bloody Harold Delph's thinking about it – he doesn't think about anything else!

'So when you see Charlie tomorrow remember you're in a position of strength. Downing Street has been really rattled by the rise of these NewLibs – we've got a proper opposition now and Charlie told me Andy's pretty scared of them. I reckon he sees you and this new department as the answer to his prayers. So when you see McD, you need to be sure they give you authority over all the departments the Home Office currently works with – police, immigration, employment, social security, health and all the rest. Don't let him get away with saying you'll have a partnership relationship with them – OK?

'Now, I think we'll need to run the department on a unit model. We'll need a parenting unit, a family unit, a new teenager unit and maybe some others too. They're going to put us in the old Cabinet Office buildings, so that's good – it was about time Andy got rid of the bloody Cabinet Office. What a waste of resources they were! It means we'll be on Downing Street's doorstep – and you can't beat that in terms of access.

'But remember, Sel, the key to success in all this is the staff. If you don't get the right people, you've had it. You'll need me for a start obviously! Right? But we'll also need a free hand in choosing the junior ministers, and all the civil servants at grade five and above. That's absolutely vital: there's no way we want to end up with a bunch of no-hopers like we had at the D of C.

'And one other thing – this is absolutely vital, Sel – McDonald needs to agree that we have access to all Home Office and police data as of right now. We can't afford to wait: that's our top demand and it's not negotiable—'

The next day Selwyn Knox got lucky.

His meeting with Charlie McDonald was a complete success.

Knox got everything he asked for from a preoccupied-looking director of Downing Street communications, who did little more than outline the aims, powers and structure of the new department before handing it over into Knox's safe-keeping. Even the demand for immediate access to the Home Office and police files went through on the nod. McDonald dictated a brief memo conferring full authority and full security clearance on the new Minister for Society and told him to use it wisely.

The announcement about the Department for Society was to be made on the following Monday and Knox would be put up for the ten-past-eight slot on the *Today* programme, followed by intensive media briefings.

According to Charlie McDonald, the date of the launch had been personally selected by Andy Sheen because it would be the sixth anniversary of New Project's accession to power. The symbolism underlined the fact that the new department was the start of a prestigious and high-profile policy shift that would be crucial to the future of Andy Sheen's government.

'Andy sees this as a way to wrest back the momentum from the NewLibs,' Charlie McDonald said. 'The Tories are history, we all know that. For too long we got used to a world where there was no opposition to worry about. But ever since Ken Clarke took the pro-Europeans out of the Tory party and linked up with the Libs and those Labour oddballs, there's been a groundswell of revival going on. Andy has been looking at the polling data and he knows the NewLibs are strong enough to beat us now. If there were an election tomorrow, we reckon the NewLibs would get in.

'And that's why so much depends on you and the Department for Society. The wars and the foreign agenda have kept us on top of the pile up to now, but that's starting to falter. So it's up to you to get the same effect with the domestic agenda – you'll need to come up with something pretty radical. Andy wants you to go and think the unthinkable, Selwyn, something bold, something big, something to get us moving again!'

As he ushered Selwyn Knox out of the door, Charlie McDonald uttered his own blend of imprecation and blessing. 'Don't forget, Selwyn, we're depending on you. What you're doing is starting a moral crusade. Yeah, that's it – a moral crusade for the salvation of Britain. You should use that. It sounds big! And presentation is everything. What you'll be doing is going to be controversial – the more controversial the better. So I say get the presentation right and the rest will follow. It's up to you now.'

Selwyn Knox didn't know it, but the reason he got such an easy ride from Charlie McDonald was that McDonald's thoughts were occupied with another matter, quite as important as the new department but with a much more pressing deadline.

He went straight to another meeting, deep in the bowels of Downing Street, where a group of political advisers and information officials had gathered and were chatting in little groups awaiting the arrival of their boss.

'Mornin' everyone – sorry to have dragged you out of the pub. Sit down, you lot. We've got a bit of business to sort out. Come on, Damon: leave Andrea alone, you're getting greasy pawmarks on her! Where's Graham? Is he coming or not? . . . OK, quick as you can. I want to get started . . . right. I've got a few questions to ask you and I want you all to think really hard about this. It's serious, OK?'

Geoff Maddle was sitting next to Charlie McDonald on the raised podium at the front of the room, spring sunshine streaming over their shoulders from a dusty pavement-level window behind them.

Geoff had known Charlie long enough to know when his mate was worried: worried enough not to have taken him completely into his confidence, which was unusual; worried enough to have called an extraordinary meeting of spin doctors and civil servants from all the Whitehall departments.

'OK, the first thing I want to establish is whether you've all had any unusual traffic from the media in the past week. Any unexpected calls, anything out of the ordinary?'

'I had the *News of the World* asking if any member of the cabinet had taken drugs or if the PM had taken drugs.'

'So did I. I think they're trying to do a spoiling story on this new Department for Society stuff. You know, "Ministers who smoked dope are now telling us how bad it is for us."'

'We've had the *Mirror* asking where our man's going on holiday this year—'

'Yeah, we had them too, Charlie. It's a round robin, I think. They're doing a "conspicuous wealth and New Project's new snobs" story.'

'They've been chasing us about the leadership question. Same old crap about when is Delph gonna be the PM and all that. I told them it was all froth and they should do something more important.'

Charlie McDonald listened to the hubbub of voices with the concentrated air of a man waiting for bad news; waiting to hear his worst suspicions confirmed. 'Right. Let's just talk about the *Mirror* stuff, can we? How many of you have had calls from the *Mirror*?'

Hands were raised by half of those present.

'OK, so quite a few of you. And was it always the same caller? Jim McGee was it?'

Everyone agreed that it was McGee.

'Now. Did all the calls start off about ministers' holiday plans?'

The consensus was that they did.

'Right. What I want you to try and remember now are the supplementaries. What did McGee ask you after he'd done the holiday questions?'

Among the civil servants, Damon Fowler, head of news at the Environment Department, was waving his hand in his usual eager-schoolboy way. Charlie McDonald thought Fowler was a self-serving asshole – he'd told Geoff as much on several occasions – but now he needed any help he could get. 'Yes, Damon. What was McGee really after?'

'Well, Charlie, I know we're not supposed to discuss ministers' movements; you've made that very clear to us and I always respect your guidelines, so I said I couldn't tell him about holidays. So then he started on about our Secretary of State's finances: he said David is quite rich, and I said, "Yes, he is; so what?" And then

McGee started asking about the other cabinet members and I said I didn't really know about them. That all went off OK. But then he got on to Andy, er – the PM, that is. And he said he was interested to discover that the PM owned two homes in the UK and also a flat in New York. Well, I sort of knew this was the truth – but I didn't know whether we were supposed to confirm it or not. But McGee seemed to know it anyway, so I told him, "Yes, that's right." And then it was his next question that puzzled me a bit. McGee said, "Well, we're always being told that Andy Sheen came from a modest family, son of a vicar and all that, and yet here we are discovering that he owns all these properties." Now I know New Project don't think wealth is anything to be ashamed of, Charlie, so I said, "So what? The PM is the PM and he's entitled to own properties, isn't he?" But McGee wouldn't let up and he said, "Do you want to know something interesting, Damon? Andy Sheen bought all those properties a long time ago. In fact, he bought the New York flat in 1981 when he was still a student – so what do you think about that?"'

Damon paused to gauge Charlie McDonald's reactions, to see whether he was going to be applauded or rebuked for the way he'd dealt with the enemy on the *Mirror*, but McDonald remained inscrutable.

'OK, Damon. What else did you tell him?'

'Oh well, that was it really, Charlie.' Damon Fowler suddenly had the impression that his chirping was not going down well with the boss and decided it might be time to shut up. Mercifully, Charlie McDonald didn't pursue him but turned instead to the others.

'Well, Damon's had quite a chat with Mr McGee, then. Anyone else had a similar conversation about Andy's finances?'

With a show of some reluctance, two other civil servants and three political advisers, including Sonya Mair, raised their hands and recounted the grillings they'd had from Jim McGee. All agreed that the initial enquiry about ministers' holidays had been just a smokescreen and that McGee's real interest had been in the Prime Minister.

Charlie McDonald frowned and started to bring the meeting to a close.

'OK, thanks very much everyone. Now I've got a favour to ask you. Can you all have a good think about any dealings you've had with Jim McGee in the past? Anyone who has anything useful they can give me about McGee – you all know the sort of thing I mean, *useful*, OK? – will you please come and see me afterwards? Anything you guys have got on the *Mirror* in general or on the editor Cliff Evans will also be gratefully received. And I need this stuff pretty sharpish. One final thing: Geoff and I are going to be dealing with this matter from now on, so any further calls you take about Andy and about his finances, just say nothing. Make a note of the questions and come and tell us. OK? Got that? Thanks very much.'

The following Monday was the anniversary of New Project's accession to power. It was Selwyn Knox's big day too.

The announcement of the new Department for Society had been leaked to the previous day's *Observer* at Sonya Mair's suggestion. She had argued that the bleeding-heart liberals at the *Guardian* and the *Obs* would be the biggest critics of the department once they'd figured out what its real agenda was. So Sonya's plan was to wrongfoot them by feeding them an exclusive story about all the social ills Britain was now suffering from, which a new department was going to be created to deal with. 'The *Observer* lot will jump for joy when we give them this stuff,' said Sonya. 'They'll do a front page saying the department's the answer to all their liberal prayers and Selwyn Knox is the new messiah. So when we actually get the department going and they discover what it's *really* about, they'll maybe have to think twice before slagging off an idea they started by praising to the heavens—'

In the event Sonya's gambit worked reasonably well. The *Observer* was cautiously encouraging and its story set the tone for Monday morning's radio, TV and press coverage. Selwyn Knox's *Today* programme interview was followed by a traipse round ITN, Sky, Channel 4, IRN and the multiple BBC outlets – all fortunately housed together in the parliamentary broadcasting centre over the road from the House of Commons – with Sonya Mair leading her boss in and out of studio after studio.

Sonya told Knox he'd done well. The interviews were largely conducted by presenters who knew very little about the new Department for Society and had had to base their questions on what little briefing she herself had given them beforehand.

The result was a media consensus that the concept behind the department was intriguing and that Selwyn Knox should be given a fair wind to make things happen.

Charlie McDonald had told Sonya there was a possibility of a joint photo op for Knox with Andy Sheen that Monday afternoon. He'd told her this would depend on whether Sheen could clear his diary; but Sonya knew what he really meant was that Downing Street would be watching the tone of the morning's media coverage before a decision was made: if Knox and the department got the thumbs up on morning radio and TV, Andy Sheen would be straining at the leash to join Selwyn in taking credit for the idea; a media thumbs down would almost certainly have meant the PM finding himself just too busy to join his new minister in dealing with the press's criticism. So Sonya was gratified when Charlie rang to say Andy would join her boss at two-thirty on

College Green. The photo op went well, the two men smiled a lot, and the Department for Society got off to as good a start as anyone could reasonably have expected.

That afternoon Selwyn Knox and Sonya Mair were settling into their new departmental offices off Whitehall, watching the cleaners clear out the last reminders of the dinosaurs from the late unlamented Cabinet Office, and discussing the key members of the team who were about to join them.

Sonya didn't beat around the bush. 'What we must make sure is that we don't end up in the same situation as at the D of C: we're agreed on that, Sel, aren't we? We need our civil servants to be absolutely loyal to us. That's the only way we'll ever get anywhere with some of the stuff Andy wants us to push through. Some of it's going to be pretty controversial and we can't afford to have officials who are doubters and trouble-makers. Am I right? OK. So you know, and I know, that the only way to do that is to make sure we have something over them. Something we can use against them if their tender consciences start troubling them and they start being a nuisance for us. Well, the access to Home Office and police files you got us off Charlie McD was well worth the effort, Sel: have a look at what I've got here. I think you'll like it—'

Sonya Mair opened her briefcase and spilled a pile of red folders onto Knox's desk.

'Pick a card! Have a look at some of the stuff I've managed to find out. It's pretty high grade, I can tell you.'

Knox gave Sonya's hand a squeeze, picked up one of the dossiers from the top of the pile and began to read aloud.

'"Robert Jenkins: age forty-three; currently Home Office director of drugs policy. Coming to us on 20 May. Married, three children—" blah, blah, blah. "First from Oxford," OK, good.

"Previous departments include Customs and Excise, Transport and—" ah-hah, this is it, isn't it, Sonya? This next bit is your freelance stuff.'

Sonya Mair smiled and pointed to a paragraph at the bottom of the page. Selwyn Knox read on.

'August 2006; in Soho – in a gay bar! Whoa! That's a good one, Sonya! Picked up by the cops – I wonder what he told his wife and three kids.'

'That's the point, he didn't tell them anything. They don't know. But we do because I took the trouble to find out. And *he* doesn't know we know! He only needs to know that if he ever gives us any trouble. Pretty handy, eh?'

'Certainly is. Can I see the others? Who's this one here? Christopher Brody from the Inland Revenue – coming to us next week. Married, two children. OK, what's the gen on him, then?'

'Look at the bottom of the page, Sel. That's where all the juicy stuff is. It's gambling with this guy. You might think they're all boring grey accountants at the Revenue, but you'd be wrong: this Brody guy has gambled himself into a bigger hole than the ones they had at Passchendaele! He's got debts to loan sharks in the East End; he's taken a second mortgage that his wife knows nothing about; and he's got two County Court judgements against him that he's kept pretty quiet. Any of that stuff could blow him sky-high if we ever needed to use it against him. And let me just show you one last one. This is the big fish, Sel. It's Robert Nottridge – Sir Robert Nottridge, actually, your new Permanent Secretary who's moving in to the office through that wall. Just have a read—'

'OK. Thanks, Sonya. "Sir Robert Nottridge: born 1953; Eton; Cambridge – nothing obvious there. Married, no children—'

'Right. Stop right there, Sel. Now look down the page. Nottridge's wife thinks he's got no children. But guess what? The old bugger's been knocking off one of his former secretaries, a girl called Miriam McLeish, who lives in a flat in Clerkenwell and – surprise, surprise! – she's got a four-year-old and a two-year-old. Claiming benefits, had to give a father's name – that's how we put two and two together. Nottridge doesn't know she put him down as the father, but it's all in the files. So we've got a double whammy on him: we can screw his relationship with little Miriam by letting on that she's named him to the Benefits Agency, and we can screw his marriage by presenting Lady Nottridge with her two little stepchildren! What do you think of that, then?'

'What do I think? I think you're quite something, Sonya! The stuff you've got in your head is priceless. It's enough to make you bullet-proof – and me too, thank God. There's no way anyone can touch us, you know that. Because we've got the ammunition to fight our way out of any corner. I honestly don't think I could survive without you, Sonya, and I'm not joking when I say that—'

Sonya grinned. 'Too right, Selly baby. Too right. So just make sure you don't cross me, then! You won't be bullet-proof from me, you know. I'm the one with the silver bullet, so you listen to what I say – OK? Right. Now there's one post we haven't talked about yet and it's an important one: with all the media work we're going to have to do for this department, we'll need someone pretty on-message as our director of communications. It's a civil service post, of course, but it's too important to leave to the usual paper-pushers. I think we need to get a journalist in, Sel. We'll have to get him through the civil service selection procedure, but I think we can manage to fix that, can't we? Is there anyone smart and malleable at the same time? I thought of Dave Sopwith – he's certainly malleable; it's just that he's such an arsehole—'

'Don't worry, Sonya. We're sorted on the communications job. That's one post I *have* thought about myself, and I've got the perfect candidate. We're going to go for the BBC politics reporter, Nigel Tonbridge – he's working on *Newsnight* at the moment, but I've known him for quite a while—'

'What? *That* Nigel Tonbridge? He's a good journalist right enough, but isn't he the guy you had a run in with, back up in Scotland?'

'Exactly right,' said Selwyn Knox. 'And that's why he's so perfect for us: I've got *plenty* on Nigel Tonbridge.'

7

CHARLIE MCDONALD and Geoff Maddle usually ended their extended working day with a couple of drinks at the Red Lion.

They were both in Downing Street every morning by half-past seven, in time to read over the papers and the radio and TV transcripts before the eight-thirty news-planning meeting. And they rarely knocked off before eight or nine in the evening. How could they? Even if there was no event for them to attend with the PM, no speech, no reception or dinner to go to, there were the TV bulletins to monitor, the late-deadline calls from journalists needing just one last piece of guidance before putting the front page to bed, and worried ministers needing a quick briefing before going on *Newsnight* or else praying Charlie's indulgence for some slip of the tongue, for some deviation from the official line while speaking to this or that hack.

After all that, the Red Lion might have seemed a strange place to seek refuge.

Just over the road from Downing Street and right opposite the old Treasury building, the Lion was the pub where Whitehall, Westminster and the fourth estate met and mingled on neutral ground. Civil servants in shabby suits were there; so were the sharply attired TV faces, the political correspondents and business hacks hoping for a repeat of the legendary Charlie Whelan's indiscretions, which had more than once thrown the stock market into turmoil. Into this bear pit Charlie McDonald and Geoff

Maddle would stride with a nonchalant, 'Hi, you lot. Who's buying?'

For Charlie and Geoff, the Red Lion served two purposes.

If they wanted to plant tomorrow's story in the minds of the press corps, this was the place to do it.

Like most people's, journalists' minds blossom and become touchingly receptive after a few drinks. It was always easier for the spin doctors to take a chosen one to the back of the taproom and whisper in his or her ear than it was to follow the formal channels of a news conference, a press release or even a telephone call in the cold sober light of next morning's newsroom.

But if Geoff and Charlie didn't have a story to peddle, if they'd had a shitty day and just wanted a bit of peace and quiet to chew things over, the Lion was still the place they headed for. On these occasions, though, they wouldn't hail the assembled crowd; they'd nod to the landlady, the endlessly helpful and unfailingly hospitable Marian, and she'd wave them to the private rooms upstairs.

Here the sultans of spin could stretch out and relax. The front room, overlooking Whitehall, was their favourite. Here they could stare hypnotically at the lazy ceiling fan as it wafted their cigarette smoke round and round the grimy, print-bedecked walls; they could help themselves to the drinks that Marian trustingly left on the narrow bar counter at the back of the room; they could escape from the storm outside and gather their frazzled thoughts.

Tonight, as so often, they smoked and drank their way through an initial nerve-calming twenty-minute oasis of luxurious silence. Glances exchanged, sporadic smiles and nods were the outward and visible signs of the inward process of mental digestion they were both going through, thought patterns seemingly following parallel trajectories as they mulled over the triumphs that lay behind or the potential pitfalls ahead.

It was Geoff who finally broke the silence.

'So what's that *Mirror* story all about, then?'

'Yeah, I was just thinking the same thing. It could be nothing—'

'It could be something, though, couldn't it?'

'Yeah. The thing that's got me a bit worried is that Andy doesn't want to talk to me about it. It's not like him.'

'Nah. What's the deal? It's that flat in New York, isn't it?'

'Possibly. I knew he had it, of course. Marie and the kids have been over there a couple of times during the school holidays. I don't think Andy uses it, though. Doesn't really speak about it much.'

'So is it just the *Mirror* on its politics-of-envy kick? You know, "Why has Andy Sheen got a luxury pad stateside while our readers live in crappy council houses?" There's not much mileage in that, is there?'

'Wouldn't have thought so—'

'Well, has McGee phoned to speak to you personally, Charlie, or is he coming at this from some sort of angle? What was he after from all the guys he's been ringing? Why did he ring Sonya Mair, for example?'

'I don't know, mate. Maybe because she knows Andy as well as anyone. I don't know. It is strange that he hasn't rung me, though.'

'It's nothing to do with the "not inhaling" story, is it? That's not going to jump up and kick us in the balls?'

'Funny you should say that. I asked Andy about that too; but he's absolutely insistent that he just did a Clinton – nothing more. And it's over thirty years ago, when he was a student at Cambridge. I can't see how that can hurt us.'

'Well, let's think it through, Charlie. So Andy smoked a bit of pot when he was at Cambridge. Right. So did everyone. OK, no big news in itself. Smoking dope didn't harm Bill Clinton; it didn't harm those Tories who put their hands up when Ann Widdecombe started rabbiting on about zero tolerance ten years ago, did it?'

'Yeah. The only thing is this new Department for Society that Andy's just got going – with Selwyn Knox, you know. It'd look bad if the papers run a story about the PM smoking dope when he's just launched his moral salvation crusade to wipe out naughty behaviour. We all need to be whiter than white at the moment—'

'Right. That'd be embarrassing, but it wouldn't be the end of the earth, would it? I don't know, Charlie. I've just got a sneaking suspicion there's something more than that going on in Jim McGee's filthy little mind.'

'Yeah, I think you might be right. Andy says we should just forget it, but I don't think it's going to go away, myself. Sometimes Andy needs us to protect him even if he doesn't know it.'

As McDonald and Maddle were ruminating in the Red Lion, Nigel Tonbridge was just beginning to feel the pressure.

The problem with *Newsnight*, he always felt, was that the ten-thirty transmission time gave you a false sense of security.

When he'd been working for News, he'd got into the rhythm of churning out piece after piece from the moment he arrived at the BBC Westminster office in the morning to the minute the Radio 4 midnight bulletin went off the air. It was hectic, but in a way it was easier. You just got your head down and went with the flow.

Newsnight gave you too much time to think. Sometimes Nigel would spend the whole day agonizing over a minor element in a story: how to phrase something; which MP to use as the main interviewee; where to go for pictures to illustrate the story. And before you knew it the time would have ticked away and the studio director would be screaming for the cut spot.

Added to that was the pressure to be different; to give a sexy new perspective on a story your viewers might already have watched four or five times on earlier news bulletins; to be hip and cool in that annoying *Newsnight* way; to appeal to the younger audience that Fred Pond the genial D-G was always banging on about.

Recently Nigel had begun to wonder if it was all really worth it.

And another thing – Nigel laughed as he caught himself muttering the telltale phrase of the archetypal ranting nutter – Nigel's 'other thing', the thing that was really starting to get to him about the new-style BBC, was the dumbing down. The seemingly endless quest to seduce a new, less sophisticated, less informed, less interested audience was becoming the bane of Nigel Tonbridge's professional life.

It wasn't just the need to sex up every story with 3-D smart-graphix and a dose of chart music, it wasn't just the pressure to expound every policy initiative in terms of 'what it means for today's urban teenager', or to explain every time you mentioned Andy Sheen that he was the Prime Minister – it was the whole new BBC mentality. In moments of soul-searching, Nigel was honest enough to admit that an additional factor in his dissatisfaction – perhaps even the most important factor – was that his face was starting not to fit.

It was over four years since he had moved from Radio Strathclyde down to Television Centre in London. On his debut as a TV News reporter, he had been acclaimed as a serious heavyweight; four years later and four years older, he was starting to feel like an old lag. He'd done his stint of car crashes, floods and crime reporting, he'd spent three months in the social affairs unit, he'd been to Brussels and he'd done two tours of duty in the various Middle East war zones.

Then he had moved to the BBC's Westminster operation, where he had been taken under the wing of the man he respected more than anyone in broadcasting.

Marc Lemaire was a brooding genius of French-Jewish descent. More than most others he had resisted the Corporation's headlong slide into infantile trivia, reality docu-soaps and news as entertainment. He had fought hard – and failed – to stop the axing of *Panorama*, *Worldview* and *Nation Matters*. He'd put up a valiant rearguard campaign against the dropping of foreign news from the television bulletins. In his own self-defining terminology, Marc Lemaire was a grown-up; but he had been fighting a losing battle with the less than grown-ups who were now running the show.

Over the months, Nigel could see his mentor becoming more and more frustrated, more and more frayed at the edges, as he watched the ineluctable decline of the Reithian ideals that once fuelled public-service broadcasting.

Marc Lemaire had taken early retirement from the BBC on his fifty-fifth birthday in 2010. The TV Centre accountants had announced they needed a thousand redundancies, and had offered beneficial terms and enhanced pensions to the staff the new bosses had fingered as dinosaurs, trouble-makers – 'old soldiers rattling their muskets' in the D-G's telling phrase. Marc's name had been at the top of the list – how could it not be? – and the names of virtually everyone else Nigel rated and respected in the Corporation had come just below it.

Since then, Nigel had found BBC Westminster increasingly inimical.

The new reporters and presenters flooding in were for the most part young and pretty – and pretty ignorant of politics, history and world affairs. But theirs were the faces that fitted at the new BBC, not Nigel's. Nigel Tonbridge's generation were starting to hear the tumbrils roll.

Tonight, for example, Nigel was supposedly cutting a four-minute spot on the problems facing British conscripts returning from the Middle East Wars.

He'd wanted to examine the financial and social issues of injuries sustained in the line of duty; of chemical poisoning from Syrian weapons plants, where previously unknown stocks of nerve gas and germ warfare agents had miraculously been discovered; of psychological traumas among the returnees.

But *Newsnight*'s highly regarded young editor, Shayna Kelvin, had told him these were issues with 'no resonance for our audience'. What she wanted – and what Nigel was now reluctantly producing – was a survey of returning squaddies to see how they rated the new music in the charts compared with what had been there when they'd left for the war, how they coped with unfaithful girlfriends and – Shayna was hoping for a little actualité TV here – how they dealt with the blokes who'd stolen their bitches.

At that moment Nigel's phone rang.

Looking back later, he realized the only reason he didn't tell Selwyn Knox to go screw himself was that his despair over the BBC and his fears for the future were at an all-time high, while his self-confidence and his resistance were at an all-time low.

Geoff Maddle's mobile had gone off in the Gents. He'd told Charlie that the toilets of the Duke of Clarence weren't the best place for a confidential chat and had gone outside to the anonymity of a busy Trafalgar Square.

'Right, mate; we're OK now. What is it?'

'I don't know what to make of it, Geoff. After we'd been talking in the Lion last night, I went back to Andy and told him to stop pissing around. I told him if there was anything else in the drugs story – or anything else he's got tucked away in his past – we needed to know about it now. I told him if there were any skeletons – any shape or any size – they could harm us pretty badly if we don't know about them and things come out in an uncontrolled way. I mentioned all the sensitivity over St Selwyn's new department, like we said, and I told him we might just be able to get away with whatever it is, if he owned up to me right away, but he just kept denying there was anything.'

'OK. Well, that's it then. Shiny Sheen is shiny clean and we can stop shitting ourselves. Right?'

'Yeah, maybe, but I've just got a funny feeling, Geoff. You know, we've always assumed Andy really is Mr Clean. So I was just a bit surprised when he wouldn't look me in the eye while I was giving him the third degree. I'm a pretty good judge of when someone's bullshitting me and I got the distinct impression Andy was covering something up. Maybe we should run a Lancelot check on him – what do you think? It's just it's a bit sensitive running Lancelot on the Prime Minister—'

'Yeah, but I think we should do it. We can't afford any surprises with Andy. We've always promoted him as such a goodie-goodie. Anything that dents that image is bad news for everyone, not just for him, but for the whole party, the whole image we've built, the whole Project.'

'Yeah, I reckon you're right. I just wanted to check that with you, mate. I'll get it done and let you know what spews out.'

'OK, but don't just go after the cannabis thing, Charlie. I want to know why McGee keeps banging on about Andy's finances and the New York apartment. Maybe you should get Damon Fowler back in for a chat. He's a wanker and he can't keep his mouth shut, but he might be a useful way to quiz McGee, assuming you don't want to talk to him directly.'

'Yeah, good idea. If I ring McGee, he'll know he's got us worried. I'll use simple Damon instead.'

It was after midnight when Nigel got home from his shift at *Newsnight*.

Joanie and the kids were all in bed, but Nigel knew he wouldn't be able to sleep. The sound of Selwyn Knox's voice – not on the radio, not on TV, but in person on the end of the phone – had shaken him more than he cared to admit.

For four years, Nigel had tried to forget the Exxington tragedy, had tried to forget little Clare O'Leary, to forget the growing terror he'd felt on hearing Knox's carefully calculated, smirking telephone speech which had killed Nigel's scoop and crushed his self-esteem.

For four years he had carried in his pocket the journalist's notebook he had been using in September 2006, the notebook with the transcript of Ian Murray's allegations, Eileen O'Leary's lament and Knox's gloating monologue.

Without him quite realizing it, the image of Selwyn Knox had become an obsession.

The memory of his own attempts to bring the guy to justice, his shame and self-loathing when he had crumbled before Knox's bullying and his subsequent rationalizations, which had half per-suaded him to believe Knox was most probably innocent – all this had become ineradicably ingrained in a corner of Nigel's psyche, a corner he had spent four years trying never to visit.

Nigel spotted the blinking light of the answering machine and flicked the Play button. Like a dogged nightmare, the grating voice he had heard in September 2006 and then heard again tonight for the first time in over four years echoed round the room.

'Hi Nigel. It's Selwyn. It was good to talk to you tonight. I'm ringing to ask if we can let bygones be bygones. I'm sorry our last conversation back in Exxington was a bit fraught. I've always rated you as a journalist, it's just you got the wrong end of the stick all those years ago. Anyway, I appreciate your integrity over the whole affair. You were big enough to realize there was never anything in those stupid allegations Ian Murray was peddling and I respect you for that. I'm sure you know Murray left the council straight after the accident on the mountain: it was pretty obvious he was accepting the blame for what went wrong – the *Express* and the *Sun* made it clear it was all his fault and I guess he was big enough to put his hand up. I feel a bit sorry for him, actually. That was the end of his career and he ended up a bit of a sad case – drink and things. Died last year, from what I heard. But you've done well, Nigel. What was it after Radio Strathclyde? A stint on the local radio desk down in London and then that posting in Brussels doing EU stories for the BBC regions. Pretty good stuff. And now here you are on national television, working just round the corner from me. Anyway, I won't beat around the bush. I want you to come and work with me on the big project I'm launching. I'm sure you've heard about it. I know you're not happy at the BBC. This is your chance to do something worthwhile, to give something back to society. Come and do it, Nigel. You won't regret it.'

Damon Fowler had been in a flurry of excitement ever since he came back from Downing Street. He had been recounting and embellishing his conversation with 'Charlie' to his colleagues in the Environment Department press office with a glow of pride: 'So Charlie asked me what I thought of Jim McGee and what I would do to deal with the *Mirror*. So I said, "We're going to have to deal with this guy sooner or later, Charlie; we're going to have to deal with him hard, and I think we should deal with him now before he can do us any harm." Charlie and I think McGee is a bastard.' Damon looked slightly shocked at his own temerity in pronouncing such a word, but he clearly felt it was the sort of language he should use to impress people and show he was one of the boys.

Damon Fowler's burgeoning self-image was about to get another boost. His phone rang and there was the voice of Charlie himself. Damon made sure his colleagues on the desks around him could hear his end of the conversation and that they were in no doubt who he was talking to.

'Yes, Charlie, I think you're dead right. That's exactly what we need to do. Of course I'll come over to Downing Street, Charlie. I can ring McGee for you, no trouble. I'll see you in about half an hour. Bye, Charlie.'

The Department for Society was starting to take shape.

Selwyn Knox and Sonya Mair had watched the new officials moving into their offices and played a private little game of matching faces to files, exchanging discreet nods and grins as they spotted the more amusing cases.

The department's top civil servant, the Permanent Secretary Sir Robert Nottridge, was due to arrive the following day: his departure from the Department for Work and Pensions had been delayed by another crisis in the long-running saga over the collapse of the UK's pension system, which had left hundreds of thousands of OAPs without income, food or housing. Knox had fixed a private meeting with Sir Robert, Sonya and himself for the next morning.

For her part, Sonya was not best pleased.

Their new department had inherited the dregs of the former Cabinet Office's press officers, the more competent among them having found themselves jobs in other departments.

Sonya had discovered an operation in disarray.

All the faults of the old regime were present in spades. The press operation was a shambles, with no strategy unit, no media-planning unit, no instant rebuttal unit and an out-of-hours cover system that left much to be desired. Jack Davenham, who had been running the information directorate on a temporary basis pending the appointment of the new director, had been in the business for twenty years and evidently felt no need to improve on what he had grown used to.

Journalists' telephone calls were regularly met with a casual 'I'll have to check and get back to you,' followed by radio silence until after the reporter's deadline had been missed. So newspapers were left to print whatever they liked about the government, with no statement to put the department's point of view or correct misleading facts.

But even worse than the lack of defensive media response was the total absence of proactive planning. Sonya was shocked to find that the department had no strategic planning unit to work up future media opportunities, to identify the best dates for future stories and to coordinate with other departments and Downing Street. This meant there were often clashes when the department tried to put out big news releases on the same day that other departments were presenting theirs.

And even worse than the organizational chaos was the attitude of the civil servants working in the directorate. The place was full of old lags working out their time until retirement who were totally uninterested in improving the way the press office operated.

As far as Sonya was concerned, the place was a shambles. It needed shaking up from top to bottom.

And to do that, Selwyn Knox told her, they needed a director of communications who would do Sonya Mair's bidding, someone who could be made to do what he was told, someone like Nigel Tonbridge.

*

Nigel talked to his wife about the phone calls from Selwyn Knox.

Joanie did not hesitate: she told him it was a great opportunity. He had been so fed up with the way the BBC was going lately that he should jump at Knox's offer. And the six-figure salary was much better, too.

Joanie was surprised when Nigel sounded diffident. And when he could not explain the reasons for his hesitation—

She asked if he had anything against Knox as a person.

Nigel was aching to tell her, to ask her advice about what had happened in Exxington.

But he couldn't: embarking on that story inevitably would have meant explaining the threat Knox had used and could still use to gain Nigel's silent connivance. Several days' thinking took Nigel little further.

Too many questions remained unanswered and – from where he was sitting – unanswerable; questions that could only ever be answered by re-entering the ambiguous world of Selwyn Knox. What was behind Knox's offer? Was it a genuine attempt at reconciliation? Was Knox trying to use Nigel in some way? Would he be stepping into a trap, into some sort of danger, if he were to accept?

He was surprised Knox had come to him after their run-in all those years ago, but he understood why Knox might regard him as useful: he had good contacts in political and media circles, they were both from the same part of the world, and Knox knew his qualities as a journalist.

On the other hand, Nigel still felt anger and shame over those events in Exxington.

The old notebook with the shorthand notes, always in his pocket, Nigel kept as a constant reminder of his own cowardice and inadequacy, a nagging self-reproach, which over the past four years had become a Hamlet-like obsession.

The more Nigel agonized, the more he rationalized, the more

he convinced himself that Knox must surely be innocent, that Knox would surely not have approached him now if he really were guilty of Clare's murder, that Nigel must indeed have tried to convict an innocent man in Exxington.

What Nigel did not enunciate to himself was that actually he liked this conclusion because it brought him a sense of relief . . . a happy release from the burden of culpability he had carried with him for four years. If Knox were innocent, then Nigel too could be freed from his own sin of omission, his own guilt by inaction.

Nigel actively wanted Knox to be innocent in order to redeem himself.

And because he wanted his own redemption so badly, he slowly convinced himself that if he accepted Knox's offer he would somehow validate Knox's innocence, he would somehow make real the construct he had built in his own mind: 'If Knox employs me, he cannot be guilty.'

In the end, Nigel's agonized reasoning brought him to the strange conviction that only by accepting Knox's offer could he set the seal on Knox's innocence – and on his own salvation from the sins of hesitation, weakness and, consequently, complicity in responsibility for Clare's death.

Nigel rang Knox's office to say he would be delighted to apply for the post of director of communications at the Department for Society.

As Damon Fowler walked into his office, Charlie McDonald was seized by a powerful wave of contempt. Little tough guy Damon, the pocket braggart who talked the talk but couldn't walk the walk, Damon the big mouth, Damon the tiny dick.

McDonald sighed and waved to Damon to sit down.

'OK, mate. Like I told you on the phone, you're going to ring McGee, tell him that you've been thinking about his call and you'd like to help him. You'll have to say you've got some grudge or other against Andy and you'd like to help the *Mirror* stitch him up or something. The main thing is to find where McGee's coming from. Try and see what his information is; see what tip-off he's had to get him started on the Andy thing, OK? I'll be listening on the other extension. And don't forget: whatever you hear in this office stays in this office. If I hear you've been blabbing about any of this, your future ends yesterday. Understood?'

Sir Robert Nottridge had been a civil servant for thirty-five years.

During that time, he had seen administrations of every political hue come and go.

He had worked with good ministers and bad ministers, good governments and bad governments.

So vast was his experience that friends told him he should write a book about it.

The reason Robert Nottridge did not do so was because he took seriously the civil servant's obligation of confidentiality, the oath of omertà that bound him and his colleagues to silence.

In long careers spent in intimate contact with government ministers, he and others like him would hear plenty of evil, see plenty of evil, but undertook to tell none of it to the outside world.

Robert Nottridge believed this was the only way the machinery of government could function. In his eyes, it was the only way ministers could allow themselves the total frankness they needed in their close, daily dealings with their Permanent Secretaries, the best of whom became a cross between father confessor, mentor and butler, the trusted receptacle of the most sensitive knowledge and opinions.

In his years at the top of the civil service, there had been two or three occasions when Robert Nottridge had felt that the malpractice of his minister or his minister's political adviser bordered on the reprehensible and the criminal. On none of those occasions did he speak out about what he had witnessed and he felt no sympathy for civil servants who did. But this dog-like loyalty did not preclude Sir Robert from having his own opinions about the governments he served.

He had despaired of the sleaze and stagnation of previous governments and had privately rejoiced when the New Project government was elected in 2005. He welcomed the new cabinet's energy, resolve and genuine idealism. It had been a good time to be in Whitehall, as the New Project broom began to sweep out the dead wood.

In their first, successful years, the new boys had enacted a swathe of sensible, reinvigorating legislation that had brought new life to the political arena. Even their increasing obsession with PR and spin and their steadily growing reputation for distorting statistics and embellishing news of their own achievements did little to dampen Sir Robert's enthusiasm. He felt this was a good reforming government that believed in what it was doing. He had supported the Middle East Wars, even when the casualties began to mount and the Allies were drawn into invading one more country after another.

His only doubts concerned the way New Project had begun to treat the civil service he believed in and loved.

Since the Northcote–Trevelyan reforms of the mid-nineteenth century had abolished the old ways of cronyism and corruption to establish a non-political, independent service appointed on merit and grounded in the highest ideals of impartiality and integrity, the civil service had loyally served governments of all stripes. In return it had been respected by them and protected from improper political pressure.

Until now no government had asked the civil service to do its political dirty work, no government had forced it to serve party interests at the expense of the wider interests of the nation.

The one flaw with New Project, Sir Robert felt, was that they were so eager to see through the work they had begun, so eager to stay in power, that they had begun to treat the civil service as their own plaything, at New Project's beck and call to help New Project get re-elected.

The antics of some of the party's infamous political advisers, the shock troops of the New Project revolution who were sent into every department to bully civil servants into toeing the New Project line, revolted Sir Robert.

The advisers, who thought they could give orders to his officials, undermining the service's prized impartiality, were anathema to him, and those who ordered civil servants to tell lies and conduct smear campaigns on behalf of the Project party were the worst of the bunch.

Now though, in 2011, Sir Robert Nottridge was prepared to give Andy Sheen and Selwyn Knox the benefit of his good will.

The idea for the new department he had been chosen to preside over struck him as evidence that the party was returning to the idealism and radical thinking it recently seemed to have lost.

His get-to-know-you chat with Selwyn Knox had gone well. He had found the minister enthusiastic and impatient to start the good work. Knox had told him to expect controversial measures from the Department for Society and Nottridge had replied that no omelette was ever made without breaking eggs. His political adviser, Sonya Mair, on the other hand, had struck Nottridge as deliberately unfriendly and cold. He had been told she had no time for civil servants, and she had taken few pains to hide it.

On the whole, though, Sir Robert Nottridge had left the meeting with a good impression of Knox. On returning to his own rooms down the old Cabinet Office corridor, he briefed his Private Secretary on what to expect.

'Knox comes across as a man of integrity, Philip. He seems motivated by idealism and not by personal ambition. I believe he may be the man to make a success of the great initiatives we are now embarking on, to bring back that honesty and generosity of spirit that has recently been dimmed in our political life. I admire him and have great hopes for him.'

For their part, when Nottridge left the room and closed the door behind him, Knox and Mair had looked at each other and burst out laughing. 'Fancy that lump of pompous bullshit having two little bastards hidden away in Clerkenwell! He doesn't look as if he had it in him!'

Nigel Tonbridge received his invitation to an interview at the civil service selection board the following week.

He was invited to submit in advance a paper on 'The Problem of Teenage Immorality and the Presentational Issues Surrounding Government Action to Tackle It'. At the selection board, he was told, there would be role play based on a 'typical situation that a director of communications may be expected to have to deal with in a major government department', and an extended interview before a panel of senior civil servants and assessors.

Nigel found the whole project somewhat daunting.

Two days before the selection board he received an unexpected phone call from Sonya Mair. 'Don't worry, Nigel. The board is going to go your way. Selwyn and I want you as our communications director and we're going to make sure we get you. Nothing has been left to chance. You're home and dry.'

That evening, Selwyn and Sonya drove to his pied-à-terre. It was here, in Dolphin Square, that the original nightingale reputedly had sung, only for the songwriter to decide eventually that Berkeley Square sounded more romantic. Nowadays the sprawling complex of apartments looked like an upmarket council block. Its less than fashionable position, on the Thames embankment next to Vauxhall Bridge, made prices affordable, while its closeness to Westminster made it a favourite place for out-of-town MPs to stay during parliamentary sessions.

Many of them, like Selwyn Knox, enjoyed the fact that wives or live-in girlfriends seldom made the effort to come and stay with them.

Sonya Mair had already uncorked a bottle of red Bordeaux and poured two large glasses. Dinner was on the table by the time she broached the subject that had been on her mind for days.

'You know, Sel, I made all the arrangements to fix that selection board for Nigel Tonbridge. Those civil servants are so prissy about their ethical independence, but you only have to know which buttons to press and they roll over as easy as anything! I went to see the HR guy who's chairing Tonbridge's board and a couple of the board members: they all figured in those dossiers I showed you, remember? So I gave them a little glimpse of what we know about their little peccadilloes and they all jumped straight into our pocket. What a surprise! So Tonbridge owes us one before he even starts the job. But look, I've been thinking. The thing I really want to be clear about is this: are you *really* sure you want Nigel Tonbridge to come and work with us? I think he's too dangerous. He could be a viper in our midst.'

Knox smiled as he replied. 'You've got it wrong, Sonya. If the guy's dangerous, where better to have him than right here where we can keep an eye on him? If we leave him at the BBC, it's going to be too tempting for him to start taking potshots at me once the department launches its crusade.'

But Sonya wasn't convinced. 'Oh, come on, Selwyn. That's

bullshit. He's had plenty of time to take a potshot at you and he hasn't. Why on earth do you want him on board now?'

Knox hesitated for a moment. 'I don't know – you need to trust me on this one, Sonya. I just have a feeling he could be important for me. That's why I'm involving him in what we're about to do. I'm making him our accomplice. I'm binding him so close to me he won't be able to bite.'

Soon, almost unnoticeably, the bottle of wine – and then another – were emptied.

As Knox stretched out by the fire, Sonya leaned across and stroked his neck. He did not respond. Sonya's hand began to slip inside his collar. He remained motionless. Now her hand was unbuttoning his shirt, reaching down to his belt, opening the buckle, slipping inside, slipping down to grasp . . .

Suddenly, Knox leapt to his feet, boiling with anger, all pretence at restraint irretrievably lost in a hail of rage and flailing fists.

'What the hell are you doing? Not that way, for Christ's sake! That's wrong, you bitch – that's not what we do. I need it how I've told you. What are you trying to do – humiliate me?'

Sonya Mair leapt back to protect herself from the blows raining down on her. 'No, Sel, no. It's not that—! I just wanted to try something normal for once . . . I'm sorry . . . no, don't hit me! Not my face . . . don't hit my face! No. No. I'll do it . . . wait . . . I'll do it, Sel . . .'

And Sonya Mair ran from Selwyn Knox's onslaught into the adjoining bedroom. When she returned, she was no longer the sophisticated, elegantly dressed, carefully made-up thirty-five-year-old who had left the room minutes earlier.

8

NIGEL'S LETTER of appointment arrived from the civil service commissioners, informing him of the grade, salary and pension rights attached to his new job.

His title was to be director of strategy and communications at the Department for Society, a grade three post entitling him to membership of the senior civil service and the First Division Association. His three-year contract was renewable by mutual consent. Under separate cover he received a genial letter from Sir Robert Nottridge, welcoming him to the department and inviting him to make an appointment for an introductory chat on his first day in post.

When Nigel phoned Sir Robert's office, an Assistant Private Secretary with a pronounced Brummie accent told him he was expected to start work a week on Monday and the Permanent Secretary could see him after morning prayers that day at ten-twenty.

After so many years at the BBC, Nigel found himself disorientated by the speed with which such defining changes in his life were being made. To BBC colleagues who quizzed him about his new job, and expressed doubts over the characters of Selwyn Knox and Sonya Mair, Nigel replied with a noncommittal shrug. He told them he'd had enough of being a political reporter, constantly on the outside looking in; he cited the example of other journalists who had gone to work for the government and who all spoke now of how closely they were involved with policy-making; and he reminded them of the respect this government accorded its communications officials as privileged participants in the inner workings of the New Project party.

Privately, he told Joanie that his greatest regret was that he would now have to abandon Sir Hubert. As a serving civil servant, he would be barred from making any publications with a political content and he felt Sir Hubert would inevitably be regarded as falling into that category.

For the past six years, Nigel had spent his spare time trying to resurrect his unfinished university thesis, which had recently blossomed into a full-length biography. During that period, Nigel had grown as fond of Sir Hubert Wakely as if he had been a living friend, rather than a long-dead nineteenth-century politician, remembered now – if he was remembered at all – solely for his role in one of Westminster's lesser political scandals.

His affinity for Sir Hubert was due partly to their shared Scottish connections and partly, Nigel sometimes felt, to his own empathy with Wakely's tendency towards melancholia and self-reproach. This darker side of Sir Hubert emerged with great clarity in the private journals he had kept during his reclusive existence at the family home of Clanwinning in Midlothian following his disgrace in 1845.

In his student days Nigel had visited Clanwinning and befriended the then owner of the house, a youngish stockbroker named McIndoe with little interest in history and no use for Wakely's journals, which had lain unopened for over a century. Mr McIndoe had been more than happy for Nigel to beaver away in the former library, which Mrs McIndoe had had converted into a solarium and mini-gym, and to copy down in longhand vast swathes of Sir Hubert's musings.

This prolonged communion with the dead politician had given

Nigel a strange insight into the Sheffield & Ironbridge scandal and the devastating effect it had had on its principal political victim. Wakely's journals began a few weeks after his resignation speech to the House of Commons in May 1845, which, he wrote, 'has left me with ringing cries of "Shame!" from my erstwhile familiars forever burned in my ears, very like we are told the visage and form of the assassin can sometimes be burned on the retina of his victim's eye, there to be retrieved after death and used by the detective seeking to resurrect the identity of the killer.'

It seemed to Nigel that Wakely regarded his life after the railway scandal as a form of living death. Nowhere did he attempt to justify his own part in the events leading up to the twenty-seven fatalities on the Crewe to Warrington line. He accepted the findings of the official inquiry that the derailment had been due to 'the buckling of the rail under the downwards pressure exerted by the passing engine on a section weakened by insufficient admixture in the iron used for its constitution'. And he refused to complain about the treatment he received when he was expelled from parliament.

At no point did Wakely ever deny that he had lied about the Northern Railways share scandal. He had failed to warn investors that the steel used for the new tracks on the Crewe to Warrington line had been ordered from the Sheffield & Ironbridge Foundry Company, despite warnings of impropriety about the firm's directors.

The investigation into the ensuing crash had established that the track failure was due to the adulteration of the iron ore used in its construction, and that Sheffield & Ironbridge had done this deliberately to save money. Wakely had tried to hide this fact in his statement to parliament. Later he had been forced to backtrack on several important aspects of his statement and had then been held up to public ridicule and forced to resign.

What puzzled Nigel was that Wakely never sought to defend his conduct or to exculpate himself. While bribes had been paid by Sheffield & Ironbridge, Wakely himself had never made any monetary gain from the affair.

The government minister who did profit – he was, it later transpired, the first cousin of Sheffield & Ironbridge's chairman – was never charged with misconduct and went on to enjoy a long and successful ministerial career. The only references to this in Wakely's journals are oblique. In the section of his diaries which he had apparently been preparing for publication as a memoir under the title, 'Animadversion on the Nature of Success and Failure', Wakely hinted at his disillusion with former colleagues. 'All I see around does seem to point at me the bitter accusing finger of failure and dishonour. Not least the bounty I see my colleagues enjoy in their careers which, though I estimate such worldly success at nought, I cannot but feel levels reproach at one such as me. I bear my shame with bitter fortitude.'

A close reading of the Wakely journals had led Nigel to conclude that Sir Hubert had other transgressions on his conscience in addition to Northern Railways. The diaries made reference to further episodes involving false statements to parliament both by the author himself and by fellow ministers.

Nigel felt perhaps the greatest merit of his own work on the Wakely case was the light it threw on the culture of lies and deceit which routinely surrounded the political life of the period. But the most shocking result of his research, and the one that affected Nigel most deeply on a personal level, was his conviction that Wakely had not died of the influenza that is customarily given as the cause of his death. From references in the later journals, Nigel had become convinced that the shame Wakely felt after 1845 had led him to plan suicide and that his death in 1852 was the result of self-poisoning with arsenic. Wakely's descendants, apparently fearful of the further disgrace this would bring on the family name, had disguised Sir Hubert's suicide in the commentaries written after his death and had kept the secret for the next century and a half.

Charlie McDonald had done his research and had gathered as much intelligence as he felt he could expect to unearth from the comfort of his Downing Street office. Now he sensed the time had come to take the initiative.

Now was the time to brief Geoff Maddle and give him full authority to get out and do something.

'So this is what I've managed to find out, Geoff. First of all, I did the Damon Fowler thing we talked about and I've got a much clearer idea of where Jim McGee and the *Mirror* are coming from. I got Damon to ring McGee and offer to help him dig the dirt on the PM. McGee was delighted: as soon as he thought Damon was going to help him rattle Andy's skeletons, he was falling over himself to explain what he's discovered so far.

'Basically, McGee has been contacted by someone who says that he's a pal of Andy's from way back and that he's got something of interest to tell the *Mirror*. McGee wouldn't tell Damon who it is, where he lives or what he's got on Andy, but I think it's someone who knew Andy at Cambridge. What I do know is that McGee's come across the Sheen-smoked-pot story, and what I think he's trying to do is turn it into something much bigger. McGee told Damon he's chasing something that could blow a few people out of the water—'

'He could be bullshitting, Charlie, he could be trying to put the wind up us. I'm not convinced McGee's got anything. He's on the City pages, remember – that's how he got the info about Andy's flat in New York. But I reckon he's trying to put his name to a big story that'll make his reputation and get him into political reporting.'

'Yeah, that's all these bloody hacks are concerned with – making their own name. All they're interested in is gossip and tittle-tattle and they couldn't give a toss about the truth. But we can't afford to take our eye off this one, Geoff. I wondered why no one had ever run a Lancelot check on Andy, so I ran the program on him like we said. It came up with nothing. Nothing, except the usual pile of opposition smears they've tried to run against him over the years, nothing to stick. What I did do, though, was go to the Police National Computer – I just did it on a hunch. And that's where I got something. Apparently, we have privileged access to the third-back-up, fail-safe hard drive, or whatever you call it, on the PNC – y'know, the one that's never wiped out however many times you pass the official eraser over it, the sort of thing that got that pop star on the child pornography charges all those years ago. Well, take a look at what it came up with: "Andrew Michael Sheen, Cambridge Magistrates' Court, 11 May 1981" – it's a conditional discharge on a drugs rap!'

'Let's see that – Andy bloody Sheen! I can't believe it. So he did inhale after all!'

'Looks that way, doesn't it? He was certainly up in court on a possession charge.'

'So do you think that's the story McGee's got? Is that what he's making all the song and dance about?'

'Could be, Geoff, but I'm still a bit suspicious. For a start, from the way he was talking to simple Damon about it, it sounded as if it was quite a bit bigger than just some hippie on a conditional discharge. And the other thing is: if that's all there is to it, why didn't Andy just put his hand up when I tackled him about it the other day? He must know we can deal with a conditional discharge – it's not going to bring the government down, for Christ's sake.'

'So have you been back and shown this to Andy?'

'No, I haven't, actually. To tell you the truth, I'm getting a bit worried about old Andrew Michael Sheen and I want to find out as much as I can before I confront him again—'

'Well, the only good thing is that McGee won't have seen this PNC stuff, Charlie. The court appearance would have been wiped off Andy's record ages ago: I don't think these things stay active for more than a few years. And if this is the only computer file that exists, then I reckon the *Mirror* haven't got anything on us. If all they've got is some guy spinning McGee a yarn to earn a few bob, they don't have a leg to stand on—'

'Yeah: *if* this is the only record of what went on in Cambridge; *if* this is the only thing that fingers Andy. I'm just worried there could be more of this stuff lying around.'

'Well, there's only one way to find out. Shall I go and have a sniff around?'

'Yeah. Thanks, Geoff. You know you're the only one I can trust to do this. Get down to Cambridge, look at the official records – police, courts, university, newspapers – and do what you can to wipe them before the media get hold of them. A bit of rewriting of history is called for here, mate. I'll give you an Official Secrets Act affidavit in case you need to keep anyone quiet over this – y'know, the old "I can tell you this, but then I have to kill you" routine—'

'That'll work with PC Plod, Charlie; but what about the guy who's been blabbing to the *Daily Mirror*?'

'Absolutely: we need to find him before he does us any more damage. So find out the truth, mate – and then destroy it! Meanwhile, I'll deal with McGee and the *Mirror*. I'm already collecting some material on Mr McGee – useful material to keep him quiet.'

Nigel had been intrigued by the idea of government departments holding morning prayers. When he arrived, early, for his first day at the Department for Society and was met in the spacious lobby of the old Cabinet Office building, his first question to the amused Assistant Private Secretary to the Permanent Secretary, who had been deputed to meet him, was met with a laugh and the explanation that this was actually civil service slang for the daily morning planning meeting, which he, Nigel, would soon be expected to chair.

Nigel's second question – a request for an explanation of the young man's own convoluted title – brought a more considered response.

'Well, the Permanent Secretary, Sir Robert, is the top civil servant in the department. He's "Permanent" because the here-today-gone-tomorrow Secretary of State (that's Knox at the moment) theoretically can't appoint him or remove him – that's what makes the civil service independent and able to offer impartial, objective advice without fear of reprimand or hope of favours from the politicians. I say theoretically, mind you, because this New Project lot are having a pretty concerted go at cowing the civil service into becoming the Whitehall arm of the Project party.

'Anyway, if you think of *Yes, Minister*, the PermSec is basically Sir Humphrey and the Secretary of State is Jim Hacker. Now, both of them have junior civil servants to run their private offices – make sure they're always well briefed for meetings, that they see all the documents they need to see, that they wash behind their ears and so on – and these are called Private Secretaries. In *Yes, Minister*, Sir Humphrey's young helper was the one whose name I can never remember – he was played by Derek Fowlds, I think – so he would be the Private Secretary to the Permanent Secretary. And then, of course, you have the Assistant Private Secretary to the Permanent Secretary, which is me, *et voilà!*'

By this time they had reached the Permanent Secretary's outer office, where a bevy of Private Secretaries – or Assistant Private Secretaries – were hunched over documents and telephones looking ostentatiously busy in anticipation of Sir Robert's return from prayers.

Nottridge himself soon strode briskly into the room, spotted Nigel and stretched out his hand. 'My dear fellow, welcome to the Department for Society. I feel as though I already know you well from your splendid career at the BBC. Do come through and have some tea. Judy, would you fetch two teas, please?'

The senior civil service operates a closely codified status system, involving the size of offices, type of desk chair and soft furnishings allocated to its members. Unremarked by Nigel's untrained eye, but a source of pride to their owner, Sir Robert's pink settee and two armchairs were arranged around a teak coffee table. Nigel sat in blissful ignorance on one chair as Sir Robert launched into his welcome speech.

'I must say you join us at an exciting time, Nigel – we're all on first-name terms here, by the way – except, of course, that one addresses the Secretary of State as "Secretary of State". As civil servants, we address the office, not the person, a fine distinction, but an important one. Where was I? Yes, an exciting time . . . I have myself been a civil servant for thirty-five years – a Permanent Secretary for twelve of them – and I have served administrations of all colours. I was saying only the other day to the Secretary of State that this New Project government has done exceptionally well overall, but I do feel its place in history will depend on the outcome of the MEWs and – of more relevance to us here – on its social legislation.

'If we in this department can assist them to revive the idealism and enthusiasm they arrived with in 2005, if we can return them to their early commitments to social justice and fairness, then I believe history will remember them kindly.

'Overall I admire the majority of the ministers in this government: you get a few bad apples in any barrel but, in general, they have been a pretty good crop. So, *courage, mon brave*! The spotlight will be on us; I know the PM regards our work as vital to the fortunes of his administration. Now, Philip will show you to your office. If you have any questions, do not hesitate to come and ask me. In the meantime, I would recommend you go and talk to the head of our policy division, a fellow called Christopher Brody, whom you will find at the far end of this very corridor. You and Christopher will be working closely together and he will be depending very heavily – as we all shall – on your presentational advice and your media expertise in our policy work—'

Nigel's head was beginning to spin from the morning's information overload as he knocked on the door of Brody's smaller but nonetheless well-appointed office. Brody was a gangly, bearded man of about fifty, fretful in his manner and with a breathless staccato speaking style. He waved Nigel to a seat on one of several hard-backed chairs drawn up to a beech veneer table squeezed into the space between his desk and the window.

'Well, welcome to the Ministry of Social Engineering. Glad to hear that you'll be keeping us all on the straight and narrow, keeping us in McDonald's good books – that's the ultimate test of success in this government as far as I can see. Get the *Daily Mail* headlines right and you get a pat on the back, that sort of thing.

'Been to see old Nottridge, have you? Not a bad sort – bit

gullible, but there are worse. I'll be frank with you: my problem with this New Project lot is the spin. If it weren't for the McDonalds and the Maddles, they could have made a fist of things.

'People believed them back in 2005; but then they decided they had to have the spin doctors in charge of everything, telling lies when they didn't need to. It's just become a bit of an obsession: why tell the truth when you can tell a lie?'

Nigel smiled wryly.

Brody was in full flow now. 'Worked OK at first, but then people began to see through it. Now, even if government press notices were approved by St Peter himself, people would say, "Where's the catch?"'

Nigel grimaced.

Brody looked him straight in the eye. 'It makes your job as communications director very tricky. You're a civil servant so *grosso modo* you're likely to be telling the truth; but I can tell you it won't be long before you'll get leant on by the political advisers to join them in a few Project party porkies.

'You'll need to be on your toes in this department because our political adviser, woman called Sonya Mair, is a particularly bad example of all that. She's already been round here breathing down my neck.

'She'll have you doing New Project's political dirty work for them and if you object she'll have a few threats to throw at you: I certainly hope you've got no skeletons in your cupboard because, if you have, she'll know all about them and she'll have no qualms in using them against you.'

Nigel felt his stomach clench in an icy knot. He looked to see if Brody had spotted his wave of panic, but Brody was still talking. 'You need to remember that she enjoys Knox's total support – you'd better watch your step with both of them.

'They're zealots, of course, right out of Andy Sheen's academy of messianic missions: the New Project lot have always had a streak of odious piety about them, but now it's become an overweening and very unattractive obsession. They believe that only God and they know what's best for society and since God won't introduce the legislation, they had better do it themselves!

'They've got a dangerous passion for social engineering and saving society – and this department has been given the green light to give it full rein. I think we'll need to keep a very close eye on that Knox fellow, or he'll be deporting the unemployed to Tasmania.'

As Brody spoke, Nigel fingered the old notebook in his pocket and felt a frisson of trepidation that the man whose words were contained within it was now leading the crusade to save society – and that he, Nigel, was working alongside him.

Geoff Maddle had half an hour to wait at King's Cross – the Cambridge train had been delayed because of rolling-stock failure – so he settled down with a coffee to scan the morning papers. Several of them were running with Knox's remarks on the responsibility he felt as he embarked on his mission to revive the moral underpinnings of society and combat the enemy within. Geoff balked at the rhetoric – it was too high flown for his taste – but he recognized that it would go down well with the PM. He tipped his hat to Nigel Tonbridge, who was now shaping Knox's media strategy and had obviously picked up pretty quickly on the sort of tone Andy Sheen was looking for.

Geoff's personal opinion of Sheen was distinctly mixed. Geoff had joined the New Project spin machine because his best mate had asked him to. But, unlike Charlie, Geoff had not been sharing Andy Sheen's political bed for the past decade and his residual loyalty to the Old Project party remained much stronger than

Charlie's. He knew, though, that he had signed up to the new party for better or for worse, and he knew too that in Cambridge he would do whatever it took to protect the reputation of its leader.

Anyway, Geoff reasoned, we've got to think about Andy Sheen the image as well as Andy Sheen the man. It's the image that *we've* created and it's the image that means something pretty important to millions of people throughout this country: who cares if the man slips a bit from the ideal, as long as the image remains intact? And, whatever I think of the man, it's my job to keep his image shiny clean: I'm not doing this for Andy Sheen, it's for the good of the party and for the good of the whole country.

Nigel Tonbridge had been in post for three weeks now. Things had gone surprisingly smoothly for the launch of such a major government department. Selwyn Knox had wisely avoided any detailed policy announcements at this early stage and had concentrated on talking up the ideological rationale behind the Department for Society.

Nigel had warned him that the press were circling the department, unsure what to make of it and reserving judgement until Knox showed his hand. The liberal media had been brought onside by the first *Observer* profile; the right-wing press were hoping the department would provide the backbone in social policy they felt this country needed.

Neither right nor left wanted to take a definitive position on Knox and his crusade until they had a better idea of his political direction and its practical application. So Nigel's media handling advice was that the Secretary of State should prolong this initial honeymoon period by keeping the hacks guessing. He arranged a series of interviews and profiles at which he advised Selwyn Knox to commit himself to as little as possible. The tone of moral mission had come from Knox himself, but otherwise Nigel felt they had had a good few weeks in media terms.

For Selwyn Knox, this was a period of phoney war, a period of consolidation before the great campaigns ahead.

He told Sonya Mair that he felt he was on the threshold of momentous events in his life; that the all-consuming force he felt within himself was at last on the point of finding an outlet, an application that would channel it to positive ends. Sonya congratulated him on a successful start to the new department's activities; in the scheme of things, she said, it could have been a lot worse.

She acknowledged the role of Nigel Tonbridge in setting the tone for the media coverage; but she could not avoid raising the same questions she had asked her boss before: was he sure Tonbridge was safe? Was he sure he had done the right thing in bringing him to work at the department? And, as on previous occasions, Knox replied that no one other than Nigel could carry out the tasks that would eventually be required of him; only Nigel could play the role that he, Selwyn Knox, would one day need him to play.

Seeing Sonya's fleeting expression of hurt, he added that she and Nigel were the two beings without whom the future he had planned for his department and for himself would not be possible.

With a little shrug, Sonya changed the subject. 'What are you doing this weekend, Sel? It would have been nice if we could have invented some conference or other and had a weekend together. The problem is that Thomas has got clients coming to dinner on Saturday and I'm going to have to stay at home and play the good wife and hostess—'

'I know. I would have preferred a weekend in a hotel with you, but I haven't been to the constituency for a while and the agent is agitating for more grass-roots activity. Constituency parties are strange: they're proud to have an MP who's near the top of the ministerial ladder, but they get jealous too. They seem to look on me as an unfaithful husband who's been lured away by the flesh pots of Westminster. And a weekend at home will help keep Ruth happy as well. She's very long-suffering, but even she gets a bit resentful when she hasn't seen me for so long.'

Geoff Maddle was having a problem with Sharon.

Sharon had been in her job for eleven years. She was clear about the rules, and she was used to applying them with a rigour that any High Court judge would have been proud of. 'I'm sorry sir. These things need to be arranged in the proper way. He's the court registrar and he can't just come and see anyone who walks in here.'

'This is very important. Is he in the office today?'

'Well, yes he is. But, as I say, I can't disturb him just like that.'

The man in the parka thought for a moment. Sharon could see the suit and tie under his rough outer jacket. The language of dress codes was speaking to her, but she was unclear how exactly to place what it was saying.

'OK. Please tell him that I'm here on official business and it's very important that I speak to him now.'

Sharon hesitated. 'Well, why don't you tell me who you are and what you need to talk to us about. Then perhaps I could—'

'No. You go and get the registrar. I'll explain to him. This is a very important matter and it's in his interest to talk to me now. I can't tell you any more than that.'

The tone was peremptory, not used to coming off second best. Sharon frowned, made a gesture of annoyance and rose reluctantly from her chair.

'Well, if you wait here I'll see what he says. I can't promise anything. All right?'

Maddle nodded and took a seat. The otherwise anonymous walls of the reception area were decorated with prints of Cambridge colleges. It reminded him of that detective series that used to be on TV: *Inspector Something*.

Maddle wasn't an Oxbridge man. It wasn't that he resented the Oxbridge types in the Government Information and Communication Service. He knew he had seen a lot more of the real world than any of them. How many of them had spent time sitting in magistrates' courts? How many of them had reported burglaries and car thefts and dangerous dog cases for a local rag?

How many of them could have come here today and done the sort of things he was about to do? Not many. Maddle was the man for this job. He was the one to tidy up the mess.

There was the scrape of a door and Sharon reappeared. 'You can go in now, sir. Mr Hodges will see you.'

Maddle walked into a comfortable, orderly office.

What surprised Nigel Tonbridge most about his new job was the level of access he had to the Secretary of State and his official engagements. Old hands in the department's press office, which Nigel was now running, told him this was a development since New Project had come to power.

In the old days, the director of communications had been just an afterthought in the policy-making process. The politicians would beaver away among themselves, taking advice from civil servants on legal and factual policy issues, but ignoring presentational questions until the policy was ready to go to parliament. Then and only then would they call in the communications director and present him with the initiative or the legislation that he was expected to go out and present to the media and public opinion.

Since 2005, according to Nigel's press officers, the process had been virtually reversed. Now PR considerations carried a much higher priority. Now no government policy was worked on without first considering advice from the director of communications on how it would play with the media. Cynics said the tail was wagging the dog.

From Nigel's point of view, the fact that civil servants working in the Government Information and Communication Service were now regarded as central to the policy-making process meant that his job involved a disconcerting intimacy with Selwyn Knox. Never a day went by without the Secretary of State calling him into his office to listen to lobby groups or attend strategy planning meetings. He was called in for private chats about policy-presentation issues or to listen in on Knox's telephone conversations with the PM and other government ministers.

Nigel's work on the Wakely case had roused his interest in what makes politicians tick; his run-in with Selwyn Knox, and his obsession with his own failure to call Knox's bluff over the death of the girl on the mountain, had left him with an unsatisfied need to explore the forces that drove this particular politician. A sense that there was unfinished business and his own dissatisfaction with himself were pushing him on.

Nigel knew Selwyn Knox must be aware of this – Knox was a shrewd, perceptive man.

The peculiar knowledge each had of the other's past history, thoughts and obsessions threw a heavy shadow of intimated significance over even the most trivial conversation. It seemed as if each man was constantly peering into the other's soul, seeking out deeper meanings in whatever was said, looking for the hidden thoughts behind every comment. It was like a continuing game of psychological chess, whose significance was known only to the two participants: each making mental thrusts and parries; each defending his inner secrets or baring his inner thoughts.

On reflection, Nigel was sure Knox must have known this would be their relationship if he invited Nigel into his professional life and he was disturbed by the thought that Knox had deliberately chosen to create the situation they were now in. Why had Knox recruited him? Why had he clasped to his bosom the one man who could read his most intimate thoughts and reveal the secrets of a past he would surely wish to conceal from the world?

Nigel could find no rational explanation for Knox's action, no explanation of why Knox had deliberately placed himself in a position of great danger – danger of exposure, danger of humiliation and danger of ultimate shame.

Geoff Maddle was on the phone to Charlie and his news was not encouraging.

'So I saw the registrar of the court, OK? And he had no idea what the hell I was talking about. He's only been there ten years. I didn't give him any details of the case, but the judge who would have dealt with Andy back in May 1981 has apparently been dead for ages. Anyway, the guy I spoke to today said there would be no written records anywhere in Cambridge as far as he knows. The only possibility would be the Police National Computer and that was extremely unlikely to have kept any information from that far back. I didn't mention that we'd already been there, done that!

'So the next thing I did was to go down to the *Cambridge Evening News* and check the archives for May that year. There was nothing in the paper, Charlie – I didn't expect there to be. That was the hippie era, wasn't it, or at least the tail end of it? There must have been conditional discharges coming out of their ears.

'What I did do, though, was make a note of who the *Evening News*'s crime correspondent was at the time, a chap called Reg Green. Then I spoke to the current hack who does the courts for them nowadays and I asked him about Green. He said Green retired in 1996. He didn't know where he was now except that he thought he had a house in Royston: that's a place a few miles out of town. Anyway, Mr R. Green of Huntingdon Road was conveniently in the phone book, so I thought I'd pay him a surprise visit.

'He's eighty and he's pretty doddery, but he did remember the Andy Sheen case – he said he'd picked up on the name when Andy was first elected PM. He seemed to think the whole thing was a bit of a laugh – obviously didn't realize it might be a bit embarrassing for a Prime Minister to have a drugs record!

'What he did say, though – and I think this might be what we're after, Charlie – is that he thought there were two defendants in that case, Andy and another student. I just wonder if that could be the guy who's been playing the *Mirror*'s Deep Throat – but even if he is, I don't have the faintest idea how we're going to find him.'

9

Even Selwyn Knox admitted he had been doubtful at first about the task he had been handed by the Prime Minister. What Andy Sheen was asking him to bring about was nothing less than a revolution in the hearts and minds of the British people, a fundamental change in the way individuals think about their relationship with and their place in society.

The more Knox reflected on the challenges that lay ahead, the more he became convinced that this momentous undertaking was to be the pinnacle of his life's work. He began to regard the Department for Society as a personal crusade to rescue Britain from all its faults and sins, in short, to rescue it from itself. He began increasingly to speak of the department as a mission of moral salvation.

Knox admitted he was unsettled by the size of the task.

He was comfortable with the aims – he had fixed his department's targets – but he remained unsure of the best way to set about realizing them.

His favourite metaphor was of himself and his fellow reformers as loving parents who find they need to correct and discipline a wayward child. He spoke of a father's love that had to be sincere but had also to be rigorous and sometimes even cruel.

He was unsettled, too, by the torrents of conflicting advice he had begun to receive from political interests, social lobby groups, the media and the many people from around the country who wrote to him in sackloads offering tales of personal experiences and recommendations for tackling the problems they had identified.

In the face of such divergent pressures, Knox had initially felt unsure about the direction his department should take.

With liberal voices urging him to enact more social welfare policies and provide more help for the disadvantaged, more understanding for offenders and sinners, while conservative forces demanded a momentous crackdown on deviant behaviour and antisocial tendencies, for a while Knox seemed to be caught in the grip of debilitating indecision over the very bases on which his crusade was to be constructed.

He knew he would soon have to start producing more than just statements of aims and intent, more than the generalist moral rhetoric he had so far employed. He felt under growing pressure to move from talk to action, to take the first concrete measures to turn plans into practice.

Finally, after several weeks of agonized hesitation, Knox was about to open his first departmental strategy meeting.

On the day he had arrived at the Department for Society, Knox had asked his top officials to prepare for this meeting. He had commissioned strategy papers from all the civil servants engaged on policy formulation. He had explained the parameters within which Andy Sheen had asked them to work and the goals he had asked them to achieve. He had stressed that he wanted his officials to 'think outside the box', to be radical in their proposals and to throw off the shackles of previous policy constraints. He told them they were operating on a green-field site – the world of social policy had begun anew on the day their department was created – and he reminded them that the PM had demanded they have the courage to think the unthinkable.

But Knox was not fooling himself. He knew all about the baggage the civil service had inherited from decades of conservative thinking – stifling caution and an ingrained unwillingness to do anything that might rock the boat.

As he scanned the faces of the officials who had taken their seats around his ministerial conference table, Selwyn Knox felt few grounds for optimism.

He instinctively mistrusted the civil service and felt he could assign virtually all those present to one of two stereotypes: those like Sir Robert Nottridge, old, staid and stifled by the dust of decades of stale civil service thinking; and those like Christopher Brody, cynical, mocking and unwilling to sign up to anything that went beyond the pragmatic and the workaday.

As he looked around the table, Knox concluded that only three of those present were capable of grasping the real issues, only he, Sonya Mair and Nigel Tonbridge, he thought, would have the breadth of understanding, the vision and the imagination to recognize the true import of what they were being called upon to do.

'Good morning, everyone. Thank you for coming. This is an important and potentially historic meeting. I hope you will not object if I open it with a brief prayer—'

As those around the table were responding with varying degrees of enthusiasm to their minister's words of holy commendation, Geoff Maddle was uttering a few choice words of his own.

The basement of the police station was dark and dirty. The low ceiling and absence of natural light reminded Geoff of the times his father had punished him as a child by locking him in the linen cupboard 'until he knew how to behave properly', a memory that had stayed with Geoff and – he thought – accounted for the claustrophobia he experienced when flying or travelling on the tube.

At the moment, though, claustrophobia was the least of his worries.

It had taken him the best part of the morning to persuade the Cambridge police that he was who he said he was and that they should allow him access to their files. The senior officer had been polite, but not over-helpful. Telephone calls to Downing Street had confirmed Geoff's identity, but the superintendent had insisted on written permission from the Home Office, and had only reluctantly settled for a faxed letter of authorization bearing the signature of the Home Secretary with the promise of a hard copy to follow by courier.

The station's record keeper – a harassed elderly sergeant who clearly had better things to do than rummage through files from thirty years ago – had categorically assured Geoff that no written records from 1981 would have been kept, unless the case had been a 'big one' or 'something special'. He said files from that time would almost certainly have been thrown out and it was 'well before we were computerized'.

Hampered by the fact that he could not reveal details of the case he was interested in, Geoff was unable to call on Sergeant Plod's assistance in sorting through the files. He had thus found himself sitting in front of a row of crumbling brown foolscap folders that filled a good thirty feet of shelf space. Decades of rummaging policemen had left big gaps in the dates of the surviving files with little attempt at chronology. By early evening, when the new shift was coming on duty at the front desk on the floor above him, Geoff decided enough was enough and told the departing sergeant that he too was calling it a day and might or might not be back in the morning.

After a morning of preliminaries, the inaugural strategy meeting of the Department for Society was going much as Selwyn Knox had foreseen.

The opening contributions, including one from Sir Robert

Nottridge, had been so predictably dull that Knox had found himself torn between anger and amusement. Nottridge's paper was so elegantly, so impeccably balanced, such a litany of 'on the one hand' and 'on the other hand', that Knox had interrupted on more than one occasion to ask Sir Robert whether he had reached any conclusions or whether he even held any views of his own on the matter.

After half an hour of exposition, the Permanent Secretary had clearly noticed the note of exasperation in Knox's voice and hastily decided to yield the floor to the department's head of policy, Christopher Brody.

Brody's paper – presented in a dry, take-it-or-leave-it tone – consisted of an overview of the precedents for social reform measures in the past decade.

He cited a growing tendency towards the application of laws regulating aspects of life that would previously have been considered private and outside the ambit of government policy, a tendency which Brody said he would, for convenience, refer to as 'legislating for human nature'.

One Secretary of State at a department then known as Social Security (a concept, Brody noted, which had subsequently disappeared not only in the name of the department, but to a large extent in practical implementation as well) had instituted cuts in state benefits to unemployed single parents, meaning, in the vast majority of cases, single mothers. The intention was to provide a political stimulus – a financial penalty in this case – to persuade members of a certain class in society to alter their behaviour. The aim of this behaviour-correcting policy was, it went without saying, to get them to stop sponging and start working.

But the fate of those policies, Brody noted, was instructive. Following protests from liberal and left-wing pressure groups, the benefit cuts were initially withdrawn and the minister was dropped from the cabinet. She had, however, blazed a trail and had implanted in the minds of the public the concept that a government – as long as it had a large majority and pure intentions – should have the right to pass legislation aimed at reforming human behaviour. 'Legislating for human nature' was becoming respectable.

And the sacrifice was not in vain.

Within the space of a year or so, the cuts were reinstated in a slightly disguised form, and similar policies were applied without major protest to several other 'difficult' classes of society.

Subsequent ministers came up with various initiatives to deal with malingerers. The young unemployed were targeted initially, then the middle-aged, then the partners of the unemployed, and finally – most daringly – the disabled. In a policy dreamt up by the then Employment Department, disabled people who were out of work were specifically targeted to demonstrate the government's seriousness of intent. Brody spoke of the 'courage' shown by a government willing to penalize people so disadvantaged by nature that they traditionally fall outside the scope of punitive policies. He said he raised his hat to an administration which believed so fervently in its mission to alter and improve human behaviour that it would even target people in wheelchairs or suffering from cerebral palsy. This, he said, was the intellectual rigour of a Robespierre applied to the modern world.

Sensing the rapidly dwindling patience of the Secretary of State, Brody listed briefly the further social engineering measures which had followed under New Project. He mentioned the withdrawal of civic rights from benefit cheats, the forced repatriation of asylum seekers who were placing an unfair burden on the welfare system, the name-and-shame campaigns to stop teenage pregnancies, the provisions to outlaw offensive or undignified sexual practices including sex outdoors, the boot camps for the hardcore unemployed, the prison schools for habitual truants, and the addict colonies for drug abusers – all measures which had been successfully introduced in recent years.

The concept of legislating for human nature – Brody concluded – had now been established as one of the natural rights of a reforming and ideologically trustworthy government.

Had he stopped at this point, Christopher Brody might just have got away with it. Selwyn Knox was perceptive enough to notice the irony in Brody's presentation, but shrewd enough probably not to make an issue of the head of policy's dumb insolence.

Brody, though, was nothing if not daring; he decided he would deliver the last paragraphs of his presentation, whether the Secretary of State liked them or not: 'In conclusion, however, at the risk of appearing a fuddy-duddy, old-thinking civil servant, I feel it would be remiss of me to end this presentation without pointing out that the smooth implementation up to now of such socially charged legislation by this government cannot – as the financial advertisements put it – be taken as any guarantee for continued plain sailing in the future.'

Brody looked up over his spectacles and smiled sweetly.

'I say this simply to point out that legislating for human nature is not as easy as one might think. Attempting to change people's behaviour is a potentially risky business. The human soul, I fear, is not a rational instrument; there is no telling how it might react to the stimuli we may wish to apply. Our social scientists could tell us that our action will necessarily meet with such and such a reaction – a reaction that will logically move society forward and increase the sum of human happiness for all concerned. We may reassure ourselves that our intentions are pure, the putative results of our actions self-evidently beneficial for the objects of our experiment, that is to say, the citizens to whom the measures are applied. And yet, because the human soul is such an imperfect, irrational and slippery target, the fear must remain that its reaction will be far from the one we predict.'

Brody looked up from his speaking notes, as if deciding whether or not to press on with his argument. His slightly raised eyebrows and faint squeeze of the lips suggested to Nigel a man who was briefly weighing up the difference between a lamb and a sheep before plunging onwards.

'So please indulge me for just a few moments if I end with Shakespeare. You will recall that in *Measure for Measure*, the Duke, a highly principled, well-intentioned ruler, has – like us – identified sin and immorality in his country. I will, if I may, just read to you how Shakespeare describes it. He says it so much better than I ever could:

> We have strict statutes, and most biting laws,
> The needful bits and curbs to headstrong weeds
> Which for this fourteen years we have let slip . . .
> Now, as fond fathers,
> Having bound up the threat'ning twigs of birch,
> Only to stick it in their children's sight
> For terror, not to use; in time the rod
> Becomes more mocked than feared; so our decrees,
> Dead to infliction, to themselves are dead.

Again Brody paused and glanced round the table as if expecting to be interrupted, hesitated slightly and continued: 'So, you see, the Duke is pained by the moral decay of society and he commands his minister Prince Angelo to wipe it out with strict legislation. I should say, by the way, that Angelo's sanctions for unchaste acts are slightly more draconian than we might be contemplating – sex outside marriage, for instance, incurs the death penalty. But, as we discover, it is Angelo's absolutism, his refusal to allow for human nature, that ultimately undoes him. Shakespeare concludes that no amount of laws can change "the blood", no amount of laws can wipe out the irrational human drives deep within us. And Angelo is undone by the very human nature – this time his own – that he had tried to legislate out of existence: "Blood thou art blood," he says, as his own uncontrollable lust makes him commit an immoral act, one of many for which he himself has prescribed the death penalty. And I suppose Angelo's fate might be a lesson to all of us here in this room today: if we cannot stamp out sin in ourselves, we can never hope to stamp out sin in others: "Judge not, that ye be not judged. For with what judgement ye judge, ye shall be judged: and with what measure ye mete, it shall be measured to you again—"'

But Knox had heard enough. He was not going to stand for such insolence from a civil servant. His voice was harsh and loud.

'That's enough! Quite enough! I am not in the habit of allowing my meetings to turn into lectures on Shakespeare, or on anything else for that matter. We are here to discuss social policy not fairy tales. I am afraid your presentation is simply not acceptable, Mr Brody. And I am not prepared to continue this discussion until we have agreed some rules of behaviour we can all abide by and respect. I am ending this meeting right now. You can all go away and think again about the way you approach these very serious issues. I am afraid I have not seen any evidence at all of the type of serious, committed thinking this department is going to need. And I can tell you, if you are not capable of producing what I need, I will not hesitate to bring in other people who are better equipped and better determined to do what I ask of them. So go now. Go and think about what I have said. You'll hear from me or from Sonya when I am ready to resume this discussion.'

*

Charlie McDonald was getting worried.

He had not heard from Geoff Maddle for forty-eight hours and he could not shake off the thought that the *Daily Mirror*, in the unprepossessing form of Jim McGee, was probably using the time to dig and delve, to accrete more dirt on Andy Sheen, to tighten its stranglehold on the windpipe of the government.

So when the phone rang and a familiar voice came on the line sounding considerably happier than in previous calls, McDonald heaved an audible sigh of relief. 'I never though I'd be so pleased to hear from you, you old bugger. What have you been up to all this time?'

'What do you mean "all this time"? I haven't stopped to draw breath, mate. And it's been worth it, I can tell you. At last, I think we're getting somewhere with this bloody story – I think I've got a lead on our second man. And we've got it because I've been hacking away in the basement of a bloody police station for the past two days. Anyway, we were right – there was another defendant up with Andy in 1981 and his name is Harvey Parks. The file on the case should have been destroyed years ago, but it wasn't. It was in a filing cabinet in the basement of the Cambridge cop shop – and I found it! And not only do we have his name; we even know where he is. Once I'd read the file, I burnt it, OK? Like we agreed. So that's all dealt with. But then I asked my friendly sergeant about Mr Harvey Parks. Turns out he's pretty well known in police circles. He lives in the last squat in Cambridge, unemployed, bit of a sad case, says my policeman. Used to be a student here, had a good career in front of him, made a lot of money developing and marketing some medical remedy or something, then he got hooked on drugs and lost it all. They've had him in the station here a few times – pleasant bloke, apparently, very intelligent, or could have been. He wouldn't be any trouble to anyone if it wasn't for the old substances: he's a junkie.'

The Secretary of State's strategy planning meeting and the disorderly circumstances under which it had been so abruptly suspended had become the talk of the department and much of Whitehall.

Civil servants who had been there lost no time in revealing what had gone on to colleagues in the various policy divisions, and they in turn were quick to email the spicy news to friends in other government departments.

It was little surprise to any of those involved that a garbled account of the flare up quickly appeared in the *Independent*. Seasoned kremlinologists noted the tone of the piece – portraying Knox as a ranting zealot – and speculated about who the source of the leak might have been. Several civil servants spent an uncomfortable day or so in fear of a summons to the Secretary of State's office, where – if challenged – they would have had some difficulty explaining their conversations and telephone records in the aftermath of the fateful meeting.

But the calls never came.

There was no leak inquiry. And when, a week later, Selwyn Knox finally reconvened the interrupted meeting he gave no indication of the rage that had overcome him when they were all previously gathered round his table.

This time, though, the Secretary of State was at pains to avoid a conflict of views with his civil servants. He achieved this largely by making sure the only views heard and minuted were his own.

His opening remarks turned into a monologue that lasted over an hour.

He began by recapping the list of social policy measures taken by the New Project government. He praised them, but concluded, 'If we look at these measures objectively, they were – I'm afraid – little more than tinkering at the edges of the problem.' He then briefly discussed the memos he had received from his officials setting out their suggestions about how to tackle the problems which had been identified as priorities. These were, he said, 'all very measured and reasonable, or, put another way, the ineffectual pap and typical half-measures of anaemic civil servants'.

What was needed now, said the Secretary of State, was not palliatives, but radical surgery, measures to tackle the underlying causes of the disease that must be applied without delay and with all available force.

'And when we have done that,' he continued, 'the symptoms will start to disappear on their own. Our first task is to identify the source of the moral rot afflicting our society. Now, when I first looked into this question, I asked myself if something fundamental had changed in the psyche of mankind. What was the cause of the uncivilized behaviour that has gripped modern society?

'Had man suddenly become evil? And had this new evil suddenly spread through our ranks, bringing with it all the adverse effects we have witnessed in the behaviour of our people?

'Had war, for instance, degraded the ethical basis of men? Had conflict in the Middle East somehow thrown our moral compass off balance?

'My answer to this was: no.

'Our experience in the past has been that war actually improved the moral qualities of those who remained at home: the Second World War saw a new coming together of civilian society in this country, a willingness to act in the best interests of society as a whole, the celebrated "pulling together" of the East End.

'My other conclusion was that the moral decline of contemporary society did not begin seven or eight years ago when war first became a dominant factor in our everyday life.

'The moral decline began long ago, but its most pernicious effects, its most dangerous threats to our society, have emerged only in recent years.

'So I ruled out transient factors. I looked deeper. And that is where I found the answer I was looking for.'

Knox surveyed his audience. His eyes radiated the triumph of a man convinced of his own wisdom.

'The answer, gentlemen, is in our parents: in the way they raise their children; in the values they inculcate into them; in the discipline they instil in them. If our parents do not raise our children in the ways of respect and responsibility, how can society ever prosper? Allow parents to raise children with antisocial attitudes and society will ipso facto suffer. It follows as night follows day. The root cause of the dropouts, scroungers, addicts and criminals who plague our society is the failure of our parents. The nest from which emanates the poison at the heart of our social decline is the parental home, where lax discipline, wrong thinking and absent fathers have thrown our society into turmoil.

'This is not rocket science, gentlemen.

'It is not an earth-shattering revelation.

'It is common sense. And common sense says this root cause must be tackled if our society is to have any hope of surviving and prospering. The rocket science – if rocket science it be – lies in making the bold, decisive step of moving from analysis to action.

'Sociologists, academics and even government ministers have identified the problem of parental failure in the past, but they have never had the courage – or, indeed, the authority – to move from merely identifying the problem to taking the action necessary to deal with it.

'Well, I can tell you that today you see before you a minister who has that courage and – thanks to the outstanding leadership of our Prime Minister, Andy Sheen – also has the power to move from words to deeds. Now, over the next days and weeks, I shall be working on practical measures to turn this vision into reality.

'And I am today commissioning you all to go away, to tear up the short-sighted, feeble policy papers you submitted to me for this meeting and to think again.

'What I need from you by the time of our next meeting is a set of radical new proposals that go to the heart of the problem I have just outlined: I need measures to ensure that our nation's homes cease to be a breeding ground for criminal and disruptive elements. I need practical policy initiatives that will ensure parents change fundamentally the way they raise society's coming generations, policy initiatives that will produce a new generation properly schooled in the needs of society, inculcated with the values we hold dear and cleansed of the undesirable attitudes that result from parental inadequacy – cleansed of the sins of the fathers.

'It is a tall order, I hear you say, and I agree with you. But think of the rewards if we succeed in this great enterprise. Think of the new society we will be helping to create. Think how we will be remembered in history. Bear all these thoughts with you as you go about your work. And come back to me with a programme we can all be proud of. I am depending on you; but most of all the society of this country is depending on you. So I leave you with a challenge. You must ask yourselves: do you have within you the motivation and energy to tackle these great issues? Do you have the force within you to make changes that will be remembered and respected for generations?

'And, so that you are in no doubt, I can tell you quite categorically that I do myself have that inner force, that power and energy, which is welling up inside me and demanding to be turned to practical effect. I have it. I hope you all do too. Thank you and get to work.'

When Harvey Parks opened the door of the rundown terraced house in the drab street on the edge of central Cambridge, Geoff Maddle had little or no idea what to expect. Nor had he decided how he would deal with Parks if he did turn out to be the informant who was tantalizing the *Mirror* with promises of dirt on Andy Sheen.

Geoff had no intention of telling Parks that he was from Downing Street – that was a no-brainer: there was no point in inflating Parks's own valuation of any story he might or might not have on Andy. Geoff had toyed with several approaches and was still not completely decided when Parks peered out at him, blinking a little in the sunlight.

'Yeah. Can I help you?'

'Harvey Parks?'

'Yeah. Who wants him?'

'You know who I am, don't you, Mr Parks?'

'Erm, no. Am I supposed to?'

'If I told you Jim McGee sent me, would that mean anything to you?'

'Aw, fuck, man. You're from the *Mirror*, aren't you? You bloody journalists – I can tell you a mile away. Look, I'm really glad you've come, man. I thought you lot were never going to get back to me. Come in – come and have a smoke or something.'

Christopher Brody had been expecting a visit from Sonya Mair and he was not disappointed. She had put her head round his door, smiled and said, 'Can I have a word?'

Now she was sitting on the edge of his desk, looking desirable in a tight black dress and heels. Despite himself, Brody felt his eyes wandering towards the expanse of white thigh that Sonya had thoughtfully placed in his line of vision. Chris knew what was about to descend on him – the wrath of a Secretary of State was not something that even he took lightly – but he did find himself thinking how much more exciting and, probably, how much more lethal, it was going to be to take his punishment from Sonya Mair than from Selwyn Knox.

'You can guess why I've come, can't you? We've both been in this game for long enough. You're probably used to taking the piss out of cabinet ministers in front of their officials. You probably think it's all a bit of a joke. And, to be fair, you're most likely right in the majority of cases.

'But what you haven't twigged, I'm afraid, Mr Brody, is that this cabinet minister isn't like all the rest of them. When Selwyn Knox embarks on something, when he talks about making things happen and getting things changed, it isn't hot air. Selwyn Knox means what he says and he believes in what he's doing.

'So you can see, can't you, Chris, that it would be very hurtful – very hurtful indeed – to have some smart-arsed civil servant with an inflated opinion of his own cleverness come in and hold the whole thing up to ridicule.

'So I'm here to tell you that you should stop being such a naughty boy. You should stop playing with things you don't understand. Because this time you are completely out of your depth.

'And just in case you don't believe me, there's one other thing you should be aware of as you go about your duties. I know you civil servants think you're all invulnerable and that you can get away with saying and doing whatever you like because the poor old minister is only here on sufferance and you're all so frightfully permanent and independent and untouchable.

'Well, in your case, Mr Brody, I'm sorry to have to tell that you're dead wrong. And that's because the minister knows all about your secret, Chris. He knows about your sad little addiction. He knows you can't pass a betting shop at two hundred yards. And he knows you've mortgaged your family's future to feed your pathetic gambling habit. And, just in case you're wondering, he knows about your criminal past too. He knows about the court judgements; he knows what you've got hanging over you. So if you want to keep in with your bosses, if you want to keep your job, if you want to keep your family, perhaps, you know exactly what you need to do. It's up to you, of course. You can carry on sabotaging the work of this department; you can carry on dumping on Selwyn – but you just need to know that if you do that, you will be shat on in a much more unpleasant, much more terminal way. Well, it's been nice talking to you. I think we understand each other. And you can take your eyes off my tits now. Byeee—'

When Sonya Mair had closed the door behind her, Chris Brody sat in silence at his desk. He knew Sonya was right: they did understand each other. And he knew he had been comprehensively thrashed by a ruthless and calculating woman. He should have been feeling humiliated. The strange thing was – and he couldn't quite pin down how or why – the experience had left him with a vague feeling of excitement and arousal.

Brody was still sitting frozen when Sonya reappeared at his door. 'And by the way, don't ever quote the Bible at him again – ever! If anyone's going to read him parables, it's me. OK?'

Geoff Maddle refused Harvey Parks's offer of a smoke and settled for a cup of PG Tips.

Geoff couldn't quite pin Parks down: his accent was upper-class Home Counties, but his clothes were from Oxfam or worse; his manners were exquisitely polite, but his language was littered with 'fuck' and 'shit'; he quoted Latin but lived in squalor. Geoff had to make a judgement on Parks; he had to figure out whether the man was a drug-sapped nutter or if some sharper intelligence was hiding behind those junkie's eyes. The way Geoff needed to play the situation, his game plan for the next hour, and perhaps the fate of the whole operation, depended on making the right call.

'So, Harvey, you had a pretty useful conversation with Jim then—'

'Yeah, useful, man. Useful. Useful for him, 'cos he knows I've got something, right? Not that useful for me, though – I told him what would be useful for me if he wanted to hear the whole story.'

Geoff was reading the signals and reading them fast. There was a tick in the first box: Parks had swallowed his visitor's claim to be from the *Mirror*, following up Jim McGee's enquiries. And there was almost a tick in the second box: Parks had told McGee he had something on Sheen, but it seemed he hadn't given him the whole story. That was good, but it was also a warning sign: it meant Parks had enough intelligence to play his hand carefully, so he probably had enough intelligence to rumble Geoff if he put a foot wrong.

'Right, Harvey, I see what you mean. It's the money, right?'

'Yeah, the money. That would be useful for me, very useful—'

'OK. I understand that. But you have to understand where Jim and I are coming from, too. We have to know that what you've got is worth it before we decide to sign any agreement with you.'

'Well, I told your pal I had something really big on old Andy Sheen – something that'll send a bit of a shiver through the marbled halls, you know?'

'Yes, that's right, Harvey. You did. But I'm the man who controls the money. I expect Jim probably told you that, didn't he? And if I'm signing a big agreement with you – and I mean big money, Harvey – I need to know exactly what we're going to get from it. You understand that, don't you? I have to be really careful before I sign anything that commits us to paying you so much money. So what I'd like to do, if you don't mind, is just to recap exactly where we're up to. We have to do this bit by bit; we each have to give something in turn and eventually we'll get to signing the big agreement – the agreement that I've got, er . . . here in my briefcase. OK? So first, what I need you to do – just to be quite clear – is to run through for my benefit exactly what you told Jim when he came to see you. Then we'll be one step down the road and I can perhaps offer you a provisional agreement on that basis, so you can then tell me the whole story about Andy Sheen and then I'll be able to sign the full agreement for you to get your money. Does that sound fair to you, Harvey?'

'Well, I guess so, man. The first step sounds pretty good to me, 'cos that's just the stuff I already told your friend when he was here before. So I'm not giving away anything of the other stuff. But then you've got to give me a provisional agreement before I give you the whole shit, OK? And then you'll see that it's pretty dramatic. And then we'll fix a price for it and sign the real agreement, OK?'

'Yes, OK. That sounds a fair way of doing business, Harvey. But you have to be completely upfront about things. So first you're going to tell me exactly what you told Jim McGee, OK?'

'Right. So what I told him is that Andy Sheen and I were the bosomest of bosom pals. We both came up to Cambridge in 1877 or 1977 or whatever. And we both got on well – like the old house on fire, you know – and what I also told him is that there were a lot of drugs around at that time, man. It was, like, the seventies, OK? So, drugs – yeah. And the thing I told your Mr McGoo was that he could reveal to the nation that clean Mr Sheen, the man who's wiping the scourge of narcotics from the nation's noses, wasn't all that clean way back when. Because in 1981, when we were both in our final year, Mr Sheen got a little summons to the Cambridge magistrates for smoking a bit of the wacky baccy. So what's that worth for starters, Mr Moneyman?'

'Yes, Harvey, that's good. That's a good start. But there's more to it than that, isn't there?'

'My dear fellow, you see into my very soul. Oh yes, my friend, there most certainly is more than that—'

'All right. And let's just be clear, now: did you tell Jim about the other, erm, material?'

'Did I tell him? Well, to be very clear: I told him there *was* more, erm, material, but I did not tell him what the more, erm, material is. And I didn't tell him that because he did not place any money on my coffee table. I trust that is clear?'

'Yes. Absolutely clear, Harvey. Now the difference between Jim McGee and me, Harvey, is that Jim is a journalist and I am a journalist but also a businessman. So I am in the happy position of being able to place the money – or at least a binding agreement about money – wherever you want it placed. And all you have to do in order for me to do that is to tell me now, in your own words, exactly what you know about Andy Sheen.'

10

SELWYN KNOX'S post-mortem on the strategy meeting was held the following day with the departmental review group in Downing Street.

Sherry Black had been named as the Department for Society's permanent contact in the Number Ten policy unit and she had brought two colleagues with her. None of them looked a day over seventeen, but all spoke with the absolute assurance and authority which was the exclusive preserve of these creatures of the Prime Minister. When Sherry Black pronounced the phrase, 'Andy wants—' or 'Andy thinks—', even the most experienced ministers and officials, some of them decades older than her, would unquestioningly concur with her every thought, comply with her every wish. They might complain privately about the arrogance of the policy unit in issuing such orders – many ministers felt the PU advisers were a little too free and easy in invoking the name of Andy Sheen for what were in many cases their own schemes and demands – but they all knew that any show of resistance would be reported back to the PM and reprisals would not be slow to follow.

For Knox, the meeting with Sherry and the Sherrettes – as Sonya had scowlingly christened them – was thus of seminal importance in getting the prime ministerial seal of approval for his reform strategy.

'Well, Selwyn, Andy thinks you are doing well so far. He likes the press coverage you've been getting. But Andy says you need to start producing some concrete initiatives now. He says you need to define a bit more clearly the direction the department is going to take.'

'Right, Sherry. I'm glad you say that. Because that's exactly what we've been discussing and that's what I want to clear with you today. We're set to introduce our first measures now, and some of them are going to be pretty controversial. Andy asked us to get tough and that's what we're going to do. We've looked at all the social-reform policies of the past few years and some of them were pretty stern, but what we're about to do will make that lot look like a Girl Guides' picnic. What we're going to do will tackle the root causes of the cancer in our society. We are going to identify the people who are to blame – the teenage mums, the absent fathers, the unemployed, the spongers, petty criminals, drug addicts, benefit cheats and asylum seekers – and we're going to ensure they do not perpetuate themselves in our society. We cannot afford to allow generation after generation of these people to contaminate our way of life. These people don't vote, of course. They're not too much of a problem in themselves. There'll be liberal voices bleating about civil liberties and protecting the weak, but decent people are sick to death of being ripped off by social security frauds and immigrants. They know teenage girls get pregnant just to get handouts and a house at taxpayers' expense. They're fed up with seeing beggars and addicts on their streets. They're terrified of the muggers looking for easy money to feed their habit. So we're going to clean things up. We're going to be like a whirlwind sweeping through the whole of society, seeking out the corrupt, the criminal, the work-shy, the lazy, the violent and the antisocial. We're going to cut them out of our society like a cancer out of a healthy body.'

Sherry nodded her approval. 'OK, Selwyn. Andy will like that.

We've got an election coming up within the next twelve months and it could be sooner rather than later. The votes we need are in the As and Bs. They're the decent people you're appealing to and they *do* vote. So the rhetoric's right and the voter targets are right. How are you going to handle the image issue, though? You're not going to make yourself popular with the liberal media; and that's where Andy will have to distance himself from you. He'll take the credit for the results you achieve, but he can't afford to be too close to the methods you're using. You'll have to stand up and take the flak on that score; you know that, don't you?'

'I do, Sherry, and you can tell Andy I'm more than happy to shield him from the brickbats. The thing is I believe in what we're doing at the department, so I'm proud to be associated with it. The image question isn't a problem for me. This country needs the firm hand of authority and I'm privileged to be the one who provides it.'

When Geoff Maddle got back to Downing Street late that evening, struggling with a thickish folder of longhand notes, a DAT recorder and a pounding headache, Charlie McDonald was in emergency conclave with officials from RAM, the Rural Affairs Ministry, discussing contingency quarantine plans to tackle the latest outbreak of GM-crop-borne tuberculosis.

After pacing up and down in the press office for half an hour, the knots in Geoff's stomach got the better of him. He poked his head into the mauve conference room to signal that Charlie had better come out soonish and hear what he had to tell him.

Charlie wrapped up his meeting and came straight out.

'Right, mate. What's the deal? What's your man in Cambridge told you?'

'It's not good news, Charlie. In fact, it's a bit of a Doomsday. I went to see this Harvey Parks guy – I've got his address and phone number and everything. And I went wired. Anyway, it turns out that Parks and Andy went to the same college together in 1977. I can't remember which one—'

'Trinity.'

'Yeah, that's it. Now they were both doing languages there, Spanish to be precise. And it seems that when you do languages at Cambridge, you do two years in your college, then you do a year abroad to practise your speaking and your accent and all that, and then you come back for a final year.'

'Yeah, I know all that, so what's it got to do with Andy and this Parks fellow?'

'I'm just coming to that. As soon as they met, Parks and Andy got to be big mates. So when it came to the year abroad they both asked to go to the same place.'

'Yeah, Spain presumably, since they were doing Spanish – doh!'

'No, mate. It's not just Spain where they speak Spanish. Andy and Parks went to Colombia in South America. They had a year teaching English at a school in Bogotá. But it seems they were doing other things as well —'

'Hang on. I'm sure Andy's CV says he did his year abroad in Spain. Have you checked?'

'Yes, I have checked. What his CV says is that he spent a year abroad studying Spanish: no mention of Spain.'

'Oh, shit. So don't tell me they were sampling the local herbs when they were in Colombia—'

'Much worse, mate. They were quite the young businessmen. According to Parks, it was all Andy's idea. Well, I'm not sure if he's telling the truth about that, but anyway the two of them got pretty pally with some pillars of the local economy—'

'Drug dealers, you mean?'

'Not drug dealers, Charlie, drug *lords*. These are the guys who keep Colombia going. It's their business that finances the national economy. It's their money that greases the palms in the local councils. They're the ones who finance local services, fund the youth clubs and the football teams; they provide the social security, such as it is, and the people love them. They drive around in flash cars with bodyguards and live in fortified compounds. The police can't touch them. It's not Brixton on a Saturday night like we used to know it; it's institutionalized big business. And that's what got Parks and Andy involved. They reckoned it was a business venture they couldn't turn down—'

'Did you say you were wired while Parks was telling you this, Geoff? Have you got it on tape?'

The walk from Number Ten along the old Cabinet Office corridor to his own department had become a well-trodden route for Selwyn Knox. Now, energized by Sherry Black's endorsement of his proposals and her agreement to fix a date for him to present them to parliament, he positively skipped along the flagstones.

Back at his desk, he called through to his Private Secretary and asked him to summon Sonya Mair, Nigel Tonbridge and Chris Brody.

'Tell Sonya to come straight in. Keep Tonbridge and Brody in the outer office until I call for them. And make sure no one tells the PermSec about this until the meetings are over, OK? I'll talk to him once we've decided everything.'

In the end, Chris Brody and Nigel waited for over an hour in Knox's outer office while Sonya and the boss were in private conclave.

Brody, who had of course seen it all before, spent the time scoffing at Knox's missionary zeal and lunatic plans, speaking loudly enough to embarrass the junior civil servants in the room and make them glance constantly towards the Secretary of State's door in case the boss could hear what was going on.

'So what do you think of this fellow, Nigel? Now you've been working here a few months, I bet he gives you the creeps, doesn't he? All his crackpot Calvinist ranting about being a father to the naughty children of the nation who've gone astray – to all the poor sods he's legislating for – makes him sound like the tsar of all the bloody Russias. They had the peasants praying to them and calling them "Our Little Father", didn't they? Well, in my humble opinion, he's going to come a cropper if he goes through with all this. I've seen it happen before. He's going to earn Andy Sheen's undying gratitude and the nation's undying hatred. As for that Sonya Night-Mair, she's a tough old thing, but even she won't be able to save him. I wouldn't be surprised if there's something going on between them, Nigel – something extra-curricular. I've seen it before, you know; ministers and their consorts – always ends in tears.'

After a struggle, Geoff Maddle located the right section in his DAT voice recording and pressed the playback button. Charlie McDonald raised his eyebrows as the muffled but comprehensible voice of Harvey Parks emerged from the machine on the table.

'It was such an accepted part of life down there, man. Everybody was involved in it or connected with it or benefited from it. It was like . . . business, you know. And here we were – young English businessmen from Cambridge – it was a natural! And it was so easy. Remember, this was before the US got paranoid about the heroin trade. There were no CIA ops helping the Colombians; no helicopters, no nothing. It was just a few local pigs and they were all paid off by the cartels. We spent our time hanging out with Ramòn Echeverria – you may not remember him, the Feds shot him a few years later – but he was Mr Big back then, man. And he was pretty cool to be with. He had money and booze and women. Everyone respected him. And everyone respected us too because we were Ramòn's pals. All that time I think he was testing us to see if we were reliable – like, did we use or didn't we? Were we discreet or did we blab? – that sort of stuff. We did bits and pieces for Ramòn while we were there and it was all a big adventure to us. We did runs down to Cali for him – never touched Medellin, that wasn't our territory, too dangerous – but all the time what Ramòn was doing was seeing if we could help him when we went back to England. And I guess we passed the test! Just before we were due to go back to Cambridge Ramòn took us out one night and told us he liked us and he trusted us – I guess he didn't know I was using; Andy wasn't, he never did – but, anyway, he told us we were going to be his representatives in England and, if we made a fist of it, for the whole of Europe. It was like an import–export business, you know: the imports were in the form of white powder and the exports were mainly pounds and guilders and pesetas.'

Geoff Maddle pressed the stop button and looked at Charlie McDonald.

'If this is true – and I think it is, Charlie – we're talking about meltdown time. According to Parks, the two of them came back to Cambridge, did their degrees like everyone else and spent their spare time setting up the whole European distribution network for Colombia's favourite export.'

When the door to the Secretary of State's inner office finally swung open and a flushed-looking Selwyn Knox appeared, Brody turned to Nigel and winked. 'Get ready now, old boy. He's about to do to us what I think he's just been doing to Ms Mair!'

Knox ushered the two of them, plus Jeremy, his Private

Secretary, into his inner office, where Sonya Mair was already installed at the head of the long conference table. Before the scraping of chairs and the rustling of papers had subsided, Knox had already begun.

'Right. Thanks for coming. I'd like you to listen carefully. We are about to launch the single most important piece of social legislation this country has seen for over a century. I have just spoken to the Prime Minister and we have been given the go-ahead for a speech to parliament in ten days' time. The centrepiece of the legislation I shall be outlining then will be something that should have been introduced long ago, something this nation *needs* to curb the self-renewing generation of antisocial elements who threaten our values and way of life. I can tell you that my priority now, and the priority for all of you present, will be the introduc-tion of radical new legislation to institute a compulsory, nation-wide Parenting Licence. It will be a simple but effective test of parenting skills, a qualification that most prospective parents will find easy to acquire, but a qualification without which parents in the future will not be authorized to produce offspring. No Parenting Licence means no right to produce children. It's simple, it's effective and it's vital to the future of our nation—'

Christopher Brody, whose face had been expressing growing degrees of incredulity, could hold back no longer: with one movement he pushed his chair away from the table, threw back his head and erupted into a prolonged guffaw.

If Charlie McDonald was shocked, he was hiding it well. His only visible reaction to Geoff Maddle's bombshell was to frown a little and scratch his head. But his thoughts were in turmoil. The memories of his Brixton childhood, his struggle to make it as a black journalist in a white man's world, his unprecedented rise to the Prime Minister's side – all this was in jeopardy. Andy

Sheen's future was hanging in the balance and so was Charlie McDonald's.

'Right, Geoff. We'll need to think. First of all, what exactly has Parks got against Andy, apart from a bunch of wild allegations, that is?'

'That's the problem, Charlie. He's got everything. Parks was the bookkeeper for the operation and basically he's kept the books! He's got a written record of everything they brought in from Colombia and of all the cash – minus their commission, of course – that went back to Echeverria in Bogotá. Half of it's in Andy's handwriting – his DNA must be all over it. And Parks has got the photos – him and Andy and all the Colombian Mr Bigs you care to name. It's a rap, Charlie, and Andy must know it. Let me play you a bit from the end of the tape. Here's what Parks has to say about Andy when they graduated and left Cambridge.'

Another bout of stop–start playback and Geoff finally found the DAT reference he was looking for.

Parks's voice emerged again like an avenging angel's. '. . . so like I say, man, Andy was getting pretty well off by now. We looked on it as a start in the business world. All the others were getting recruited by McKinsey's, but we had our own little business venture and business was booming. We rarely had anything to do with the actual merchandise, of course. That was brought in by the mules. But the amount of money that passed through our rooms, man, it was mind-blowing! We disguised it all as a medicines and pharmaceuticals trade. Pharmaceuticals! Yeah – anyway, I squandered all my money – I was already a user when we came back from Colombia and it just got worse. Andy Sheen, though, he was smart. He had to launder his part of the bread, so what did he do? He went and bought a luxury bloody flat in New York! There aren't many students who can do that, are there?'

*

Selwyn Knox fixed Chris Brody with a withering glare.

Brody was a hard man, but even he felt a chill run down his spine and his guffaw stuck in his throat. Sonya Mair gave him a sharp look full of threat; for the rest of the meeting Brody sat in silence.

'So, if Mr Brody has finished now, I would like to explain the thinking behind this measure. Perhaps then you will see why it is not only justified and sensible, but also vital and inevitable. You need to know that the Parenting Licence is aimed at a certain class of people. These are the parents who didn't and don't want their children, people who have their children inadvertently because of a lack of education, by mistake as it were. You can see them everywhere you go. The way they treat their children betrays the resentment they feel for the burden of parenthood; they cannot disguise it. And their resentment is all too readily felt by their unwanted offspring. This sort of parenting breeds resentful young people with a chip on their shoulder, the social malcontents who plague this country today.

'Put at its simplest, the new Parenting Licence will be a caring and compassionate way of prompting these people to reflect before they rush into something that they, their children and ultimately society itself will regret. Now I am not naive, despite what Mr Brody and others may think. I know there will be resistance to what we are proposing. I know people will compare our policies to the social engineering of Soviet Russia or Nazi Germany. But nothing could be further from the truth! These are humane, compassionate policies. The requirements for acquiring the Parenting Licence will be laughably simple. All they will involve will be watching a few government-produced DVDs, a couple of half-hour classes with an official government adviser and the completion of a questionnaire. It isn't a big test by any stretch of the imagination and if you are the right sort of person you will get through it easily. But what it will do is make people think twice before rushing into parenthood. It will make them reflect on the responsibilities they will have towards their off-spring and towards society. In the cases we are specifically target-ing, it will – I believe – help reduce the numbers of unwanted babies and consequently the numbers of potential future crimi-nals, addicts and scroungers.

Knox paused and gave a half-smile of satisfaction: his audience was interested, intrigued – now he could hook them.

'At first sight, what I am proposing today may seem outlandish, but reflect for a moment before condemning these measures. You will remember that several years ago in the Sexual Offences Bill we moved to outlaw many forms of sex, including sex outdoors and in public places. That was a good start. And the people of this country realized that implementing the Bill was the right thing to do. Now I believe we must go further; but we must be clear about our objectives; we must be clear about what we cannot do and would not wish to do. We cannot, for example, outlaw sex outside marriage, much as we might think it right to do so. We cannot forbid people to have sex, nor would we want to – that is clear. However much we believe that certain classes of people should be prevented from reproducing and perpetuating the ills they have visited on society, however carefully we would pledge to choose those who would be subject to the law, I believe such a measure would not be practicably enforceable. Nor are we talking about enforced sterilization, even for the most undesirable classes of society. That is not something that this country is ready for, although I believe the practice exists in some southern states of the USA for destitute black women – among others – who are taken into the care of state-run institutions. Actually, could someone check on that please and let me know? If it is true, it could be very useful ammunition—

'Anyway, what we are doing is simply introducing a Parenting Licence, a humanely enforced educational programme for people's own good.

'Decent people will have no problem with the concept or with the actual act of obtaining their Licence. The tests will be easy for them to pass and will be an opportunity for them to prove their credentials as good citizens. It is the undesirables who will either fail the Parental Licence tests or seek to avoid taking them. These are the people the Licence is aimed at. These are the people we wish to discourage from producing undesirable offspring.

'In sum, we must send a message to decent people that this programme is not aimed at them. It is aimed at those elements in society whom decent folk fear, despise or wish to see removed, people who don't contribute anything positive to society – and, I may add, don't vote.'

Geoff Maddle thought Charlie McDonald was taking the news about Andy Sheen's criminal past remarkably calmly. Maddle himself was in the grip of incipient panic and he was strangely perturbed that McDonald did not seem to share his alarm.

'I don't know what you're so calm about, Charlie. This is nuclear. And don't go thinking that Parks is just a harmless druggie because he isn't. One thing he let drop – and I had no idea about this, maybe you did? – is that Andy has been sending Parks money every month since 1997. 1997, Charlie! That's the year Andy started his career in politics. It's too much of a coincidence that the payments started then. Andy hasn't been sending Parks money out of the goodness of his heart. He's been sending it to keep Parks quiet. It's blackmail money. Andy's been paying the guy off—'

'Yeah, it certainly looks that way. So why has Parks gone to the media now? Isn't he happy with what Andy's been paying him?'

'No, it's not enough for him, that's the problem. Parks has found he's needing more and more money to feed his habit and he couldn't get it from Andy. That's why he approached Jim McGee from the *Mirror*. McGee gave him a few quid and the promise of more. But now he's after big bucks for selling his story. If the *Mirror* won't deal, he's talking about going to the *Mail*. He's no idiot, Charlie. I've kept him quiet for now by giving him five hundred pounds in cash and what he thinks is a contract with the *Mirror* that'll earn him eighty thousand quid for his story. But when he realizes I've been stringing him along, he'll be off to your old paper like a shot, and the *Mail* will lap it up for sure—'

'OK, Geoff, we need to stay calm over this one. Let's have a think. For a start, it's pretty strange this hasn't come out before. How has Andy got away with it up to now?'

'Well, Parks has kept quiet because Andy was paying him, obviously . . . And when they were dealing back then, Parks says they had Mr Ramòn breathing down their necks, so they weren't going to be boasting about what they were doing. And anyway, they were never "hands on". They weren't the ones on the street corners selling the stuff, so no one knew what they were up to. I don't think they even felt they were doing anything wrong: for them it was like a venture capital business enterprise, with a product people wanted and they could supply. Their only slip was the court appearance on that minor possession charge and, as we know, they got away with it. It certainly didn't do them any harm: in those days, half the student population of the UK was up on possession charges.'

Charlie McDonald looked at Geoff, passed his hand over his face and sighed briefly.

'OK, Geoff. I guess it's make-your-mind-up time on this one.'

The following day Selwyn Knox summoned his director of policy for a private meeting with himself and Sonya Mair. Christopher

Brody did not make any trouble, not even when he was tasked with identifying the priority target groups for the parenting unit's new programmes. Knox told him to trawl the police, Home Office, employment and benefit agency databases. He told him to prioritize people with criminal records, single parents, registered and unregistered addicts, asylum seekers and the homeless. In addition, he was told to run a series of focus groups among social As and Bs with the aim of testing public opinion over who they would most like to see targeted for the new Parenting Licence. Brody shrugged and went away to get on with it.

In a parallel meeting, Nigel Tonbridge was told that he must prepare the ground for the parenting unit by stirring up public revulsion over recent examples of parental cruelty, neglect and abuse. He was instructed to compile a dossier of the most horrific cases, starting with the tale of the little girl who had been tortured to death by her parents. Knox told him he should include the more recent examples of children locked in cupboards and left to starve, the young twins who died on a hot summer's day in their child seats with the car windows closed, and the little boy who died of hypothermia after being deliberately locked out of his house overnight in winter. Nigel was told he must ensure the media ran features listing all the most outrageous details of deficient parental behaviour and linking them with unplanned pregnancies and absent fathers. Knox had already spoken to the department's statisticians and he handed Nigel a sheaf of figures proving that the highest rates of unemployment, criminality, alcoholism and antisocial behaviour are found among children from dysfunctional and single-parent families. Nigel looked searchingly at Selwyn Knox, seemed on the point of saying something, but picked up the dossier and left the room without a word.

*

SPIN

Four days later, the *Cambridge Evening News* carried a brief item recording the death of a drug addict in a house near the city centre. Harvey Parks was described as a former student of the university, who had once had a promising career as a businessman. In recent years, said the paper, neighbours in Dove End Street, where he lived, had found Parks to be quiet and reclusive, but always polite and friendly. The Cambridge coroner had recorded the cause of death as heart failure brought on by a drug overdose; there were no suspicious circumstances.

Nigel arrived first and took the more comfortable bench seat against the wall. Tagliano's was one of several central London restaurants he used regularly for these lunchtime meetings with journalists. In the months he'd been at the Department for Society, he had never really enjoyed the artificial intimacy conferred by sharing bread with reporters, who in many cases were his former colleagues and acquaintances. Their meetings were inevitably strained. He knew they regarded him with mixed feelings: a hack who had gone over to the government, poacher turned gamekeeper, as they constantly reminded him. But he knew also that these seasoned correspondents retained a residual and illogical conviction that they could trust Nigel: in their eyes he had been one of them, a journalist, and therefore he was more likely to tell them the truth than the other PR reps vying to sell them a story. He blushed inside as he reflected on the naivety of this, especially when his task was to convince his lunch partner of policies he himself disapproved of. Nigel was about to curtain-raise a Knox initiative that he regarded with the deepest suspicion, that troubled even his long-blunted conscience.

'Hi, Nigel. Sorry I'm a bit late. I was doing the Andy Sheen New Transport for New Britain initiative – giving it a pretty good write-up, you'll be pleased to hear. Have you ordered anything yet? That wine looks nice—'

Dave Sopwith was among the easiest of the Fleet Street polcorrs for Nigel to deal with. His journalism consisted largely of reproducing what the government told him, so he had been the obvious choice to kick off the grooming of public opinion over the Parenting Licence.

Even Sopwith couldn't hide a gasp of surprise when Nigel told him what was being proposed. 'But, Nige, how are you going to get people to accept something like that? And how are you going to administer it? OK, look: I can see it's a good idea to slash the numbers of these problem children who turn into problem adults, but how the hell are you going to force people to sit this parent trap or whatever you're calling it?'

'Dave, you know I'm a civil servant. You know I can't leak details of government policy initiatives. On the other hand, I can see you're interested in this story and the department wants to help you. If you can just hold your horses for ten minutes, I'm expecting someone to join us and I think she may be able to fill you in on what's being proposed. OK?'

'Yeah, sure, Nige. Whatever you say—'

Ten minutes later, right on cue, Tagliano's was graced by the elegant, head-turning entrance of Sonya Mair. As Sonya glided through the crowded restaurant towards their table, Nigel stood up and took his leave of a fidgety Dave Sopwith. 'All right, Dave, nice to have seen you. I expect you won't mind me leaving you in Sonya's hands, will you? Give me a ring later if anything isn't clear.'

Sonya Mair slid into Nigel's vacated seat and gave Dave Sopwith a melting smile.

Charlie McDonald and Geoff Maddle felt that at last things were now beginning to move in the right direction.

Over lunch in the private upstairs room of the Red Lion, McDonald was assessing the danger still remaining, the poison as yet undrawn from the Andy Sheen story, now that the key prosecution witness was gone.

'So Parks is out of the picture. OK. That's lucky for us, Geoff—'

Geoff Maddle gave a half smile. 'Lucky – yeah, I suppose you could say that. Junkies and overdoses – happens every day.'

'Yeah, it does. So, that's the first thing in our favour. McGee's hand is weaker than it was. He got no documentation off Parks and all the written evidence, all the photos from Parks's files, have been Hoovered and trashed, right?'

'Right.'

'So what has McGee got? Parks told him about the conditional discharge, but he's got no corroborating evidence, nothing on paper. Right?'

'Yeah. You took care of the Police National Computer, Charlie, and I burned the paper record from the Cambridge cop shop.'

'OK. So, if you were McGee, what would you do now? You know there's a story out there somewhere, but you can't stand it up. You're pretty sure Parks was telling the truth about the court appearance and you strongly suspect there was much more where that came from. So do you run the line about the conditional discharge and hope it'll flush out the rest of the dirt?'

'I don't know. He's got to be worried about Andy suing him for libel, especially as he can't call on Parks to support the story any more. I reckon McGee's in pretty bad shape.'

'Yeah, I think he is too. But I don't want to take any chances with him, especially as we've come this far already. I don't think we can risk leaving him out there to shoot at us. What do you reckon?'

'I don't know, Charlie. Depends what you've got on McGee, I suppose.'

'Well, funny you should mention that, actually. Because I've taken the sensible precaution of gathering ammunition on Mr McGee: there's easily enough to get our retaliation in first. You know I was trawling for dirt on the guy? Well, it turns out there's plenty about. You remember the story back in 2005 about financial journalists and that insider-dealing scam? They'd buy up shares and then tip them in their column so the price sky-rocketed? Well, some of them got the chop, but it seems Mr McGee managed to get away with it. And, guess what? Since then, he's been doing it again and no one's been able to catch him.'

'Sounds good, Charlie. But what's the evidence for it?'

'The evidence is the lovely Sonya Mair! Among all the others she's charmed over the years, she has been – how shall I put it? – very close to an important insider at the *Mirror* who knows about McGee's little money-spinner. He's even told Sonya about McGee's latest wheeze, a nice bit of insider trading on the DRE deal. Apparently, McGee bought thousands of DRE shares at rock bottom, just before they got clearance to sell off to EES and go into bio-engineering. Do you think I should ring and mention this to Mr McGee?'

'Well, when you put it like that, Charlie, it does seem sensible.'

'Listen, Dave, I'm talking to you off the record, OK?' Sonya squeezed Dave Sopwith's arm. 'What I'm telling you now you need to pin on unnamed but reliable sources close to the government.'

'Of course, Sonya. You know you can trust me.'

'Yes I do know that and I appreciate it. But it's especially important with this story. Because what I'm telling you won't be announced to parliament for another week, I'm technically breaching parliamentary privilege by even talking to you. The Speaker won't like it if this can be traced back to the department and you know how het up Mick McPaddywhack can get!'

'Trust me, Sonya. Just tell me what you want me to write and I'll do it for you.'

'Thanks, Dave. Now, I think you've got the rationale behind what we're doing. The main thing is for you to print all the horror stories of parental inadequacy in the dossiers that Nigel gave you. You need to use his statistics to show exactly who these people are and which social categories they come from. And you need to write the article so your readers recognize how important it is to stop them overrunning our society and our values. We need to have the public demanding decisive action – crying out for our Parenting Licence by the time we make the announcement. I think that's a message *Chronicle* readers will welcome, don't you?'

'Oh, absolutely, Sonya. Don't worry about that. We'll give it a good show. But I'm still not clear how you're going to administer this thing.'

'All right, Dave. As far as the mechanics are concerned, I can give you a broad outline but not the fine details. Selwyn needs to keep those for his speech. What you need to write is that the Parenting Licence is an idea whose time has come. It will be welcomed by all right-thinking people and it is so self-evidently in everyone's interest that the vast majority of prospective parents will need no prompting to sit and pass the simple tests it involves. After all, we sit an exam before we can drive a car, don't we? And how much greater is the responsibility involved in being a parent? I think the comparison is clear, don't you? What you can say, though, is that the government recognizes there will be some people who resent the PL or try to evade their responsibilities. On that, you should just write that there will be a carrot-and-stick approach to the hardest cases: the carrot will be free advice from professional government counsellors and help with how to be a good parent. The stick will be in the form of sanctions, but I can't give you anything concrete on those yet: it would be too obvious that the whole thing has come from inside the department. All right?'

'Yes, of course, Sonya. But could you just answer one question for me? What about people who get pregnant by mistake? You know, good, decent people who just make a slip?'

'Well, this might sound harsh, but we have to be realistic: the whole point of the Parenting Licence is to stop slips and mistakes because slips and mistakes are where the future problems for society all come from. People have to learn to behave responsibly. Unplanned pregnancies are what we are trying to wipe out. But we're not unreasonable, Dave. If good, decent people find they are expecting, they can of course come and sit the PL in the months before the child is born. We are even considering post-facto PL tests, but there's been no agreement on those yet. We're reasonable people, Dave, but we have to make sure this initiative is taken seriously.'

Charlie McDonald was a relieved man.

Jim McGee's agreement to drop his investigations into the Andy Sheen drugs story had restored McDonald's usual good humour, which colleagues thought had deserted him in recent days.

Now, sitting in Downing Street with an Arsenal mug full of strong tea, he was sharing a laugh with an equally relieved Geoff Maddle. The first target for their wit had been the PM himself and those cabinet members who had been in the news recently. Then they had been through the documents that had accumulated in Charlie's in tray during the Jim McGee interlude and exchanged scathing witticisms about their authors. Now they were reading a file from the US State Department, which set out the case for Jeb Bush's strongly held belief that the Allies should extend their zone of permanent occupation to Afghanistan and northern Pakistan.

Charlie remarked casually that one way to convince Andy to agree might be to mention the local trade in certain substances and both men collapsed in a fit of giggles.

Their hilarity was still in full flow when Charlie's secretary called through to say she had the Director-General of the BBC on the phone. By now, Charlie's mood was such that the prospect of a chat with Fred Pond seemed to promise even more amusement, and he gestured to Geoff to listen in on the spare extension.

'Well hello, Fred,' Charlie smirked into the telephone, 'to what do I owe this signal honour?'

'Ahm, bit tricky, Charlie. Bit tricky. Need to tell you something. Not good news I'm afraid.'

'Oh, come on, Fred. It can't be that bad. What's our favourite D-G got to worry about?'

'Ahm, well. Problem is people are talking, Charlie. Having a go at me and the chairman. Sure you've seen it in the press. Saying we're too close to you chaps. Too soft on the New Project government after all that fuss with the chemical weapons inquiry. Not impartial—'

'And there's nothing wrong with that, Fred. You keep it up! You and Mervyn are our best assets.'

Charlie and Geoff were finding it hard to keep a straight face.

'Ahm, quite. Problem is, the press know about the donations from Mervyn and me. Saying we're New Project stooges. That sort of thing—'

'Oh, surely not, Fred!'

'Ahm, 'fraid so, Charlie. Have to do something to prove we're impartial. Having to screen a bit of a political drama. Bit of a drama based on New Project's first decade in power. Two-parter. Called *The Product*. About the way New Project gets marketed and sold by you spin-doctor chaps. All spin, no substance. Bit critical, I'm afraid—'

Charlie looked at Geoff, grinned broadly and gave a theatrical frown into the telephone. 'Now, now, Fred! We can't be having that, can we?'

'Ahm, got to do it, Charlie. Sorry. Got to. Don't worry, though. Bit of a con trick. Publicizing it as an outspoken attack on New Project's ethics – show Mervyn and I are even handed – not soft on the government. Actually, we're making sure *The Product* is a damp squib. Dead boring. People'll think we're criticizing New Project, but it's so tedious no one will sit through it. So nothing to worry about. They'll be bored to death. Hope that's OK with you, Charlie. You will tell Andy, won't you?'

The fun that had seemingly vanished from the spin doctors' lives had at last returned.

Charlie McDonald was back on form and ready to tackle the remaining letters in his overflowing in tray.

'Let's see what we've got in here, Geoff. Who else can give us a laugh? Ah, talk of the devil, here's one from the lovely Cliff Evans at the *Mirror*. I wonder if his boys have had any more ideas for good share tips? Oh, hang on . . . oh, shit! . . . This isn't funny, mate. Have a look at this—'

Geoff Maddle scanned the letter in Charlie McDonald's hand and grimaced.

Cliff Evans was writing to say that it had come to his attention that Prime Minister Andy Sheen had concealed a drugs conviction in his past and that the *Mirror* was intending to run the story the following Monday. Evans's letter admitted that he had no written evidence of the PM's conditional discharge, but said that as editor he was sufficiently convinced of the story's veracity to be prepared to run with it.

Geoff Maddle's immediate response was angry. 'McGee promised he'd drop this, Charlie. But they're still running it. We need to screw McGee now!'

'No, it's gone beyond McGee. The editor's found out and he's the one we need to reckon with now.'

'Bloody hell, Charlie. Why is all this happening to us? It never would have happened when Tony Blair was Prime Minister. He and Alastair Campbell played things straight.'

'Maybe, Geoff, but we're here now and we need to deal with Cliff Evans. What do you think?'

'I think he's bullshitting us. Look, he says himself he can't stand the story up. I bet he'd never risk running it. He's trying to panic us or blackmail us into giving him something.'

'Mmm. I suspect you're right, Geoff. But can we take the risk? That's the question. I suppose we could just let him run the Sheen-smoked-dope story. It'd be embarrassing but it wouldn't be fatal. The danger with any drug story, though, is that it could bring all sorts of things out of the woodwork, it could open a whole can of woodworms. I think we need to play safe, we need to negotiate with Evans. What do you think?'

'Well, maybe. Yeah. You might be right, Charlie. What can we offer him as a sweetener, though?'

'It shouldn't take too much. Evans doesn't know the real story about Andy so he doesn't know his bargaining power. He'll probably settle for a bit of a scoop from us in return for dropping the drugs thing.'

'Yeah. What, though? What can we give him?'

'Well, maybe I can think of something. How old is Marie Sheen now? About thirty-nine?'

'Forty-one last birthday, mate. Why?'

'Hmm. It could work, but it'll need a woman's touch. I think we'll get Sonya to give us a hand with this one.'

Nigel Tonbridge had spent his week carefully leaking details of Selwyn Knox's impending policy launch to various newspapers and broadcasters. As is often the case with major announcements, the broad lines of the Parenting Licence had now been reported and picked over in the media well in advance of its official presentation to parliament. The object of this was to lessen the shock of such a radical initiative and to forestall the firestorm that might otherwise engulf the Secretary of State on launch day. In addition, Knox now had a good idea of the reaction he could expect and the questions he would be asked when he rose to his feet the following Monday. Nigel had few qualms about this breach of parliamentary etiquette, but he did have real and growing concerns about the aims of the policies he was helping to promote. The more he reflected on the work he was doing for the department, the more he was puzzled by Knox's motives in bringing him to work there. Nigel was sure Knox was aware of the distaste he felt both for him and for his policies and he had become increasingly convinced that Knox had had another, hidden motive for recruiting him. In his more fanciful moments Nigel had begun to suspect that Knox wanted him close by solely because of their shared experience in Exxington; he was the only one who shared the intimate burden that haunted Knox's every waking moment – the knowledge of past sins. At times, Nigel wondered if Knox had brought him close because somewhere deep down he longed for Nigel to expose him, to unmask the darkness within him. Did Selwyn Knox have a purpose for Nigel? An unexpressed desire for the painful light of exposure? A death wish that only Nigel could grant?

*

SPIN

At Charlie McDonald's suggestion, Sonya Mair rang Cliff Evans and told him he needed to drop his misguided allegations of a drugs offence in Andy Sheen's past. For a start, they were completely untrue. For another thing, the *Mirror* had no evidence and no witnesses for the story, and if Evans ever did run it, Downing Street would see him in court. But just because she liked him Sonya said she was also offering a trade-off in the form of an exclusive. Evans said he was prepared to deal and Sonya gave him the scoop on Marie Sheen's late and unexpected pregnancy. The next day, the *Mirror* splashed this on the front page. No mention of drugs and the Prime Minister ever saw the light of day.

11

NIGEL TONBRIDGE felt himself sinking into one of his periodic bouts of self-loathing. He had suffered from them long enough to recognize their onset and had learned from experience to resign himself to their chill embrace.

Joanie said his black-dog episodes had got worse since he turned forty; Nigel joked about the male menopause.

Familiarity had taught him the symptoms, perhaps the causes, but never any solutions. His bouts of depression flooded him with self-doubt, convinced him of his own worthlessness, of the waste he had made of his life.

As a young man, Nigel had never had time for self-examination. He had been focused on the next story, searching for the elusive scoop, rising up the ladder of journalistic success. He had had a goal and a defining purpose.

Promotion, praise, fame and money were an easy structure against which to judge his worth. As at school, success and failure were well marked out; things seemed comprehensible, generally fair, always transparent. And while he was progressing towards the next target – the next correspondent's post, the next pay rise, more recognition – he felt he was on course and was satisfied.

But in recent years the stable points in his life had been kicked away. Now the ready-made, prêt-à-porter values against which he had measured himself, the fixed targets, were all gone.

In his bouts of depression, Nigel felt at sea in a world without benchmarks. Now he had to create his own moral checkpoints, define his own acts of courage or cowardice, success or failure, good or bad behaviour. And he did not like it; he had to judge himself and he had no idea how to.

Now he lay awake in the middle of the night, recalling with regret the certainties and energy of the past, looking with trepidation on the challenges of the future, tormenting himself with the memory of what had passed between him and his father – the secret he had concealed from everyone, including even his wife, but which Selwyn Knox had once intimated he had somehow uncovered.

It was in this state of mind that Nigel now tried to confront the dilemma which had begun to obsess him.

The immediate trigger was clear. In recent weeks, he had begun to feel increasingly uncomfortable with the responsibility Knox had given him for promoting the department's policies. In meetings with journalists, Nigel had heard himself describing how Knox's ideas would cleanse and regenerate society, how they would restore moral values and bring people together. And as he spoke, he had realized with growing clarity that he loathed and detested the policies Knox was proposing. He felt gripped by a deep internal contradiction between his own views and the propaganda he heard himself spouting – and he had no idea how to resolve it.

His first reaction was to use the 'obeying orders' strategy: he was a civil servant so he could not object to the official policies of his minister, he had to accept and promote them unquestioningly because his minister told him to do so. The civil servant's code, as understood by Nottridge and most of the others he worked with, was to do blindly and die blindly. Their consciences, if they had them, were eased by the service's vow of unquestioning loyalty.

But Nigel's conscience would not go so quietly.

He began to think of himself as the only man who could halt the progress of Knox's insidious policies, the last remaining Hollywood superhero who could save the world from the evil genius at the helm of the Department for Society! He laughed, but the wrestling with his conscience continued.

'Hello, Nigel? It's Jeremy here. The Secretary of State would like you to come up to his office in half an hour. We've got an NCCL delegation arriving for a chat about the new Parenting Licence, among other things. They'll be here at ten o'clock. Can I tell him that's OK with you?'

The delegation, it turned out, was in fact a coalition of concerned activists, led by the National Council for Civil Liberties but embracing other campaigning bodies such as the League of Churches, the Humanist Council and the Fellowship of Human Responsibility.

Their spokesman, Alastair Barber, was an NCCL lawyer with twenty years' experience of civil rights issues and a string of successes in opposing government policies that he and his colleagues saw as a threat to freedom of speech or action. He had led the campaign to oppose mandatory fingerprinting and DNA sampling of the whole population; he had fought and won when the Home Secretary had proposed the return of the death penalty; he had opposed but failed to halt the return of universal military service.

Now Alastair Barber made no secret of his outrage at the leaked stories in the press foreshadowing the policies which Knox was about to announce.

'Well, thanks for seeing us, Mr Knox. At least you've done us the courtesy of hearing what we have to say. I just hope you'll take note of the alarm and anger that has been generated by the stories about your Parenting Licence proposals.

'First, I would like to put on record that the NCCL and the

other groups represented here today have deep concerns about the whole concept of a Parenting Licence.

'We feel it infringes basic personal freedoms. This country has a proud tradition of guaranteeing liberties to citizens to the extent that they do not impinge on the liberty of others. And this is a principle that goes back as far as Mill and Hume and Locke.

'We are, however, realists.

We recognize that public opinion today is such that revulsion against crime and the antisocial phenomena plaguing our society has fostered popular support for your proposals where it probably would not have existed in the past.

'We are even prepared to concede that the damage inflicted on society by the elements you are seeking to curb may theoretically justify certain proposals to curtail civil liberties in order to protect the liberty of others.

'I say this to show that we are approaching this discussion with a reasonable and open mind; and I hope you will respond in kind.

'After extensive debate, and in light of the arguments I have just outlined, we have decided we will not oppose the overall principle of your proposals.

'What we are determined to do, though, is ensure you are held to account in everything you do, that the details of the legislation you introduce are compatible with the protection of the weak and the vulnerable in society. We are determined to police this legislation in all its minutiae, Mr Knox, and to oppose it wherever it oversteps the limits of acceptable civilized law.

'So I'd like to start, if I may, with a series of questions, and my colleague here will minute your responses.

'I should tell you, also, that if we are not satisfied with the undertakings you give us in reply to our concerns, we will have no hesitation in taking this issue to direct action and to popular protests on the streets.

'I hope it will not come to that, however; it is in your hands to give us the assurances we require if we are to avoid such an outcome.

'Now, the first undertaking we need is that the obligation to pass the PL will be applied equally and fairly to all social groups and that there is no intent deliberately to target specific social categories.'

'Yes, Mr Barber, I can give you that absolute assurance.'

Selwyn Knox was firm and frank: he looked Alastair Barber in the eye; he was a man to be trusted.

'Thank you. The second assurance we need is that proper counselling will be made available to all who need it and that there will be no penalization of those who fail. In other words, that this will be a programme enacted with a carrot, not a stick.'

Again, Selwyn Knox was frank. 'Yes, I can give you that assurance.'

Barber looked slightly surprised, relieved even. 'Thank you. We also need an undertaking that there will be no stigmatization of single parents, children born out of wedlock, asylum seekers or other disadvantaged groups.'

'I can give you that undertaking. The programme will be compassionate and benign. All we are seeking is the enhanced well-being of those who are affected by it.'

'Thank you, Mr Knox. We have several other concerns that I will send to you in writing. But I do have one major assurance I shall require from you now if the NCCL is to give its provisional approval for your plans. I must have a categorical undertaking from you that the data you gather from the PL programme will not be misused in any way. You will understand that the people most likely to come under the aegis of your parenting counsellors will be vulnerable groups, many of them from ethnic minorities, whose mother tongue may not be English; people who have difficulties coping with authority, difficulties of a financial, addictive or legal nature. Can you give me your word as a government minister and as a man of honour that your department does not intend to share the information these people vouchsafe in confidence to your advisers with agencies such as the police, immigration or tax authorities, agencies where such data could be used to penalize the participants of your Parental Guidance scheme?'

'Mr Barber, I can give you that undertaking and I am prepared to stand by my word. I shall do my utmost to satisfy your concerns and I hope as a result that you will accept the good intentions behind my PL proposals. I hesitate to mention religious beliefs in such distinguished company, but I am – like Andy Sheen – a committed Christian and I can assure you that my conscience is clear. All the measures I am proposing are of the highest moral standard; all are conceived solely for the good of the people they will apply to.'

'Thank you once again then, Mr Knox.' Alastair Barber looked delighted, overjoyed almost, with the outcome of what had promised to be a difficult meeting. 'I accept your assurances on behalf of all those I represent and I can tell you that the NCCL at least is now prepared to give its provisional approval to your plans. Thank you.'

As the NCCL delegation left the room, Selwyn Knox signalled to Nigel and Sonya to remain behind.

Nigel's first reaction was to congratulate Knox on the reasonableness of his approach and on the assurances he had given about the Parenting Programme, but Knox and Sonya Mair were already rummaging through files of papers and pulling out documents which they proceeded to lay on the conference table.

'OK, Nigel, you need to move fast.' Knox looked up and put his finger to his lips to silence Nigel's half-uttered remarks.

'Barber's not going to be happy when he finds out what we're really up to with this PL programme, so we've got to make sure he doesn't start turning nasty on us—'

'Wait a minute, Selwyn.' Nigel looked questioningly at his boss: 'What do you mean "what we're really up to"? You just gave him a pretty clear picture of how the programme—'

'Oh, come on, Nigel. Don't be as wet as you look. All that softly, softly stuff – that's just to buy us a bit of time. You don't think we're really going to keep all those promises, do you? We can't run this programme with bleeding hearts and woolly liberal do-gooders. But we do need to keep Barber in check and fortunately Sonya has come up with the means to do it. The documents I've got here are Mr Alastair Barber's CSA records and they don't make pretty reading. Look, this one shows the Child Support Agency has had to chase missed alimony payments from A. Barber esq. on at least three occasions. The man isn't a responsible parent, Nigel, and he's certainly not the sort of person who should be lecturing the government on how to run its parenting unit. Now I think it would be quite helpful if you were to get the first of these documents to a friendly journalist and then let Alastair Barber know that we are thinking about including him on our Dead-Beat Dads list. Do you think you could do that, please?'

Only much later that morning was Nigel Tonbridge able to bring some sort of order to his thoughts.

He had had time to reflect on the Secretary of State's request and he knew he was now approaching a line which, if he crossed it, would draw him irrevocably into Knox's enchanted inner circle.

He walked into Sonya Mair's office and closed the door behind him.

'Sonya, I have to talk to you. You know I've been loyal over this PL initiative. I've done all the press work, I've toed the departmental line, I've supported him even when I've had serious doubts about what he's proposing. But there are some things he really shouldn't ask me to do. This Alastair Barber thing is too much. It's a smear campaign against the guy and it's not something I should be doing. I'm a civil servant: I'm not here to do Selwyn's political dirty work.'

Sonya Mair looked pityingly at him. 'Don't be a prat. The Barber job has to be done and you should be grateful Selwyn has chosen you to do it. It means he trusts you, he wants you to be part of the team, Nigel. He's showing his faith in you. So don't start having pangs of conscience now, you're in too deep for that—'

'Oh? And what's that supposed to mean exactly?' Nigel's voice was sharp and strained.

'It means you're in too deep, Nigel. You weren't parading your prissy conscience when you got your selection board rigged for you, were you? You didn't come over all coy then, did you? So don't think you can start lecturing us on moral values now. OK?'

Nigel's head began to spin. Sonya was threatening him and making no secret of it. His hands felt chill and his heart was pounding. Sonya was right, of course: if it were ever revealed that the board had been rigged, he would be out of his job in no time. But then, he told himself, it wasn't his idea to rig the board. Maybe not, but he had acquiesced in it. And how could he cope if he were to lose his job? The BBC would never take him back. What could he do?

In his current state of self-doubt, Nigel felt overwhelmed by Sonya Mair's ruthless self-assurance. Instead of standing his ground, he turned to her for some sort of explanation, some sort of answer to the questions that had been obsessing him for weeks.

'Look Sonya, I can't cope with this right now. I've got a lot on my plate. And I need to know some things from you. Some things only you can tell me. For a start, do you understand why Knox decided to recruit me? He knew I was never going to be on board for all this messianic mission stuff – and why does he insist on letting me see all the dirty tricks he gets up to? Why does he always parade the dark side of what he's doing? It's as if he actively wants me to know how devious and twisted he is.'

Sonya Mair looked at Nigel and for a fleeting moment he thought he saw a glimpse of recognition, a glimpse of sympathy. But her reply was cold and harsh.

'Look, Nigel, you're no different from all the other civil servants here. It's your duty to do what the Secretary of State tells you. So don't start thinking you're something special. And stop trying to analyse Selwyn. He's in charge here. He's a force of nature – he can get things done while other people just flounder around. It doesn't matter if he crosses a few lines and tramples on a few outdated notions of propriety. You do what he tells you to do. OK? It's the end result that counts.'

Nigel walked slowly northwards towards Trafalgar Square. He was meeting Joanie for lunch at the National Gallery. The removal of traffic and unauthorized pedestrians under the Congestion and Security Measures Act had turned Whitehall into something between a village high street and a ghost town.

The bright sunshine was helping marginally to clear his head. 'Perhaps Sonya was right,' he thought. 'Maybe Knox really is just a bully, maybe the reason he wants me to know about all his dirty tricks is just his way of bragging, to show me he's the boss, that he can do what he likes, that I can't stop him—'

But something still did not make sense.

'It's as if he wants me to see all the evil he's capable of,' Nigel thought. 'But why? Is he proud of his sins? Is he taunting me? Is he showing me that he got away with Exxington because I was too weak to stop him?'

Joanie saw him across the restaurant and waved. As he approached her table, Nigel gave a little grimace and sank into his chair.

'Hi. Bad day, I'm afraid—'

Joanie knew Nigel was suffering since he had taken his new job. She knew the Department for Society was getting him down. But she did not know the reasons and Nigel had shown no signs of sharing them with her.

'What is it, Nigel? It's something serious, isn't it? You've been down for weeks now.'

Nigel looked at Joanie and felt all the love and affection that twenty years of partnership had created between them. After Sonya Mair's predatory, threatening presence, Joanie's goodness shone like a beacon.

'It is, Joanie. It is—'

'It's that Selwyn Knox, isn't it?'

'Yeah. It is.'

'He's creepy. Those dead eyes . . . that mad, ranting way he talks. He's getting you worried, isn't he? Do you want to tell me about it?'

'Yeah, I do. I can't say I understand it myself, though, really.'

'I know you don't agree with some of his policies. Is that it?'

'That's part of it. But there's more to it than that. I suppose all civil servants have times when they don't agree with their minister. But this is more. It's to do with the man himself, Joanie. I can't figure him out. At times, he seems such a good man, so inspired and so enthused with the love of humanity – he genuinely seems to believe in what he's doing. At others, he seems so cynical. So ruthless, so, well, so immoral.'

'Is he asking you to do things you don't agree with, Nigel?'

'Yeah, he is. Things no civil servant should be asked to do. Smear campaigns and blackmail. But it's more than that, even – I can't quite pin it down. It's something to do with the way he treats *me* in particular. He seems to have something about me.'

'Is it to do with that little girl who died up on the mountain? That was the first time you had anything to do with Knox, wasn't it?'

'Yes, it was.' Nigel looked anxiously at Joanie's face to see how much she had figured out about his run-in with Knox back in Exxington. 'You know, Joanie, I think it does have something to do with that. It's strange: he's never mentioned Exxington the whole time I've been working with him, but I'm always aware – and I think he's always aware – that it overshadows everything we do and everything we talk about.'

'Do you think he feels guilty about Clare O'Leary? It wasn't his fault, was it? I thought Ian Murray took the blame.'

'Yes. Yes, he did. There's something I can't explain, Joanie. Something difficult there—'

From her reaction, Nigel saw that Joanie had no inkling of his secret, the secret Knox had used against him to ensure his silence back in Exxington. He felt relief, but also regret, as he heard Joanie move the conversation away from him and back to Knox.

'So what does he say to you, Nigel? What does he want from you?'

'It's not even so much what he says. It's more the way he behaves with me, Joanie. Look, the really strange thing is that he seems to make a point of deliberately letting me know the underhand, dirty tricks he gets up to – all the shadowy manoeuvring, all the lies and the cheating. And I can't understand why. Everyone says he's a calculating politician, but if he is, why

SPIN

doesn't he keep his secrets to himself? Why is he showing me – a stranger, a potential enemy – the worst side of himself? Why is he giving me ammunition I could use against him? There's no logic to it—'

'It's because he knows you disapprove of him and he's worried about what you might think or do. He wants you to know about those things because he wants to draw you in. If he can make you part of them, you can't denounce him. Isn't that what's behind it?'

'Yeah, I did think that. At first, that's exactly what I thought: he's parading all his sins for me to see because he wants to make me his accomplice; to prove he can get away with it and I can do nothing to stop him.

'But now I'm not sure it's like that, it's more complicated. It's as if he wants me to know something that's hidden deep inside him and he can't get out of. You know, he's overbearing and bullying, and he does his best to intimidate everyone he works with. But at the same time he's somehow pathetic and weak – I can't explain it, Joanie.'

'Well, I'm not sure I feel much sympathy for him. I don't know him like you do, but one thing's clear, which is that you shouldn't get involved. Don't get lured into his schemes. As soon as you do one little thing that's wrong, as soon as you give him one little thing he can use to threaten you, you'll be lost. He'll exploit every weakness, every little fault, to draw you deeper and deeper in. If I were you, I'd go and report this smear campaign thing straight away. Isn't there someone in charge of propriety and that sort of thing for the civil service?'

'Yeah, it's Nottridge, the PermSec. I have been thinking of going to see him.'

'Well, do it now. Go as soon as you get back.'

*

Nigel's meeting with Sir Robert Nottridge that afternoon was one of those difficult, stilted conversations at which the civil service excels.

Even before Nigel had taken his place on the Permanent Secretary's pink settee and placed his cup on the teak coffee table, Nottridge had sensed that his director of communications was bringing him trouble and he listened to Nigel's tale with the air of a man who would rather not hear what he was being told.

'I'm sorry to trouble you with this, Robert,' Nigel began tentatively. 'I wouldn't have come to you if I thought there was another way of resolving it. But I have to tell you that I have grave concerns about the behaviour of the Secretary of State and his political adviser—'

'Ah yes, Nigel. We all have these feelings from time to time. You were right to come to me. I find these things can generally be resolved without too much fuss. But do, please, carry on. Tell me what's troubling you, old chap.'

'Right. Thanks, Robert. It's quite a lot of things, actually. But let me give you an example. You know he had a delegation from the NCCL here this morning—'

'Ah, yes. You were invited to attend the meeting, were you? Strangely, I did not learn of it myself until it had already finished. No matter. Please continue.'

'Well, I was impressed by the Secretary of State's attitude during the meeting. He seemed very reasonable indeed. They were asking him to give some quite detailed undertakings about the new Parenting Licence – reassurances that it will be administered sensitively, that sort of thing. And he just kept saying, "Yes, I agree." He gave them every assurance they asked him for.'

'Well, that's quite excellent. And I think it speaks well of the Secretary of State: I do believe some of the criticisms of him have been rather exaggerated, you know.'

'Yes, but that's not my point. What I'm worried about is what happened afterwards. He had me and Sonya in, and he basically said he'd been lying to the NCCL and he wasn't going to keep any of the promises he'd made.'

'Ah, I see. Well, you know, Nigel, these things happen and it's rarely quite as black and white as we may think. Politics is the art of the sensible, old chap. I'm sure he didn't mean to say he was telling lies. I suspect he was just refining what exactly he was prepared to do for the NCCL and he'll come up with a compromise that keeps everyone happy. I wouldn't worry about it if I were you, you know.'

'Well, that may be the case with other ministers, but Knox was absolutely blatant about this, Robert. He told me he'd lied to buy time until the PL is passed into law. And the worst thing is he then asked me to take part in a smear campaign to keep the NCCL guy quiet – Alastair Barber.'

'Now, now, Nigel. I'm afraid I must stop you there. One important thing I have learned in my many years in the service is that we have to take care to be moderate in our language. Smear campaigns are not something we should allege lightly, you know—'

'He asked me to leak details of Barber's CSA records to the press to scare him into keeping quiet. If that isn't a smear campaign, I don't know what is.'

'Well, let's just reflect for a moment. The Secretary of State may well have had a perfectly honourable motive. He may have just been—'

'He didn't, Robert. He's had Sonya Mair trawling through their Lancelot computer to dig the dirt on one of their political opponents and he's asked me, a civil servant, to leak it. It seems pretty clear-cut to me.'

'Oh, Nigel, in my experience, these things are never quite as clear-cut as they first appear. Politics is a grey art, you know, and we have to consider many things before we go flying off the handle. We need to keep constantly in mind, for instance, that we have to work with our minister on a continuing basis: we can't go accusing him of impropriety, or we'd never get on with him again. And where would that leave us? In the past there have been cases of ministers falling out with their Permanent Secretary and not exchanging a word with him for a year or more, and that's no way to work, Nigel. It can bring the whole department to its knees. I'm certainly not going to let that happen at the DfS.'

'I know what the dangers are and I know you have gone out of your way to be conciliatory towards Selwyn, to make every possible allowance for him. And that's laudable, obviously. But it can't mean we have to turn a blind eye to malpractice in the department. That's in no one's interest—'

'Well, I'm afraid sometimes we have to do things we are not entirely proud of because we have to keep the bigger picture in mind. I'm sorry to have to tell you that I do not regard this case as warranting any further action and I must ask you to return to your desk and carry on with your duties.'

Nigel blinked. Nottridge looked disturbingly serene.

'Let me be clear about this, Permanent Secretary. I have told you about a blatant breach of propriety by the Secretary of State and you are telling me to ignore it.'

'Oh, Nigel, I know it sounds difficult but, believe me, these things happen many times over the years and we have to get used to them. During the course of my career I have been outraged by some of the things I have witnessed. There was all the sleaze under the Conservatives, you know, and then all the deceitfulness under the next government. Few people remember it now, but the Stephen Byers and Jo Moore case, for instance, stirred up tremendous passions. But governments always protect their own,

Nigel. And in this case they'll protect Knox and spin against you. Don't stand on your principles and think you can speak out. They'll tear you to pieces. Your career will be over—'

'I understand what you are saying, Robert. But don't you think that's an argument for greater courage and integrity from us? If we'd made a fuss over all the little things, we might have been able to stop the lying over the big things: things like persuading the country to invade the Middle East when there was no real evidence war was necessary?'

'Ah, there, Nigel, I am afraid you go beyond my competencies. War is not one of my subjects. I am more concerned with your well-being, old chap, with your career and – I'll admit it – with mine. I am not ashamed to say that the post of cabinet secretary falls vacant this year and I am regarded as one of the leading candidates to fill it. As you will appreciate, I have been given charge of the Department for Society as a crucial test of my abilities and I intend to pass that test, Nigel. I intend to maintain good relations with my Secretary of State and stable working practices in my department. So I fear I cannot countenance any idea of confronting the minister and Sonya Mair over this. And I strongly advise you to put the thought right out of your head.'

In Downing Street at that moment, Charlie McDonald and Geoff Maddle were meeting Sonya Mair to plan Selwyn Knox's parliamentary launch of the new Parenting Licence the following Tuesday. After congratulating Sonya on the smooth passage the PL had enjoyed so far, Charlie enquired about Nigel Tonbridge. Sonya said she and Knox had got him under control, but suggested Charlie might want to call him in for a pep talk. For her part, she congratulated McDonald on the disappearance of the Andy Sheen drugs story, but asked how he now intended to get round the problem of Marie's magical disappearing pregnancy.

'Easy,' Charlie said. 'We just ring old Sopwith and give him the exclusive on Marie's tragic miscarriage!'

Sonya and Geoff laughed, but McDonald put his finger to his lips. 'Andy's not very happy about the way we used Marie on this one, but he can stuff it. We did him a bigger favour than he knows, and one day we might have to call it back in from him.'

12

It was one of those days when the crowded Chamber was abuzz with expectation a full hour before the main event.

The Foreign Secretary announcing the breakdown of yet another round of peace talks on the MEWs was like the warm-up bout at a heavyweight title fight: MPs' attention was desultory, their thoughts had turned to the bill topper ahead, and their lips silently mouthed the speeches they had rehearsed to welcome or excoriate Selwyn Knox's notorious Parenting Licence.

When Knox rose the noise was deafening. Speaker McFadyen's bar-room brogue was barely audible above the cries of 'Bravo' and 'Shame' that rained down from both sides of the House.

'Order! Order, I say! The Secretary of State for Society – order! The Right Honourable Gentleman must be heard. Order!'

From his perch high in the Press Gallery, Nigel Tonbridge surveyed the packed government benches below. His now practised eye suggested that Selwyn Knox had a reasonable majority of back-benchers behind him, although the antis were making more noise than their numbers might have warranted.

Since the opposition benches were on his side of the Chamber and below his line of vision, Nigel found it hard to judge the mood among the NewLibs. He knew the leadership had latched onto the NCCL's endorsement of the PL to give it their support, but the party's MPs were notoriously and endearingly independent minded and it was all but impossible to guess which way they would swing.

The few remaining Tories were solidly behind Knox, whom Nigel reckoned would probably take the vote with a little to spare.

Much, though, would depend on the speech, and Nigel knew Selwyn had spent the weekend and most of the previous day in conclave with McDonald, Maddle and Mair, polishing it until it shone like a platinum wedding ring.

'Mr Speaker, Honourable Members—'. Knox's words were met with another cacophony of cries. He yielded. Speaker McFadyen called for order. Knox rose again. 'I come here today to announce a policy that will change our society—'

Shouts of 'And not for the better!' were drowned out by a chorus of 'Hear, hear!'

Knox stood impassively, waiting for a lull. His eyes scanned the benches opposite; his shrewd politician's brain was calculating the mood of the House, doing the arithmetic that would judge his speech, calibrating the tone he needed to strike.

'The Honourable Gentleman shouts "Not for the better", but I wonder what society he is living in. I ask him: is society today the society we would wish to live in? Is it the place we want our children to grow up in? Are we content with a society where people live in fear? Fear of the mugger, the drug addict, the burglar?'

Knox had the gift of pitching his speech to the mood of the moment, making it sound like a spontaneous response to the concerns of the Chamber.

'I ask the Honourable Gentleman: is he content to see towns and cities where people live in isolation, not knowing their neighbours, fearing human contact with their fellow citizens? Where a man will not come to the aid of others because he no longer feels part of the society he lives in?'

Knox was in his stride now. 'A world where the glue of social cohesion has melted away, leaving individuals alone, cut off from humankind because of the fear and suspicion that haunt our society? Where children are failed, abandoned, abused and neglected by their parents? Where teenage girls become pregnant but do not want the child? Where young men get their girlfriends pregnant and refuse to take responsibility for what they have done? Where fathers walk out on their families and fail to support the wife and children they have abandoned?'

The Chamber was quiet now. Knox had passed the first test: his audience was listening.

'So, I say to my honourable colleagues, this is not a society I wish to live in. Nor is it the society my constituents wish to live in. Nor – I am convinced of this – is it the sort of society the people of this country wish to live in.'

The rattle of approbation that swept the House told Knox his audience had warmed to his rhetoric. Now it was time to hit them with the detail.

Knox's adumbration of the measures he was promising was fast and polished, delivered in a relaxed, even tone whose confidence suggested that he at least had no doubts of his ability to deliver on the tasks he had set himself: to tackle the underlying causes of criminality and antisocial behaviour; to regenerate society; to save society from itself.

He listed the penalties he planned to introduce to crack down on absent fathers, single mothers, teenage pregnancies, asylum seekers, the unemployed and the other antisocial elements. He saved his master stroke to the end. The Parenting Licence was what MPs had come to hear about and he did not disappoint them. He outlined the training programme prospective parents would have to undergo before conceiving. He listed the skills they would have to prove they had acquired before the PL would be granted. And he announced that a vast network of counsellors and advisers would be set up to visit problem cases and explain the rights and responsibilities of being a parent. Knox drew gasps as he detailed the scale of the project and the number of counselling jobs it would create.

But as well as the carrot, he added with a slight smile on his lips, there would also be a stick. As well as rights, there would also be responsibilities and, in some cases, people would have to be made to live up to them.

There would, for example, be sanctions on anyone who became pregnant without a proper licence. These would involve the withdrawal of certain state benefits, remedial schooling and the obligation to acquire the PL retrospectively. The fabric of society, Knox said, must be based on every generation's respect for parents, and on future parents' realization of the responsibility they took on when planning to bring a child into the world. Without this there could be no self-respect and no social cohesion.

When it finally came, his conclusion was rousing and drew approval from all parts of the Chamber. 'So I say this to the doubters among you, to the jeerers and the mockers: New Project is not afraid to talk of responsibility and morality, despite liberal voices sneering about "social engineering" and lack of compassion. Because what this society needs is authority. For too long now people have been used to a system that has grown lax, that has fallen into disrepute, that has lost its bite. And, oh! I am not fooling myself. Some people won't like it when authority is restored. They'll resent me for the discipline I introduce. But it has to be done. The figure of the parent, the symbol of the father, must once again become the source of authority and respect in the lives of individuals and in society. I endorse this new order as a man, as a minister and as a champion of paternal government for all our citizens.'

When the vote was taken, the Parenting Licence was passed with a larger than expected majority.

A late amendment providing for enforced abortions 'in extreme cases only' was voted through virtually unremarked.

An hour after the vote Selwyn Knox was still on a high. Adrenalin was coursing through him as he sat slumped in his darkened MP's office high on the narrow upper corridor of the Palace of Westminster. He was waiting for Sonya Mair to finish her rounds of back-benchers, to finish proffering thanks to those who voted for and admonishing those who voted against.

Another hour passed before Sonya came through the door. He was immediately clutching her, pulling her onto the patched and worn sofa in the corner of his office.

'Sonya, we did it. This is the greatest moment of my career so far—'

Knox was buzzing.

'And they bought it, Sonya. We prepared the way and they bought it. The liberals didn't baulk even when we told them how tough we're going to be. They bought it all. And what they don't know is that we've pulled off a double win: if they think all these new counsellors and advisers are going to be agony aunts and uncles, they're even greener than we thought! The adviser network is a godsend for us. Just think, the cases they'll be concentrating on, the "difficult" cases, the under class – they're the people we need to watch the closest. The advisers will be there to gather the information we need – on the scroungers, the dole cheats, the petty criminals, the drug users. They'll be my eyes and ears, penetrating every home, every nest of crime and discontent. And they'll be my early-warning system: these people may think the counsellors are there to dish out help and fluffy words, but they're much more than that! They're my way to stamp out antisocial behaviour before it happens—'

Sonya smiled and put her arms round Knox's neck. 'Don't you

think that's just the tiniest bit sneaky, Selwyn? Don't you think our clients on the Parenting Programme might be just the tiniest bit resentful?'

'No, they won't be, that's the beauty of it. They won't even know they're being watched. These people are my errant children, Sonya, and I need to keep an eye on them. In time, they'll come to know me as a father figure; a father who watches over them, who penetrates their innermost thoughts—'

As Knox spoke, swept onwards by excitement and euphoria, Sonya Mair was slowly sinking to her knees in front of him.

'When I swoop to stop them misbehaving, they won't know how I get the information I use to discipline them. But they will know I have that information. That I know everything about them – their innermost thoughts. I'll know what they are going to do before they do—'

Now she needed no prompting. Now she knew what he wanted. Now she was taking on the role she knew he loved the best.

'And in time they'll respect me for being the authority and discipline they need in their lives, the discipline they never had before I came to them.'

As Knox talked on and on, in front of him Sonya was becoming the childlike figure of the girl he loved the most, the girl he loved to hurt, the girl he loved to smother with love.

'They never had it because their parents didn't discipline them. Because their parents didn't love them . . . and you know, Sonya, I do love them. It's because I love them so much that I have to discipline them. I have to do it. I have no choice. I can't hold back. And they'll love me for it – they'll look on me as a father, Sonya. They'll thank me—'

*

It was nearly daybreak and the first cleaners and messengers were stirring in the great Palace when Selwyn Knox emerged from his fit, a changed man now, his appetites satisfied, his rage calmed. Now he looked with wondering affection on the soft naked form beside him; now he tended her bruised and lacerated flesh with love; now his tears flowed and he opened his innermost thoughts.

'Oh, Sonya,' he whispered tenderly, 'I feel a force swelling inside me, a great power of nature that must see the day.'

The intensity of the physical and emotional high that had enveloped him was pushing Knox to spill the contents of his heart.

'I can't repress it. It's an energy I can't control, an energy for good or for evil – I don't know which. And I'm powerless before it. I welcome it – I fear it – and I know I must be responsible for the impact it makes. The power of my own nature, the strength of this energy within me, sometimes it terrifies me, Sonya. And that's why I need you to stay with me. Alone, I can't control it. That's why I have bound you to me, you and Nigel. You are the only ones who can help me, help me channel the forces within me that are bursting onto the world. You and Nigel understand me; you and he hold the keys to my nature, you and he can shape me, for evil or for good.'

Nigel Tonbridge showed his Government Information and Communication Service pass at the gates of Downing Street and followed the police constable's directions to the fast-track security clearance: it was quicker than the procedure for non-government visitors, but Nigel sometimes regretted not being given the souvenir slippers they could take away with them.

Once inside Number Ten, he turned left to the ground-floor press office and knocked on the door to the panelled antechamber where Charlie McDonald's secretary was sitting typing.

'Oh, hello, Nigel. You can go in straight away: he's expecting you.'

As Nigel entered, McDonald looked up from a file on his desk, smiled and said, 'Sit down. I won't be a minute: I'm just perfecting my *EastEnders* strategy.'

Nigel had no idea what Charlie was talking about, but did as he was told.

A beaming Charlie McDonald, white teeth shining in his rich black face, eventually took off his wristwatch and placed it on the table – a signal that he was taking time out from business matters and honouring Nigel with a conversation friend to friend.

'Well, Nigel, we're all well pleased with you. You've done a great job getting old Selwyn such a good press on this Parenting Licence thing. I have to tell you I was pretty worried when Andy and Sel came up with it, but it seems to be going down a treat. And Andy's grateful, too. I've got a note from him here that he wants me to pass on to you and Selwyn and Sonya and all the team. Now, where is it? Ah, yes; here it is: "I regard the initiatives from the Department for Society as the keystone of our domestic policy. If this government is to be remembered for one thing, I want it to be for the rebirth of a moral society in this country. I believe we will be held to account on this by future generations and by God. My thanks go to all of you who are helping to make this possible." Pretty heavy stuff, eh, Nigel? What do you think of that, then?'

Nigel nodded his appreciation, but he could not suppress the nervous reaction that often overtook him in moments of emotion or stress. Instinctively, his hand reached into his jacket pocket to thumb the pages of the old notebook he constantly carried with him.

His response to Charlie McDonald's question was similarly

unpremeditated. 'I think it's great, Charlie. But are you really sure Selwyn's the right man to be in charge of all this?'

A look of amused enlightenment passed over McDonald's beaming face.

'Ah, so that's it, is it? You're feeling the Knox effect! Not very pleasant, is it? A bit creepy, eh? Well, don't worry about that, mate. Everyone feels the same, but it doesn't make him a bad minister.'

'Well, I'm not saying that. I'm just—'

'I'll let you in on a little secret, one that's really helped me in this job.' Charlie McDonald was in expansive mood and he wanted Nigel to share it.

'Basically, a politician's personality is irrelevant. What matters is his image, and that's something that has to be created by people like you and me. Once we've done that, it can be manipulated quite easily and quite independently of the man himself. And I'll give you a tip. Go and read a book that helps me at times like this. It's called *The Hitler Myth* and it's by a historian called Ian Kershaw. If you don't believe what I've just been saying, you will do once you've read it.'

Nigel's face was evidently expressing such horror at this suggestion that McDonald stopped himself to laugh.

'I'm not comparing anyone to Hitler, you idiot. All I'm saying is the techniques are still valid: you cover over the reality of the politician, the man, with a veneer, an image – something you can create and control. You'll understand if you read the book: Kershaw says the Hitler image, the brand, got stronger and stronger until it was the only thing left that united the regime and the country. No matter how many Germans had doubts about what the Nazis were doing, there was always ninety per cent or more who approved of Hitler, or – rather – of the Hitler image they'd been presented with. Think about it, Nige! It's a pretty powerful tool. We use it with Andy, although we don't talk too much about it, of course. You know, Kershaw says that eventually the image wrapped around the Führer got so solid and so permanent that the man underneath it just shrivelled up until there was only a black hole. There was no real person left – just a shell, a cocoon, a myth. And that's how I think of your guy Knox sometimes, you know. He's allowed himself to become the image we've created for him so completely that his existence as a man has had all the juice sucked out of it! Sometimes I look into his eyes and I'm looking into empty sockets. They've got that blank look, like Himmler's eyes – have you seen them in photos?'

Nigel nodded, acknowledging the aptness of the comparison.

McDonald laughed again. 'You know, Nigel, people say Knox is inscrutable, but I'm telling you there's really just nothing there. He only lives when he's being the mask we made for him. He's not a man like you and me, Nige; he's a black hole! I think he only exists for his politics, for his ambition, for his ruthlessness: he's become the image we created for him and the man underneath has vanished. Sometimes I think he's worn the mask for so long that it's stuck to his skin, and if ever we pulled the mask off everything else would come away with it. There'd be nothing underneath! As far as Selwyn Knox is concerned, I can tell you: the man has not just become the mask, the man has been replaced by the mask! And that's great because it makes him untouchable – an untouchable weapon, Nigel. You can't get to him as a man because there's no man there to get to.'

Nigel Tonbridge trudged down the old Cabinet Office corridor with a heavy heart. He felt as if he'd undergone a Kafka-like transmutation into a modern-day Chicken Lickin from the children's stories he used to read his daughter . . . Chicken Lickin, whom he remembered as the only animal in the farmyard to see that the sun was falling out of the sky and was about to immolate the known world. And everywhere Chicken Lickin turned to raise the alarm she was told to go away and stop being so silly.

As Nigel arrived back at the DfS deep in thought, his secretary lifted her hand and gestured towards his office in a mime of early warning. Inside he was surprised to find Chris Brody and an unknown visitor sitting at his table, evidently awaiting his return. Brody made as if to speak, but was forestalled by the stranger.

'Mr Tonbridge, is it? I'm glad you're back. I've just been having a bit of trouble with your colleague here and I'm rather hoping you can help me.'

Nigel looked at Brody, who shrugged and made a helpless gesture.

The visitor continued. 'As I explained to Mr Brody, I'm from the Home Office, currently attached to the Metropolitan anti-terror unit and homeland security division, and I need a bit of help from you. I have told Mr Brody that I need to see the lists of priority targets for your Good Parenting scheme and your Parenting Licence programmes, but he doesn't seem to want to help me.'

Nigel frowned. 'And why exactly do you need to see our lists?'

'Because *we* have an interest in those sorts of people, too. There must be masses of Arabs and Asians on those lists, masses of asylum seekers who've gone to ground. People who laugh at the idea of carrying an identity card, all those cases that have slipped through our nets and have got caught in yours. And I don't have to tell you why we're interested in those people. The anti-terror programme is the number one priority for all of us now.'

Nigel made an effort to keep an open mind. 'So if we give you these lists, what exactly do you intend to do with them?'

'Basically, we need them for surveillance purposes. We've got to use every lead we can get to track these people down. But don't worry, we won't publicize the fact we're using your data. You'll be safe on that.'

Nigel thought for a moment and looked at Brody, who was pulling a face. He made up his mind. 'No, I'm sorry. I can't agree to your request. For a start, these are confidential files. It would be wrong under the Data Protection Act for me to hand them over. And it'd be immoral for me to do it. We're trying to help these people, not betray their confidence.' The official tried to interject, but Nigel was in full flow. 'There are a lot of vulnerable people on those lists. They've told us a lot about themselves – very personal details – because they thought we were there to help them, not to hand them over to the Special Branch. OK, you might find one or two dodgy cases, but essentially these are innocent, disadvantaged people who need help, not the police on their backs.'

Nigel could see that his arguments were making little impression, so he tried another tack. 'And, anyway, think about the danger it'd put our inspectors in: if it gets around that being on the Good Parenting list means you're under state surveillance, think how our advisers are going to be met when they visit people. They'll be treated with suspicion, with threats, with violence even. Who knows what might happen? No, I'm sorry, these lists are my responsibility and there's no way I can divulge them. You'll have to go back and say the answer's no.'

The visitor looked distinctly unimpressed. 'OK, mate, if that's your attitude. But don't think this'll be the last you hear of this. You lot need to start living in the real world.'

The following morning Nigel was running late. He was due to meet the Secretary of State in the foyer at nine a.m. to leave for the Dead-Beat Dads launch at the old workhouse in Whitechapel, but he had been held up by a morning prayers meeting that refused to die. As he hurriedly gathered up his briefing documents in the press office, he glanced at the morning papers and burst out laughing as he saw the front-page tabloid stories proclaiming that Andy Sheen was intervening on behalf of Wayne Mitchell. Wayne, of course, was Grant's teenage son, who had mysteriously appeared as if from nowhere a few months earlier and whose reputation had now been falsely tarred by association with his father. Wayne had been wrongly imprisoned for a crime he did not commit, and the viewing population was outraged at his fate.

Nigel now realized what Charlie McDonald had been talking about the previous day: in Wayne's arrest, he had spotted an opportunity to demonstrate that the PM was a man of the people, that he shared their concerns, especially about a character in *EastEnders*.

Nigel read the headline on the *Sun*'s story, 'Sheen Says: Don't Visit the Sins of the Fathers on Our Youngsters', and winced at the way it mimicked the rhetoric of his own department.

Even as he admired Charlie McDonald's cheeky wit, Nigel's disquiet increased. What sort of government is this, he thought, that wants to distract us into a fantasy world where Prime Ministers intervene in soap operas? What are they trying to distract us *from*?

He knew his position as a civil servant meant he should not speak out publicly about his minister's malpractice, but no one he talked to about his worries seemed minded to do anything. He felt the familiar beginnings of the depression he was prey to.

He was coming to the conclusion that he must tackle Knox directly, that he should demand an explanation for all the suspicions he was harbouring. He felt McDonald was partly right when he spoke of Knox as a 'black hole', but he feared an even more repulsive reality beneath it. And into this reality Nigel felt he must now peer.

Glenn, the chauffeur, spotted Nigel running down the stairs and motioned to him to get a move on. Selwyn Knox was already in the back of the ministerial Jaguar and the heightened security alert – Amber Special – meant they would have to hurry to make it through the roadblocks to reach Whitechapel by nine forty-five.

The journey passed largely in silence.

The precautions over Alastair Barber and the NCCL had had the desired effect, but Knox was evidently aware that Nigel's reluctance had meant it was Sonya Mair who had carried out the leaks and the warnings.

Knox made no direct reference to this, but Nigel sensed he was annoyed.

In the strained atmosphere in the Jaguar, Nigel had the distinct impression that Knox was silently willing him to broach the subjects that were so much on his mind, to throw down the challenge that Nigel had long been contemplating. But neither man made the first step and the understandings or misunderstandings between them remained unspoken.

The Dead-Beat Dads launch went well.

It had been Knox's own idea to set up the Name and Shame website and he had taken a personal interest in giving the initiative a particularly high profile.

To the strains of 'Love Will Keep Us Together', the DfS's unofficial but popular theme music and a strobe flashing the department's official watchword, 'Respect the fathers and society will respect you', Knox bounded up to the high table of what was once the Whitechapel workhouse's communal refectory.

To the delight of the fifty or so journalists present, he proceeded to give a demonstration of how the site would work.

In a 3-D plasma-ball projected above the audience's heads, he called up at random several of the two million case histories the website contained.

The first few were fairly standard exposés of absent fathers who had failed to keep up with child-support payments, showing their face images, current addresses, bank records, a sentimental life story of the children they had abandoned, and concluding with a section where the children themselves were encouraged to express the pain and resentment they felt over their failure-father's behaviour.

The next example was the official exposé of a man who had got his girlfriend pregnant and then left her for another woman. The blurb included the name and address of the seductress and the fact that the man had infected his child's mother with herpes and gonorrhoea.

When Knox was asked why so many of the case histories he had chosen to show were from ethnic minorities, he smiled smugly and said it just showed how much non-whites were statistically likely to figure as DBDs. Later in his presentation he drew the journalists' attention to the notes at the end of each case history, which revealed those subjects who were HIV positive, drug addicts or criminals with a court record.

Knox took questions and was bringing the press conference to a close when the GBC TV crew asked him to project one final case history to use on the evening news. Knox said he was happy to oblige and hit a button that called up the file on a Mr Alastair Barber.

In the crush of bodies in the corridor after the event, Nigel could see the high regard Knox was held in by the media. Journalists crowding round him to expound their own tales of inadequate fathers and abandoned children were met with unfeigned sympathy and practical advice on how to contribute to the DfS's new Internet database, which would record and excoriate social failings of many different types and categories.

Nigel was already at the exit door and had signalled to Glenn to start the engine, when a reporter he did not recognize asked a casual question about Knox's relationship with his own father. For a fleeting moment Nigel saw hesitation on his boss's face and a flash of consternation in his eyes before Knox replied flatly that his father was dead. The reporter said he was sorry and Knox jumped into the Jaguar.

As they crawled along Upper Thames Street, sitting side by side in the back of the car, Nigel sensed an opening.

'I need to ask you something, Selwyn. Why did you say your father was dead? He isn't, is he? I saw the letters from him that came to you at the department. You chucked them in the bin, didn't you?'

Knox stared straight ahead. His stillness suggested he was expecting the question, had been preparing himself for it. He did not turn his head, but Nigel noted a tremor in his jaw.

'No, Nigel, he's not dead, at least not in the sense you mean it. He's alive somewhere – alive for someone, I suppose. But for me he's dead.'

Nigel saw a moistness in Knox's eye, and then his conscious effort to draw back from the intimacy that had suddenly opened between them. 'And, ah, if you get any more media enquiries about my family – about anything in my private life – I would be grateful if you could make clear that it is completely off-limits: tell them it's off-limits and then tell me who's been asking. All right?'

Nigel thought for a moment. A catharsis was beginning to shape itself and he could either provoke it or withdraw.

'Yes, of course I'll tell them. But with the work you're doing, the family measures and all that involves, don't you think the media might see your private life as fair game? And if they do, don't you think I should know about anything in it that could cause us a problem? Is there anything you need to tell me, Selwyn, anything you want to tell me?'

The atmosphere was charged. Both men felt the conversation was leading them onward towards subjects they feared, but somehow felt compelled to address.

When Knox turned to Nigel, his eyes were wet with tears. 'Sonya has been talking to me, Nigel. You asked her why I got you to come and work with me, didn't you? Why I sought you out after what happened in Exxington? I'm not quite sure myself. We're from the same part of the world, aren't we, so we understand each other in that sense. But perhaps we understand each other in a different way, too? There are things from the past I share with you that I don't share with any other living being. We have common memories – do we also have a common understanding of what matters in our lives? Sometimes I think we are both bearing burdens – the weight of the past. Perhaps we also feel the weight of the present and the burden of what might come in the future.'

Nigel knew they were getting close to something important. He knew he must push Knox to explain. 'How do you mean, the burden of the future?'

'I feel a great power within me, Nigel. But it's an ambiguous power. And bearing the responsibility for it is a great burden. If I can't control it, it could be a terrifying destructive force. I don't know if I'm capable of controlling it and that's why I have bound you and Sonya to me. I feel that you have the power to release me from the burden I bear; you alone have that power – I don't have it – Sonya may, but she doesn't know it. And in the same way, maybe I have the power to release you from the burden you are bearing.'

Nigel looked at Knox and half-understood the meaning of his words. He had a troubling sense that Knox was trying to confess something, to relieve himself of a weight that oppressed him, or perhaps prompting Nigel to relieve him of it.

He knew he hated much about Knox and what he stood for, but now he was less certain that Knox was responsible for the death of the girl on the mountain, less certain that the burden oppressing him was the burden from Exxington in 2006. Nigel felt a flush of relief that he had not gone public with his suspicions about Knox; a brief pang of solidarity with the man.

Nigel heard himself talking about his own parents. About his father who endured excruciating pain during the two years he had suffered from motor neurone disease. About his agonized discussions with his mother. About their eventual decision to help his father. About the dose of morphine. About the death that followed mercifully and peacefully.

'That's how it happened, Selwyn. I've never told anyone. Not even Joanie. But somehow you knew about it back there in Exxington, and you used it to scare me. We both have power over each other, don't we, Selwyn? But if one of us pulls the trigger, I think we both die.'

13

NIGEL'S SUMMONSES to the Secretary of State usually came in the form of a phone call or an email from one of the civil servants in his private office.

This time Sonya Mair rang.

Normally their meetings were attended by Knox's Private Secretary, who kept a formal record of the discussion.

This time Nigel found himself alone with Knox and Mair.

It did not take him long to understand the reason why.

Knox's manner was brisk and impersonal; he was no longer the hesitant, confiding man who had opened his heart the previous week in the back of the Jaguar.

'Right, Nigel, Sonya and I have been talking. We can both understand why you had your doubts about handing over the Good Parenting lists to the homeland security people. You were right to point out the difficulties. But now I'm telling you the anti-terror measures must be our absolute priority and they have to take precedence.'

Nigel could tell Knox was set on re-establishing his authority, so he sought to step back from confrontation.

'Of course, Selwyn. Of course that's right. But I'm just trying to be practical. If we hand over the lists, we'll compromise the whole PL programme: think how clients are going to react to our advisers if they know they're working for the police – they'll stop cooperating with us, there'll be a backlash and the counsellors will become targets for violence—'

But Knox was in no mood for reason.

'I'm sorry, Nigel, get real. These counsellors aren't Samaritans. They're already collecting information for me. We're using them to fight drug-dealers, shirkers and benefit fraud; and don't tell me you didn't know. All this means is they'll also be helping wipe out the terrorists and infiltrators. I can't see the problem.'

In the face of this intransigence, Nigel's own reasonableness began to waver.

'Well, the problem is when we get one of our counsellors attacked and killed—'

Knox was losing patience.

'Look, the PM wants this and we're going to give it to him. Sometimes people have to suffer. So we may lose a few counsellors, but what's the problem if that helps save the country from terrorists? We don't want a repeat of the ricin poisoning or the tube bombings, do we?'

'Of course not—'

'So think about it. Let's say we don't give them the lists. We stand on our principles: we protect the privacy of the single mums, the scroungers and the addicts and, yes, we save a few of our people. But then what? The terrorists launch another attack, we get another two thousand deaths – and then we find the bastards who did it were staying at the house of an Arab couple on our lists. They were in our sights and we let them go. So another two thousand decent British people are dead and we're to blame. How do you feel about that?'

Nigel was starting to feel in danger of losing it.

'Don't patronize me, Sel. I know what the issues are. But giving them our lists isn't going to stop the terrorists. And you can't trample on people's civil rights just because it might stop something worse happening.'

Knox was entering his grim, calm mode, fixing Nigel with his stare, making it clear he was ready to crush Nigel once he'd finished his little speech.

Nigel ploughed on. 'Look, Selwyn, of course you might stop the terrorists if you turn the whole country into a police state, if you take away every human right, every freedom. But what's the end that justifies those means? We'll have turned ourselves into tyrants. We'll have become the intolerant, bigoted despots we accuse the fundamentalists of being. OK, we might stop a terrorist bombing; we might protect society from physical violence. But what sort of society would we be preserving? A shackled, cowering society of slaves ruled by bullying potentates sitting in fortified offices in Westminster completely removed from reality? Removed from contact with, or sympathy for the people they say they're protecting?'

Now they were glaring at each other, now neither would give way.

They had threatened each other, now they would have to see it through.

Knox's eyes had the emptiness of a gambler's, a poker player staking his future on the outcome of one hand. The blank indifference, the disdain on his face, were calling Nigel, demanding to see his cards.

He was unblinkingly, terrifyingly calm and Nigel could not match him.

Nigel fingered the notebook in his pocket, hesitated and walked out.

An hour later, Sonya Mair was in Nigel's office, her back against his door, a silent reminder he was trapped.

'And this time, Nigel, you do it. No running off to Nottridge, no squealing, no wriggling. This time Selwyn's going to push the button.'

'What does that mean?'

'It means if you don't do it you're dead meat. He's got a written record of your machinations to rig the civil service selection board and it'll be on its way to Dave Sopwith at the *Chronicle*. You'll be out on your backside. And what a shame that would be for you and for Mrs Tonbridge and the kids. Who'd be paying the fees at that little public school you've got them into? And the two hundred thousand mortgage on that nice Victorian house in Battersea? I don't think Joanie would be too pleased—'

Nigel hesitated and Mair saw it.

'Come on, Nigel. Don't make a fuss. It's not worth it. You're not going to go public and make a big show of principle over this. Downing Street would crucify you. You wouldn't get any sympathy. And, anyway, think what we're asking you. You know we have to fight the terrorists. We're talking about people's lives now, not just some little smear campaign. Handing over the lists would be an act of public service. OK, you'd put a few counsellors at risk, but you'd be protecting society. You don't have to feel bad about it, you'd be doing the right thing – and you'd be saving yourself and your family a nasty bit of bother.'

'Look, Sonya, I'll have to think about it. And if I do give you the lists, it needs to be in confidence – between you, me and Selwyn.'

Sonya smiled.

'That's the stuff, Nige. I knew you'd make the right decision. Come on board with us: help save society. You know it makes sense.'

'I said I'll think about it.'

'OK. But don't think too long. I need the disks in my office this afternoon.'

That afternoon, in Sonya's office, Nigel was looking for something in return, some explanation of the world he felt he was slowly being sucked into.

'I think you know what I need, Sonya. I need to know what Knox expects from me, what he wants me to do. You know everything that goes on in the man's mind, the same way he and I recognize each other's thoughts. So what is it that's bound us into this triangle? And who's pulling the strings? Is it you? Or Knox? Who holds the cards?'

'I don't know what you mean, Nigel—'

'I think you do. I think you and he both know I've got one card – and it's a big one. I don't know if I can ever play it. But the strange thing is I sometimes get the impression he actually wants me to: do you feel that? He hides nothing from me because he wants me to see his secrets. He wants me to see his ruthlessness, his conflicts and his pain. And he wants me to *judge* him. He's showing me the contradictions and darkness inside him because he wants me to be his *judge* – is he trying to goad me into blowing the whistle, Sonya? Does he *want* me to expose him?'

'You understand some things, Nigel. But not everything. Selwyn's a good man. He has ideals and great plans. He's inspired by noble motives. And he's a Christian. He believes society can be brought back from the moral death it's sunk into. He believes people can be redeemed; he believes in salvation.'

'And what about himself? Does he believe *he* can be redeemed?'

'All I can tell you, Nigel, is that when he and I are together, he asks me to read to him from the gospel, and when I read the story of Lazarus, he cries.'

Nigel recognized in Sonya's words the need he knew Knox was feeling, the need to explain and excuse, to reveal the truth about himself and be held in the balance.

'That's it, Sonya. Selwyn wants us to be his judges. I tried and failed to judge him five years ago in Exxington. Now he wants us to complete that process. But he's asking us to do the impossible. I don't know if the devil can be judged. Can the devil be pardoned? Can he be redeemed?'

Nigel left, not knowing whether Sonya really believed what she had told him.

Could she really think Knox was a force for goodness and purity? Or was she spinning the usual cynical lies? And if she knew Knox was evil, why did she stay with him? Was she addicted to the man? To the power he wielded and she shared? Or was she too scared to leave him? His thoughts about Sonya, about her intentions towards him, remained ambivalent. Nothing was resolved.

The *Mail on Sunday* dropped through Nigel's letterbox with a thump. Usually it woke the household, provoking angry barking from the dog and howls of protest from the children, but today the kids slept on.

Over breakfast, Nigel and Joanie flicked through the sections one by one. Nigel was immersed in the arts coverage, trying vainly to take his mind off the stress that had followed him home from the department. Joanie had the news section and was reading out extracts from a follow-up article on Marie Sheen's miscarriage. She had skipped the front-page story on the Internet paedophile investigations: so many similar tales had been doing the rounds in recent months that today Joanie hadn't bothered to read past the first paragraph.

When Nigel eventually got the news section, his eye alighted on a line that grabbed his attention. 'Among the twelve thousand names included on the credit-card lists confiscated from the Meet-a-Babe Agency of Bethnal Green, police sources say they have found several leading businessmen, actors, barristers, MPs and a serving government minister.'

He gestured to Joanie and began to read aloud. 'The sources, who have seen the confiscated lists, have not revealed the identity of those involved and a police investigation is currently under way. They caution that some of the names used by clients of the agency, which allegedly supplied both paedophile pornography and access to under-age child prostitutes, are clearly false. But the vast majority of customers using the services of Meet-a-Babe did not bother to disguise their identity, in the mistaken belief that their credit-card details would remain confidential—'

Joanie looked at Nigel and grimaced. 'I can guess who some of the MPs are, can't you? And I bet the minister is old Trautberg: he's always given me the creeps.'

The following morning, Selwyn Knox was in Charlie McDonald's study in Downing Street. The conversation had been strained and Knox was starting to lose patience.

'Charlie, I told you I only used the agency for research purposes. We're doing a lot of work around child abuse for the Good Parenting programme and I needed to see some of the things these paedophiles get up to. It was for official business—'

'Right, so you registered what you were doing with the Data Authority before you started logging on, did you?'

'I told you, Charlie. I didn't do that because I'm a cabinet minister. I shouldn't need to have to do that—'

'And you used official departmental credit lines to pay the site fees?'

'No. I've explained all this. I used my own credit card because it was more convenient.'

'And how many transactions do the lists confiscated from the agency show you've run up?'

'Well, quite a few, obviously. This is a long-term project—'

'Look, I want to help you, Selwyn. But you're not making it easy. You know as well as I do that your record with these Meet-a-Babe people dates back to before you ever went to the Department for Society.'

'Charlie, I want you to think carefully about this. You know how much store Andy sets by what I'm doing at the DfS. You know how much he values me. I know Andy will want to protect my good name and protect the department.'

'Yeah, sure, Selwyn, but—'

'Wait till I've finished, Charlie. You need to think this through. Andy will expect you to do that. Now, the *Mail on Sunday* haven't seen the actual lists. They were tipped off by some low-grade twerp at the Met, and the police have taken him out and dealt with him. The lists are safe now; there aren't going to be any more leaks. So that's the first thing. The second thing is the Trautberg factor. You know as well as I do that people have thought for years that Trautberg's a pervert. The press would have written the story ages ago if they hadn't been scared of what you guys would say. So when people read the story yesterday, everybody, but everybody, assumed it was him.'

'Yeah; you're right there, Sel. Melanie fingered him straight away—'

'See what I mean? So let's think, Charlie: what's the silver lining in all this? Trautberg's an Old Project dinosaur. The last of them. Andy's been wanting to get him out of the cabinet and out of his hair for years. He hasn't done it because the Old Left have backed Trautberg. But do you think they'd still back him if the media were fingering him for this Meet-a-Babe story? It's a gift, Charlie. Andy needs to take it – for his own good.'

Down the hall from McDonald's study Andy Sheen was enjoying a cappuccino with a prawn sandwich as he ran through the sit-reps from the government delivery departments.

He'd seemed rather gloomy in recent weeks, so his secretary was pleased to hear him chuckling.

She didn't know the cause of his good humour, but Andy Sheen had just read the report from the Department of Commerce detailing the filing DRE was about to make to declare itself officially bankrupt. The report writer traced the DRE management's travails from the time they'd used the billions of pounds from the sale of their defence business to buy a string of bio-engineering and human-cloning firms in the USA. Two months later their biggest purchase, HumanBioTech Solutions of Lincoln, Nebraska, had been shown to be the brainchild of tricksters, based on technology that was little more than a fake and accounting practices riddled with scams.

The US regulatory authorities had shut them down, with a disastrous impact on the new DRE. Lord Willans and Tim Stilwell were being sued by thousands of investors and were personally bankrupt.

As a side-bar on the story, the government analyst who'd compiled the D of C report had added a note about Jim McGee of the *Daily Mirror*. 'This financial journalist,' said the report, 'was the newspaper's specialist on DRE. He personally sold thousands of shares before writing the front-page story which ignited the adverse speculation about DRE's fortunes and sparked the disastrous share-price collapse. As in previous instances, insider trading by Mr McGee is suspected but not proven.'

*

Andy Sheen was still chuckling when Charlie McDonald threw open his door and lurched up to his desk in a foul mood.

'Andy, we've got trouble with Selwyn. He's in my office now and he wants me to ask you something.'

For Selwyn Knox, left to pace the boards in Charlie McDonald's office, the waiting was agony. His thoughts flitted wildly from the personal friendship Andy Sheen had always shown him – they were both Christians and both believers in the moral imperative to improve mankind – to the catastrophic incongruity of the offences now stacked against his name.

One moment he found himself hoping and believing that Andy's personal goodness and the affection he had for his Minister for Society would persuade him to take the Trautberg route; the next he was in a gut-churning turmoil of despair, foreseeing his own political death and personal disgrace. How could the good name of a reforming minister, he kept asking himself, be squared with public whispers, with insinuations of immorality and worse?

As the minutes stuttered onwards and McDonald's desk clock ticked off half an hour, then three-quarters, then a full hour, Knox began to understand his fate was sealed: if Andy were going to save him, he would have come by now to embrace his errant minister, to absolve him of blame and pardon his trespasses.

But Andy Sheen did not come.

Charlie McDonald came back alone and Selwyn Knox knew his chance of salvation had gone.

'I'm really sorry, Sel' – Knox noted that McDonald's face showed no signs of being sorry – 'but Andy says it's no dice: we're going to have to let you go.'

McDonald talked; Knox heard him without taking it in; his thoughts were in meltdown.

'There's no way we could keep the story quiet in the long run,

Selwyn. Trautberg would kick up a fuss; people would find out it was you; it'd do incalculable damage to our moral revival campaign. I'm really sorry, but you just can't expect to stay on as Minister for Society with such a sword hanging over you.'

Knox began to sense that McDonald had stitched him up to the PM.

'It didn't matter when no one knew what you were up to, Sel – when it was all a secret. But it's a different matter now it's in danger of getting out.'

Knox made a last attempt to save himself, to postpone the judgement that was about to strike him down.

'OK, Charlie. Look. Let's forget the Trautberg thing completely. But why can't you just tell the police to wipe my name off the lists, destroy the credit-card records and drop the investigation? I'll chuck the laptop in the Thames. It wouldn't hurt anyone, Charlie, and it'd save the DfS's reputation – it'd allow us to carry on with the work we're doing for Andy and for the party.'

'Selwyn, I hear what you're saying, believe me. It's not going to be easy announcing what's happened to you. It'll hurt the department. But it'll lance the boil. Andy just can't take the risk of being seen to protect a paedophile. Andy loves you, but you've got to appreciate the party has to be absolutely ruthless in defending its own long-term interests. The cause we're pursuing is too important and individuals have to be sacrificed if they get in the way.'

Nigel Tonbridge had been due to see the Secretary of State at eleven.

At ten to, the Diary Secretary rang from Private Office to tell him that Knox still wasn't back from Downing Street so he'd have to wait on standby.

Nigel asked her the reason for the hold-up, and she said they were as puzzled as he was: all they knew was that the SoS was in a one-to-one with Charlie McDonald. His earlier meetings had already had to be rescheduled.

Nigel shrugged and went back to the search he had been carrying out on his personal 3DVD.

After years using the same machine, he had been amazed to find that he had accumulated over two thousand Sound'n'Vision files and he'd finally decided it was time to start weeding them out. The only trouble was that each SnV file he examined seemed to hold memories strong enough to make him want to view it before electing to keep or delete. He had viewed SnVs of old press conferences he had attended, interviews he had carried out as a journalist and even the planning meetings he had been to in the early part of his government career.

Mixed in with the official files were sequences from his private life, mainly of the kids at birthday parties, school plays and sports competitions, but also of himself and Joanie when they had wanted to make an e-record of moments that had seemed important at the time, but which now had the inconsequential charm of forgotten voices chattering from the past.

All of them had sparked recollections that kept him occupied throughout the morning and made him neglect his departmental updates and the messages accumulating in his 3-D e-tray.

The SnVs of his late father were particularly poignant.

In the 3-D plasma ball he was projecting over his desk, Nigel watched the frail old man walk towards him as if he were about to walk out of the screen and back into his son's life. He heard his father's voice as he had always remembered it, telling him of episodes from his own youth – swimming in the Thames, returning from Korea, visiting Scotland on holiday, meeting Nigel's mother – all stories Nigel had heard him recount in life.

His phone rang and it was the Diary Secretary again, saying

the SoS was back but had gone into a private meeting with Sonya Mair.

He had asked for all his appointments to be cancelled. Nigel could stand down.

Sonya had never seen her boss so agitated as when he came back from Downing Street that morning.

She watched his distress.

She listened to him in silence.

She thought of the consequences for Knox, for herself, for the party, for society.

She told him she could save him. She told him what he must do.

Nigel opened the SnVs of himself and his mother discussing endlessly the cruel illness that had struck his father and how best they could help him. His mother's distress seemed even more stark than he remembered it in life. He was thankful the files ended a day or so before mother and son had carried out the decision they both knew was right, but both had buried deep in the dark corners of their psyches which they now tried never to visit. Nigel pressed the Delete-All button and watched the SnVs disappear into the void.

Knox rang Charlie McDonald to say he needed to see him again.

He was running down the corridor gripped by a nervous exultation he had not known since walking out to face the cameras five years earlier – at a house in Exxington.

Knox was hyperventilating; he told McDonald he knew about the drugs.

His chest was tight; he knew about Harvey Parks.

He gulped for air; Sonya had told him everything.

His hands were chill, his vision blurring; he knew Sonya had been made to kill the story.

Little blows of nausea were hitting him in the back of the neck; he really thought McDonald should talk again to Andy Sheen.

Cold, clammy sweat was forming on his palms; he really thought McDonald should do it right away – now!

This time, Charlie McDonald returned within minutes.

Knox spun round to face him.

McDonald looked at the floor. 'You can go and see Andy now, Selwyn. He says it's all right for you to come to him. You're saved.'

As Knox left the room, Charlie McDonald's secretary ran in with a live telephone, indicating urgently that he'd better take the call.

It was the Home Secretary, Jimmy Kelso.

McDonald listened; his face darkened; his frown grew deeper.

After five minutes of Kelso's whining explanations, McDonald snapped.

The information officers in the adjoining room heard his voice rise menacingly above the hubbub of the press office.

'You keep your pecker in your pocket, you randy goat! You ditch your tart and you stay married – or you can wave goodbye to your cabinet job, mate!'

On the other end of the line, Jimmy Kelso listened in flabbergasted silence.

14

Things were getting difficult in Downing Street.

Andy Sheen was slow to chide. He was quick to bless. But the close shave over Harvey Parks's drugs stories and the pressure of Selwyn Knox's transgressions had seriously displeased him. He had let it be known that vengeance would be his; those close to him were waiting for payback time.

Charlie McDonald had stored away his usual insurance against any fallout that might come in his direction. He felt safe personally, but there was a growing feeling that backs were to the wall in Number Ten. In recent months the joshing and joking had become strained. Now they had the air of febrile whistling in a darkened world, awaiting the impact of an onrushing asteroid.

Charlie and Geoff Maddle were doing their best to keep smiling. With the benefit of retrospect, McDonald's retelling of events had even taken on a patina of humour.

'Poor old Kelso had no idea what had hit him,' he would tell Geoff. 'I was over the top, of course, but don't forget I'd just come back from dealing with the pervy vicar and I can tell you I was raging, mate. I cleared it with Andy, though: he's got no time for ministers screwing their secretaries, never mind wanting to marry them! Ever since Kelso's been meek as a lamb – just caved in, basically. You know, it reminds me of Goebbels in 1938 – he wanted to leave his wife to go off with a Czech actress, but Hitler vetoed it on the grounds of "moral responsibility". Ha! Moral responsibility, there's a laugh. Course, poor Magda Goebbels would've been better off if he *had* buggered off: she ended up swallowing poison with him and their six kids and Adolf in the bunker.'

Now Charlie McDonald's laugh was loud and grim.

Nigel Tonbridge, too, had tried to come to terms with the way things were. Unlike Charlie McDonald, though, he was finding it hard to see the funny side.

Nigel had noticed Selwyn Knox's affection for him had become more demonstrative since he had agreed to hand over the Parenting lists. It seemed that the homeland security people had been using information from the DfS's counsellors to good effect and several arrests had apparently been made.

Knox himself seemed on the crest of a wave.

After some administrative problems in the first few months of its existence, his Parenting Licence had been deemed a success and the figures looked good. Official statistics showed a healthy majority of new births were now occurring to parents who had taken and passed the PL short course, designed for couples in the later stages of pregnancy, or had taken the full licence retrospectively. And increasing numbers of prospective parents were now signing up for training in advance of conception.

Talk in the department that Selwyn Knox might have been the minister implicated in the Internet child pornography investigations had quickly died away. On instructions from Downing Street, the police had refused to rule out Frederick Trautberg's name from their enquiries and his guilt was universally assumed.

Knox himself was now invited to attend weekly meetings with Andrew Sheen and Charlie McDonald, an apparent sign of prime ministerial blessing that other ministers regarded with unconcealed envy.

But Nigel's relationship with his boss had grown complex.

For both men it now encompassed hatred, fear and suspicion, with an undertone of complicity and mutual dependence. Nigel continued to sense that Knox expected something from him and was offering him the veiled promise of something in return.

As Christmas approached, Nigel was seized by the nagging conviction that something had to give. He felt increasing pressure to resolve the unarticulated stand-off with Knox and made up his mind to have it out with him.

The DfS's 2011 Christmas party was a difficult affair.

Half the department, the true believers, had come in a mood of genuine festive joy, determined to celebrate the successes of the PL and the social experiments they had helped to mastermind. The other half were the weaklings and the cynics: officials like Robert Nottridge, who went along with Knox for reasons of civil service loyalty or personal self-interest, or like Christopher Brody, who feared and despised Knox's policies but kept quiet for their own unspoken reasons.

Both factions were well represented in the department's conference room for after-work drinks – Moldovan beer and the cheap Ukrainian wine that had flooded London since the former Soviet republics joined the EU – and afterwards at the Crown and Unicorn, where the more energetic continued the festivities or the sorrow-drowning.

Knox had not appeared at either venue, but his representative on earth, as Brody liked to call her, was conspicuous by her very attentive, listening presence.

Only towards the end of the evening did Nigel realize he had been drinking steadily and that he was now in a surprisingly jovial mood. Without being exactly drunk, he had reached a state of mind in which the world was beginning to appear manageable and his colleagues in the bar seemed just the sort of people he wanted to share his most intimate moments with.

As closing time approached and the party-goers disappeared out of the door, Nigel found himself sitting alone in a dark corner of the bar.

He was vaguely steeling himself for the cold tube journey home when he sensed a presence – a whiff of perfume, a rustle of silk, perhaps – on the bench seat next to him. Nigel had not noticed Sonya Mair for the latter part of the evening, but she was here now and she had evidently been waiting to talk to him alone.

'Are you all right, Nigel? How are things?'

Nigel might be the worse for beer, but the feel of Sonya's hand caressing his arm was enough to ring alarm bells.

'Fine thanks, Sonya. Yourself?'

'Mmm. All right, I suppose. Were you talking to anyone interesting tonight?'

Nigel's suspicions grew: interrogation by Sonya Mair under these circumstances was not a prospect he relished. 'No, not really. Just the usual suspects—'

'Did you talk to Selwyn at all?'

'No, I didn't see him all evening. Was he here?'

'I meant on the telephone. He's away. Gone off to Ruth. He's spending Christmas with her up in Scotland.'

Nigel noted the regret in Sonya's voice, but had enough presence of mind to avoid sympathy. 'Well, everyone seems to have called it a day. I suppose we'd better be heading off ourselves, don't you think?'

Sonya looked at him thoughtfully.

In less than a nanosecond, the perceptions vouchsafed only to the very drunk flashed through his mind in a series of bewildering illuminations: 'Sonya Mair is Knox's mistress,' he thought. 'Of course she is – that's why she's jealous of Ruth. She's missing him this weekend. She's coming on to me—'

Nigel's consternation at what he had caught himself thinking, coupled with the alarming thought that Sonya could probably read his mind, left him barely able to take in what she was saying.

'Don't go just yet, Nigel. I need to talk to you. Can you stay a bit longer?'

From the front door, Chris Brody, wrapped in scarf and woolly hat, waved a cheery goodbye in their direction and shouted something vaguely scabrous. Realizing Sonya's hand was still on his arm, Nigel waved sheepishly as Brody winked and departed.

'Well, I don't know, Sonya. I should be getting home. Shouldn't you—?'

Sonya's reply was suddenly earnest; the flirting at least momentarily gone. 'I should, but I don't want to. I can't face it at the moment, Nigel. Would you stay and talk to me? Please?'

Nigel mumbled something about the pub closing and getting thrown out on the street, but he was wavering.

'Look, you don't have to if you don't want to. I know you're probably thinking: what the hell is she up to? Well, I'm not up to anything. I've had a bit to drink; you've had a bit to drink. I just thought we could talk to each other for once, instead of trying to scare each other off—'

Her voice wavered. 'Actually, Nigel, I don't know who I can turn to if you won't—'

Even in his tipsy state, Nigel marvelled at Sonya. Either her appeal to him was genuine, or she was a mistress of the dissembler's art. Either way, he thought, she was a very attractive woman.

'All right, Sonya, it's all right. But where can we go? We can't stay here.'

'Don't worry about that. I've got somewhere we can go. And I've got something I need to show you.'

Unsteadily, they rose to their feet; unsteadily, they walked out onto the pavement. As they climbed into the back of a taxi, Sonya called to the driver, 'Dolphin Square, please. We're going to Dolphin Square.'

Christopher Brody got home after midnight.

The house was quiet and he went straight to the small study on the mezzanine between the first and second floors.

The image of Nigel with Sonya Mair's hand on his arm had stayed with Brody throughout his train journey, on his walk from the station, and was there still as he sat and watched the computer screen flicker into life.

Brody hit the keyboard and began to type. It was something he felt he had to do. He addressed the memo to Nigel Tonbridge.

Selwyn Knox and Ruth Leeming had finished their dinner and were sitting in front of the TV. Ruth had been looking forward to seeing him. He managed to get up to Scotland so rarely these days. Now he was here, though, he seemed distant and uninterested. She caught him looking away distractedly as she spoke. When she asked what was wrong, he snapped at her. The man she had lived with and called her partner was here at her side, but Ruth could see his thoughts were not with her. His eyes were cold as he told her things were getting complicated in London and he might not be able to stay for Christmas after all.

Brody hit the Send button and the memo winged its way through ethernet cables, through routers and switchers, wired and wireless message paths, girdling half the globe before plopping virtually into Nigel's unmanned, unscanned 3-D e-tray.

From: Christopher Brody, Dir. of Policy
To: Nigel Tonbridge, Dir. of Comms
Sent: 17 December 2011
Subject: SoS; Polit.Adv; contradictions

Dear Nigel,

I reflect on the beliefs which unite and define the monoliths of recent political thought.

I observe that the great enlightenment currents of the last hundred years have been predicated on the innate perfectibility of man.

Communism, Nazism, Maoism have preached that man can be saved.

But that premise has been the greatest instrument of human self-destruction ever invented.

Germany, the USSR, Eastern Europe, Cambodia.

Where politicians believe – or claim to believe – humankind can be perfected, they tend not to falter even at the gates of the concentration camp.

Knox is drawn to this line of reasoning, as is Sheen.

The humanist enlightenment has become an orthodoxy for many, a fanaticism for some.

These latter have seized on the death of God to replace His unshakeable truths with their own.

And their self-belief gives them the right to use every means to impose their utopias.

It gives them the right to despise the people in whose name their utopia is pursued.

They identify with the downtrodden, in whose name they claim to speak, but despise them at the same time.

And here is the flaw.

In their comfortable, self-righteous world, they feel a slight but constant ache.

An ache that nags and cannot be excised; a tremor that shakes the ground beneath them.

If visions of human goodness fuel their fanaticism, knowledge of the worm in the apple serves as an uncomfortable brake on their plans.

Knox claims to believe in human goodness, but when he looks within himself he sees something different.

He sees in himself the innate fault in man; the original sin that invalidates his politics.

He is committed to his party's brand of utopianism, but he himself bears the mark of Cain.

If he himself is proof of original sin, how can he believe in the perfectibility of man?

He cannot reconcile the two: he is trying to accelerate and brake at the same time.

He cannot resolve the contradiction and it has worn him out.

Knox is a sinner; humankind is sinful. So the question he asks himself is: can Knox be saved? Can the devil be redeemed?

And if the devil is pardoned, what is his place in the new utopia?

Knox understands the conflict between perfectibility and sin, between certainty and doubt.

For an intelligent man in a position of power, this has become a struggle between self-justification and self-hatred.

Vindication through unthinking fanaticism has become his only chance to avenge his own pain.

And it makes him dangerous.

The purpose of this memo is to warn you of this danger.

It is a systemic political danger, but also a personal danger to you, Nigel.

So where I began with the political, I finish with the personal.

By the time you read this memo, you will have formed your own views of Sonya Mair. Tonight I saw you in circumstances that caused me some concern.

What is my conclusion?

The doctrine of unlimited human perfection is the instrument of unlimited self-immolation.

The only antidote, as Kant says, is unlimited respect for the sacred core of the individual. My conclusion is that you should not lose sight of this, Nigel.

I hope you find this helpful.

Christopher Brody

Nigel had little recollection of the taxi ride through Parliament Square, along Millbank, past Tate Britain.

He heard Sonya talk, but he barely responded.

It was her hand on his arm that monopolized his attention; he could not decide whether it was the hand of friendship, the hand of supplication, or the hand of the jailer leading him forcefully to his fate.

The taxi drew into the courtyard and Sonya took control. She paid the fare; she led him into the foyer. She drew him into the lift; she unlocked the door of the third-floor apartment.

In the living room, he saw the photos and mementos; he had already guessed whose flat this was.

Sonya put her arms round his neck and kissed him.

The kiss was tender, almost chaste. Nigel could not discern its meaning.

Sonya moulded herself to him. He felt her body warm against his.

She flowed into his embrace. He could feel the beating of her heart.

Nigel waited. Waited for Sonya to take the lead.

He both desired her and feared her.

Sonya spoke. 'Nigel, I need to tell you something, show you something. Come through here.'

In the bedroom, Sonya opened a wardrobe and Nigel saw Selwyn Knox's sharp, elegant suits. Sonya bent to open the clothes drawer and Nigel saw the crumpled school uniform of an adolescent girl, saw the piles of photographs, the magazines, the downloaded images of children.

His face expressed his horror.

Sonya seized his hand and began to cry. 'I'm lonely, Nigel. He's the one—. There's no warmth in his world. I just needed some warmth.'

Nigel remembered the *Mail on Sunday*'s story; he remembered the government's tacit fingering of Fred Trautberg as the paedophile minister and he was seized with revulsion. Revulsion at the culture of lies that now ruled the government, at Selwyn Knox and at the life that Sonya had let herself be drawn into.

It seemed Sonya had read his thoughts. She began to plead for his indulgence. 'Nigel, don't look at me like that. Please don't blame me, Nigel. He's the one. I'm cut off from human warmth. There's no warmth in his world.'

But months of dealing with a different Sonya Mair, with a hard, scheming, dangerous Sonya, had left Nigel wary. 'Why don't you go back to your husband, Sonya? Go back to Thomas.'

'It's too late for that, Nigel. Selwyn's a hard master. He demands devotion. He's needed me all for himself – and now I've lost everything, cut myself off from everything and everyone.'

'But why did you do it? What reason—?'

'You know Selwyn. You know how strong he is. He has such massive energy welling inside him, bursting, exploding. And he needs me – it's partly a sexual thing – I think you've guessed that—'

'But what sort of sex, Sonya? What do you call all this—?'

He gestured at the child's clothing and photographs on the floor.

'It's something I can't explain. It's horrifying, but it's fascinating at the same time. It's to do with sex, but it's about power as well. Don't judge me. You know the power Selwyn offers us – the importance, the significance; He says the power we wield gives a meaning to life.'

'And are you happy with that? Are you content to be part of that?'

'Yes … perhaps … I don't know. Selwyn says power is lonely and I believe him. He has no other life, no other meaning. If his politics fail, then he fails and there's no right of appeal. They're like a sect of fanatical believers – Selwyn, McDonald, Maddle, Sheen – and I've let myself become part of it. It's exciting, it's arousing, but in the end it's deadly. There's an emptiness at the heart of their power, a lack of values, a lack of substance. Selwyn knows that and he suffers. But he wants to draw others into his loneliness. He's in a deep well of loneliness, Nigel, and he's trying to pull me – and probably you – into it, too. He's pulling us in to alleviate his pain, but he's pulling us in to drown with him.'

Sonya collected herself and sighed. She looked at Nigel. 'But you, I suppose you should go back to your life, back to Joanie. Don't make the same mistake as me – I haven't resisted him, but maybe you can. I see you fight against his pull and I want to see if maybe I can scramble back up out of the well, too.

'But how? We need to save ourselves from his power and we need to save others from it.'

Listening to Sonya, Nigel realized that his decision was made. He knew now that he must go back up to Exxington; back to find the truth about Selwyn Knox. Again, she read his thoughts. Again, she smiled sadly.

'I want to leave him, you know. I've had enough of his power and his exploitation. But I'm worried how he'll take it—'

'Do you mean violence, Sonya? Are you worried about what he'll do to you?'

'No, Nigel, it's him. I'm worried he won't be able to live without me.'

Nigel woke with a sore head and cursed the Lord Iveagh.

As he raised himself gingerly on his elbow, a brief sensation of dizziness sent him falling deeply, endlessly back into his pillow.

He shook himself to find his balance; looked around him.

It was a moment before he knew where he was.

The clock said ten a.m. He was alone in his bedroom at home.

By the side of the bed he reached for the telephone and rang Sonya Mair's mobile number.

'Sonya – Sonya, is that you? Are you all right? You're still there, aren't you? Still at Knox's? Yes, I think I'm OK. I'm at home. I've no idea how I got here. Joanie's gone out to work already and the kids are at school. Listen, I wasn't joking when I said I was going up to Exxington. I need to find out the truth about what happened there. You want me to do it as well, don't you? I'll make the calls today. We're going up to my mother's for Christmas next week. I'll see what I can find out while I'm there. But don't you do anything precipitate, Sonya. Don't tell him you're leaving him. Wait at least until I get back. I don't want anything to happen to you—'

For the first time in five years Nigel opened the notebook that had lain in his pocket since the death of Clare O'Leary.

For the first time since 2006, he reread his notes and transcripts, his case interviews and his half-written stories. He reread the bewildered sorrow of Eileen O'Leary, Eileen Bates, who had known him in primary school, who had just lost her daughter; he read the unused testimony of Ian Murray, pointing the finger at Knox; and he read the transcript of Knox's own cynical telephone message warning him off the case.

Nigel picked up the telephone and dialled a number in the west of Scotland.

He heard the familiar, cigarette-blackened voice of his first mentor in journalism. He asked George Young for a favour.

'Yes, George, the names of all the children on the trip that day and their current addresses if you can get them. I'm mainly interested in anyone who's still living locally. Most of them would be in their early twenties now. Clare was the youngest and she was twelve back then . . . Yes, I know it's tricky, but you're a journalist, George: that's what we're supposed to be good at, remember? And you're retired now; it'll give you something to do to keep you out of the pub. All right? Thanks, George. I'm coming up next week, I'll see you then.'

Nigel did not see Sonya Mair in the two days before his departure. She had called the department to say she was sick and would be back after Christmas.

When he thought about her it was with a mixture of pity and affection, anxiety and desire. He felt the warmth of her arms on his neck and the scent of her breath on his lips.

He felt her absence.

He did not ring her. She did not ring him.

But the day before Nigel was leaving for Exxington, a hand-written note appeared on his desk. He asked his secretary where it had come from, but she said she'd been on lunch break and hadn't seen who brought it.

In a neat, slanting hand, Sonya wrote of her feelings for Nigel, of her gratitude for the kindness he had shown her and of her fears for his safety if he were to cross Selwyn Knox:

> *I don't need to tell you, Nigel: Selwyn is a force of nature. He fascinates me, he overwhelms me and I enjoy that feeling, but he also scares me. I admire the good things, the benefits his energy can bring the world, but I also fear the damage his power can cause. He is human in his faults and sins, but superhuman in the strength he possesses. He sees you and me as his safety valves. In my case for the sex, certainly, and you because you are the only one who has the power to restrain him if the forces within him run out of control. You have the knowledge and the power to bring it to a halt. You are his executioner, Nigel; an executioner he needs by him for the time when he reaches the irredeemable point of disaster for himself and for those whose lives he controls. He knows he is not strong enough to stop the forces welling up within him; he cannot take the axe to his own neck; but he knows you can. He needs you to do that, Nigel – and he feels he can push you into wielding that axe at the moment he needs to bring the whole process to an end.*

Nigel and Joanie went up to Exxington once or twice a year.

Joanie's parents were dead and the children enjoyed a week being spoiled by their remaining grandmother.

The car journey on the new Toll-Way from London to

Glasgow had been remarkably smooth despite the snow. Joanie felt her husband was a little quieter than usual, wrapped up in his own thoughts, but she didn't say anything and Nigel didn't volunteer an explanation.

On the first evening of their stay he said he was going to see George Young in the Exxington Arms; he thought Joanie would find it boring and she said she was happy to look after the children.

Two days later Nigel went out again.

This time it was not the Exxington he was heading for, but a different pub on the rundown south side of town.

Nigel found himself walking through streets he had never seen before, through the industrial estates of Exxington's under class, through lowering canyons of abandoned factories, across a rubble-strewn landscape where workers' houses had been razed under Knox's Clean-Sweep policies.

By the time he arrived at Bratten Street dusk had fallen.

The street was a strange oasis – a single row of terraced houses among the acres of demolished streets. It stood like a lone tooth in a toothless mouth; a random relic of some apocalyptic air raid.

The street lights were beginning to glow.

Outside the Eagle and Child the pub sign swung in the wind. The eagle gently bore the naked child in its claws, soaring, flying, fixed for ever mid wing-flap, suspended in space and time.

He sat at the bar and ordered an orange juice.

The room was empty apart from an elderly man in overalls in the corner, contemplating his pint.

Nigel waited.

He had told Cathy he would be wearing a leather jacket and green scarf; she could not miss him.

She had told him not to expect too much from her: she had been living in a hostel for the homeless since coming out of the young offenders' institution a year earlier; she had blonde hair and was pretty sure to have a ciggie in her mouth.

Nigel spotted her as soon as she came into the bar.

He waved her over and said, 'Cathy? Cathy James? Thanks very much for coming. George said you would. Can I buy you a drink?'

Nigel bought himself a pint and Cathy a vodka.

As they walked across the cigarette-strewn floor to a corner table, Nigel looked at Cathy and felt a pang of pity.

She was not pretty, but she had a fragile, vulnerable look to her. Her bleached hair was straggly and unkempt, her clothes were dirty, she had the glazed eyes of an addict.

Nigel found his imagination rewinding to the putative Cathy of five years earlier: to the young girl magically unwound from the years of trouble that had brought her to where she was today, an unspoilt girl looking with hope to the years ahead, foreseeing love, friendship, a career, unaware of what fate had written for her future; setting out on a trip to Ben Donnan with the Exxington District Council youth scheme.

What fate had decreed such a fall for Cathy James?

What had changed her from the hopeful, trusting girl to the addicted ex-offender before him now?

Nigel recalled the memo Christopher Brody had sent him the night he himself had been led from another pub by Sonya Mair, led away to Knox's lair in Dolphin Square.

He thought of Brody's mysterious, ambivalent exegesis of original sin, his quasi-celebration of this blight man was born to, of sin as an affirmation of humanity, innate imperfection as a token of human defiance in the face of Knox and Sheen's implacable insistence on perfection, the flawed humanity that negates the princely Angelo's strident fanaticism.

And he wondered now if Cathy's fall was the fruit of original sin.

Was Cathy's fate already decided when she set out for the mountains back in 2006?

Was her destiny already inscribed in the book of life?

Was it written in her DNA?

After a few drinks, which Nigel paid for, Cathy recounted her life: the schoolgirl jobs in the Exxington supermarkets; her liaison with Billy, the dealer; her first experiences with drugs; the abortion; the thieving to pay for her habit; the months inside; and now the hostel for the destitute; the abuse from the warders who used her body and the inmates who used her gear.

Nigel probed gently.

He asked her about the abuse, asked her if she had been abused as a child.

Cathy thought for a moment, then asked him who he meant in particular.

Nigel mentioned the death of Clare O'Leary.

She hesitated, looked at him with a question in her eyes.

Nigel said, 'Do you want to tell me something about that day, Cathy? About the day you and Clare and the councillors went up on Ben Donnan? About what happened to Clare?'

Still Cathy looked at him.

He could see her formulating her thoughts, struggling to tell him the truth she had hidden within her for so many years. At last she asked, 'Who was he? That councillor – what was his name?'

Nigel sighed. 'His name was Knox, Selwyn Knox.'

As he pronounced the name, Nigel saw Cathy's eyes fill with relief.

'Yeah, that's him,' she said. 'He's the one who abused us. He abused Clare, he abused me and he abused the other girls. He was known for it. We were terrified of him.'

Nigel sensed he was at last nearing the truth; the truth he should have uncovered five years before, but had not had the courage to pursue. He felt a great weight begin to lift from his mind. The conscience that had tormented him for so long slowly began to ease.

'Thank you, Cathy. Thank you for having the courage to tell me that. And can you tell me anything about the way Clare died? Was Knox with her when she went missing?'

Nigel saw Cathy hesitate again, look at him intently, reflect before taking the plunge.

'Yeah. He killed her. Selwyn Knox killed Clare! I've been too scared to say. Too scared he'd come and get me if I grassed him up. But now I've said it. Now I've told you. Is that what you wanted to hear?'

Nigel took Cathy's hand gently in his.

He told her not to get upset, not to worry. He would protect her. She didn't need to fear Selwyn Knox any more.

Now he would deal with Selwyn Knox and Cathy could find some peace; now at last she could overcome the terrible memory that had haunted her for so long.

Nigel and Joanie had four days left in Exxington.

He spent another couple of evenings out of the house.

He gave Cathy James as much money as he could afford and told her to use it to leave the hostel and get a flat, to make sure she kept away from the dealers and the abusers, to get herself clean, to drag herself out of the blight she had been born to.

Nigel thought a lot about Cathy.

He thought of her as if she were his own daughter.

SPIN

He prayed she would use the help he had given her to better herself, to rise above the vices she had fallen into.

And he went back to London to expose Selwyn Knox as the perverted threat to humankind that he was.

15

WHEN NIGEL returned to London, his first thought was to find Sonya and tell her what he had discovered in Exxington.

In the period between Christmas and New Year most government departments are skeleton staffed and when he went in to the office, the DfS was like the *Mary Celeste*. Sonya was not at her desk.

He was surprised by the wave of disappointment he felt at not seeing her. He called her mobile and got no reply. He called again. Then again. And again.

By the end of the day he found himself strangely desperate to talk to her. He rang her home number, but got only her disgruntled husband, who told him he hadn't seen Sonya for nearly two weeks.

Nigel spent the following days unsuccessfully trying to contact Sonya and preparing for the showdown with Knox.

A few days later Knox suddenly appeared in Nigel's office.

The shock of seeing him threw Nigel into a panic.

For all his preparations, he was alarmed that their meeting had been thrust on him so unexpectedly.

Knox's first remark plunged him into turmoil. 'Sonya tells me you saw her before Christmas and that you've got something you want to talk to me about.'

Nigel's eyes went dim, he felt faint.

Had Sonya been deliberately leading him on? Had she been in

it with Knox all along? And what about everything she had said to him that evening? Was it all lies and deceit?

Knox fixed him with a probing stare.

Nigel saw triumph and mockery in his face. He saw there was no way back. 'I don't know what you mean about Sonya, Selwyn. But it's true I need to talk to you. And I think you know what it's about.'

'I have no idea, Nigel. Why don't you tell me?'

Knox was worryingly calm. His eyes were blank, the empty eyes of the dead. Behind them, Nigel felt a vacuum sucking him in, pulling him down.

'All right, I will tell you. I'll tell you about the lies and the cheating. The evil you've instilled into the way the government treats people in this country. The evil within yourself. The paedophile pornography. The way you abuse Sonya and God knows who else. The way you abused and murdered Clare O'Leary.'

If Nigel had been expecting his words to shake Knox, to provoke a breakdown, a confession, a catharsis, he was to be disappointed. Knox's expression did not flicker.

'Well, Nigel, that's all very interesting. And what do you propose to do about it?'

'I let you off the hook once before, Selwyn. I'm not going to do it again. I intend to talk to the Prime Minister and the cabinet secretary. And if they won't do anything to stop you, I'll do it myself. I'll go to the papers, I'll tell them the truth—'

Knox smiled.

'I wouldn't do that, Nigel. Have you forgotten our pact? I have covered for you, covered up your cheating at the civil service board, and in return you've acted in the best interests of the country and the best interests of Nigel Tonbridge. I don't think that's the sort of story you'd like to see in the papers, is it?'

Nigel had been expecting Knox to threaten him. This time, he was ready for it. 'Well, I'll just have to live with that, Selwyn. We all make mistakes. We're all guilty of something, I suppose; and we all have to live with the consequences of what we've done. But it's a question of distinguishing between degrees of guilt, between the sins all men inherit and the evil some of us make for ourselves—'

Knox smiled again. 'And what about your sins, Nigel? What about your misuse of the confidential information you obtained in the course of your official duties? What about the way you misused the Parenting lists for your own material advantage?'

'What? I misused them? It was you who forced me to hand the lists over, Selwyn. It was you who misused them.'

'Well, I'm afraid that's not what Dave Sopwith will be writing in the *Chronicle*. He'll write what I tell him to write.'

'Look, Selwyn, this is nonsense. The game's up. You can't bully your way out of it this time. You do what you like to me – I'm going to tell . . .'

'Whatever I like? Well then, what if I were to tell the Attorney-General about the way you murdered your father? About the inheritance you so desperately needed? About the poison—?'

Nigel looked at Knox in terror.

'What are you saying? I told you why we did that. It wasn't murder. It was pity. It was mercy.'

'That's not the way your confession sounded to me. I heard you break down and admit everything. I can remember it quite clearly.'

'My God – you liar. You can't do that to me.'

'Just try me, Nigel. I can't let you stand in my way. The work I'm doing is much too important for that.'

'No, Selwyn, it's the work you're doing that I have to stop. It's the evil you're creating at the heart of this government, the way you're subverting everything good and human in our society. I can't stand by and let you—'

'I don't think you have much option, actually. You probably don't know this, but your efforts to destroy the evidence against you were a failure. You may think you wiped the SnVs of you and your mother plotting to murder your poor father, but you didn't think about the back-up copies on the hard drive, did you? Fortunately, I now have them all nice and safe. It won't be pleasant for your mother to stand trial, but it'll be so much worse for you. In this country people treasure respect for a father more than almost anything: I've made sure of that since I came to the DfS. You *murdered* your father, Nigel, and I can show you no mercy. You'll find yourself in front of a court that has only horror and revulsion for patricides. I'd like you to reflect on that. Take your time. Don't do anything rash. And then come and see me on Monday.'

It was not a happy New Year in Downing Street.

Andrew Sheen and Charlie McDonald were beginning to feel like 3-D chess players, fighting off assaults from all directions, forever trying to shore up their beleaguered defences against incoming threats from unpredictable sources.

Their weekly meetings with Selwyn Knox allowed them to keep one danger at least under surveillance.

Fred Trautberg's agreement to step down following the Internet paedophilia allegations had prompted McDonald to observe that he must have had something even more awful in his closet to persuade him to go so quietly. But it had got Knox off the hook and for the moment at least had staved off his threat to blab about Andy Sheen's former Colombian connections.

McDonald felt the stalemate with Knox was fragile, though, and Number Ten were plotting to find ways to secure their hold over him. In recent weeks they'd been pushing him to come forward with a new initiative for the DfS, something big and radical, in the hope it would either keep him occupied and out of trouble or would prove so controversial he would eventually hang himself.

But if the threat from Knox was in abeyance, the spectre of Cliff Evans at the *Daily Mirror* had risen again with a vengeance.

McDonald suspected Evans had either realized that the Marie Sheen pregnancy scoop had been a charade and was feeling aggrieved, or that he was simply chancing his arm in the way good editors tend to.

Whatever the reason, Evans had resurrected Jim McGee's story about the PM's appearance on possession charges and was threatening to run it on New Year's Day. Geoff Maddle was strongly of the opinion that it was a bit of blackmail by the *Mirror* and that Evans would never risk a libel suit for such a half-baked story.

But McDonald was not inclined to call his bluff.

He had spoken to Evans and asked what it would take to get the *Mirror* to forget completely and for ever about Andy Sheen's disputed past.

Evans had told him it would take something big, certainly much bigger than a phantom pregnancy; and McDonald was now wondering if he could kill two birds with one stone.

In Charlie's office he and Geoff Maddle were weighing Dewi Jones in the balance. It had happened on Boxing Day, and Charlie and Geoff both knew Dewi had been full of festive spirit. But still, Clapham Common—! The two spin doctors burst into laughter. The image of a tipsy Dewi Jones caught with a strange man on Clapham Common on a snowy Boxing Day at three in the morning seemed so incongruous that they momentarily forgot about the repercussions and gave way to a bout of nervous hilarity.

It was McDonald who cut it short.

'Look, Geoff, the bottom line is we need to kill this drugs thing once and for all. We tried with the pregnancy story but that was a washout. This time we need to give the *Mirror* something big to shut them up. And the only thing I can think of is Dewi Jones. It'd mean the end of Dewi's career, his marriage for sure, and – you know the state he's in – it could drive him over the edge. It's not a call we can make on our own. We'll need to ask Andy; and that means we'll have to tell him how close he's been to seeing his Colombian drugs story in the press. I'll go and tell him. He'll have to make the decision.'

An hour later McDonald reappeared.

'Andy says we give them Dewi.'

A very different Selwyn Knox ushered Nigel into his office on Monday morning. Nigel was struck by the change in him over the space of just one weekend. The belligerent, bullying self-confidence had disappeared: he now appeared diminished, deflated. Instead of fighting for his life, he seemed resigned to his fate, almost willing the axe to fall.

He sat silent, immobile at his desk, his lassitude was all-enveloping.

For his part, Nigel had returned in fighting mood. He was determined to act, but first he wanted answers from Knox.

'So you saw Sonya, Selwyn. Where is she?'

'No I didn't. I have no idea where she is.'

'But you said you saw her, Selwyn. You said you saw her and she told you I wanted to talk to you.'

'You're wrong. I haven't seen Sonya for weeks. Not since before I went away for Christmas.'

Knox's lie filled Nigel with a presentiment of horror. Suddenly he thought he knew why Sonya had not answered her mobile, why she had not returned his calls, why her husband had not seen her . . .

But now Knox was beginning to talk. After the silence, his words were spilling out in a torrent. Nigel listened, fascinated, horrified.

'I've been bearing a burden, Nigel. The burden of the extraordinary man. The weight of responsibility lies heavy on my shoulders. You know I am responsible for the downtrodden and the neglected, for the disinherited and the insulted. I am responsible for their well-being and their salvation. I am responsible for them, Nigel, like a father for his children. But there's one thing you and I both know, something we've learned from our work together in this department: fathers can stumble, they can be weak, they can fail their children. My burden is that at times I have betrayed the faith they had in me, I have let them down.'

Nigel looked at Knox and saw a broken man, a man who had recognized his accuser and now wanted him to hear his confession.

'You know the way children expect so much from their father? They invest so much faith in him. He's an infallible guide, a man with no weaknesses, no failings. They see him as a god. So the father feels the burden of expectation, he cannot slip from the ideal of perfection his children have made him – it would destroy them. But reflect, Nigel: a father is a man and no man is free of weakness, free of inadequacies. So the faith placed in him is an expectation he can never satisfy. And when the father slips from the ideal, the pain is immense. His children are devastated; the depth of his self-reproach, his torment and self-loathing can never be described. He's in hell, Nigel. He feels cast out by men. His loneliness is profound.'

Knox spoke and Nigel listened in silence, waiting to hear the confirmation of what he feared to hear, the confirmation of what Knox had done with Sonya, why she had disappeared.

'Yes, there is evil within me, Nigel. Evil alongside all the forces for good. I know that. I recall the harm I have done and I am ashamed. I shudder when I think of it. I picture the man who did this harm, but I cannot recognize him. It is not me, Nigel; it is another. I know it was my hand that inflicted the pain, but I cannot connect that hand with the hand you see before you now. I did harm. I am capable of evil. But the evil is not me. I am not responsible for its presence. So am I to be damned for something which is not me? For the sin that was visited on me, for what was written?'

As Nigel listened, Christopher Brody's memo came to mind, with its unanswered questions. Can Knox be pardoned? Can the devil be redeemed?

But Knox was pressing on, carried forward on a torrent of words.

'I am saying this to you, Nigel, because I know you too have failed; you understand what I am going through. You too have been bearing the burden of inadequacies and omissions. You feel what I feel. That is why we understand each other, even though you may not wish to admit it.'

Now, at last, Nigel was beginning to understand: Sonya had been right – he *was* asking Nigel to be his executioner.

'And how can the father be saved from his agony? How can he be redeemed? The only person who can understand his torment is the man who has shared his path of sorrow, who shares his past. Only that man can know the horror he is suffering. But not even that man can save him, Nigel. It is too late for that. The best he can hope for now is that a fellow sufferer will take pity on him and bring an end to his suffering—'

Knox rose to his feet and began walking to the door.

Nigel made to call him back, but Knox raised his finger to his lips to forestall him. 'I am going now, Nigel. If you want answers, come and see me tonight at my flat. You know where it is. You have slept in my bed. Come and see me there.'

Nigel spent the rest of the day in the agony that stems from doubt and fear; from an overwhelming feeling that a terrible task lay ahead of him, a task he could no longer avoid but dreaded even to contemplate. His calls to Sonya's mobile still brought no response and he had several times picked up the phone to report her disappearance to the police before thinking better of it. He had enough self-awareness to recognize the complex tricks his mind was playing to postpone that first dreadful step into the pitiless territory of denunciation and public confrontation.

Nigel rang the bell by Selwyn Knox's door on the third floor of Dolphin Square and heard the sound of shuffling feet.

The door opened and he walked into the apartment he had visited two weeks earlier. Now it seemed changed, unkempt, unsettled in the way a rumpled bed speaks of the passions and exertions that helped unmake it. Looking uneasily round the darkened room, he saw a picture on the wall off balance, books open on the floor, a chair leaning queasily against the table. Knox had walked ahead of Nigel towards the single table lamp. As he turned and faced him, Nigel saw his face was scratched and bloody.

Nigel feared the horrors ahead of him.

Knox passed his hand over his face and said, 'Do it, do it now. You see what it is. I'm sinking under this. I can't bear it. I can't stop myself. It's an addiction, Nigel. An addiction. Like the poor addicts we berate and punish, I can no more free myself from this drug than they can from theirs. Free me. Please free me from this—'

Panicking, Nigel advanced into the dark room and tripped over an upturned coffee table. He cursed then yelled at Knox. 'Where's Sonya, Selwyn? What have you done with her? Have you done the same to her as you did to poor Clare O'Leary?'

'You should have stopped me. I told you I can't control the forces in me. I can't be responsible for what I might do. You'd be helping me, Nigel. The burden of sin isn't easy. Take it off me. Put an end to this.'

'Where's Sonya? Tell me where Sonya is—'

'It'd be an act of mercy, Nigel. You did it for your father. We spend our lives trying to perfect others, trying to save them from themselves, but who will save me?'

A low moan came from the bedroom. Nigel pushed Knox aside and rushed through the door. On the double bed, Sonya lay gagged and bound, her face was bloody, her eyes black and swollen, stained with mascara and tears.

Three days later in Downing Street Andrew Sheen and Charlie McDonald were still trying to bring some order to the chaos that threatened to engulf them. McDonald was rallying his boss, attempting to banish the air of defeatism that had recently crept into Sheen's manner.

'Look, Andy, the main thing is Sonya doesn't want to press charges. She doesn't want to hurt Selwyn. I don't know why after what he did to her, but she's devoted to the guy. Selwyn's up against it, though: Nigel Tonbridge has got it in for him. Knox says Tonbridge has been threatening him. Knox won't admit it, but I reckon Tonbridge has discovered something pretty dirty about old Selwyn; something more than just kiddy porn and the way he treats Sonya. But Tonbridge is weak, Andy. He hasn't blown the whistle and I don't think he'll ever have the balls to. He's under Sonya's spell – I reckon he'll listen to what Sonya tells him. Knox is tricky, though. We'd dump the guy if we could, but we've hitched ourselves to him so tightly that if he goes down we go down too. Knox knows too much about us, Andy. He knows too much about you. Sonya's been his eyes and ears; without her, he wouldn't last long and that's for sure. Anyway, we're going to have to stand up for Knox and screw poor old Nigel Tonbridge. We'll have to do the dirty on him – smear campaign, the usual stuff. We need to stitch him up before he starts to blab.'

16

IT WAS messy. It was painful.

Nigel had seen the cabinet secretary.

Sir Thomas had told him he was not responsible for this sort of thing, but would pass the information on to the Prime Minister.

Nigel had asked for a meeting with the Prime Minister.

He had been told to talk instead to Charlie McDonald, who questioned him at length about what he knew, about what documents he had, and about the names of his sources and informants.

Nigel had gone to the police, who told him they had already been made aware of his allegations and that the matter was being dealt with at the highest levels of government.

Then there was silence.

Knox had told his Private Office he would be in his constituency and out of touch until parliament reassembled.

Sonya was back at her husband's, who was answering the phone with a curt refusal to pass on any message.

And Nigel's repeated calls to Charlie McDonald were fielded by a secretary who made increasingly less convincing excuses for why he could not come to the phone.

Nigel and Joanie's agonized discussions about what to do next went round in endless circles.

They knew the acute sensitivity surrounding the allegations about Knox, they knew the dangers involved in going public, and they knew the machinations that were certainly going on in Downing Street to make sure Nigel kept quiet.

He had had enough experience of the ruthless cynicism of McDonald and the Number Ten spin doctors to know they would make his life very uncomfortable if he stuck to his guns.

In the end, his decision was based on a dawning certainty that Downing Street had no intention of dealing with Knox and were even now preparing their cover-up operation. The longer he waited, Nigel realized, the more time he was giving them to find ways to discredit him and rubbish his revelations.

The moment Nigel called Rob Tyler at the *Sunday Telegraph* late on Tuesday evening, things started to move with breathtaking speed.

Tyler listened briefly to Nigel's story and told him to wait at home – he would be round in half an hour.

When he arrived he had another journalist with him, whom Nigel also knew, and a staff photographer.

The four of them sat with Joanie over cups of coffee for the next six hours telling and retelling the stories of Selwyn Knox's misdeeds, checking dates and places, listing the documentary evidence for each episode in the litany of lies, firming up the sequence of events for the Exxington story, exchanging exclamations of recognition as they independently recalled more examples of the minister's duplicity, and shaking their heads in shared bewilderment at Sonya's role.

By the time the clock of St Luke's next door struck three o'clock on Wednesday morning, Tyler and his associate were satisfied they had enough for a Sunday splash in the review section and a front-page write-off in the main paper.

They asked Nigel to make himself available in the intervening days to answer any further questions; and as they walked out of the front door into the frost-tinged early morning, Tyler turned and said, 'I don't want to sound melodramatic, Nigel, but I think you should stay away from work for the rest of the week. I know what Downing Street are capable of when they're in a corner and this is going to put them in a tighter corner than they've ever been in. I think you need to protect yourself and your family.'

From that sleepless Tuesday night to the eve of publication, Nigel and Joanie lived in the breathless anticipation that often precedes great turning points in people's lives.

Every moment together now seemed charged with significance; they lived like condemned prisoners, treasuring the smallest things others take for granted.

Joanie never referred to the warning Tyler had given; she never questioned Nigel's decision to speak out.

She knew that what he was doing was right – following his conscience, where others had washed their hands and made excuses – but she also knew his actions would unleash the wrath of a powerful and angry government.

And she feared the coming of the storm.

At nine o'clock on Saturday evening it came.

The first phone call was from Jennie Bennett of the *Independent on Sunday*, chirping her amazement at the *Telegraph* splash and asking Nigel if it was all true. He said it was. Jennie checked a few details and said she had to dash to write the story for the *Indie*'s late editions.

After that the phone never stopped ringing.

Next on the line was Joe Clancy at the *Sunday Express*, doing his 'Gorr-blimey, guvnor' turn and telling Nigel the *Telegraph* had written up the story 'like bloody *War and Peace*'. Clancy wanted something fresh for his follow-up, more juicy bits about Selwyn the Perv to titillate his readers, but Nigel replied wearily that he'd revealed everything in the original story. Clancy said OK and told Nigel he would get it onto the front page of the second edition.

Then came Dave Sopwith. His tone was reproachful and wheedling.

'Read your stuff in the *Telegraph*, Nigel. Looks a bit dodgy to me. Just been talking to Charlie. Government says it's a pack of lies. Seems you've got yourself in a bit of bother. We all know you've been plotting against Selwyn – you don't like him, do you? Looks like you've set out to stitch the poor bloke up, doesn't it – inventing all that nonsense about him.'

'Look, Dave. Everything I said to the *Telegraph* is true. It's up to you whether you believe it or not – there's enough evidence. You shouldn't believe what your master's voice tells you every time—'

'Oh, I see, Nigel. Are you accusing the *Chronicle* of telling lies for Charlie McDonald? I'll quote you on that.'

'Don't be juvenile, Dave. This is important—'

'And I suppose you got paid for talking to the *Telegraph*, didn't you? How much did you get for your Judas act? Fifty thousand, sixty thousand?'

'Look, Dave, stop right there. I'm doing this as a matter of principle, in the public interest. I took no money for it.'

'Oh, well, you may say that, but it's not what my sources tell me and I'll be going with them when I write my story for Monday.'

Nigel gave up in despair.

He knew the lengths to which some journalists would go in order to curry favour with Downing Street, and Dave Sopwith was the worst.

At least, he told Joanie, they had now had a taste of what McDonald and Sheen were going to throw at them.

By one a.m. the papers had all got their stories for the late editions and Nigel had turned down interview requests from myriad radio and television producers, who had rung to say they were leading on the Knox story and would he appear live on their programmes. Nigel recognized most of them; many were former colleagues. But he told all of them that he didn't want this to turn into a media circus, that he had said what he had to say and now it was up to the government to put its house in order.

Joanie was already in bed when the phone rang again at two a.m. Nigel picked it up and heard the grim voice of Charlie McDonald.

'Tonbridge? I know that's you. Well, let me tell you something. You've had it, mate; you're dead meat.'

The line went dead before Nigel could collect his wits to reply.

The next morning, Sunday, Nigel and Joanie were woken by their twelve-year-old daughter telling them to look out of the window.

When Nigel sleepily opened the curtains, he was amazed to see thirty or forty journalists, photographers and television crews besieging the house.

His heart sank and his stomach cramped in knots of fear.

At that moment he realized exactly what he had unleashed by speaking out, how great was the public interest in anyone who had the courage to blow the whistle on this overbearing government, but also how much anxiety, unhappiness and – possibly – danger his actions were destined to cause himself, his wife and his children.

Cut adrift by the civil service, cold-shouldered by Downing Street, about to be locked out of his department and cursed by Charlie McDonald, Nigel was shocked by the sense of isolation that seized him in its icy fingers.

He closed the bedroom curtains and fought back a pang of regret that he had ever agreed to speak to the *Sunday Telegraph*.

Nigel had enough knowledge of the mass media to recognize that the almost universal unanimity in the coverage of his revelations about Selwyn Knox that Sunday morning was a startlingly rare phenomenon.

The tone in all the papers, on the radio and television was one of approval for what he had done and condemnation of the deceitfulness that most of the commentators agreed now characterized this government.

Only on the events in Exxington did they show a certain reticence: there seemed to be a certain wariness about a story implicating a cabinet minister in murder.

The press pack outside Nigel's house turned out to be jovial and friendly. He found he knew many of them from his time in the BBC Political Unit and he soon got to know the others as he went in and out of the house to a chorus of banter.

They weren't slow to let him know what they thought about Selwyn Knox and about the Downing Street spin machine, sentiments they repeated in more restrained language in their published articles.

Messages of support rained down on Nigel from his neighbours and, since his photograph was in most of the Sunday papers, from complete strangers who approved of what he had done.

Downing Street's fightback began on Monday morning.

Dave Sopwith's article in the *Chronicle* was headlined 'Greedy Civil Servant Took Money to Frame Boss' and claimed Nigel had deliberately lied to seek revenge on a minister who had passed him over for promotion.

Ominously, the article quoted 'government sources', who said

Tonbridge was reportedly being investigated for tax evasion and could soon be facing prosecution.

On the *Today* programme, the Education Secretary, Ron 'Fatty' Clegg, huffed and puffed about despicable civil servants who abused the information they received from their work in government to pursue personal vendettas against ministers. He called for legislation to introduce prison terms for any who made unauthorized statements in future.

Of Knox himself, however, there was no sign.

Reporters despatched to his constituency failed to find any trace of him; his apartment in Dolphin Square and Ruth Leeming's house in Scotland were fruitlessly staked out round the clock; of necessity the TV news bulletins continued to use library pictures of the vanishing minister; and the DfS refused to answer any questions about his whereabouts.

Reading between the lines, Nigel suspected Downing Street were hesitating over how to play the story. They could either concentrate their efforts on discrediting Nigel without actively defending Selwyn, in which case Knox would probably be kept out of sight and quietly allowed to resign when the fuss had died down. Or they could go the whole hog and mount a concerted defence of their man. This would mean pushing Knox into the spotlight, attempting to trash Nigel's allegations one by one and staging a public confrontation between the minister and his accuser.

Three days into the story and with the controversy showing no sign of abating, it became abundantly clear they were going for the second, nuclear, option.

On Wednesday morning Downing Street offered Selwyn Knox to every radio and television outlet, and they all leapt gratefully at the chance to enflame the controversy further.

The questioning was hostile, but Knox had been coached well

by the spin doctors and had clearly been given the green light to tell any untruth he needed to defend himself.

In response to every suggestion of wrongdoing, he simply issued a categorical denial. Listening to him, Nigel was amazed at the implacable, bare-faced temerity of his lying. In some TV interviews his top lip seemed to sweat a little and his eyes swivelled nervously, but otherwise it was a Rolls-Royce performance; impressive in its chutzpah, ominous in the way it upped the stakes.

Downing Street's transition from defence to aggression was not slow in coming.

It was ferocious in its intensity.

In a slickly coordinated campaign, statement followed statement.

First Sonya Mair, her face now healed or covered over with make-up, was thrust in front of the cameras to choke back tears and deny Knox had ever laid a finger on her.

Nigel watched her praise 'Selwyn's goodness and Christian idealism' and thought of those videos released by the terrorist captors of Allied servicemen in the MEWs: it was impossible to tell if she was speaking of her own free will or reading from a prepared script at knife-point.

The following day the police issued a statement ruling Knox out of their Internet paedophilia investigations and specifically denying he had ever been a suspect in the death of Clare O'Leary.

As for Knox's 'alleged lying and political misconduct', a series of cabinet ministers leapt to defend his integrity, culminating in a statement from Andy Sheen giving him his 'full backing and support' and concluding, 'Selwyn Knox will continue to be an important and trusted member of the cabinet.'

The point was underlined by a highly publicized photocall on the steps of Number Ten, where the smiles and backslapping between the two men concluded with a slightly surprised-looking Andy Sheen being given a kiss on the cheek by his triumphantly vindicated minister.

Nigel could not help marvelling at the confidence that had returned to Knox's manner: after the humbled, broken man he had last seen in Dolphin Square, this was another bewildering peripeteia. He could not fathom the way Knox swung from one extreme to another in such short order: it was as though he were two completely different people.

Meanwhile the government's strident support for Knox and Charlie Mcdonald's shameless smear campaign against Nigel had muddied the waters in the media coverage. Several journalists rang Nigel to check Downing Street's allegations against him and most refused to run them, but others didn't bother and simply went into print.

Pro-Downing Street stalwarts like Dave Sopwith had concluded long ago that Nigel was the villain of the story and Knox the maligned hero. Most of the rest of the papers and the BBC continued to favour Nigel's version of events, but Charlie McDonald's clever campaign of allegations and innuendo meant that the unanimity of support and trust Nigel had initially and rightfully enjoyed had been undermined.

Not content with denouncing Nigel's claims about Knox, Charlie McDonald was pressing ahead with a character-assassination campaign. Nigel was pilloried as an embittered traitor who had tried to vilify a decent, honest minister. He was 'exposed' as a secret NewLib sympathizer who had 'deliberately infiltrated the civil service to sabotage the government's vital policies of moral salvation'.

After another week of unrelenting vilification, Downing Street issued a statement saying that the Minister for Society, Selwyn Knox, would be bringing an action for libel against the disgraced former civil servant, Nigel Tonbridge, and would be demanding punitive damages.

At the same time the Attorney-General announced with a flourish that a case was to be brought in the public interest against Nigel George Tonbridge and his mother Elizabeth Jane Tonbridge, née Dalziel, that they did knowingly conspire to cause the death of Percival Tonbridge by the administration of a mortal dose of a harmful substance.

To remove any doubt, the announcement pointed out that Nigel Tonbridge would be facing a charge of patricide.

The government's attacks and the hail of announcements hit Nigel like hammer blows.

His life fell apart.

From being a heroic whistle-blower, respected and congratulated, he had suddenly become an outcast, a pariah: he had killed his father; he had libelled a minister.

And he didn't have the means or the will to fight back.

He didn't have the stomach to slug it out in radio and television interviews.

He refused all requests for a response to Downing Street's smears and closeted himself with Joanie and the children in their house, which remained besieged by journalists and photographers.

Friends had started to regard him with mistrust, neighbours turned against him, strangers talked about him with contempt.

Downing Street had set out to destroy Nigel and they were succeeding.

He was under intense psychological pressure, close to collapse.

It was in this frame of mind that Chris Brody found Nigel when he knocked on his door, called his name through a tentatively opened letterbox and slipped inside to the flashes of news cameras and shouted questions from the throng on the pavement outside.

Nigel and Joanie both said how grateful they were to see a friendly face.

Brody then told them that the DfS had instructed its staff to avoid contact with the Tonbridges, but he had never let the department run his life and he wasn't going to start now.

He said the first few days after Nigel's revelations had been pandemonium.

Those who knew what Knox was capable of expressed their admiration for Nigel's courage in speaking out against him, but few were willing to add their names to the roll of Knox's accusers.

Most of them feared Knox would be back in avenging-angel mode, and when Downing Street launched their campaign of vilification against Nigel they were proved right.

On his return from his extended Christmas break, the Secretary of State had at first kept a low profile. And apart from her brief stage-managed statement to a gaggle of carefully vetted TV crews, Sonya Mair had not been seen at all.

Now though, Brody said, Knox was starting to get back into his stride.

He had circulated an internal SnV to all in the department, which showed him sitting confidently at his desk, poring over new legislative proposals and looking up to the camera to smile and say, 'The work goes on. Now it is time to draw a line and put recent events behind us. Some individuals in this department have shown they were not committed to the work we are doing here and, indeed, were determined to sabotage it and undermine their minister. That episode is over. Now it is time to move on.'

When Nigel expressed his amazement at the way Knox seemed able to gloss over such damning revelations and carry on as though nothing had happened, Brody laughed. 'What can I say? Knox is not a man, he's a political machine. Knox-the-image is flawless, unfeeling, infallible. The mask doesn't slip, Nigel—'

Nigel disagreed. 'You might be right, Chris, except that I have seen two Selwyn Knoxes: there's Knox the psychopath, the lunatic social engineer; and there's Knox the idealist seeking the best for society – Sonya recognized that in him. There's the fanatical, unbending dictator, and there's the broken wreck looking for support from me and Sonya and anyone who'll offer it. How can he be two such extremes? How can he be such different people?'

Again Brody smiled. 'Didn't you read my memo? Knox has evil in him, but he says he's not responsible for it. He says he fights against it, but he knows it's a fight he can't win. He's suffering in himself. His sins torment him. He may have tried to excise his conscience, but like the nerve at the root of a tooth it's still there and it puts him in agony.

'The problem for him is that his policies are selling people an invitation to a perfect world – a world without sin; but he knows he himself has no place in that world. He's like the suicide bombers, Nigel: he knows there's no Nirvana for him, but his reward will be here on earth after he's gone. The perfect earthly paradise he's created will be his vindication, his legacy and – perhaps – his vengeance.'

Selwyn Knox arrived for his weekly meeting at Downing Street in a state of some excitement.

He knew the idea he was bringing with him would impress Andrew Sheen and Charlie McDonald; he knew it was a big idea, an idea that could outstrip even the Parenting Licence in the impact it would have.

'Andy, Charlie, listen to this. You remember Jack Willans and Tim Stilwell? You remember they threw all DRE's billions into those bio-engineering firms in the States? And then it all began to fall apart and it looked like they were going bust? Well, they may not have thrown it away after all! They came to see me a month ago – before all that nonsense with Nigel Tonbridge – and I've been talking to them ever since about an idea that could revolutionize our social policy!

'It seems their work on gene therapy has turned up trumps after all. One of their outfits has found something that could rescue them and us with them! It's a fantastic breakthrough, Andy. DRE have identified the gene markers for antisocial and deviant behaviour, and in the last three weeks they've successfully taken out UK and world patents on the technology that does it. The possibilities are endless! DRE can now identify which individuals have a propensity for crime and social disruption. And we can use that technology. Last month I reached an agreement with Willans and Stilwell that they would make their research available to us so we could test it against a selection of known criminals. We used it on petty crooks in the prisons – without telling them what we were doing, of course – and we compared that to tests on a control group of ordinary, decent people. The results were amazing! The accuracy of the gene predictor was ninety-eight per cent among those with criminal pasts. Among the control group of decent citizens, only four per cent had the criminal gene. Think about it! We have in our hands the ability to separate the population into sheep and goats! We can identify those who are tainted with original sin, if you like, and those who are not. And we have the means to wipe out original sin. It's the chance of a lifetime! We have the power to completely transform society, to create a new world, a better world – dare I say it? – a perfect world! We remove those who are tainted with sin and we preserve those who are free from it, those who are innocent.

'And it's easy, Andy.

'If we incorporate this technology into our Parenting Licence programme, we can take DNA samples of the whole population: we can identify those with the gene and we can stop them reproducing. It's a panacea. We stop crime and antisocial activity at one blow. We wipe out deviant behaviour. And, don't forget, the legislation we got through parliament last year gives us the right to enforce abortions in extreme cases. The beauty is that the legislation does not define an "extreme case": we can make that definition ourselves. We can define it as those who carry the criminal gene! Couples who might produce criminals can be stopped. And in the future we might want to take it even further: those parts of the population with the strongest gene markers for criminality could be confined in preventive detention. We could take them out of circulation; we could stop them breeding. If we apply all these measures rigorously, we could wipe out crime for ever in the space of just one generation. There would be protests, of course – there were protests over the PL – but it would be easy to face the liberals down. All we have to say is that we need to put up with a short period of restrictions (they would call it repression, I suppose) to achieve an eternity of bliss: an eternity without crime, without social disruption, without discontent, without unhappiness. It's paradise on earth and we can achieve it, Andy.'

When Knox had left the room, Andrew Sheen turned to Charlie McDonald with a quizzical look. 'What to do you think, Charlie? It sounds a bit radical, but then people said the same about his Parenting Licence. Do you think Selwyn may have come up with another winner?'

Charlie McDonald winced. 'No, I don't, Andy. I think Selwyn's lost it. I think he's in danger of getting himself consigned to the loony bin of history – and us with him. I think we need to do something about it.'

17

SELWYN KNOX'S suicide note was typewritten.

The police said this was unusual, but not unknown.

A long, exultant passage about his political career ended with an impassioned encomium on his proposals for compulsory DNA tests to identify the crime gene and remove potential future criminals from society.

The forensic experts suggested that Knox had broken off at this point and resumed typing some time later when the document switched from the political to the personal and the tone became despondent.

It gave voice to his doubts about the morality of the policies he was advocating. It suggested he was haunted by the thought that his legislation was destroying the cohesive bonds of human solidarity and human warmth. He talked at length about original sin.

A message for his political adviser, Sonya Mair, suggested there might have been a disagreement in the days before his death, and concluded by saying he could not live without her. He thanked his director of communications, Nigel Tonbridge, 'for understanding me and what I needed from you'. Perhaps surprisingly, there was no message for his long-time partner and common-law wife, Ruth Leeming.

The news of Selwyn Knox's suicide was broken by a BBC presenter on *Breakfast* news.

The announcement interrupted a live follow-up on the Corporation's latest reality television series, *Big Sister*, in which the BBC invited attractive, large-bosomed young women to spend a week in a hermetically sealed house with a team of teenage boys, whose task it was to persuade the female contestants to reveal their breasts to the many cameras which covered every corner of the house, including the toilets. The rules specified that the boys must not use physical force and that live sex was not permitted between the participants. The latest controversy had been about young Mark, who had allegedly broken both these rules – and in fact had broken rule one to help him break rule two.

The *Breakfast* news audience was being polled to determine whether Mark should suffer any sanctions – possibly a prison term – on leaving the *Big Sister* house and returning to the real world.

The voting was getting tense, and the BBC audience did not take kindly to the announcer interrupting with a boring announcement about an old geezer who had topped himself.

For Nigel Tonbridge, the relief was intense.

In practical terms, Knox's death meant that he no longer had a libel case to answer. Despite Andy Sheen's recent revisions, the law still held that the dead could not be libelled.

With Knox unable to testify about the alleged confession on the patricide charge, Nigel's lawyer seized the opportunity to request immediate dismissal of the case. After some hurried discussions with Number Ten, the Attorney-General wrote back to say the charge would be left to lie on file, but no further action would be taken.

And, most importantly, Knox's suicide restored Nigel's reputation at a stroke.

In the eyes of the media and of the world, the decision to take his own life confirmed that Knox was guilty and that all Nigel's allegations about him must have been true.

By extension, it confirmed Nigel's innocence.

It confirmed he had been right to denounce Knox. It confirmed he was, after all, a jolly good fellow.

Once again, the weathercock of public sentiment swung in his favour.

No longer was he an outcast, a reviled and lonely man suspected of the worst imaginable crimes.

He was restored to his status of hero; he was respected and admired by one and all.

He was vindicated, fêted by the media as a man of principle, a courageous whistle-blower.

Such was its violence and speed that Nigel found himself almost amused by the cartoon-like ferocity of the reversal that shook his life and threw him from one extreme of emotion to another.

It reminded him of the moment towards the end of *The Duchess of Malfi* when Webster has his mass murderer explain a particularly acute plot swing as 'a contrivance such as I have oft observed in plays'.

It was hard to believe, but for Nigel these successive and alarming reverses of fortune were happening in real life.

In Downing Street the panic was boundless.

For one thing, Knox's suicide had brought the wrath of the media down on all their heads. The widespread acceptance that Knox was guilty as charged had pointed up the extent of the lies Number Ten had told to defend him and to vilify Nigel Tonbridge.

For journalists who had been on the receiving end of the New

Project spin doctors' mendacity, it was payback time. Accumulated resentment at all their insults, deceit and double-dealing was being thrown back at Sheen and McDonald with considerable interest.

The pressure on the Prime Minister to explain why he had protected a known paedophile and suspected murderer and kept him in his cabinet was becoming intense. Even Dave Sopwith ventured a veiled criticism, not exactly biting the hand that fed him, but certainly giving it a good flick with the edge of his tongue.

The siege mentality that had begun to grip Downing Street even before Christmas was now reaching its apogee.

The anti-terror cordon around Number Ten, with its razor wire, police security emplacements and two-and-a-half-ton concrete blocks to keep out the car bombers was a reminder to the gloomier minded among them of the minefields, tank-traps, and blockhouses round the Hitler bunker in 1945.

Its occupants were protected from the outside world, but also effectively cut off from it – cut off from the people they claimed to rule, to save and to cherish; cut off from reality.

For privacy from the flapping ears of junior staff, the PM and his closest aides were now holding most of their meetings in the complex of fortified rooms underneath Downing Street, which had originally been intended for use in a terrorist emergency. It was rumoured that many of them were sleeping there as well. But now, like the Soviet troops in Berlin in 1945, the real world was pouring in.

And, like Eva Braun, Sonya Mair had refused the offer of a safe flight out of the bunker to putative safety in exile.

After her televised statement supporting Selwyn Knox, she had refused to return Nigel's calls. She had not talked to him since the night he had discovered her gagged and bound on Knox's bed in Dolphin Square, and she would not talk to him now.

Instead, she had rallied to the defence of the besieged Prime Minister and his entourage. When the massed ranks of political journalists and reporters signed a resolution condemning the lies and deceit which Charlie McDonald and Geoff Maddle had been responsible for during their years in power and refused to attend Downing Street briefings 'unless and until these individuals are removed from their posts', Sonya was offered and eventually accepted the poisoned chalice of taking over their duties. On the day she officially took on the thankless task of official Downing Street spokesperson, Sonya sent Nigel a one-line email, which read:

I'm sorry. I couldn't climb out of the well. SM

One of Sonya's first jobs was to deal with her old friend Cliff Evans.

Emboldened by the media frenzy, the editor of the *Daily Mirror* had spotted his chance.

The opportunity to bring down not just a cabinet minister, but the Prime Minister himself, was too much for him to resist.

He ran the story under the headline: 'Cabinet of Perverts Led by Drug Dealer?'

The question mark had been inserted at the insistence of the paper's lawyers, but within hours of the story hitting the streets it was clear this precaution had been unnecessary.

The *Mirror*'s news desk received more than a dozen phone calls from former Cambridge students, contemporaries of Andrew

Sheen in the 1970s, who remembered the Sheen–Parks partnership and each of whom brought important new details to fill out Jim McGee's initially tentative story.

The following morning, as the other nationals wrote follow-ups to the *Mirror*'s first-day lead, Cliff Evans was able to print the triumphant banner: '*Mirror* Proved Right: Sheen was Drug Fiend'.

Under a shared byline, McGee and Evans revealed the full extent of Andrew Sheen's drug-related profiteering; his 'student links with Colombian racketeers and murderers' and the narcotics-funded purchase of the New York flat, 'still owned by Sheen and used regularly by Marie and his unwitting children'.

The story was the number-one lead in every newspaper; the number-one topic of discussion on every TV bulletin and current affairs programme.

Perhaps to deflect the public's attention, Downing Street launched a new offensive in the MEWs, throwing hundreds of troops into a suicide mission against al-Qaeda's fortified mountain strongholds. But this did nothing to lessen the intensity of the drugs coverage, and it led several commentators to reflect on Andrew Sheen's 'despicable, ruthless sacrifice of innocent lives in his twisted attempt to save his own skin'.

Sonya Mair rang Cliff Evans in a foul temper.

She reminded him of the deal they had agreed, first over Marie's pregnancy and then again over the late Dewi Jones. She cursed Evans for his duplicity and dishonesty, for breaking his promise to kill the story, for betraying her personally.

But Evans replied, 'I'm sorry, love. You should know better than anyone: if you think you can sin and get away with it unpunished, you're fooling yourself. You know our sins always come back.'

*

And Cliff Evans was quickly proved right.

The combination of the revelations about Selwyn Knox and the bombshell of Andrew Sheen's student transgressions was always going to be too much for a government which had built its politics on the premise of moral perfection; which had anchored its self-proclaimed right to impose demanding standards on the whole nation to the firm ground of its own irreproachable, saintly wisdom.

The growing perception that the cabinet really was the preserve of perverts and criminals did not take long to bring the government down.

As the invading wave of public disgust and anger rose higher and higher over the Downing Street bunker, Andrew Sheen reached for the political cyanide.

His resignation was announced on the same day the general election was called.

The pundits were united in predicting that the resurgent NewLib party would sweep the board.

18

GALLING AS it might have been for Downing Street, Andrew Sheen's misfortune was Nigel Tonbridge's silver lining.

Taking their lead from the *Daily Mail*, whose banner headline had proclaimed him 'The Honest Man Who Brought Down Cabinet of Crooks', the media were busy turning Nigel into a popular hero.

He was invited to appear on radio and television discussion programmes, chat shows and panel games; he was profiled in newspapers and magazines; he received lucrative job offers in journalism and public relations; he was promised silly money if he would write his memoirs or reveal his 'true story' to *Hi There!* magazine.

Despite his frequently repeated protestation that he had only been following his conscience when he blew the whistle on Selwyn Knox and that any honest man would have done the same, Nigel could not help feeling secret satisfaction at the respect and vindication he was enjoying.

While he was sometimes embarrassed by the fuss being made of him, he now woke every morning to a deep wave of relief that the nightmare weeks of persecution were over, that he could walk down the street without fearing the disapproving glances of passing strangers, that he could answer the telephone without wondering if it would be news of more vilification by Downing Street.

Nigel and Joanie knew that the trials of the past months had brought them closer than ever. Now the only thing troubling Nigel's idyll of vindicated contentment was a message on his answering machine.

He had discovered it late one night when he and Joanie returned from the cinema.

He had played it once, played it again, listened to it six or seven times.

The words were clear: what he was trying to divine was the meaning, the hidden intention behind the woman's voice asking him to call her as soon as possible.

'You know who this is,' said the voice and Nigel did know.

'You know how to reach me,' said the voice and Nigel did know.

'You know what this is about,' said the voice, but Nigel did not know, or at least he told himself he did not know, did not want to know.

He erased the message before Joanie could hear it and went to bed.

Three days passed before Nigel mustered enough resolve to pick up the telephone and return the call. Three days of foreboding, in which the redoubled efforts he felt himself making to enjoy the life he and Joanie were sharing signalled the fragility he sensed within the idyll.

His delay had been the product of fear, he knew. Fear of re-opening the nightmare of the past months, fear of talking again to the woman who was forever linked to the world of Selwyn Knox.

His call was answered by a man's voice. It sounded rude, uncaring; the tone was brusque.

Nigel waited.

He heard footsteps on a stone floor, then whispered conversation.

He heard someone pick up the receiver.

He recognized the voice immediately, the voice of a young woman.

'Nigel? Is that you? Yeah, it's Cathy here. Thanks for ringing. I didn't know if you would. Anyway, the thing is I need to see you. No, I can't speak on the phone. I need to see you. Can you come up here to the Eagle and Child? Well, as soon as you can. It's urgent.'

On Bratten Street the eagle was still flying; the child still cradled improbably, eternally, in its claws.

Nigel was convinced of the truth of all he had believed about Knox, everything he had accused him of.

Of course he was.

The man's suicide had blown away any lingering doubts.

But coming back here to Exxington seemed wrong.

It seemed like treading on someone's grave, revisiting something that should not be reopened.

Cathy was already in the bar when Nigel entered. He had the impression she might have been drinking for some time. She seemed upset.

As he saw her, Nigel felt again a pang of pity; the involuntary sensation that she could easily have been his daughter.

He saw her clothes were still ragged and thought to himself she had not done much with the money he had given her.

He saw the telltale, distant look still in her eyes.

Cathy offered to buy Nigel a drink. He said he would get the round and she asked for a double.

Their conversation was awkward.

Cathy talked about her life and the hardships she was enduring. She said she had been thrown out of the hostel a few days after Nigel had phoned her.

She had already lived as a street person in the past and she was starting to get used to it again.

Nigel felt oppressed by the dirt and gloom of the pub. He sensed Cathy was going to ask him for more money and was making his mind up how he would respond.

In the meantime, he went to the bar and brought back two more vodkas.

Cathy asked him how he was feeling after the controversy over Selwyn Knox. She asked him why Knox had killed himself. He said he didn't know.

Cathy talked about Clare O'Leary. Nigel was beginning to feel uncomfortable about where the conversation was leading.

He asked her why she had needed to see him so urgently.

She asked him for another drink.

Nigel came back with two more vodkas and Cathy gulped hers down.

'I needed to see you, Nigel. I needed to tell you something – I needed to tell you he didn't kill her.'

Nigel looked at her intently.

She was waiting for him to respond.

Nigel drained his vodka.

'Cathy, you told me he killed Clare. You told me—'

'Yeah, I know I did. I told you a lot of things.'

'What do you mean? You mean you told me—?'

'I mean he didn't kill her and he didn't abuse her. He didn't abuse me.'

Nigel felt his hands turn to ice.

'But you told me, Cathy. You said Selwyn Knox abused you and Clare and the other girls. You said he was a child molester.'

'I know I did. I said it because I wanted to please you. I knew that was what you wanted me to say. I could tell. And I wanted you to give me money, Nigel. That's why I said it.'

Nigel felt the vodka kick in. His head was feeling dangerously light.

'OK, so you didn't see him abuse Clare up in the mountains. You didn't see him kill her. But that doesn't mean—'

Cathy burst into tears.

'I said he didn't molest her, I said he didn't kill her. I know he didn't.'

'But how can you know? That's the point. We can't know what—'

'Yes we can. That's what I'm trying to tell you. I *saw* Clare O'Leary fall off the cliff. I was there. I saw her. And I ran away. I ran away because I thought they'd say it was my fault. I never told anyone. I was scared. I was fourteen—'

Nigel gulped down his vodka and went to order another.

Terror seized him as he walked to the bar, panic that he had hounded Knox, driven him to his death.

Nigel returned with the drinks, tried a last time.

'Cathy, this is very important. Are you sure what you're telling me is true? I believed you last time and now you say you were lying.'

Cathy wiped her eyes.

'I was lying then. I told you, I needed the money off you. But now the guy's killed himself, Nigel. He killed himself—'

Nigel looked at Cathy; he knew she was telling the truth.

He thought of the last time they had sat here.

He remembered how she had hesitated over the story of abuse and murder.

He kicked himself that he hadn't realized, had allowed himself to believe her. Kicked himself that he had let her push him into denouncing Knox, into locking horns with such dangerous opponents, initiating such a frightening process with such a catastrophic outcome.

Nigel's stomach cramped with fear: fear of the ramifications of what he had just heard.

His thoughts in turmoil, he barely heard what Cathy was saying. He registered the word money and looked up at her.

'I'm an addict, Nigel. I can't give it up. I spent the money you gave me on more gear. But I need more. I need money to feed my habit. I'm already on the street. It means going on the game or going back to Billy and thieving. It'll be the death of me, Nigel, unless you give me more.'

Nigel looked at her in astonishment.

'But, you've just told me you lied to me. You've put me in trouble up to my neck, Cathy. Why should I give you more money? You can't be serious—'

'I think you should give it me, Nigel. I need it. You're my only hope. And there's something else, don't forget: if I go to the police and say that Knox didn't kill Clare, say you were telling lies, what'll that do for you? It won't be good for you, will it? I need the money, Nigel. Give it me and I'll keep quiet. Give it me and I'll never tell anyone what I've just told you.'

Nigel gulped his vodka.

His thoughts were scrambling. He knew the trap he was in.

This time Cathy was telling the truth, there could be no doubt. He knew that danger lay ahead.

In his fuddled state, the anger and disgust he felt with himself turned on the girl beside him.

How could she have deceived him? He had trusted her like his own daughter.

He had tried to help her, given her money and advice.

He had tried to redeem her from the sin she had fallen into.

And she could have responded, she could have improved herself, saved herself.

She could have joined the better society the government was building.

But she had refused to change, refused to pull herself up out of the trough, out of the blight she was born to.

She had been too attached to her faults, too addicted to the imperfections of her type.

Now Nigel's faith was shaken – if Cathy was false, who could he trust?

Was the whole of humankind tainted with deceit? With original sin? Was it written?

Preordained?

Was it in our DNA?

Nigel was getting more drunk.

He had no plan.

Clarity gone.

No fixed idea.

The juggernaut of vengeance was stalking him.

The juggernaut wore the face of Selwyn Knox, Andy Sheen, Charlie McDonald.

He knew he had to play for time.

But how?

'Come on, Cathy. I've got no money on me. Let's find a cash machine.'

They left the pub's smoky warmth.

Out into the street.

End of Bratten Street.

End of the last remaining terrace of houses.

Beyond the last terrace.

Onto the plains of rubble.

Here houses had been bulldozed.

Here lives and memories had been swept away.

Swept under the rubble.

The end of the terrace.

The end of civilization.

Where the wasteland began.

Now Nigel was walking.

With Cathy.

Slowly crossing the waste ground.

Thinking of Knox.

Turning it all over in his mind.

Knox was dead.

Thoughts in turmoil.

He was to blame.

Despair gripped.

But through swirling emotion, rational thought began.

Cling to it.

Like a drowning man to a branch in the river.

'Keep straight . . . think it through . . . what it means . . . for you, for Joanie . . . for the kids.

'If this gets out, you're finished . . . more vilification . . . more trashing in the media . . . can you cope? Dead meat . . . persecuted the Minister for Salvation . . . killed the man who would redeem our sins and save our souls.'

Nigel shuddered.

Get a grip.

'Wait, wait. Get it straight! Knox was dangerous . . . the child pornography . . . the paedophilia . . . and his policies . . . they were the source of the poison, the lies . . . he needed to die . . . his death brought renewal . . . elections . . . maybe the NewLibs . . . some integrity again?'

In his confusion, Nigel saw himself as the slayer of the hydra; but hydra-like, new danger was springing from the decapitated head of Selwyn Knox.

'As long as McDonald isn't allowed to reinvent Knox . . . to trade on his memory. If Cathy clears him of the murder, it'll be Knox the martyr! Knox the saint! Knox of blessed memory. They'll use it to re-ignite his political legacy . . . they'll raise themselves from his funeral pyre.'

The vodka filled Nigel's bloodstream.

He was walking unsteadily.

Thinking unsteadily.

The thought that Knox could be resurrected even now buzzed in his head.

He glanced at Cathy.

Could she be kept quiet?

Not by paying her blackmail demands. That was for sure.

Then how?

What if she were to die here?

Now.

On this waste ground.

Nigel found himself thinking:

'She'd be just one more vagrant.

'Left for dead in the wasteland.

'No one would miss her.

'And the good that would come from it.

'The good for the country.

'Immeasurable—'

Now they were approaching the centre of the waste ground, stumbling over the levelled ruins of former streets and houses – streets and houses razed under Knox's Clean-Sweep; razed to wipe out Britain's sink estates, the nests of crime and evil tainting society.

Without looking, Nigel whispered, 'Cathy, have you got any family – parents still alive?'

'Nah. They're dead. I'm all on my own.'

Nigel glanced at her.

Ragged clothes.

Glazed expression.

Needle-tortured arms . . .

. . . and he felt such sympathy that tears pricked his eyes.

'These are the people Knox was destroying,' he thought. 'These are the poor, the disinherited. He was "phasing them out" . . . in the name of social cleansing! Get rid of people like Cathy and you get rid of the procreators of crime, the source of discontent that troubles decent society . . . that's what the New Project wanted. That's what it'll do if it gets back in again now.'

Nigel felt his head throb, lightning flashed behind his eyes.

The months of pressure, the battering his psyche had taken, the strain of the burden that lay upon his shoulders . . .

He looked around as they stumbled forward across the rubble.

This was no ordinary waste ground.

It stretched for miles, no one to be seen.

It was a graveyard and here they were alone . . . at the very centre of the wasteland.

Nigel glanced again at Cathy.

He pitied her. He loved her.

People like her died every day on waste grounds like this.

The fruits of sins past, the seeds of sins to come.

Nigel felt the vodka kicking in, warming his body against the bitter cold.

He took hold of Cathy's hand with tenderness and compassion.

He led her forward . . .

Nigel remembered little more after that.

He had no idea how he had walked back to his hotel.

No idea how he had walked through the lobby, climbed the stairs, fallen into bed.

He vaguely remembered the night – the ominous dreams of blood, Britain washed by a sea of blood.

The people were drowning in the blood, but was it blood that was killing them? Or was it blood that was washing away their sins? Washing away their old life, the imperfections of what had gone before?

Nigel couldn't work it out.

When he came to, he realized the TV had been left burning through the night.

As he surfaced from his subterranean nightmare world, Fiona Thomas was reading the headlines.

'Election countdown, and with five days to go, polls show the NewLibs have an almost unassailable lead. Barring any major upset, any major reverse, the UK will have its first NewLib government in less than a week from now.'

Nigel heard the news, heard it with joy – and with pain.

Why was he not rejoicing?

What veiled memory from the night before was holding him back? Stopping him celebrating? Clouding his thoughts?

Nigel racked his vodka-deadened memory, then remembered Cathy, remembered the secret she held over him.

In a sudden flood, he remembered his own thoughts, his temptation in the wasteland.

The memory convulsed him with shock and horror.

With dawning dread, he realized he could recall nothing after he took her hand.

Why could he not remember?

And how could he have harboured such thoughts?

Contemplated such a deed? To kill Cathy.

These were the thoughts of a Knox, the demonic sophistry Knox would have used to justify his own evil actions.

Had he killed Cathy to save himself?

In a panic of fear and self-revulsion, Nigel strained to remember what had passed between him and Cathy, he berated himself for even thinking of harming her.

'What have I done? What was I thinking? Of course people tell lies. People aren't perfect. She told lies, she has her faults, she's human. Perfection exists only in Knox's empty, sterile projects; perfection means the end of humanity. We may aspire to the angels, but the ancient human law says we end with the beasts. It's not my place to sit in judgement. The Lord said vengeance was His, not mine, not Andy Sheen's, not Charlie McDonald's. Knox had his faults, had his sins, he was human. So if God pardons Cathy, does He also pardon Knox? Will the devil be saved?'

Nigel sat up in horror.

His hotel room was in disarray.

Cups and plates were broken on the floor.

But where was Cathy?

What had become of her after the moment when his memory grew dim?

Nigel looked at the floor beside his bed.

There, covered by a hotel blanket.

Blood on her forehead.

He looked again.

Cathy was there. Breathing lightly. Sleeping. Innocent, like a twelve-year-old child.

His eyes clouded with tears of release.

He felt in his pocket and opened the notebook from Exxington, from all those years before.

He thumbed the pages and turned to the notes of his interview with Eileen O'Leary. He read her lament for the daughter she had lost and now would remember forever fixed in a single moment, the moment of waking from the depths of sleep.

'And when I wake her in the morning,' he read in his faded shorthand, 'she is a child waking from a dream. Her eyes shine; she blinks off the night; all her worldliness is washed away. When she opens her eyes and she's soft with sleep, she's suddenly back to the little one she used to be. And then you can see that inside she's still the same; still full of goodness and simplicity and love.'

After all the spin, Nigel thought, after all the lies, all the deception, all the ambition, all the calculation, all the cruelty, there was only one thing that mattered. Compassion was the only hope.

He smiled at Cathy, stirring by the side of his bed.

OTHER BOOKS
AVAILABLE FROM PAN MACMILLAN

ADRIAN MATTHEWS
THE APOTHECARY'S HOUSE   1 4050 4657 0   £12.99

MARTIN CRUZ SMITH
WOLVES EAT DOGS   0 333 90750 7   £17.99

ANDY OAKES
DRAGON'S EYE   0 330 43196 X   £6.99

ARTURO PÉREZ-REVERTE
THE QUEEN OF THE SOUTH   0 330 41313 9   £16.99

All Pan Macmillan titles can be ordered from our website,
www.panmacmillan.com, or from your local bookshop
and are also available by post from:

Bookpost, PO Box 29, Douglas, Isle of Man IM99 1BQ
Credit cards accepted. For details:
Telephone: 01624 677237
Fax: 01624 670923
E-mail: bookshop@enterprise.net
www.bookpost.co.uk

Free postage and packing in the United Kingdom

Prices shown above were correct at the time of going to press.
Pan Macmillan reserve the right to show new retail prices on covers
which may differ from those previously advertised in the text
or elsewhere.